The Prince of Destiny

David Vonderheide

Table of Contents

Map of Haxter

~Prologue~

THROUGH THE HOWLING WIND and blinding snow, one might not have been able to spot the dilapidated shack shuttering against the late winter gales, as it sat perched on the ravine's edge, as if ready to jump. No light shone out from the sole window, nearly covered by the thick blankets of snow, already draped over the encampment by a fierce storm. It showed no signs of letting up.

A man, clothed in nothing but rags, if one dared to call the tattered bits of cloth rags, waded through the deep snow, tripping and stumbling towards the structure on the ridge line. A gust of bone-chilling air swirled up around the man and the shack, snatching snow from the ground and swirling it across the barren plain. The man collapsed to the ground, crying in pain as the cold tore at his bare flesh, sucking the warmth of life from him, bit by bit.

He lay there, cold and still, when from the window of the shack, a glimmer of light danced across the snow, venturing into the dangerous storm.

"The mission went almost as planned, Master," said a hooded figure, whose skin failed to make an appearance underneath his robe and tattoos. He stood next to two others, dressed in the same hooded robes.

"*Almost* as planned, Tawassa?" The voice was soothing, peaceful, coaxing, but the three men could sense the anger it was hiding. The words emanated from a throne, which was turned away from three men, who cowered before it like criminals before the guillotine.

"Yes, Master."

"Please elaborate, Tawassa." The voice was losing its gentle tone. This sentence was said with an edge as sharp as a dagger.

Tawassa, dreading his Master's response to the answer, fell to the ground, begging. "Master, please spare me! It wasn't me! I wasn't any of us! It-"

"Silence, you imbecile!" roared the voice, unable to control its anger anymore. The throne spun around. "Frin!"

The man to the right of Tawassa stepped forward, removed his hood, and kowtowed in front of his Master. Frin was shorter than Tawassa, stockier, too. His forearms were covered with lizard-like scales.

"Master," said Frin.

"Get up, you scaly fool, and tell me what happened," spat the Master.

"You see, Master, when we set fire to the castle, we couldn't find the baby anywhere."

"Fools! Three of the most powerful people in all the land, and you can't even capture a baby." The Master's voice dripped with disappointment and disdain. Frin was struggling to hold his gaze.

"But Master-"

"I don't want to hear it!" With that, the Master picked up Frin by his shirt and flung him across the room where he came to a sliding halt. "Oxlo, did you at least kill Lady Relwasa?"

The third and final figure spoke, his deathly black robe flowing behind him as he took a step forward. "Yes, Master. She was killed right before the lord's eyes, like you asked."

"At least you idiots did something right. But what about the baby?"

"The kidnapper we hired betrayed us and made off with the baby."

"Why did you hire someone to do the job I sent you to do?" asked the Master, with a frustraded tone.

"I...I believed that the...the burning down the castle would require both...both Frin and Tawassa," stuttered Oxlo.

"But why did you think *you* needed to be helping? You're a Sage of Water," said the Master.

"I thought that...that Frin and Tawassa would require some of my energy to maintain the...the fire."

"Well, I need to move past the fact that you all are clearly morons. Do you have any idea of where he escaped?"

"We have reason to believe he escaped and is hiding in the Ozreek Mountains with the baby."

"Well, why are you here? Capture this traitor and bring him and the baby to me!" The three men started to turn and walked towards the door. Before they left, their Master called out, "And don't fail me this time."

All seemed well that day. The sky was cloudless, the air was warm. The land of Haxter with all its many kingdoms continued as normal... until the volcano shot out flaming debris and lava, smoke rising from the mountain. What the onlookers did not know was that during that eruption, four special objects were spewed from the fires that day. Items that would later determine the fate of the world.

Part I
The Gii Games

Chapter 1
Professor Prince

FEDRADIN

FEDRADIN WALKED OUT OF the Craggy Keep. He stuck his bastard sword in its sheath and tucked his dagger in the back of his boot. He fidgeted with his leather pouch until it was right where he wanted.

It was a beautiful day, a taste of what was to come that spring. Birds chirped in the trees, sheep bleated as they were shepherded across the pastures, the snowmelt trickled down the path, and the breeze was scented with just a hint of warmth.

Narven, the capital of its namesake fief, was perched in the towering Ozreek Mountains. The fief of Narven abstained from most warfare in Haxter, due to its coinless treasuries and weak army. But even though it wasn't strong, the Narvish went about their business with pride and diligence.

Unfortunately, being a Narv during the time of war wasn't effective, for they always preferred science and exploration to warfare. When the humans arrived in the lush land of Haxter hundreds of years ago, they started warring over territory, and Narven had to keep migrating to avoid getting destroyed by rival kingdoms. Finally, Narven settled in the mountains while one particularly strong kingdom triumphed over the others, and in victory, joined its five fellow kingdoms into the Human Empire. There were five fiefs of the Empire: Narven, Gii, Swenvip, Viven and Borave. All of the fiefs had specialties.

The Narvish had become experts at one thing, and that was exterminating the many monsters and magical creatures that roamed the land of Haxter. After migrating for so long, there were no monsters they hadn't come across, no beasts strange to them. From aurvoraxes to zelts, the Narvish had seen it all, killed it all. Many of the other kingdoms of the many races of Haxter called upon them for help when it came to monsters.

Prince Fedradin Quickblade of Narven, the heir to the Narvish seat after his cousin, Thereeko, trained a specialized

13

group of monster exterminators called Ridders. The Ridders eliminated every kind of monster there was.

Fedradin took in a deep breath of the fresh air. A few days ago he had turned twenty, twenty years without a mother or father. Instead, he was raised in the castle, by the castellan, Scholars, and his cousin.

When his father had committed suicide, after his mother, Relwasa died while saving Fedradin from a fire, Fedradin was too young to rule by himself; he was merely a baby. The Narvish Council decided against a regent. Instead, they appointed Thereeko, Fedradin's father, Lord Zantor's, nephew as Lord of Narven. Fedradin had no title. He was not the son of a lord, otherwise known as a lordlun, yet still an heir to a fief. When one day, as a child, Fedradin flung a plate of burned bacon, denouncing it as 'too charred to eat,' Thereeko had said he was acting like a little Prince. The title stuck.

Prince Fedradin didn't mind not having parents or not being a lord -or lordlun for that matter. He was independent and didn't like responsibility -besides leading the Ridders— shirking it whenever possible.

Fedradin's azure eyes looked around at the fields near him. Farmers were just bringing out livestock, a least the few that had survived the winter. Fedradin's black hair tousled in the wind, and he flattened it with his small hand. He passed a farmer, and it was apparent that Fedradin was shorter by a few inches. They greeted each other and went on their way. Fedradin brushed his cheek and realized he had not shaved the stubble emerging near his low cheekbone, so he pulled a knife out from his boot and began to do so with a muscular arm. Finally he arrived at his destination.

Fedradin spent most of his time training his Ridders in a small arena outside of the wall that surrounded the Craggy Keep. Inside, benches lined the left wall. Extending out from the benches, there were a few lanes each separated by a foot-high wall. In the middle of each lane there stood a dummy.

"Today, we will be taking on nolls," announced Fedradin. Many people were gathered around him, listening intently. Fedradin pulled out a huge book with gold lettering on the cover, which read: *A Narv's Research on Monsters and Magical Things by Lord Assawat the Wanderer*. "'*A noll is a humanoid creature that is a strict follower of the Demisio religion, which is the belief of the demon prophet, Erch. Nolls spend their time waiting for the return of their leader by hunting in packs for lone humans. They have a very doglike appearance, with red fur and a long tail, but usually wear armor and carry axes. They also stand on two legs, are eight feet tall, and weigh three hundred pounds. Weaknesses include an intense fear of fire and the susceptibility to being poisoned by silver. Nolls are from the Subplane of Leaves. They have to use plane portals to navigate from their original plane to the Base Plane or the Plane of Earth. They cannot travel to any other planes. They live in forests with a moderate climate on both planes.'* So, any questions?"

A hand shot up. Its owner was a young woman, with chestnut hair, and green eyes.

"Aren't you the new recruit?" asked Fedradin, when he pointed at her to take her question.

"Yes. My name is Bev," she said very precisely, in an eager-to-please, yet disciplined tone.

"Well, Bev, what's your question?"

"I don't understand portals and planes."

"What are you confused by specifically?"

"All of it."

"'Right. In essence, planes are different levels of existence, stacked one on top of each other. For the most part, planes don't connect. Portals are the exception. They are open to certain creatures that originate from the plane to which the portal is connected and act as tears to allow for travel. Subplanes are linked to other planes more directly than portals, and travel between them is simpler.

"We know of the Base Plane -this plane, and the only plane humans can access, since we originated here-, the Certzol, Szrek, the Elemental Planes: Fire, Earth, Wind, and Water, all the Elemental Planes' Subplanes: Leaves, Ice, Swamp, and Grassland, the Chaos, Celestial, and Chthonic. For some reason, no portals bond to the Chthonic."

"Where did Draslupp come from? He's a Domer right?" asked Axto, a shorter man with dark skin and dark hair, the classic features of a man from Shang-Li, also known as the Jade Island. Axto was a medic for the Ridders. He was no Scholar, trained in the arts of healing only by his father, who had been training as a Scholar until his recent, unexpected death.

"Actually, Draslupp is one hundred percent human," said Fedradin. "His ability to turn invisible comes from...well no one knows what. The condition is found in only a few humans."

Suddenly, Draslupp, a young boy with dirty blond hair, who'd been in attendance since the lesson began, disappeared.

"See?" came Draslupp's voice. A murmur of excitement went through the crowd. A moment later, Draslupp reappeared. "The Domer Dark Ages, when we were exterminated, has left our kind few and far between. I barely survived myself. My family wasn't as lucky." Draslupp looked down. It was obvious the memories were still painful for him. Fedradin tried to change the topic of conversation.

"Anything else?" asked Fedradin. No one raised a hand. "'Right, now, Misk, could you turn these dummies into nolls?"

A lanky, red headed man with freckles and an odd twitch in the side of his face waved his wand, and the dummies began to vibrate. The cloth covering the dummies began to grow brown fur. Their heads started growing elongated snouts, and sharp fangs shot out from both sides, yellow eyes popping out, while large ears emerged. The arms grew longer, and developed claws. The legs stretched out too, and their hands transformed into large paws. A tail burst its way out the back of the dummies, and swished back and forth. Finally, large battle-axes materialized in their hands. Some gave their new weapons test swings. Others tossed them from hand to hand, deep in thought -or as much thought as one can be in as a bipedal dog, for that was how they now appeared.

"Bev, these are simulation dummies. I had my wizards specially design them for the Ridders. It cost me a fortune and I have no idea how it works, but if you get hurt or die while fighting, you're good as new when the simulation is cut."

"Will I feel pain?" asked Bev, nervous.

"Only if the noll injures you," replied Fedradin, turning to address the rest of the class. "Everyone get into a lane and take out your weapons."

Fedradin and Misk paced down the line. The first man charged forward. He had greasy black hair, green eyes and small ears. The noll swung its axe downwards. The man spun away from it, the axe striking the ground. The man gave the beast a kick. The noll crashed to the ground, and the man yanked the axe out of the noll's hands. The monster scrambled backwards, but before it could get far, the man brought the axe down on its neck, decapitating it instantly. Misk waved his wand and the noll's body got up, collected its head and axe, and returned to its starting position.

"Kekk, remember how I said that nolls are poisoned by silver? You have a silver weapon don't you?" asked Fedradin.

"Yes. My dagger is," muttered Kekk.

"Use that. It's much safer."

Fedradin moved on. A woman with blondish-white hair and long legs was next.

"Whenever you're ready, Shah." She stepped forward. The noll jogged towards her, swinging its axe menacingly. Shah reached into her pouch, and pulled out a stick. She flicked the top of it, and it burst into flames. The noll's eyes went wide. It backed up, and Shah pulled out a silver dagger. In one quick motion she lunged forward, and slit the noll's neck. She extinguished the flame, put her dagger back into its pouch and retreated backwards.

"Very impressive Shah," said Fedradin. He started to walk away, but then remembered something. He spun around, "Oh, and Shah."

"Yes?"

"I asked the Boravian ambassador about you going to Borave and setting up a Ridders business."

"What did he say?"

"He said that he wants you to start as soon as possible."

"So he said yes?" asked Shah, getting excited.

"Yes he did," said Fedradin.

"When do I leave?" asked Shah.

"The Boravian ambassador already left, so you will just have to make plans of your own. But as soon as possible, I image."

"Thank you for teaching me, Fedradin!" She said, and kissed him on the cheek. Fedradin couldn't help it when a little color came to his cheeks.

"I would suggest waiting a week or two, you know, to let winter pass and the snow on the roads melt down south."

Fedradin continued to pace the lanes and witnessed many other attempts at trying to kill the noll, like Yexico, a plump, unathletic man trying to perform a kick and finding himself with an axe in his side; Axto driving his halberd through the middle of a noll; Bev pounding a noll mercilessly with her quarterstaff; and Draslupp tickling the noll -while being invisible of course- then shooting it with an arrow. The final stop was the Ridders' second wizard, Dethroid. There wasn't much to see. A quick white spell from his wand tore the head from the noll's body.

"Alright, Misk, create a few more nolls for each person, I'll practice with Yexico here," said Fedradin. Yexico flushed. Misk waved his wand and the nolls tripled. Hardly anyone was paying attention to the nolls, instead watching Fedradin and Yexico practice. It happened nearly every class.

"Now Yexico, the first thing you want to do is disarm the noll," said Fedradin. Yexico managed to nod, embarrassed by the Ridders watching him. Fedradin walked forward to Yexico's noll. The noll swung its axe, Fedradin moved aside, and removed both its arms from one swing of his sword.

"That's one way. My favorite way is this," said Fedradin. After Misk waved his wand, and the noll's arms snapped back into place, Fedradin tossed the axe back to the noll, which caught the weapon and swung it once more. Fedradin caught the wooden shaft on the side of his sword, slid it up the pole to the axehead, twisted his blade and pulled the weapon from the noll's hands.

"Everyone has their own way," said Fedradin, "You just need to get creative. After you disarm it, go for the kill. Got it Yexico?"

Yexico murmured his acknowledgment.

"'Right, Misk. Give me a challenge!" said Fedradin. Misk waved his wand. The noll in front of Fedradin started duplicating into fifteen different nolls. From the ground, a vapor rose up. At first glance, Fedradin assumed it was a vampire. His sword was blessed by the Rotnazian Church, and he had holy water in his pouch, so he wasn't worried.

The nolls circled him. On the outside of the circle, the mist twirled around and around. Suddenly a noll jumped forward, its axe pulled back, ready to strike. Fedradin cleanly sliced its head off before it could strike.

"Hypocrite!" yelled Yexico, "You didn't disarm it!" Fedradin resisted the urge to tell Yexico the disarming trick was only for beginners. Two more nolls lunged forward from either side of the circle. Fedradin jumped back right before they reached him, and he stuck out his foot so a noll tripped. The nolls' heads collided with a sickening crunch as one fell forward, and they dropped their axes. Fedradin pulled out a dagger and quickly slit their throats as they reeled backwards. He spared a glance at the mist. It seemed to be taking form. It wasn't a vampire. Catoblepas maybe? But catoblepas mist looked different...

An axe blade whizzed past his head. Spinning around, he was face to face with a noll. He stabbed his dagger into the noll's chest, and it fell back on the ground. Ripping out his dagger, Fedradin felt movement behind him. He ducked in the nick of time. An axe soared over his head. He turned and aimed a kick at the noll's knees, which buckled. Fedradin took the opportunity to stab it with his sword. Five nolls were down. He rotated three hundred sixty degrees, to find all ten nolls were closing in. The mist, he decided, was not of a catoblepas. What had Misk challenged him with?

Fedradin started charging towards one side of the rapidly shrinking circle. The nolls on the side he was running towards stopped, girding for Fedradin's attack. In a millisecond, Fedradin changed direction, and ran at the other side. He dove between two, unsuspecting nolls, hit the ground in a roll and got back up. The nolls were all standing right next to each other, confused, so Fedradin attacked, swinging his sword madly, killing six nolls. When he began to feel overwhelmed, he retreated.

Suddenly, there was a terrible din. Fedradin looked at the mist, but it was no longer that. It was a huge ball with bat-like wings, claws, a droopy mouth with huge fangs, and a trail of ash, dirt and grit coming off the back. It floated in midair. Fedradin had no idea what it was.

Chapter 2
Of Belks and Baks

FEDRADIN

THE MONSTER BROUGHT ITS claws down where Fedradin was last standing. Jumping away, he twirled around in midair. A noll was standing less than three feet away from him. With a swipe of his sword, the noll crumpled, no longer in possession of a head.

Fedradin looked at Misk. The wizard looked slightly befuddled.

"What the hell is that thing?" yelled Fedradin. Misk looked up.

"It's a noll!" called Misk.

"You idiot, I mean the big ball of smoke!"

"Oh! Interesting creature! I'll look for it in the book." Fedradin saw a beam light of in the corner of his eye. Instinctively, he dove away from it. Not a second later, the same spot was missing a large chunk of stone, smoke rising from the hole. The unidentified monster roared, and shot another beam out of its eye. Fedradin repeated the process of dodging the beam.

"Misk, what did you create?"

"How should I know? It's not in the book! "

"You created it, gnome brains!" Fedradin stabbed another noll. Running forward, he took out the remaining two with a single sweep of his sword. He turned back to the smoke-monster.

Fedradin leapt up, slashing down with his sword. With an almost lazy motion, the monster batted Fedradin away with the back of its claw. Fedradin came crashing down onto the floor, amidst the many gasps of other people.

"Fedradin, I don't think I made that monster!" shouted Misk.

"Then why is it there?"

"Fedradin, I think that monster is real!"

Fedradin dove out of the way of two beams.

"If you think it's real, cut the simulation!" A few second passed. Fedradin dodged two more swipes of the mysterious monster. "Misk! Are you going to cut the simulation?"

"I did!"

Fedradin shrugged. He was always up for a challenge, but he would have to be careful around the real monster, because it could actually hurt him. He kept dodging the beams and claw swipes of the monster, until finally an opportunity opened up. It stopped attacking Fedradin for just a second, so it could let out a loud roar. As it roared, Fedradin stabbed his sword straight into its body. The sound that emanated from its throat changed from an aggressive roar to a cry of pain.

"All to action!" shouted Fedradin. "You'll get more training out of this than with those simulation dummies!"

The Ridders leapt into action, shooting the monster with arrows, throwing axes, or shooting fireballs. With the sudden onslaught, the monster backed away from the angry Ridders as they attacked. Almost everyone had hurt the monster in some way, when Fedradin tired of the battle.

"Misk, Dethroid! Use a killing spell!" shouted Fedradin. The two wizards pointed their wands at each other. Slowly an orange sphere formed in between them. Once it grew to about three feet in diameter, both wizards flicked their wands at the beast. An orange beam flew out of the ball and at the monster. The beam hit the monster, and it crashed to the ground, dead.

Dethroid pulled up his wand and the orange ball disappeared. Misk fell to the floor, convulsing.

"Misk!" shouted Fedradin.

"Axto, take him to the Wing. Go with him Shah," said Dethroid. The two Ridders immediately grabbed Misk and lifted him onto their shoulders. They respected Dethroid almost as much as Fedradin, and with Fedradin not barking commands they followed Dethroid's lead.

"The hell was that thing?" shouted Yexico.

"I believe that to be a belk," said Dethroid.

"A what?" said Fedradin, pacing around the Ridders' arena.

"They're from the Plane of Air. They enjoy hunting in Osup, my home country."

"Explains why they're not in the book," said Fedradin.

"Why?" asked Bev.

"As you know, Osup is the country just off the shore of Haxter. Lord Assawat recorded all the monsters in *Haxter*."

"What happened to Misk?" asked Bev, changing the topic.

Dethroid answered. "So many questions! A killing spell is the most dangerous spell a wizard can perform. With only one wizard, the odds of creating a working spell and living are slim to none."

"Why?" asked Bev.

"Killing spells have always been cursed. When a wizard uses one alone, the spell backfires and kills him. When two use a killing spell, it is a rare occurance that either dies."

"But Misk will be okay?" asked Yexico.

"He should be. Let me beat you to your next question. A wizard who is killed with a backfiring killing spell will transform into a bak."

"Here it is in the book," said Fedradin. "*A bak, an undead wizard who has been killed by his own killing spell, is a formidable foe. The dead wizard will rise at the next full moon as a bak. With the powers of whomever it was before, it also bears a petrifying touch. Living in almost any environment, it will join up with bands of bak and other undead abominations. Baks have a humanoid appearance, with a long, thin face, slits for eyes, gray skin, and a small mouth. They have no known religion. If anything, they may follow Demisio. To fight, use holy water and blessed weapons. Baks travel to no planes other than the Base Plane.*'"

The church bells tolled, signaling the end of an hour.

"Fedradin, class is over," said Kekk, pacing nervously by the door.

"'Right, everyone dismissed. I'll look after the store.'"

Chapter 3
Ridiculous Requests

FEDRADIN

FEDRADIN MADE A STOP before he arrived at the store that he and the Ridders owned. It was the church, a large stone structure just outside the Craggy Keep. Stained glass pictures on the sides of the building depicted a man in various situations, such as holding a sword in the air, the sign of the four elements in his palms, clutching the head of a monster with hundreds of eyes and large fangs, and of course a triangle for the Gods. Fedradin entered the church, where he found himself among rows of pews. All the pews faced towards a statue of the same man who was shown on the stained glass windows, with the faces of the three dieties etched into the wall behind him. Fedradin bowed and went on his way.

He had just visited a Rotnazian Church, part of a religion that worshipped the prophet Rotnaz, who drove back the hoards of goblins during the Goblin Wars. Afterwards, he ascended into the heavens, leaving Haxter behind.

The Rotnazian Church trained three types of servants: Scholars, Knights, and Lear. The Scholars administered medicine, observed the stars, mapped the world, and were overall in charge of science. The Knights were trained to fight for the church, but since the church was not involved in every conflict, they fought for many different sides. The Lear were the children of Learon, who preached the religion to others.

The religion celebrated three main gods. Mank, the god of the Scholars. He was the god one prayed to for enlightenment or knowledge. Wearon, the god of the Knights. He was the god one prayed to for courage or power. And finally, Laeron, the god of the Lear. She was the god one prayed to for luck or forgiveness.

Fedradin walking slightly farther and approached the bottom of a staircase, etched into the side of a towering mountain. The spray from the sea crashing against the headlands left the stairs soaked and slippery. Perched precariously on a cliff, *Bits and Pieces* marked the end of the dangerous path. It was a medium-sized structure, round, and made mostly of wood, overlooking the narrow Narvish Bay on one side, and the sparkling Narven Lake on the other. The door was wooden, with a welcoming sign on the front. Inside, the store smelled of termite-eaten wood, along with a slight odor of decaying meat. A tattered, Mazleki rug covered the majority of the floor, which only showed through the rips and tears in the rug. It had been a gift from his uncle, Spencyr, when his parents died.

There were rows and rows of shelves, some so close together that it was impossible to tell where one shelf's merchandise ended and the other's began. The shelves were separated only in one place, where a large window overlooked Narven Lake on the right, and another large window on the left overlooked the Narvish Bay. Piled on the shelves were many different parts of various monsters, including minotaur horns, griffon feathers, dead medusa snake hair, hydra scales, nemean lion hides, goblin knuckles, brax eyes, nightbeast tusk and much more. In the center of the room was a counter; scattered on top of it were many papers, which told of the pieces in the store and their prices. Because many of Fedradin's customers were illiterate, Fedradin often had to read the papers aloud. Behind the counter there was a vault, which contained valuable pieces of weaponry and armor. There was also a shelf behind the counter with cages that contained fairies, sprites and zelts. Two small, wooden chairs were placed in front of the counter so Fedradin could bargain with his customers. Fedradin sat behind the counter, sketching a belk carefully on a piece of parchment.

The door opened. Fedradin put his quill down, and slid the parchment into a drawer. An older, hunchbacked, albino man walked in leaning heavily on his cane, his red eyes darting back and forth. A long, iron sword hung in his belt with a large, a shiny diamond on the pommel, an expensive and rather odd embellishment, but the lack of a bond hanging from his swordbelt revealed he was no knight.

When men were knighted, they were given a ring. Knights could link more rings together when they defeated another knight or made him yield. They would take his bond and add it to their own.

"Can I help you?" Fedradin asked.

"Yes, you can," said the man. "First, I need some hooves."

"What kind? We have satyr hooves, a few catoblepas hooves, um, hippogriff, griffon, minotaur..."

"I need two blackmare hooves to be exact."

Fedradin blinked twice and said, "Sorry?"

"Said I'll need two blackmare hooves," said the man, growing impatient.

"Well, because there are about ten blackmares in Haxter, we don't have those." Fedradin pulled out *A Narv's Research on Monsters*. He flipped to the page he was looking for and looked down a picture of a flaming, black horse. He showed it to his customer. "You mean this, right?" The man nodded.

"Well, what next?"

"Do you have a tara scale?"

"Do you know *anything* about monsters?" asked Fedradin, genuinely curious.

"No, I was given a list of things I am to get."

"Well, a tara happens to be the offspring of the chinside and the Great Lizard, and there happens to be about *two* of them in the entire world." said Fedradin.

Fedradin sighed and opened his book to a page with what looked like a large turtle, standing at the height of a war elephant, with deadly claws and fangs. "We're talking about this monster?"

"Unfortunately, yes. This is pretty pointless, but do you have thirty-six unicorn tail hairs?"

"No, unfortunately we just ran out," said Fedradin in a sarcastic tone.

"Please don't get angry at me. One last thing. I'll need two cups of hir blood and four pints of ogre hair oil as a Core."

"May I ask what potion you're creating?"

"I don't really know myself. I'm collecting this for, um, someone else."

"*This* hir?" Fedradin flashed him a picture of a serpentine creature with ten legs.

"You got it."

"Well, we don't have it. Ogre hair oil though, never heard of that as a Core before. Don't have it either."

"Well, that's the rarest of what I need." The man then proceeded to purchase giant hair, bugbear eyeball, grint tentacle, orc tongue, and kobold scales.

"That will be fifteen fellyers, one lazone, and an oplopeck," said Fedradin.

"All I have here are fellyers. Here's sixteen." The man passed over many circular gold coins with holes in the middle. An inscription along the circumference spelled out, "one fellyer." Fedradin reached down and pulled out nine oplopecks -square copper coins with a snake inscripted on them- and three lazones - triangular silver coins with the picture of a boar- in change. The man turned to leave.

"I just have to ask. Do you have a remor bezoar?"

"No, but are you thinking of *this* remor?" asked Fedradin, showing a picture of, what appeared to be, an overgrown worm with a dangerous maw with sharp teeth, spikes down its back and hundreds of small spiked legs. It had a color of pinkish-purple.

"Why do you do that?"

"Amazing how many people mix up monsters."

"Well, bye..." The man turned and walked out the door. Fedradin's eyes narrowed in suspicion and befuddlement. What elder who knew nothing about monsters ran errands for someone else? And why were Fedradin's fairies fluttering around in panic? After a few seconds, when the fairies settled down, Fedradin shrugged and went back to sketching the belk.

THE ALBINO

The albino angrily hurled the items he had recently purchased off the edge of the cliff. Another failure. He didn't want to have to acquire all the items he had requested on his own, but it didn't look like he had much of a choice. He stood up straight, relief after faking being a hunchback. He took a deep breath, pulled out a golden amulet from his jerkin, squeezed it in his palm, smiled to himself...

and disappeared without a trace.

Chapter 4
The Invitation

FEDRADIN

LATER THAT NIGHT, FEDRADIN closed down his shop. He had a well-drawn picture of a belk, and as much information as he knew about it written beneath. He was undecided about adding it to the book.

He strolled down the stairs deep in thought about potions and belks. He was thinking so hard that he almost missed the black shape flying at him on the stairs. He narrowly sidestepped it, his hand going to his sword hilt.

"Sorry!" the man exclaimed. "Do you know if *Bits and Pieces* is still open?"

"It is not," Fedradin let go of his hilt. "Though I think I can help you. I am Prince Fedradin," he said, extending his hand. The man shook it vigorously.

"Just the man I wanted to see!" the man released his grip on Fedradin's hand. "I am Ambassador Cecil, of the Fiefdom of Gii."

"Come inside; there we can talk properly," said Fedradin. Cecil nodded eagerly. The two walked down the long flight of steps. They approached the front of the castle. A few guards were stationed in front of the portcullis.

"Halt!" yelled a guard. Fedradin and Cecil stopped. He squinted, and when he recognized Fedradin, the guard called for the portcullis to be raised. Fedradin and Cecil passed through it. The two walked down winding corridors and up twisting stairs, passing bowing servants and other nobles. Finally, they arrived at Fedradin's solar.

"Here we are," said Fedradin. He opened the door, and Cecil walked in.

"Wow!" exclaimed Cecil. The walls of his study were plastered in pictures of monsters. One large sketch of a dragon covered an entire wall. A dragon hadn't been seen since the Conquest of the Dragons, when the humans, elves and dwarves, the first inhabitants of Haxter, banded together to drive the cruel dragons from their land.

On the right, there was a bay window, overlooking the mountains. There was a desk at the back of the room, flanked by a bookshelf. Fedradin seated himself behind the desk. The room smelled strongly of pine.

"Ambassador, please have a seat," said Fedradin, gesturing at the armchairs in front of him.

"Please just call me Cecil." He sat down.

"Well then, Cecil, what brings you to Narven?"

Cecil replied, "Well, in Gii, we have been doing a bit of scouting."

"Scouting for what?"

"Please be patient, Prince Quickblade. We have been looking for the best warriors in all the land. We observed you this morning take on fifteen nolls, and a...belk you said?" said Cecil.

"Yes. I would like to know how you observed my class this morning, Cecil."

"We observed you by scrying."

"The hell is that?"

"It's a process by which wizards or witches can observe something or someone very far away. Or very close by for that matter. The distance is irrelevant."

"So you're saying you were spying on me?" said Fedradin, indignantly.

"Well, we were watching you without you knowing."

"I consider that spying, how about you?" said Fedradin, rising in his seat slightly.

"No! Lord Uslo of Gii had permission!" cried Cecil.

"From who? From one of my Ridders?"

"No, from Lord Thereeko!"

"Why would Thereeko let Uslo spy on me?" wondered Fedradin aloud.

"I don't know why he did, but he did, so let's get to it. Gii has decided to start a competition to find the most powerful warrior in all of Haxter."

Fedradin was not impressed. "I know of many tournaments and tourneys like this. Why will this one be different?"

"Ah, the many tournaments you know of are restricted to humans."

"So this competition will also include, what, the dwarves?"

"Not just that." Cecil smirked.

"The chultra, too?"

"Not just those two races either." Fedradin wanted to slap the smug look off Cecil's face.

"Are you planning to invite all of the-" Fedradin was interrupted.

"Yes, if you were about to say we will invite all who have just signed the *Treaty of the Nine Races*." The Treaty was a document ratified between nine powerful races in Haxter: humans, elves, dwarves, flayers, animal cultures, Keshnul, Grefture, chultra, and svaadi, after they had worked together to quell the uprising of Osup. The Osupenese attempted to take Tinne, a port city on the Gulf of Amber during the Battle of Amber, but failed. The rest had been butchery of the whaling warriors as they fought with spears and harpoons. The tenth major race of Haxter, the seafaring Sant, had declined to ratify the agreement.

The Treaty settled a few key disagreements between the races -such as humans poaching in the chultras' sacred Grove of Ancestors-, abolished slavery in Haxter, fianced the Road that connected Haxter, and established the secular League of Nine Races, or the LNR. It developed a standard language for Haxter, which was already shared between the elves, dwarves, humans, Grefture, Keshnul, and animal cultures and known as Common, Commonspeak, or the Commontongue. It was renamed to Leaguespeak. It set up the government of cities outside kingdom boundries, which would be known as Leaguetowns.

The TNR dictated that the rulers of the races meet from time to time to discuss the issues of the day, and it also gave the framework of how the races had to treat each other. It did not end the War of Gems between the elfish and dwarfish, because neither side was willing to compromise over their territory disputes. It had been decided that the two races could settle the disagreement on the battlefield, the winner claiming the disputed land, the ore-rich Crack.

"So, how exactly do you plan to do the inviting? Are you going to pick a couple of warriors from each race?" Fedradin leaned forward, intrigued.

"Precisely. We will invite three teams from each race, a team being four warriors. Well actually, three teams from each race will make it to the quarter finals, but we'll explain all of the rules later."

Fedradin closed his eyes and shook his head. "The Treaty has only been in effect for a few months, and many of the things that the races have agreed to do as compromise have not been accomplished yet. For example, the landowners of the Breadbasket refuse to free their slaves. I can only see harm coming out of this."

"How so?"

"Well, if competition gets out of hand, there will be anger, which will lead to wars breaking out, destroying the supposedly endless reign of peace the Treaty was meant to create. The War of Gems shows no sign of abating, and I fear the Treaty is already doomed to fail. These Games will not help our rapidly deteriorating state."

"An interesting perspective. We at Gii see it exactly opposite. A competition provides the races with another outlet for settling disagreements."

Fedradin took a deep breath, for he was beginning to lose his composure. "How can you think mere *games* will settle border disputes, discrimination in Leaguetowns, and dishonor of the laws set by the LNR?"

"If we buld the tradition that glory at the Games is more important than glory earned at war, the races will be able to settle everything they need to settle with these Games."

"What if one race betrays the LNR?"

"They will be excluded from the Games, earning no glory, therefore, being punished."

"Harsh," he said sarcastically. Fedradin sat back down in his chair contemplating the proposal. "Wouldn't I need a knighthood to compete?"

"I don't know why you don't have one. I watched you fight. But no, you don't need to be a knight, especially since the flayers, chultra, and svaadi are competing." The flayers, chultra, and svaadi did not worship Rotnazian, and therefore could not earn a knighthood from the Floating Chapel.

Fedradin rubbed his forehead as he thought. "I still think your idea is absolutely ridiculous and will accomplish nothing, but, I am willing to compete if there's something in it for me."

"Is a grand prize of fifty thousand fellyers sufficient?"

Chapter 5
The Elfish Princess

BREETEX

"ELVES! ELVES ARE UPON us!" The voice came from the Rotnazian Church, accompanied by the sounding of a warhorn.

Greul Breetex was jolted awake by the call. Groping around in the dark, the dwarf grabbed his axe. He walked over to his mirror, pulled on some chainmail, plate and a helm. A yak had been etched into his armor, the sigil of his platoon. The dwarf that stared back at him had brown hair, dark brown eyes, tan skin and no beard, a strange fashion choice in the world of dwarves. He rushed outside.

The cobblestone streets of the dwarfish city, Alta, were filled with dwarves who had donned the same attire as Breetex and carried similar weapons. Breetex quickened his pace and arrived at the outside wall of the city. He looked over the edge. What he saw amazed and frightened him at the same time.

At least five hundred elves were gathered around the city. Archers with deadly precision stood in the back, carrying yew longbows. The small creatures looked amusing wielding weapons taller than themselves. His smile was wiped from his face when he remembered their bows could outdistance the spruce and oak dwarfish bows by half. At the front, more muscular elves carried deadly looking maces, pikes, spears, and morningstars. The rest carried an assortment of weapons. Swords, slings, axes, it made no difference, they all could kill. Breetex saw the parley between the dwarves and elves forming on the battlefield. Breetex didn't need to wait for the verdict. He knew what the elves were after.

Breetex darted through Alta, his destination, the warehouse. He weaved in between alarmed dwarves until he reached it. Breetex entered the warehouse, where he saw boxes pilled high, full of food, weapons, and other various surplus. He made his way to the back corner of the building. Fighting his way through cobwebs, he threw boxes and relics to the side until he found what he wanted. He walked in on a small clearing of boxes. There, eating an apple, sat a beautiful she-elf.

She had brown hair and green eyes. She was wearing a black skirt and shirt. She was very small. Her eyes darted upward when Breetex entered. She let out a small gasp, then relaxed.

"Breetex, warn me before you do that again!" she scolded. Her voice was strong, unlike her appearance.

"I couldn't warn you. What if someone else was in here, Aserax?"

"I heard the warhorns. Why would anybody be in here now?"

"Well, keep your voice down, just in case," said Breetex, though he knew she was right, like usual.

"Okay," said Aserax, lowering her voice. "What were the horns about?"

"The elves. They've tracked you down."

"How? I'm supposed to be dead!" said Aserax.

"I don't know, but that doesn't matter now. What matters is that we get you out of here safely."

"Where would we go?"

"There's a tournament in Gii, if we can get there, maybe I can win us some fellyers to travel to Osup or Mazlek or Stentor."

"But how will we escape here in the first place?"

Breetex smiled. "I have a plan."

Chapter 6
The Two Groups of Gimlocks

FEDRADIN

THE MIST ALMOST COMPLETELY enveloped the small hut leaning precariously on the side of a hill. The hut had a small wooden porch in front that one could tell was rotten and eaten by termites just by looking at it. Two windows were on either side of the door, and a small stone chimney protruded from the roof. A few trees could be made out, branches large and droopy, as if to block the hut from view. On the hill, a small deer, frail and almost unable to walk stumbled around before finding a patch of grass to eat. In the hut, one of the windows was lit with a flickering, dull glow, from a candle guttering out. Wisps of smoke came trickling out of the chimney as the fire started to die down. A slight drizzle came down on the hut and the trees, making the previously droopy branches hang even lower. Through the clouds, the moonlight was visible, distorted through the haze of clouds. As the deer grazed, a small silhouette crept in. In its hand was some kind of weapon, but it was hard to tell what. When it appeared, the deer tried to run, but instead tripped and collapsed to the ground. It proceeded to snort and growl fiercely, and the noise tripled, amplified by the silence around it. Quickly, the silhouette ran forward and killed the deer. The silhouette beckoned with its hand, and two more silhouettes also crept in. One was as small, or smaller than the first one, and the other one dwarfed both of them, showing just how small the first two were. As the first three approached the front door of the hut, a forth figure, as big as the third, inched its way across the hill, shaking its head. The first three intruders were on the porch, about to open the front door, when it burst open and three animal figures tackled the three first figures. A figure came out after the animals, and looked up directly at... Fedradin woke with a start.

He commonly had dreams like that. Dethroid said it was nothing. But Fedradin thought they were odd, they felt so real; it was like he was actually there, or had been there, like déjà vu. Misk also said the dreams were nothing. Fedradin shook his head.

If his most trusted wizards told him that they didn't mean anything, they didn't.

Fedradin got dressed and grabbed his weapons. His book was tucked under his arm, his sword in sheath, his pouch secured on his shoulder. He was headed down to the Ridders' arena, where he had taught the day before. When Fedradin arrived, he was proud to see that his Ridders were already sparring on the stage, overlooking the lanes that stretched out on the floor below. Once his Ridders took notice, they focused their attention on him.

"'Right," said Fedradin, "before we begin with *marauders-*" he let the words sink in for dramatic effect, "I have a question about the belk we encountered yesterday. They're not in the book as you know, and I was wondering if I should I add them."

Draslupp piped up. "It's called '*A Narv's Research on Monsters and Magical Things.*' You're A Narv. It's your research on monsters and magical things. I think you should add it."

Shah said, "I think you should add it, but get credit for it too."

"I think," said Axto, "that you should add more pages at the end of the book with a note that explains you wrote it."

A murmur of agreement went through the crowd. "'Right, so I'll do that. Now onto the marauders." Fedradin opened his book and read: "'*The marauder is a vicious planetraveling creature, which means it can travel to and from certain planes at any time it desires, without the restraints of having to use portals. It has a distinct appearance. It is purplish in color, with a long, barbed tail. It has a ridge down its spine, and big feet with claws. Its head is most distinct; protruding off the body, it is triangularly shaped, the point of the triangle facing outwards, with a large mouth underneath the point. It has large fangs, and its eyes sit opposite each other behind the mouth. It carries no weapons but its fangs, claws and tail. Its skin is relatively tough, but it has no other armor. It follows no religion whatsoever, it just lives day to day killing prey in the Base Plane, then heading back to the Certzol Plane. It is craven though; any sign of danger and it flees to its home. Your best defense is to use acid or fire to scare it back to the Certzol Plane.*' 'Right then, who's up for fighting these ethereal marauders?" A half-hearted cheer rose up.

"Dethroid, because Misk is in the hospital, you're in charge of making the simulation dummies," said Fedradin. Dethroid waved his wand high above his head, and the dummies began their transformation into ethereal marauders. Fedradin's Ridders started fighting their enemies. Some highlights were when an invisible Draslupp picked the monster's nose with a dagger and when Shah chased the marauder around with her Enchanted Torch.

The Ridders practiced battling multiple ethereal marauders. After they completed their challenge, Dethroid challenged them with new monsters. After all the Ridders were done, Fedradin announced that the Ridders would be starting gimlocks.

"The hell is a gimlock?" asked Kekk.

"Well," started Fedradin.

"Here it comes," Draslupp 'whispered.'

Fedradin shot him a dirty glance, but there was no real anger behind it. "According to the book, *'A gimlock is a humanoid monster. They can be divided into two main groups. One group is in positive agreement with humans who live in Keshnulian cities along with planeblood, half celestial, halflings, and other gimlocks. They act as slaves, but do all their work voluntarily. The other group consists of followers of the Demisio religion (worshippers of the demon prophet, Erch). They, like nolls, live and hunt in the woods for prey, particularly for lone humans. Their skin is a pale purple; they have large, red ears; and black hair. They wear loincloths and carry crudely fashioned axes. Their defenses are long, sharp fingernails, sharp teeth, and their axes. If you must fight one, disarm them first. Without its axe, it flees from battle. The gimlocks originated in the Subplane of Leaves, and they use the portals to navigate to and from their original plane and the Base Plane.'*

" 'Right, any questions?" There were none.

The Ridders walked back to their lanes, and started battling the simulated gimlocks. After they finished with the gimlocks, they battled multiple gimlocks at once. They were finishing when Cecil burst through the door, red in the face.

Chapter 7
A Dire Situation

FEDRADIN

"HELP!" YELLED CECIL. FEDRADIN turned and looked at him. "Guards...chasing...me!"

"Why?" asked Fedradin.

"Think...I...stole...bread," said Cecil through heavy breaths. As soon as he finished his sentence, four guards burst in, pikes held high. They looked around, spotted Cecil, and charged.

"Hey, hey, hey!" shouted Fedradin, standing in between the guards and Cecil. "What the hell is going on here?"

"He stole bread from the kitchen!" yelled the guard in an accusatory voice.

"I didn't! I swear!" said Cecil, throwing his hands in the air.

"Leave him alone," said Fedradin. "You have better things to do than chase down ambassadors from Gii."

"But the bread is gone! Someone took it!" shouted the guard, not backing down.

"That's an order!" said Fedradin.

The guard muttered, "You're not even a lordlun," but walked away anyhow.

Cecil collapsed to one of the benches, breathing hard. "Thanks," he managed to blut out, in between breaths. After a few moments, he could talk again. "Well, even though I didn't come here for this exact purpose," said Cecil, "I need to know your decision on the competition. Gii is around a day's journey from here, and if we don't leave soon, we'll be late. It starts the day after next, you do realize."

"I was about to tell my Ridders about that, when you burst through the door," said Fedradin.

"What competition is he talking about?" asked Bev.

"Cecil can tell you," said Fedradin. Cecil went on to explain the tournament to the Ridders. "You all can come with me if you so desire and if you do, you'll get some of the prize money if we win, but I need to know which three of you will compete with me

37

in the Gii Games. To decide this, I have thought of a friendly little game myself."

"Sounds fun," said Draslupp. Fedradin walked over to Dethroid.

"First things first, start them off with some dire animals," whispered Fedradin.

"Any type in particular?" asked Dethroid, in a whispered response.

"I'm thinking for Draslupp, a few wolverines. We need to challenge that invisible nuisance. The rest should get, um, a boar or two, I suppose."

"Sounds great." Dethroid waved his wand. In one lane, the dummy was transforming into five large wolverines, with glowing yellow eyes, and spikes on their backs. The rest of the lanes had two oversized boars, each with two sets of large tusks and a swath of black hair on its back.

"Fedradin, are you fighting the wolverines?" asked Draslupp.

"Nope, you are."

"What?"

"You're fighting those five dire wolverines because you're a Domer."

"It's not fair!"

"Once everyone else can turn invisible, they'll get the same challenge."

Draslupp grunted his ascent, tired of arguing a losing point.

"'Right then, let's hear about dire animals!" announced Fedradin. Draslupp rolled his eyes. "'*Dire animals are animals that are bigger and more ferocious than the animal they resemble. James of Dire and Thunderflash (a group of sorcerers, alchemists, and other types of wizards) created them. James of Dire is responsible for many animals in Haxter, including mimics, zelts and possibly even the Legendary Eight.'* Now that you have a little back story, get into your lines and wait for me."

The Ridders walked to their respective lines, looking at Bev, who was first to compete. Fedradin walked up to her, Dethroid at his side. Yexico came up to Fedradin.

"Fedradin, have you ever told us of this 'Legendary Eight' you mentioned?"

Fedradin cocked his head. "Maybe I haven't. You see, when Thunderflash was in existence, I was not born yet, but from what I have gathered, they were a very mysterious society. The only thing anyone knew about Thunderflash was that they created monsters. Some said it was for an army. Others said it was because they were wicked people and liked torturing animals.

"Regardless of their reasoning behind their actions, when rumors started pouring in about ferocious monsters, and the rumors began to gather credibility, fingers started getting pointed at Thunderflash. To prove them wrong, James of Dire himself went out into the wild to kill the monsters. He never returned from his journey.

"Once people surmised he had been killed by the monsters, the rumors began to get more and more fantastic. One rumor even told of gigantic chickens terrorizing the farms out in Borave, which of course was completely untrue, though I can't say I've never had an encounter with a gigantic chicken. That's a story for another time. Finally, a Lear by the name of Finadek went to see the monsters for himself. He was gone for over five years, when he finally crawled back to his monastery in the Sumier Mountains. He wrote a book called, '*The Legendary Eight.*' He wrote about the monsters he had seen all across Haxter and how they guarded a treasure beyond imagination.

"Most people thought that his story was complete hogwash, and it was never widely accepted. Still today, some people continue the search for the Legendary Eight and Finadek's Treasure."

"Oh. Thanks Fedradin," said Yexico. Fedradin merely nodded and looked to Bev.

"On your mark, Bev," said Fedradin.

Bev nodded, and drew her quarterstaff. The boars looked at their foe, and lowered their tusks. Bev walked forward and feinted to her left. As the boars reacted to her feint, she hit one of the boars under the chin. The boar backed up, and as it did, the second boar charged her. Bev leapt in the air, just barely clearing the boar and pulled a dagger from her belt with her free hand. The second boar, the one Bev had jumped, looked around in confusion. The first boar charged her once again, tusks lowered. Wielding a dagger in one hand and a quarterstaff in another, Bev smacked the boar's head and tusks away from her with her weapon. She brought her dagger down across the boar's neck. The boar stumbled away, bleeding out and nearly dead.

The second boar ran at her from behind. Bev, celebrating her victory, was caught unaware. The boar gored her with both its tusks, and Bev was knocked to the ground. The boar started trampling her.

"'Right, 'right. Dethroid, cut the simulation," said Fedradin. Dethroid waved his wand. The boar disappeared, and Bev got up, unscathed. "Sorry Bev, you will only get two of the six points. There were two points for each boar, then two points for getting out unharmed." Bev sighed and brushed her hair out of her eyes.

Fedradin walked to Yexico. "Just try your best, Yexico," said Fedradin.

"Thanks, but I know the only reason you let me come here is because you owe my father," said Yexico.

"You know that's not true," said Fedradin. Actually, it was. When Fedradin was about seventeen, Fedradin had been in the habit of getting in trouble because with no guardians, he could do whatever he wanted. One day, Fedradin's friend from the castle, Junike, had made a bet with him, that Fedradin couldn't break into Yexico's father's estate in the mountain pastures and steal something. Fedradin, bored with sitting in the castle all day, decided to take the bet with Junike. They went out to the house late one night, when all the lights were out. Fedradin decided the best way to go about breaking into the building was to sneak up through the sheep fields surrounding it and go in the sidedoor. Fedradin opened the gate and began running towards the mansion. He got to the sidedoor and tested the lock to find the door was open. He entered the building and began his search to find something impressive to bring back to Junike. He was skulking around the house, when he heard the sound of someone going down the stairs.

"Who's there?" called out Binneau, Yexico's father.

Fedradin immediately turned around and ran for the door. When Binneau heard Fedradin run, he pursued. Fedradin sprinted through the sheep fields and ran out the gate with Junike. Binneau gave up the chase and started yelling. The yells startled the sheep, and they began to run towards the gate, which

Fedradin had failed to close in his haste. All the sheep escaped, and Binneau was left with nothing.

The next morning, Binneau called for whoever had let his sheep escape to reveal themselves. Apparently, someone had seen Junike leave the castle late on the night of the escaped sheep. They told Binneau, and with no other suspects, Binneau accused Junike. As an influential elder, he was able to successfully call for a public flogging. Unfortunately, Junike didn't survive his whipping. Fedradin, grief-stricken about losing Junike, told Binneau that he was the one who let the sheep out. To avoid public humiliation at the fact that he had had the wrong person killed, Binneau, instead of flogging Fedradin, told Fedradin that he would eventually need to do something to pay back the cost of the sheep. That time came when, Yexico, despite all of his physical barriers, set his mind to fight monsters for a living, after Fedradin established the Ridders.

Yexico stepped forward, and pulled out a baselard, or a large knife with an 'I' shaped handle. A boar noticed him. Yexico looked down, moving his feet slightly in order to fix his posture, before looking up and bracing himself. The boar charged. Yexico stabbed with his short sword, but his timing was off, he was too early, and he missed horribly. The boar's horns collided with Yexico's stomach.

"Cut it," said Fedradin. Dethroid waved his wand. "I'm sorry, Yexico. Zero."

"Kekk, you next," said Dethroid, taking charge, as Fedradin gave advice to Yexico, adjusting Yexico's grip on the weapon. Kekk stepped forward and pulled out two poniards. A poniard was a dagger that was designed to be thrown.

Kekk immediately hurled one of the poniards at one of the boars. The blade spun handle over blade before it perfectly struck the boar in the side of the neck. The boar lurched at Kekk for a couple of steps, but then collapsed in a heap and died.

Kekk threw his second blade at the second boar. The poniard flipped through the air once again, but Kekk's timing was slightly off and the poniard's wooden handle bounced harmlessly off the boar's thick hide. The boar, full of anger, charged at Kekk. Kekk's eyes grew wide. When the boar reached him, he tried to jump over it, mimicking Bev. In midair, one of the boar's tusks clipped one of Kekk's legs. The blow to Kekk sent him crashing into the stone floor. The boar, realizing what had happened, turned around and charged at Kekk. It brought its tusks down, and Kekk barley managed to roll to one side and stand up. The boar's tusks got stuck in the stone for a moment, and that gave Kekk time to pull out his dagger. As soon as the boar looked up, Kekk stabbed it through the eye with his dagger. Once he was sure the boar was dead, he looked up at Fedradin, awaiting feedback.

"Nice job, Kekk. You have some injury to the back of your leg, but otherwise, that was almost flawless." Fedradin left, leaving Kekk squatting on the ground, breathing heavily, waiting for the adrenaline to wear off. Fedradin arrived at the next line.

"Shah, it is your turn." Shah took out her whip and short sword. She cracked the whip, daring one of the boars to approach. The boar on the right took the bait, and it charged at her. Shah rolled to the side, then struck the boar in the eye. The boar reared up and roared. While its head was up, Shah slit the boar's throat. Meanwhile, the second boar charged at Shah. As soon as the first boar crumpled to the ground dead, she leaped over the second, delivering a kick to its head. The boar reeled backwards, and Shah lunged with her short sword and stabbed the boar through the heart. While she did this, Shah grabbed her dagger, and slit the boar's throat. The boar fell to the ground. Shah pulled back her hair, picked up her weapons, and walked back to the bench.

"Shah, you never disappoint," said Fedradin. He continued on to the next person in line, Axto. He was slightly pale in the face.

"Axto, are you ready?" asked Fedradin. Axto nodded nervously.

The boars at the end of his lane snapped into action. In synchrony, they charged at Axto. Axto stabbed his halberd at the charging boars, but at neither in particular. It found its mark in the boar on the right's neck. He left his weapon after it failed to dislodge from the boar's neck. Axto quickly spun away from the second charging creature to avoid being gored.

The boar turned around, charging again. Axto tried to pull his halberd out of the dead boar's neck once more, but to no avail. Axto let go of the halberd and drew his falchion from his belt.

This nasty blade was of medium length and curved slightly at the end. It could easily be mistaken for a machete.

By then, the boar had almost reached Axto, who jumped over the corpse of the first boar. The second boar tried to follow him, but tripped on the body of the first boar. Axto lunged with his falchion and cut the boar's head off.

Fedradin walked over, "I'm impressed, Axto. You had some very close calls, though, but otherwise, it was great." Fedradin continued to the last line. There stood Draslupp. "Draslupp, show them how it's done!"

Draslupp walked forward, his knuckles white from gripping his bow so hard. Draslupp closed his eyes, and his body and clothes disappeared. A few seconds later his bow and quiver disappeared.

"Dethroid, does anything Draslupp touches turn invisible?" asked Fedradin. Fedradin realized he should have had this question a year earlier, when he had taken in Draslupp.

"No. He can expend energy to turn whatever he touches invisible. His body and clothes can turn invisible without him noticing because his clothes and body don't require very much energy to do so. Weapons and things he holds onto takes energy to turn imperceptible, more energy for larger items," replied Dethroid, whose eyes were focused on Draslupp.

"You seem to know a lot about Domers."

"My uncle, aunt, and cousins were all Domers."

"Were?"

"Murdered."

"I'm sorry."

"I'm not."

Fedradin gave him a quizzical look. Dethroid made no intention of expanding on the idea. "Let's just watch Draslupp," said Dethroid. Fedradin gave Dethroid one last searching glance before turning his attention to Draslupp, or the lane in which Draslupp was supposedly fighting. Fedradin didn't even know if Draslupp was there, because Draslupp was invisible.

Suddenly, a distinct knife cut appeared on the first wolverine. The wolverine tried to jump back, but an invisible force was pulling it to the ground, restraining it. Suddenly, its head twisted all the way around, and it crumpled, its neck broken.

A few seconds later, another wolverine fell over, a dagger protruding from its eye.

"He must've just thrown his dagger," said Fedradin.

"Either that or he doesn't have enough energy to keep the knife invisible," said Dethroid.

The other three wolverines were extremely on edge. They paced around, swiping the air with their claws and sniffing the air. This went on for many minutes.

"What's he doing?" asked Fedradin.

"Probably trying to nock an invisible arrow on an invisible bowstring. You can imagine how hard that could be," said Dethroid.

Suddenly, a bow and arrow appeared in the air. The arrow moved slightly and the notch on the end of the arrow grasped the bowstring. The two weapons disappeared, but it was enough for a wolverine to leap at the area Draslupp was taking up. The arrow became visible and moved towards the wolverine. The wolverine batted it away with its paw.

"He's in trouble," said Dethroid.

Dethroid was right. The wolverine appeared to be colliding with an invisible wall. Draslupp flickered, and he became visible. The wolverine came in for the killing bite, but Draslupp caught its head and snapped its neck. He threw away the body and got to his feet, but by that time both wolverines were next to him. They knocked him back down to the floor, and started ripping at him with teeth and claws.

"Dethroid, please cut the simulation," said Fedradin. Dethroid waved his wand and the wolverines vanished and Draslupp got up unharmed. "I'll give you four points for that."

"Only four?" asked Draslupp.

"You can turn invisible. I expected you to *at least* wound all of them."

"That's a lot to expect!"

"Well, you can turn invisible," said Fedradin. Draslupp just sighed and walked away. "'Right, who's up for some flying monsters?"

Chapter 8
The Wizard

KERWAN

KERWAN, A YOUNG MAN of about eighteen, done with his training as an apprentice and ready to go out and face the world as a full wizard, was sitting apprehensively on his horse's saddle. On this particular day, Kerwan had decided to take up one last adventure with his master and role model, Biggs.

He glanced down at a puddle on the ground. Kerwan liked what he saw in the reflection. A lively looking man stared back at him. The man had short, ebon hair. Kerwan flexed. The man in the reflection had fairly large muscles, at least that's what it seemed like to Kerwan. He wasn't a grotesquely muscular man and was actually tall and thin, the muscles on his arm disproportionate to the rest of his body. He had bright, sparkling blue eyes and a nose with a spattering of freckles. Under his right eye, he had a red birthmark, which was shaped like a horseshoe.

Kerwan was waiting for his master, Biggs, and Biggs's new apprentice, Utka. Utka was a small boy with an annoying voice and eyes that were different colors, green and blue. He was prone to empty and vain talk. Kerwan had yet to see the boy actually become adroit at anything.

When Utka and Biggs finally came out of the stone structure, Kerwan dismounted his horse and walked over to them.

"What took you two so long?" asked Kerwan, somewhat angrily. "We were supposed to leave New Swenvip almost an hour ago!"

"I'm sorry!" cried Utka. "I wanted to learn more about the wand!"

"What did you want to learn about it?" asked Kerwan.

"I wanted to know why wizards need to carry them."

"That's a simple question, Utka," said Kerwan, "Wizards need wands to tap into the natural magic that surrounds and flows around every being. Humans aren't magical, for the most part, and only a select few humans have the ability to even come close to utilizing the magic. Those who are magical can't access magic without help. That's where wands come in."

"That's what Biggs said."

"Obviously. He's the master."

"Boys, boys, boys. Yoer's far away from here. The longer we wait, the longer we have to trek in the dark," said Biggs.

"Yes! Let's go!" cried Kerwan.

"I'm really good at horse riding so we shouldn't be behind schedule for long," said Utka, much to Kerwan's annoyance.

The three wizards mounted their horses, and as they did so, Utka slipped and fell face first onto the muddy paddock they were in.

"My boots are muddy. That's why I slipped."

Kerwan sighed and pulled out his warhammer. It was a basic weapon that looked like an oversized hammer, with two usable sides: one was a flat side, meant for bludgeoning, and the other had a sharp spike. Biggs unsheathed his Stentorik scimitar. The backsword's blade curved slightly, the shape it made looking like a crescent moon. At the very end, the blade narrowed down to a sharp point. Utka had his pike out. All of them also carried twisted pieces of wood, their wands.

"Remember, you two," came the voice of Biggs, "We are carrying a very special crystal. Our mission is to deliver this piece of magic to the High Wizard Rine who is currently dwelling in Yoer." The high wizard was the most skilled wizard in the Haxter, the leader of the Wizard Guild, which was based in Swenvip.

The horses started down the Road into Swenvip Swamp. "Master," asked Utka, "What does this crystal do?"

"I would tell you if I knew, Utka, but unfortunately, that little piece of information has been kept from even me."

"Why are we escorting it around so cautiously if we don't even know what it does?"

"The short answer, Kerwan and I are being paid many fellyers to do so."

"So I take it that the crystal was discovered around here?" asked Kerwan.

"Yes, it was found on the shores of Lake Swenvip. It could've washed in from anywhere because it was near where the

Mendelgar feeds the lake. The crystal has a unique air about it, which of course is a strong natural magic."

The three traversed the first quarter mile in great time. Kerwan determined that if they continued their pace, they would arrive at Yoer by early afternoon.

The next two hours proved uneventful. Kerwan entertained himself with the thought that soon his official initiation ceremony would occur, and he would be admitted to the world of magic as a full wizard, having completed his training as apprentice with Biggs. Despite the name, a wizard did not gain any more powers by becoming a full wizard; it was only an honorary term. Only until wizards became a full wizard were they regarded as real ones and treated as such. The next step of a wizard's life was to become a master and train apprentices, but many traveled around Haxter to see the many wonders of the land before doing so.

Biggs had trained a number of other apprentices, most of whom accomplished nothing, though there were a few exceptions. One of them discovered a vital use for stranglevine berry, which was to instantly heal any poisoning and help with open wounds. Another wrote a famous book on mysterious magical relics entitled, *The Lost Treasures*. The rest just had settled down and started training apprentices, like Biggs had done. At most Biggs could handle two apprentices at a time. Currently, Biggs was training Utka and another child named Quynn who was unable to come on the mission because of a jousting injury he incurred while at a tourney near Narven. He was still in Narven's hospital wing. Kerwan had been trained with another child, named Neomie who died when she fell off her horse and down a cliff when they were exploring the Kzit Mountains. It was a shame, because Biggs had to argue vehemently to have a girl trained. She was the first female wizard apprentice ever. At that time, Biggs was too far along training Kerwan to get another apprentice.

Finally, the three stopped for lunch at a clearing in the swamp, which had lots of knolls, and an algae covered pool of water in one corner of it. The trees that surrounded it all leaned in over the top of the defoliated area, to create a sort of roof made of leaves, so when the sunlight came through it was dappled and dyed green. The trio dismounted from their horses and sat on a dry log to lunch. The smell of seawater came riding upon the westward gusts of wind. Kerwan reached into his pocket and pulled out a strip of venison, a handful of berries and an apple. Biggs pulled out a similar lunch. Utka, following suit, pulled out the same provisions.

"Master," asked Utka, "touching on the reason of why humans have wands, has any human ever not needed a wand?"

"Well, the reason that wizards can't tap into their natural magic is because we have not been around long enough for our bodies to become one with the magic. It is expected that in time, we wizards not only shall be able to freely use magic, but regular humans may also be able to. So, the answer to your question would be no, not yet."

"Master, what about the Sages you told me about? Couldn't they use magic without help?" asked Kerwan.

"Ah, I thought you might bring up Sages. There is probably nothing that you will come across in your studies, Utka, which is more interesting than the Sages."

"Actually I thought that the most interesting subject was sorcery," murmured Kerwan. Biggs shot him a dirty look, bit a large chunk of venison off his strip, swallowed, and continued.

"Sages are not proven to be real, but widely accepted as being real because they show up in many, many myths from ancient cultures. One book, written by some Lear, titled *The Spawn of the Mountain*, has a detailed account of Sages. In the book, they are told to be mortal, though powerful; hungry for power, yet merciful; compassionate, yet unstoppable. Sages can supposedly live for eons because of their slow aging, though they can be killed by anything that can kill a mortal. Generally, a Sage's quickened reflexes and bolstered bodies help them avoid death by murder and disease. These beings are also believed to be created during times of strife. Most Sages are said to be good, but some became corrupt. Never has a Sage been any race but human. You asked if they could use magic freely, but they can't. It is rumored that certain items allow them to tap into the flow of elemental natural magic. So even Sages need help to use magic. Of course, all this is just from a very old book."

"According to the book, are any of them alive today?" asked Utka.

"Yes. Three Sages, written about in *The Spawn of the Mountain* and by soldiers in a variety of different wars, are believed to still be alive. They have all vanished. One is the Narv, Tawassa, who was a Sage of Fire. The second is a Boravian Prince, Olxo, also known as the Shadow Prince. He was, or possibly is, a Sage of Water. He was born recently, during the Boravian Revolt. Being a lordlun beforehand, he was given the title of 'prince'. The third is Frin Firehand of Swenvip. He was also a Sage of Fire. All of the Sages are believed to have been created at different times, but banded together and became corrupt for unknown reasons. They are called the Minions."

"What became of all of them?"

"No one knows."

The three finished their lunch. They were about to ride off again, when a roar sounded from close by. Biggs had his wand and scimitar pointed in the direction of the din in seconds. Kerwan scrambled to follow Biggs's lead with his warhammer. Utka, who was not prepared at all, dove behind a knoll in fear. Suddenly, the trees in front of the wizards were knocked over. Two twelve foot tall, bipedal turtle-resembling creatures with tentacles coming off each arm walked into the clearing.

"What are those monsters?" Kerwan exclaimed.

"Turteilem. We must be next to a nest, for generally they're not hostile. Watch out for the tentacles, they'll paralyze you!"

One of the turteila swung a fist at Kerwan. Kerwan ducked the blow, before falling face first to avoid being paralyzed by the tentacles. Getting up with his warhammer in hand, Kerwan struck the turteila in its ribs. A loud crunch ensued, and the turteila fell back with a gurgling roar of pain.

The second turteila swung its fist at Kerwan. Biggs leapt forward and sliced off its tentacles in one swipe. The turteila's fist stopped in mid-air, and it stumbled back, almost immediately swinging its uninjured fist at Biggs catching him unawares. Biggs flew through the air, landing in a puddle of swamp water close to Utka. Kerwan waited to see if Biggs would rise, but he didn't. A paralyzing tentacle must have hit Biggs.

As he felt the wind caused by a fist flying by his head, Kerwan snapped back to the battle. Both turteilem had recovered and were charging towards Kerwan. Quickly, Kerwan sent a beam of black light out of his wand. The light hit the ground in front of the turteilem and there was an explosion, knocking both turteilem back. Kerwan ran to the side of Biggs, and started muttering a spell.

"What are you doing?" asked Utka.

The sudden outburst startled Kerwan, who cursed because he lost his concentration on the spell. "I'm trying to unparalyze Biggs!" yelled Kerwan in reply. "Now, if those monsters get close, tell me."

A second passed. "They're really close," said Utka.

"Then do something!" yelled Kerwan, not looking up at the approaching monsters. "We need Biggs to win this fight!" Kerwan brought his attention back to his task at hand; Biggs was needed, and Utka was fairly good at distracting things. Kerwan muttered the last few lines of his spell, and Biggs started to waken.

"What happened?" asked Biggs weakly.

"You were paralyzed, Master. Now we must get back to our fight, for Utka won't be able to hold them off for long," replied Kerwan.

"Utka isn't going to use magic, is he?" asked Biggs, suddenly alert, eyes wide. At that precise moment, the ground shook and a deafening explosion made Biggs and Kerwan cover their ears.

"Well, I didn't know you haven't started training him yet!" yelled Kerwan, who immediately knew what had happened. The scene before the two wizards was the swamp as it was before, except that the turteilem were dead, lying in a massive hole. Utka was passed out, lying over the top of a knoll, his wand in his hand.

"Why would you even take the chance?" said Biggs as he put his hand on his forehead, in frustration.

"I don't know! Why else would you have given him a wand?"

Biggs ran over to Utka's limp body, checking for a pulse.

"Thank the gods he's alive. Kerwan go get me the gorp."

Kerwan jogged over to Biggs's purse and opened it up. Inside, he sorted through extra wands, Enchanted Torches, and acid in bottles designed for throwing until he found a ball of food filled with nuts, berries, pieces of meat and bits of chocolate stuck together with lard, sugar and honey. It looked disgusting. Kerwan brought the food over to Biggs, who tore off a piece and force-fed it to Utka. Slowly, he came to. Biggs kept feeding Utka more of the food until Utka was alert.

"What happened..." murmured Utka.

"I'll explain later. You'll feel better after you finish this," said Biggs, handing Utka another piece of gorp. Utka took a bite.

"Ugh! This tastes terrible!"

"It will reenergize you. It might taste bad, but you still need to eat it," said Biggs. Biggs turned to Kerwan and said, "Fetch some water."

So Kerwan went down to the pond, holding a bucket. As he arrived at the pond, he startled a frog, which leapt into the water. It swam to end of the pond and buried itself under some mud. Kerwan scooped up a bucket full of water where the water seemed cleanest, and he walked back to Biggs and Utka.

By this time, Utka had mostly recovered and was talking to Biggs.

"I still don't understand what happened to me," said Utka.

"Utka, I haven't taught you how to use magic yet-"

"But I thought that was why I was picked to be your apprentice. Because I could do magic," interrupted Utka.

"No, you were picked because you have the *capability* to do magic. I have to teach how to actually use it. Anyway, when you tried to use magic, you somehow managed to tap into the natural flow of magic, but you had no idea how to take the magic safely. When you tried to fend off the turteilem, you took too much magic. As you know- well, actually you *don't* know -it takes energy to take magic out of its natural flow. When you took that large amount of magic out of the flow, almost all of your energy was used up. If you had used all your energy, you would have died in a second."

"Why didn't I die?"

"Somehow, you innately knew how to turn that magic into a spell, and when that happens, you stop taking magic. Unfortunately, you took so much magic that it drained enough of your energy to knock you out. The only advantage to this situation is that your spell killed the turteilem."

"So I'm good at magic?" asked Utka.

"It's about time you were good at something," muttered Kerwan, though Utka could hear him.

"That's enough, Kerwan, I'm tired of taking your insults!" yelled Utka, fists in the air. "Bet I could knock you out in half a minute!"

"Utka, please don't-" Before Kerwan could finish his sentence, Utka was flying at him, swinging his fists madly. Kerwan quickly placed his bucket of water down, and braced himself. Kerwan caught one of Utka's fists, dodged the other, reached for it and grabbed it too, and flipped Utka over his head. Utka landed on the ground with a loud thud.

"Look who's on the ground in thirty seconds now?" said Kerwan, as he reached down and picked up the bucket. He handed it to Biggs, who took it with a sigh. "Really? You've had him for a couple weeks. Have you taught him anything?"

Chapter 9
The Flight to Gii

BREETEX

WITH A KNIFE PRESSED against her neck, Breetex led Aserax out of the warehouse. Dwarves that saw him gasped and moved out of his way. He was three quarters of the way to the front of Alta when he heard a dwarf shout, "They want the Princess!" Before Breetex could react, another dwarf yelled, "She's over here! Breetex has her!"

The diplomats soon surrounded Breetex.

"Breetex, how did you acquire the Princess?" asked one dwarf.

"I kidnapped her when we raided Reedil," lied Breetex.

"And why were we not informed of this, Greul Breetex?" asked the same dwarf.

"I will explain everything after we neutralize the current situation," said Breetex.

"But-"

"Please, Yentrical Dixie, I will explain later. It is a long story, and right now is not the time for me to explain it."

"Greul Breetex, I expect the explanation the moment this is over." Dixie turned and continued walking. Breetex overheard him conversing with the other dwarves about what they wanted in return for the Princess.

Breetex leaned over to Aserax, his voice hardly above a breath, "Take out the first elf, then run east as fast as you can." Aserax nodded, her nod unnoticed by everyone except Breetex.

They arrived at the gates of Alta, its white stone walls extending in either direction. One of the dwarves accompanying Dixie pushed the gates open.

"We have the Princess. Stand back, drop your weapons, or she dies," announced Dixie. The elves looked over, and grudgingly dropped their weapons. The clamor of an entire army disarming was quite a din.

"What do you want for her?" asked the elf standing in front of the rest. Breetex brought Aserax in front of Dixie, so all the elves could see the dagger pressed to her throat. Dixie procured out a piece of parchment, and pulled it in front of his own face.

Dixie cleared his throat. "The dwarfish council, in return for Princess Aserax, wants..." Dixie was interrupted by a loud shout of "Now!" from Breetex.

Aserax slammed her knee into the groin of the elf. He fell over in excruciating pain. Aserax sprinted away from the two armies as fast as she could.

At the same time, Breetex punched at Dixie's face, ripping through his parchment and making contact with his nose with a sickening crunch. Breetex pulled his fist back, and it was covered in blood. He took off running, right behind Aserax.

In the confusion, the opposing armies bellowed war cries, assuming the other army to have turned aggressive. Breetex heard the twang of bow strings being released and then cries of the dwarves being hit, the clang of metal on metal, and the crunch of dwarves' boots after leaping over the walls to join the fight. Breetex knew it all too well. He heard the galloping of the cavalry, and the barking of the dwarves' bargests. Throughout it all, no matter what, Breetex just kept running.

Aserax was reminded of something as she listened to the battle raging behind her. "My bow!" Breetex smiled.

"This bow?" he procured the pieces of a disassembled bow from underneath his plate. Aserax's face lit up. "I'm not an idiot."

Chapter 10

A Carriage Pulled by Squirrels

FEDRADIN

THEY WERE OFF WITH little time to spare. The competition had taken longer than Fedradin had thought because of a tight race between Kekk and Axto for the third spot. After many extra competitions, Kekk claimed it. Draslupp and Shah had easily claimed the first two. Dethroid had not been able to compete in the competition, because wizards were not allowed to compete at the Gii Games, according to Cecil.

Fedradin, Cecil, the Ridders, and a few guards had climbed into a carriage. The carriage was pulled by two white horses and was covered in bison hide. On one side, a cut in the hide had been made to give the Ridders some air and also so they could see out. The city of Gii was about fifty miles from the city of Narven, so it would take the majority of the day. The carriage was on its way by noon.

When they were about two hours into their trip, they came out of the Ozreek Mountains. Slowly, the road transitioned from a rocky, elevated consistency to a soft, flat, dirt road. Almost all of the Ridders sighed at one point or another, as the transition let them become much more comfortable, for they no longer were bounced around by the large stones that dotted the mountain road.

About another hour into the forest, the Ridders pulled up next to another carriage at an intersection. The inntown that marked the crossroads was teeming. Bev peered out the opening to get a good look at the carriage next to them. It looked like the Ridders' carriage, except two human-sized squirrels pulled it along.

"What the hell?" Bev said.

"What?" said Fedradin, looking up from reading his book of monsters. He was currently studying the yaun, a rare race of half-human-half-snake creatures. They were evil and vicious and participated in warfare commonly.

55

"Are yaks supposed to be able to stand up?" said Bev. She looked more closely, "And *talk*?"

Yexico came over to the opening to see out of it. "Bev's right," he said. "That's certainly odd."

Cecil, who had been resting -or had appeared to be resting, for he had put his hat down over his eyes— removed his hat, shrugged off some of his grogginess, and said, "Perhaps you are looking at a team from the animal cultures? One of the nine races?"

"Animal cultures?" asked Bev.

"Oh right!" exclaimed Shah. "Fedradin taught us about them!"

"So I did," said Fedradin. "Do you want to explain, or should I find them in the book?"

"No, no. I can explain this. I need to practice for Borave," said Shah, turning back to the Ridders, "The animal cultures are a race of creatures that are from the Szrek Plane, which is closely related to the Certzol plane. Like all monsters and magical things, they found a portal and moved to the Base Plane." When Shah did not add more, Fedradin took over.

"There are five types: Yakio, Wolvio, Beaverio, Squirrelio and Lizario. Each looks like a different, giant animal; the name of the animal they look like is found in their names. Lizario are mainly the outcast of the rest of the species, for they are not as intelligent or civilized as the rest of their brethren. Though, there is a branch of intelligent Lizario, as I just found out," said Fedradin, "They are called yaun, though they are the most shunned of all the animal cultures."

"Wait, I thought there were six types," said Yexico, "Aren't Formiant the sixth?"

"No, Formiant are from the Plane of Earth, were they roamed the desert. They have moved to the Base Plane from there and have tried to colonize Haxter, if any of you have remember of the Formiant attacks in east Viven a while back. I was hardly eight years of age when the Empire drove them and their allies, the abeils, thri-kreen, and xii to Qassar after they attacked Haxter from their home planes.

"Anyway, you might think that Formiant are from the animal cultures because of their resemblance to ants, but they are not."

Another two hours went by, the Ridders chatting about yaun and tactics, when a band of kobolds wandered past their carriage. While it happened, all the Ridders watched out the window, having never seen a real kobold, only the simulation dummies mimicking their appearances. Cecil sat in the corner seemingly uneasy with the situation. Fedradin asked if anything was wrong, but Cecil waved him off.

Two more hours, and the carriage slowed to a stop.

"Congratulations, everyone," said Fedradin, standing up. "We made it here safely."

Suddenly, a garbled, inhuman voice came from outside, "Mcs no woulds bc sos surcs."

Chapter 11
Plans

NINETEEN YEARS EARLIER

THE MINIONS GATHERED IN a crowded in a corner. Their Master stood in front of them, screaming in rage, spittle flying off his lips with every word.

"A baby! A damn baby! And three of the most powerful men in the world?" he screamed incredulously, "A baby."

Oxlo spoke up. "And a wizard." The Master spun with his arm outstretched and his palm facing outwards. He pointed his palm at Oxlo. The air around Oxlo became almost...visible in a way, standing apart due to a certain thickness the other air lacked. It formed around Oxlo and proceeded to fling him across the room. Oxlo slammed into a stone wall and slumped to the ground.

"Would anyone else like to say anything?" The Master looked around. "Now, I can't kill you all for this failure, though I would if you were not Sages."

"Is that because you need us or because you can't kill us?" muttered Oxlo from across the room. The Master pointed a finger at the wall. The stone from the wall shot outward, hitting Oxlo's back before he could get up. The wall returned to its normal position. The Master spat on Oxlo's sprawled body.

"It is neither of those reasons, actually. I am not threatened by your powers as a Sage, they just help me accomplish my mission. I could replace you any time I see fit., You three would fail to beat me in any fight in any situation. I keep you around because you are *useful*. You do my bidding like dogs because you fear me, and can carry out jobs I find...distasteful myself.

"Understand, Oxlo?" said the Master, looking down, "You are still disposable, almost as much as my slaves." At that precise moment, a human slave walked in carrying a tray of food. Without looking behind him, the Master pointed his palm at the door, and a rock, appearing out of nowhere, flew at the slave, who was caught unaware. The rock smashed into his skull, and he fell over backwards, dead.

"Now, even though you fools managed to let that baby and that wizard escape my grasp, my plans for revenge must go on." The Master pulled out a sheet of paper. "Now-" He was cut off by the door slamming open. The Master snarled and looked up. A human, dressed in a chainmail with a short sword in his sheath and carrying a small wooden box, was in the doorway.

"Master, we just..." His voice trailed off as he picked his way around the crumpled body of the slave.

"Yes?" Noticing the fear growing in the man's eyes, the Master added. "Don't worry, you haven't displeased me yet. Unlike some..." His eyes flicked towards Oxlo, leaving them there for a heart-stopping moment.

The man walked to a table in the center of the room and dropped his box. He reached to open it, but the Master pushed him aside and greedily tore off the lid. As it clattered on the stone floor, the Master pulled out a glowing blue orb.

"What is this?" demanded the Master

"You pushed me!" said the man indignantly.

One of the Minions gasped. In a second, the Master had the man pinned to the wall with one hand, and a fireball growing and floating above the other. Slowly the rage faded from the Master's eyes and he let the man fall to the floor.

"I suggest you drop the attitude. These men can and will tell you; bad things will happen if you get on my wrong side. You better hope you impress me with this blue ball, or you might find yourself in a rather...undesirable situation."

The man got up, rage at the Master still present. "The orb is a Prophecy, Master. Using the Device, I stole a Prophecy going to the baby."

"What does it say?"

Without saying anything, the man grabbed the orb, and threw it on the ground. It shattered on impact, spraying a white mist everywhere. When the mist cleared, a scroll was left in its place. "It has not been read, because we thought that you would like to be the first. We all know how much you like to be first," said the man.

"I warned you," growled the Master, who raised a palm. Fire erupted out of his hand, directed straight at the man. For a moment or two, the man screamed. Another moment or two later, the smell of burnt flesh filled the air. "No need for him anymore. Tawassa, could you go fetch someone to clean up our...friends here?" Tawassa barely managed a nod, before darting out of the room. "Oxlo, Frin, you're more or less the brains of this operation. Besides me of course. Help me figure out this prophecy." Oxlo bent down and picked up the scroll. He unraveled it and set it on the table. He read:

> To lead. To fight. What must be done to find what is destined to be found. If he dies, never will they be found. But what is to be found, one must wonder? Oh, yes. Hidden away for the power is too great. The power? You wonder again. In the sea of death, despair and misery is where you will wander.

"Only a little vague..." said Frin.

"Shush!" shouted the Master. Oxlo and Frin looked at him while he thought for a moment or two until Tawassa opened the door. All three men looked over while Tawassa pointed out the bodies of the men to two slaves, who hurried to clean up the mess. When Tawassa saw the three men crowded around the scroll, he got curious.

"What?" he asked. Oxlo reread the prophecy. Tawassa thought for a moment then said. "I don't think we're supposed to kill the baby."

"Really?" said Frin.

"No need for sarcasm."

"No need to be an idiot."

"Gentlemen, Tawassa said something that needed to be said, even though we've all figured it out," said the Master.

"Master, I think that's the *only* thing we've figured out. That and this person needs to find something."

"Whatever he must find, I want," said the Master. "I have some theories as to what it is, but I need time to work them out. For the time being, until he is old enough to find this item, I want you three to find him, make sure he is safe, and never let him leave our sights. Use whatever you need to; you have my permission to take whatever you need from the Heart. When he is old enough, we will turn him to our side. All we have to do now is wait." The Minions hurried to the door.

"Master, what is your mission?" asked Tawassa before leaving the room.

"Revenge. Sweet revenge."

Chapter 12
The Bronze Knife

KERWAN

UTKA, KERWAN, AND BIGGS galloped into Yoer at their expected time of two hours before midnight, the pace had slowed since the attack. Biggs had lectured Utka about magic and wand safety until the trio had a run-in with a pesky render. It chased them for a mile or two before giving up and returning to its lair. After that, Biggs had moved on to lecture Utka about the proper precautions one must take when fighting and observing monsters. These discussions fascinated Utka, as they had Kerwan five years previously. Unfortunately, having to listen to the same speech twice (especially from Biggs with his monotonic voice) was incredibly painful.

"...and that's why I no longer have a brother," finished Biggs.

"I don't really know what he was expecting when he walked into the chinside's cave," said Kerwan. "I've heard that story a few times now and I still don't really understand."

Biggs ignored the comment. "The moral is that you treat monsters with respect."

"Or that robbing Haxter's most deadly creature is a bad idea."

Again, Biggs ignored the comment. "So here is the great town of Yoer." Biggs made a sweeping motion with his hand to draw more attention to the cluster of dilapidated wood -and a few stone -buildings all facing a beautiful two-story masterpiece of a building, the white marble gleaming in the moonlight. A few crannogs dotted the outskirts of the town for protection.

"I wonder where Rine is staying," said Kerwan sarcastically.

"Obviously the marble building, stupid," said Utka. "Where else would the High Wizard stay?"

"Ever heard of sarcasm?"

"Obviously."

"Boys, please stop. We made it here safely and we should be glad for that," said Biggs.

The trio hopped down off their horses smoothly -except for Utka who managed to get caught on the stirrups.

"Oh, and, Utka... I forgot to congratulate you on your record best of only falling off your horse four times during our trip," said Kerwan.

"Not my fault! My horse was...my saddle was too...um..." stammered Utka as he tried to free his pants from the saddle. When he managed to do so, he fell on the ground, face first. They walked their horses to a fence and tethered them there.

"Be nice, Kerwan," said Biggs.

"Yes, Master," said Kerwan in a joking, servile tone, bowing sarcastically. Kerwan started off towards one of the shacks that seemed slightly nicer than the others, even though that didn't mean much for this particular town.

"Where are you going?" asked Biggs.

"My time with you is over. I'm a Full Wizard now," said Kerwan. "Not exactly officially, but my ceremony will happen any time. Now, I'm going to buy some things at that market for when I get back to Swenvip."

"So you won't be riding back with us?" asked Biggs.

"No."

"At least then go with my blessing and this." Biggs walked forward and handed Kerwan a bronze dagger. He placed a hand on Kerwan's forehead and said, "May you use this dagger to keep you safe, and may luck find you wherever you may be." Biggs dropped his hand, and the two embraced.

"Do I get a dagger?" asked Utka. "I'm really good at fighting with them."

"Goodbye to you too, annoying little Utka," said Kerwan, looking down. With that Kerwan turned around and headed to the market. He walked up the steps in front of the building, and entered through the side door.

Inside, there was no one in sight, even at the counter where obviously someone should have been. The room was oddly shaped, with many corners and nooks. Kerwan started looking around. He passed by a large selection of books. He noticed a hand-copied manuscript of that monster book he always heard about, and the book titled *The Known World* by the same author, Assawat the Wanderer. Assawat wrote about his travels, including a list of the five glories of man, and the five glories of nature. The glories of man were the Grandwall in the

Westerlands, the Floating Chapel in the Quoll Mountains, the Fraze Pyramid in Widow's Desert, Fort Haxter on Lake Balgastar and Sitnalta on the Mendelgar Bay. The glories of nature were the Floating Mountains of Quoll, the Boiling Island, Dragonsback Ridge, the Silver Sentinels, and Mount Sage.

On the shelf, there was also a rewritten manuscript of the *Complete List of Spells* by Anarto the Great, one of the best wizards ever to live. Kerwan was impressed by the collection of books; he assumed the only reason they were inside the run-down shop was for the High Wizard.

As he flipped through the spellbook, he felt a pair of eyes watching him. He spun quickly, as he saw a flash of black as someone -or something- ducked behind a shelf of Summoner Orbs directly behind him.

Kerwan's new knife trembled. Maybe Biggs had created it with the intentions that it moved when danger or conflict was imminent? That was just a hunch, though.

Better safe than sorry.

Kerwan pulled out his wand, but kept a hand on the knife. Still, the feeling of his trusted warhammer on his back comforted him in a way like nothing else. He slowly moved until he was at the edge of the shelf. He waited a moment before leaping forward with his knife and wand pointed at where he supposed the thing was hiding.

"Aaah!" he shouted, maybe as a war cry, or maybe out of fear. Maybe just to break the silence that was beginning to make him insane. But nothing was there. Was Kerwan being paranoid? Was he hallucinating? Was that mushroom he ate on the voyage poisonous? He put his knife in its sheath and tucked his wand away. Maybe the store was closed, but the owner's cat was still here. But were there any cats that big? Could it have been a dire cat or a mngwa? As Kerwan thought, he caught another glimpse of movement out of the corner of his eye again. But this time it moved with a hostile intent, not to hide. And it was not a cat.

Kerwan pulled out his wand, but he wasn't fast enough, and whatever it was crashed into him, knocking him into the shelf. The shelf didn't fall, but rocked, and the orbs came crashing down. One of them must have hit Kerwan's assailant, for the grip from it went loose for a second. Kerwan took the opportunity and kicked his way free. As he got up, so did his assailant. They stood face to face, and Kerwan could see with whom he was fighting.

A tall man, wearing a black robe with a large hood shadowing his face, pointed a particularly warped wand at Kerwan. The hood cast the majority of the man's head in darkness, but a large red tattoo of a gust of wind on his bald forehead gleamed outward.

"Can I help you?" Kerwan shouted angrily.

The man in the robe simply snarled. He flicked his wand and out shot a black spell. Kerwan reacted quickly and projected a green shield to block it. The beam bounced off and crashed into a shelf displaying swords, most likely enchanted, but it didn't stop them flying everywhere as the beam exploded, destroying the shelf. One landed point down in the floor right in front Kerwan. He quickly shot a few white beams at the man, who flattened himself as the beams hit a shelf containing poison detectors, glass vials full of a liquid that turned any poisoned drinks green, which fell to the ground and shattered upon impact as the shelf crumbled.

Kerwan tried to draw his warhammer, but it caught on its leather straps as the man climbed to his feet. The man charged, a tremble from his knife, a sudden idea. Kerwan let go of his warhammer -which untangled itself and dropped to the ground- and he pulled the sword in front of him from the ground. He swung the blade, but the man was able to sidestep it, slamming his fist into Kerwan's forearm. Kerwan, with a cry of pain, dropped his weapon. Instinctively, he lashed out with his own fist, landing a blow on the man's temple, sending him to the ground.

As the man got back up, Kerwan picked up and charged with his warhammer. He swung it towards the hooded man, but the man managed to roll away and scramble to his feet. Kerwan swung again. The man pulled back, but Kerwan clipped him in the sternum with the flat side of his warhammer. A crack of bone, and the man fell backwards into the glass and wood debris. Kerwan approached again him and swung the warhammer down at the hooded man's skull.

BIGGS

Biggs and Utka walked up to the marble house's door. Biggs was slightly choked up about having Kerwan leave, but he tried to put on a relaxed face as they made their presence known with a gilded doorknocker. He was pretty sure he had Utka fooled, but the High Wizard would probably see right through him.

It didn't matter. Did it? Even if Rine would see him as weak would it be a bad thing? *Would* he even see Biggs as weak? The thoughts ran through his head. He wasn't even aware of the time passing, until Utka tugged on the sleeve of his shirt.

"Master, he's not answering."

Biggs knocked harder and said, "High Wizard! Are you there?" They waited a few more minutes, and still no answer. They heard a crash from inside the store Kerwan had disappeared to. Biggs turned.

"Ah, Kerwan. Must have been trying to get something off the top shelf," said Utka. A flash of black, and an explosion from the store. Three white flashes, and the sound of items falling.

"No, something's wrong," said Biggs. "We need the High Wizard." Biggs pushed against the door, but unfortunately it was locked. Biggs pulled his wand out and tapped the lock, while muttering something. When he finished, the door swung inward.

Inside there was a long hallway with small bits of furniture to the side that ended in a large room. "Be careful, Utka."

They slowly walked down the hall, Biggs with his scimitar and wand and Utka with his pike.

"I'm really good at sneaking."

"Hush, child." Almost directly after Biggs finished speaking, Utka tripped on a chair, and fell to the ground. Biggs grabbed him and lifted him to his feet roughly.

By this time, they had entered the large chamber. Two couches faced one another at the end of the room, in front of the fireplace. To the right a staircase led up to the second floor. Biggs saw Rine, a short, plump man with grizzled brown hair, gagged up and tied to a chair on the left. Rine's eyes widened, and his head jerked to the side, in an attempt to get Biggs to notice something. Just then, Biggs caught something in his peripheral vision. A flash of movement.

Biggs spun around and slashed with his scimitar, but his elbow collided with the top of Utka's head, rendering the swing useless. The man whom Biggs had tried to attack leapt back.

"Ow! Master!" yelled Utka, clutching his head. Biggs grabbed Utka's collar and threw him away.

"Find cover!" Biggs yelled, as he projected a green shield to block a black spell. The spell rebounded straight back at the man, who jumped to the side. The spell smashed into the marble wall, sending pieces of marble flying everywhere. When the debris cleared, there was a hole in the wall.

Biggs got up before the man, and saw him clearly for the first time. The man was dressed in a black robe, with a large hood. A red tattoo shone clearly from the top of his head. It looked like a gust of wind.

KERWAN

In the split second before Kerwan's warhammer finished its swing, Kerwan saw the man's eyes glow red.

And then the man disappeared, leaving only a little wind.

Kerwan's warhammer crashed into the ground, creating a hole in the wooden floor, the swampy ground visible through it. He quickly pulled the warhammer out of the floor, but before he could turn around to try to find his assailant, he felt a foot collide with the back of his head. Kerwan fell to the ground, dropping his warhammer.

The man landed on top of Kerwan, and Kerwan just managed to roll over to face the man.

"Give...me...crystal," the man seethed.

"Don't...have...it," struggled Kerwan, for the man was now pushing his elbow into Kerwan's windpipe.

"Liar!" shouted the man, who loosened his elbow on Kerwan's throat, but pulled out a poniard. Kerwan's dagger trembled.

I know I'm in danger, thank you very much, knife thought Kerwan, who pulled it out.

Just in time, too.

The man slashed down with the poniard, and Kerwan just managed to block it with the bronze knife. The poniard bounced away from Kerwan, and Kerwan stabbed upwards with his. He nicked the man's shoulder, after the man deflected the knife away from his jugular with a calloused hand. Then the man stabbed, and Kerwan rolled his head away to avoid being stabbed through the eye, but the man still punctured his ear. Kerwan yelped, stabbing at the man. This went on for a while, until Kerwan had been stabbed twice in the ear, and nicked once in the temple and the man was stabbed in the shoulder a few times, and slashed once across the cheek. At this point, they were both tired and bloody, Kerwan more than his assailant.

"Hello? I heard some awful noises in here," came a voice from the door.

The man looked up, Kerwan pushing him off and jumping to his feet. Before the man could get up, Kerwan planted his foot in the man's stomach. He raised his warhammer and swung, the man throwing his hands up to protect his head, which caught the majority of the blow, but the hammer still clipped the side of his head. Kerwan kicked the man away.

"What is happening in there?" the voice came again, this time followed by footsteps.

Kerwan tried to ignore the voice and focus on his current battle. He took a step closer to the man, and he swung the warhammer. Before the warhammer hit the man, he vanished, Kerwan striking the ground.

Suddenly, an explosion that could only have come from a black spell. Biggs and Utka were in trouble. Kerwan involuntarily glanced over at the source of the noise. He realized it was a mistake as soon as he did it. But it was too late. He felt the poniard slide across his back, but luckily his jerkin took most of the cut. But it still cut him a little and it hurt.

Kerwan cried out in pain. He avoided falling to his knees, but another lunge was coming. He put his hand out to stop the blow, and he closed his eyes, bracing for the inevitable pain in his palm. But it never came. Instead he heard the familiar sound of metal on metal, and he opened his eyes. The bronze dagger was in his hand. And it had blocked the poniard. The look in the hooded man's eyes showed that something out of the ordinary had just happened.

Thank you, weird knife.

BIGGS

Biggs quickly fired a purple spell at man he was fighting. As the beam neared the man, it splintered into a bunch of different pieces shaped like spikes. The man pulled up a green shield, and the spikes impaled themselves in that. While the man was ducking behind his shield, Biggs leapt forward with his scimitar. The man dropped his shield and looked for Biggs. What he saw was Biggs charging with his scimitar.

The man, sensing the danger of the situation, vanished in a gust of wind.

And reappeared right next to Biggs. Biggs slashed again. A gust of wind, and the man was gone. A moment later, Biggs heard a chuckle behind him. Biggs spun and lashed out with his scimitar, but again the man managed to elude him by vanishing.

Suddenly, two feet smashed into the small of his back. Biggs fell forward, but rolled so that he landed on his back, face up. The man jumped, intending to land on top of Biggs, so Biggs stuck out his scimitar. Seeing that, the man disappeared. Biggs leapt to his feet.

And the man reappeared behind Biggs. Luckily Biggs was ready this time. He leapt up, and he feinted with his sword. The man vanished, and Biggs swung his sword behind him, so that when the man reappeared, he would do so in front of a razor sharp blade.

The plan worked, and the man fell to the ground with a giant gash in his side. He groaned in pain, but Biggs had delivered a fatal wound.

"You... made... very... powerful...enemy," managed the man through his pain. "Now...you...die."

"From who? You?" Without waiting for an answer, Biggs slammed the heel of his foot into the man's neck. The man whimpered from pain. Biggs walked away from the crumpled body of the man, and called, "Utka? Utka where are you?"

"Looking for Utka, are you?" came a voice. Biggs looked up, and saw Utka and another, similar looking man on the staircase. The man held a knife to Utka's throat.

"What do you want with the boy?" demanded Biggs.

"I want nothing from the boy, I want something from you."

"And what is it you want?" asked Biggs

"The crystal. Give me the crystal," said the man, in a commanding voice.

"Why do you want the crystal? If you take it, the whole Human Empire will seek to destroy you."

"But without the help of your beloved Rine?" cooed the man, who pulled out his wand and fired a purple spell at Rine. The spell split up into six different spikes, each imbedding itself deep in Rine's back and neck. The dead wizard's head slumped forwards, the body held by the binds tying him to the chair.

"Now you've done it! The whole world is going to be in outrage after this. They will track you down and kill you."

"But how will you know where to find me?" cooed the man.

"Oh, please. You're trying to act like I don't recognize the tattoo on the man who just attacked me. You are from the cult of Desert Wind. And it seems like you've picked up some talents." Biggs was referencing his assailant's ability to disappear. The man was a little shocked at Bigg's inside knowledge, so Biggs continued. "If you're so intent on taking my crystal, why don't you fight me one on one, with honor."

"You see here, Wizard. If I don't bring home the crystal, I fail my religion. I don't care about honor, I care about pleasing my gods." The man leaned forwards. "Fortunately for you, my gods also specify that I mustn't back down from any fight." The man took his knife away from Utka's neck, and Utka sprinted out the door. "Now about that fight." The man clapped his hands, and Biggs was seized by two similarly men.

"You..." Biggs said, condescendingly, even though he knew he never should have believed the man in the first place.

"I know," said the man, "I'm despicable."

KERWAN

An old woman came into view.

"What is...Oh, gods above," gasped the woman as she saw the knife fight. She watched with her hands over her mouth for a while, until Kerwan slashed the man's cheek. "Stop this! Stop this at once!" she screamed.

The man quickly pulled out his wand, and he shot a yellow beam at the woman. The beam hit her, and she became entangled in a yellow bond. The woman screamed insults, but no profanity.

But as the man shot the spell, Kerwan charged. He slapped the man's dagger out his way with his hand and slammed into him, shoulders first. The man went flying, and he landed on a display of enchanted scabbards and quivers. Kerwan raised his knife, and then feinted a stab. The man disappeared, but Kerwan swung his knife behind him, and it connected with the man's stomach. Kerwan dropped the knife, took out his warhammer, swung around and smashed the man in the top of the head with the sharp end. The man fell over, nearly dead.

The woman shrieked. "You murderer! You monster! Someone help me! Murder! Murder!" A few seconds later, her binds went undone, as the man died, extricating her.

"Lady, I would be happy to replace those binds if you don't shut up," said Kerwan before leaving the store.

"For your information, my name is Maghin, and I run the store you just destroyed!" she shouted after him.

When he got outside, he didn't see either of his counterparts. He looked around, and started heading for the marble house. Right as he was about to get there, Utka sprinted out.

"Help! Help!" he shouted. "They're going to kill Biggs!"

Chapter 13
To Cross a Bridge

FEDRADIN

"**AND WHAT MAKES YOU** think you can stop us?" asked Fedradin. He was standing outside his carriage with the rest of his Ridders. They were at the beginning of a rope bridge, which they needed to cross it to get to Gii. The bridge was about sixty feet long, strung between two cliffs. Looking down, a river under it. The bridge was missing some of its wooden planks, which may have been in part because an obese troll was standing in the middle of the bridge.

The troll had an extremely ugly face; teeth sticking out this way and that, small horns breaking through its skin in bizarre places, and only one ear that just barely clung to its head, most of it torn off, with its counterpart completely missing. Its skin was of a green hue, though, contrary to popular belief of green being their natural skin tone, it was due to the troll's poor hygiene. The troll wore only a filthy loincloth, which its stomach rolls nearly overtook. One of its hands clutched a wooden club, with nails and sharp teeth shoved through the end, where they poked out the opposite sides, making a deadly weapon.

"Wells," said the troll. "Me sees dat yous no cans passes mes on dis bwidge. Yous haves tos fights me."

"What if I cut the bridge?"

The troll hesitated, then said with sudden candor, "Yous nos can cuts dis bwidge. Yous no woulds bes able tos cwoss."

"'Right, you're not as stupid as I thought," said Fedradin, then in an undertone, "But, very, very close." Back to his normal voice, "But what if I cut it anyway? You would still die, even though I cut 'dis bwidge.'"

The troll was completely baffled. At this point, the animal culture's carriage rolled up. A yak, dressed in a full suit of armor, and carrying an axe stepped out of the carriage.

"What's the problem?" asked the yak, with a heavy accent.

"Mountain Troll. The things are getting dumber by the year," said Fedradin. Fedradin gestured to the troll, who was conveniently picking its nose, deep in thought and probe.

"And this is a problem? Why not kill it?" asked the yak.

"Believe me, if I wanted to kill it, it would be dead. I'm just slightly worried that when we try to fight on the bridge, the bridge won't support us."

"I see. So what should we be a-doing about this?"

"Do you have any wizards or magicians with you?"

The yak looked confused. "You're not allowed to bring wizards to this competition."

"No, you can bring them, they just can't compete. So you don't have any?"

"We do not."

"Damn." Fedradin pursed his lips. After a moment, he called, "Dethroid?" Dethroid looked up from his debate with Yexico. The point of contestation: whether or not the mushroom Yexico had picked was poisonous. "Come over here please."

"Excuse me, Yexico. All I'm saying is that if you had hallucinations while picking it, it's not going to be good for you," said Dethroid.

"Dethroid, do you think that you have enough power to pick up the troll and throw him over the edge?"

Dethroid looked at the troll. "Depends. How much do you think it weighs?"

"Do they make numbers that high?" joked Fedradin, then seriously, "One thousand, thousand five hundred pounds?"

Dethroid considered for a moment. "I *could*, but if I don't clear the rope that's acting like the handles, he could pull the entire thing down."

The yak piped up, "Could you stun the troll and pull him here?"

Dethroid rubbed his eyes with both hands. "Good idea, but..."

"But what?" asked Fedradin.

"I've never had to deal with this much fat before. I don't know if my spell can reach through his gut."

"Are you serious?" asked Fedradin.

"Unfortunately, yes."

"Try, at least," said the yak.

"Alright," said Dethroid. Dethroid walked over to the bridge. "Hey, ugly!"

The troll looked up from examining its club like it never had seen it before. Dethroid flicked his wand, and a yellow beam erupted from the end of it. The beam hit the troll square in the chest. The troll grabbed at where the beam hit it, and then started to freeze -with an occasional spasm from an arm or a leg. After a few seconds of this, the troll fell over backwards. As it landed, more wooden planks fell out. Yellow strands of light shot out and entangled the troll. Dethroid pulled back with his wand, and troll slowly inched its way towards the end of the bridge, a yellow string attached to Dethroid's wand.

"Wow. He actually responded to 'ugly,'" said Dethroid.

Finally, the massive troll was completely off the bridge. Kekk walked up to the troll. He crouched over it, took its pulse, and pulled out a poniard. He raised the weapon up to stab, but at that precise moment the troll's eyes opened. He saw the knife, and rolled his head to one side. The poniard missed the troll's eyes, but sliced off its previously wounded ear.

"Aaaargh!" bellowed the troll, who grabbed Kekk and threw him away. Kekk crashed to the ground near the carriages. The troll leapt to its feet, and lumbered over to Kekk. He raised his club for the finishing blow, but suddenly a gash appeared on its cheek. The troll threw up both hands to cover its face, but it let go of its club, and it flew forwards through the air, until its flight was stopped, and it bounced to the ground. Right where it stopped flying, a man appeared, in the middle of falling to the ground. Draslupp was unconscious.

When the troll lowered its hands, a few arrows embedded themselves in his rolls of fat. None came even close to the head. Ignoring the arrows, the troll, who figured out who had hurt it, lumbered over to the unconscious form of Draslupp. A yellow beam collided with the troll. It jerked around a bit -one arm spasm hitting Yexico who was trying to sneak up behind it— but it didn't freeze. It picked up its club.

Fedradin surveyed the scene: an enraged troll roaring over an unconscious Domer, flickering between visibility and invisibility; a man sprawled out behind the troll, but not unconscious; horses crazed with panic; Ridders spread out, trying to figure out how best to proceed; and of course enormous animals, attempting to enter the fight safely. The troll stopped its roaring, and looked down at Draslupp, with a sudden interest. Based on that, Fedradin knew what he must do.

Fedradin leapt into the battle with his sword drawn. The troll was looking down at Draslupp, so Fedradin quickly slashed the troll a few times. The troll roared. It slowly turned and while it was doing that, Fedradin dove between the troll's legs. Fedradin grabbed Draslupp and started pulling him towards the animal culture's carriage.

By now, the troll had figured out what had happened. He spun around and charged at Fedradin, club raised. When the troll reached Fedradin, Fedradin was at the carriage. Fedradin threw Draslupp away from him, right as the troll brought its club down. Fedradin tried to flatten himself, but the club grazed Fedradin in his upper, right back. Fedradin felt the painful bite of the teeth and nails as the raked down his back. He yelled out in pain, and crawled away as far as he could. He twisted his body so that he could see the troll, a murderous look on its face. Fedradin raised his sword, with the hope to block the club.

Suddenly, Shah leapt forward. She clutched a knife in one hand, and her lit enchanted torch in the other. When the troll saw her, its eyes went wide with fear.

"Good job, Shah!" Fedradin shouted weakly. "Trolls are afraid of fire!"

Fedradin felt hands grasp his shoulders, and he was pulled away from the battle. He looked up to see the yak from before. The yak sat Fedradin up, took his shirt off and examined him. While this was happening, Fedradin tried to twist to see the battle. That move sent pain up his back, but not enough to stop him from performing the action.

He saw that Axto, Bev, and a large bipedal wolf had jumped in to the battle; Kekk and Yexico were dusting themselves off on the sideline; and Draslupp was being tended to by Dethroid. Axto, Bev, the wolverio and Shah were now basically chasing the troll. Bev had also pulled out an enchanted torch, and when the troll ever made a hostile move towards the Ridders, the wolf would scratch it, or Axto would slice it with his halberd. Sometimes both.

It took Fedradin, mind slightly numbed by pain, a few moments to notice what they were doing. The four were driving the troll to the edge of the cliff. When it was about a foot away, a beaverio ran forward and pushed the troll as hard as it could. The troll stumbled and fell over the cliff.

The crowd erupted in cheers. As soon as the chaos began to die down, Fedradin called out for an injury check. Fedradin had the worst injury, it turned out. Draslupp had a slice on his cheek and a bump on his head, Yexico was scraped by the troll's fingernails, and the beaverio was hit with the back of the club when the troll fell. When he was finished, Axto and Dethroid came over to him.

"I'm no Scholar, but I think I can cast a few healing spells," said Dethroid. He bent over and started tapping away on Fedradin's back with his wand. After a few moments he said, "Well, I managed to clean it and more or less patch it up. Axto'll do the rest."

Axto walked over with some cream in a small, glass bottle. "Here," said Axto. "This cream should reduce pain, swelling and infection." Axto rubbed it on, and it felt like heaven. Fedradin got up and started walking around.

Fedradin was tapped on the shoulder. He turned around to find the yak standing there.

"I don't think we have been properly introduced," said the yak. "I'm Yuntile Stronghoof."

"Prince Fedradin Quickblade," replied Fedradin.

"That was very courageous of you to go a-saving that boy," said the Yakio.

"He's my student, ergo my responsibility," said Fedradin.

"It was still brave," said the yak.

"Thank you," said Fedradin. "But we should get going now."

"I agree."

The two groups, since they had to abandon their carriages to cross the bridge, gathered up their belongings and started to cross the bridge, one at a time. No one got hurt crossing, but when Yuntile stepped on where the troll had been standing, the wooden plank broke and fell into the river far below.

Fedradin paused for a moment on his way across the bridge, looking down the canyon that seemed to go on forever. On its steep, sandstone cliffs, a few brave trees grasped for life, some having lost the battle a long time ago. Just as he was about to continue, he noticed a rainbow across the canyon and smiled. He had never seen anything like it.

When they crossed the bridge and rounded a curve in the road, Fedradin looked up.

"Here we are at Gii," said Fedradin, "Finally."

Chapter 14
A Whole New World

ASERAX

GII WAS LARGE AND confusing. Large and confusing was not how the dwarves or elves built their cities. Granted most things are large to four or five-foot high dwarves and elves, but still, it was confusing to everyone of normal size and that was not good for Aserax.

A thick wall in the shape of a diamond surrounded Gii. At each of the four points, a heavy portcullis was positioned over the door, and a number of inattentive guards -ranging from zero to twelve, instead of the required eight, based on which soldiers decided to show up- guarded the doors, or at least they were supposed to. Many played cards and drank instead. After the doors, there were busy markets.

The markets ran parallel to the wall all the way around the city, where there was absolutely no order. People came, set up shops, sold their wares, and left a few fellyers richer at the end of the day. Some days -according to Breetex— the markets would swarm with people and shop owners to buy discounted items. Slaves were illegally sold, even with many more guards who came to maintain order. These events were called Taars. Regular days and Taars, that was how it was supposed to work. Instead, the crowds were mostly of solicitors, thieves, criminals, drug dealers, and monster distributers that roamed the markets, instead of customers. Very few guards wandered around to maintain order -it was widely known that the guards that did come to the markets mostly came for the drugs and alcohol- so if a shop owner caught a thief -usually a starving child- no one stopped him from slicing off a hand...or worse. Breetex said he had seen some people with missing ears, noses, teeth, even eyes. Murder, robberies, and kidnapping weren't unheard of. It wasn't hard. So many people milling about that it was easy to stick a knife in someone's back, even in broad daylight. And once it got dark, the markets got dangerous.

The markets slowly faded into small housing developments, called the slums, where richer peasants and peddlers lived. Most lived outside the city. Inns dotted the streets, as well as taverns and alehouses. The slums went along the perimeter of the markets. The houses were in poor shape. Many had holes in their roofs, broken windows, and cracked walls. Some, abandoned ones, were in even worse condition, with roofs completely caved in and collapsed walls. The slums had many of the same problems the markets had, albeit with much heavily guarded territories. It wasn't uncommon for fights over territories to happen between gangs.

When Breetex gave Aserax a brief history after he'd spent a few days there, he said it became an increasing problem for the royals to have to pass through the markets and slums. That reached its zenith when a Lord Tiug III was killed after being mistaken for a customer that owed money to a drug dealer. To fix the problem, widow Lady Saled built something called the "Noble Passage." At the main gate, if one was a noble, the guards gave the noble admittance to an underground passage that lead to the castle.

But before the castle, and after the slums, were the richer housing developments along the perimeter. These developments were much nicer than the slums. With manses, mansions, and grand apartments, the richer merchants and landlords lived there. To stop crime from spreading into the developments, a wall had been put up along the border of the slums and developments. The wall was not heavily guarded, and only really there to discourage crime. It was, for the most part, ineffective. Nevertheless, the developments weren't as chaotic as the market and slums, but still the streets curved in weird places and cleaner taverns and nicer shops dotted the streets unsystematically.

The developments ended abruptly at a wall that was big, but smaller than Gii's outer wall. A large gate allowed access to the castle, but this gate was guarded actively by a minimum of sixteen guards. More security was added during big events. The Gii Games was one of them.

Aserax and Breetex were staying outside the city, in one of the new developments that had been built to put up the spectators coming for the Games. The new developments were like little towns, but made up of only inns and a general store. The rooms were tiny and cramped, but very cheap.

Aserax was sitting in their room, still digesting the fact that she had betrayed her race for Breetex. But she was happy and that was all that mattered. Right? She remembered when she'd met him.

It was back before the War of Gems had broken out. Breetex was the son of a dwarfish ambassador to the elfish capital of Axler, and Aserax, of course, was the princess daughter of the king and queen of the elves.

Breetex had always been left outside the castle, for he was not allowed inside during the discussions. It hadn't been long before Aserax noticed him, and started to play with him in the courtyard. This went on for years, the two of them playing as their parents did business, and Breetex and Aserax began to age. It was then that they fell in love, and all was right until war broke out violently and suddenly over simple territory disputes. Breetex was whisked away from Aserax by his father, and Aserax was engaged against her will to an elf she didn't love, by the name of Poltax. From then on, they had to meet in secret, deciding that they would run away together. They had made a plan, one that would take years to implement.

But they did it.

They had run away together and here they were now. Aserax sighed. This was a good idea...this was a good idea...

Breetex walked out of the room after saying goodbye. He prohibited her from leaving with him, for if any human was familiar with the War of Gems, they would be able to recognize her, Aserax, the princess of the elfish race. Plus, more and more dwarves and elves were arriving each day for the Games. Aserax had argued that the dwarves might be able to recognize him, being a Greul and all. Breetex had laughed and said that Greul was only the fourth highest ranking in the dwarfish military, and many dwarves were Gruels. Also, Breetex said that he looked like every other dwarf -he had even started growing a beard, no more than pachy stubble at the moment- so he was undistinguishable from the rest. Aserax replied that she also looked like many elves, but Breetex laughed and told her she was much prettier than all the other elves in Haxter. Aserax sighed,

80

Breetex kissed her on the forehead, and he was gone. Another day alone in the room.

Luckily for her, there was a window in the room. Through the window she could see the path that led to one of the gates that led into Gii. It also happened to be the main gate, so all the important guests passed through there to use the Noble Passage. She spent the twelve hours without Breetex glued to the window, watching birds fly by, deer and elk run around and graze on grass, and of course the people sauntering into Gii for the infamous markets they could not resist. Aserax saw the Wrethig of the Flayers with his mate and team of warriors; she saw two teams of Grefture gallop by including three centaurs, two satyrs, and one faun; she saw a parade of svaadi; but the most stunning of all were the Keshnul. The Keshnul consisted mostly of creatures in close relation with the celestials, an elite group that lived on their own plane, the Celestial Plane. Their beautiful golden hair and stunningly blue eyes were breathtaking.

One of things Aserax noticed was that it seemed the warriors never had any carriages, and on occasion a few were injured slightly. One of the most noticeable parades of warriors she saw was when many humans, decked out in armor, marched into Gii followed by a number of gigantic animals.

Whenever Aserax wasn't sitting by the window, like when any elves marched into Gii, or rainy days when she could hardly see out the window, she wondered about Breetex. Breetex never said outright what job he had found in the markets, and whenever she asked, he always muttered something about selling pets.

Aserax watched a fly buzz around the room for the rest of the day, until Breetex came home.

Chapter 15
An Acquired Taste

FEDRADIN

THEY HAD FINALLY MADE it. Night was falling, but here they were. When they passed the main gate, the guards gave them each a slip of paper, which gave them access to the Warrior Village just outside the stadium. Cecil left them by the main gate, giving them directions to the Village. But after a long and rough trip, the Ridders were out to have a bit of fun before going to bed. But as they set out, unbeknownst to Fedradin, they would have three distinct tastes of the Giin lifestyle.

As they passed into the markets, the first thing they saw was trouble. A small, dark-skinned Mazleki boy, maybe seven years old, was being held by a big, beefy man. The boy wore nothing more than rags wound tightly around his chest and loins. The rags were much too small, and through them, Fedradin could see the boy's ribs sticking out.

The man wore a shirt so dirty and stained, Fedradin had no idea what the original color of the shirt was. A large, bushy mustache was coming close to taking over his mouth full of yellowed teeth, and a long, unkempt beard hung down all the way to the man's breast. The man had a tight grip on the boy's arm.

"This little *scum*, this brat, just tried to steal a strip of beef from me!" yelled the man. People looked up from their shopping and started to gather around the man. The boy struggled against the man's grip, and the man slapped the boy hard across the face. Stunned, the boy stopped squirming. "Now, of course he didn't get away with it. So instead, he ate the piece of meat right on the spot! Let this be a warning to all ye who dare try to take things they don't pay for." The man, with his free hand, grabbed his butcher's cleaver.

"Wait!" Fedradin yelled, as the man raised his knife. "Don't hurt that boy! I'll pay for the meat he ate."

"And let the boy off the hook? He needs to learn what he did was wrong!"

"He knows it's wrong! But he's starving! Look at his ribs!"

"I don't care! If he died of starvation tomorrow, I would be happy!"

"You are a cruel man. Now, will you take me up on my offer, or will you harm the boy?"

The man weighed his options, looking from Fedradin's pouch to the boy, considering. "As much as I like money, and even though I need it..." The man brought the cleaver down on the boy's wrist. The boy let out a scream of pain. The man let go of the boy who fell to the ground, his hand left twitching on the man's table. "It will be hard for him to steal without his hand."

And that was Fedradin's first taste of Gii.

After the shopkeeper and the starving boy incident, Fedradin and the Ridders started trying to enjoy themselves. They bought some spirits and started to have a good time. They wandered around, going into little magical shops and buying all sorts of items. Axto bought a dragon knuckle that glowed different colors on command, Bev bought a grip for her quarterstaff that vibrated if she was being flanked, and Draslupp picked up a map of the known world.

Then came Fedradin's second taste of Gii.

A performer was in the streets, with admiring spectators around him. He juggled, swallowed a sword, sat on a bed of nails, and finally, he breathed fire to the delight of the crowd.

"Whoa," murmured Draslupp, amazed.

Fedradin turned. "Impressive," he said. "You didn't even notice the cutpurse." Draslupp looked down to see a small boy slicing through the straps on Draslupp's purse. The cutpurse darted away when Draslupp lashed out at him, the contents of Draslupp's purse spilling out onto the street as Draslupp gave chase through the crowd.

Fedsradin's third taste of Gii came not much later.

When he turned a corner in the markets, another crowd of people was gathered around. Fedradin pushed through the crowd until he could see. The rest of the Ridders did the same.

The crowd had gathered around a clearing, in which two men stood at opposite ends. One of the men was an older man, clutching a cane with a trembling grip. The other was a young, bulky man. In the middle, two monsters were locked in combat.

In the whirl of confusion, Fedradin couldn't tell what monsters they were, until they broke apart.

The creature closer to the old man looked like a big lump of clay with two sunken in eyes, a squashed up nose, and bloody, pointed teeth. Fedradin guessed that the blood on its teeth was not its own. It crouched on two arms and two legs, with two wings unfurled out to the sides. Fedradin recognized it immediately. It was a homunculus, a monster created by wizards to do their bidding. It was a difficult thing to do, create a homunculus, that is. Misk had said that one had to use sorcery to do it, which was an incredibly hard task.

The homunculus had severe burns on it, which Fedradin linked to the fact that a magmum stood not five yards away. The magmum was a beast from the Plane of Fire. It looked like a young child, but a bit smaller. Its skin was completely red, with scorch marks and fire coming out in some places, like on the top of the head, small of the back, and palms of the hands. It had clawed hands and clawed feet. Fedradin was impressed with the younger man. He must have spent hours trying to catch that magmum as it came out of a portal, looking for treasure. Catching a magmum was hard enough, let alone training it to fight.

"What the hell is that?" said Bev, probably wondering about the magmum.

"I think it's an azzet," said Draslupp.

"No, it's a fire imp," said Shah.

Pretty close guesses thought Fedradin.

"No, you're both wrong, it's a Salamander. You know, the thing that rules the Plane of Fire," said Yexico.

Not so much.

The battle started again. The magmum ran forward and leapt at the homunculus. The homunculus took off into the air, but slightly too late, as the magmum raked the homunculus's underbelly with its flaming claw. The homunculus let out a horrible scream and fell out of the sky. It landed on its back, but managed to flip back over right as the magmum leapt again. The homunculus this time charged instead of fleeing. It caught the magmum in the chest with a claw. The homunculus's momentum carried forward and through the magmum's legs.

The two monsters spun around and charged again, but this time the homunculus took to the air, early enough that the magmum missed with a blow with its flaming hands. The magmum leapt again and tried to pull the homunculus out of the air, but it was too high for the magmum to reach. As it reached its zenith, it did a nose dive, and landed on top of the magmum, which was still in midair, and the homunculus began using everything, teeth and claws, to rip at the magmum's head.

The magmum landed, legs crumpling beneath it, and the homunculus landed on top of the magmum, moving its attack to the magmum's belly. The magmum recovered quickly and roared, before the homunculus could begin tearing at its underbelly. Fire came spewing out of every pore in the magmum's body. The homunculus yelped in pain and flew away. The magmum was ready and leapt onto the homunculus, pinning it to the ground. The homunculus struggled, but couldn't break the grip that the magmum had on its shoulders. The homunculus started screeching, and Fedradin could see why. Smoke was rising off the skin of the homunculus.

Fedradin elbowed a dwarf next to him. "Is your money on the homunculus?"

"Yes, why?" said the dwarf, eyes fixed on the battle. "That homunculus can break that grip. I've seen battles where that's happened."

"A magmum's grip? Because when that magmum applies the lick, it's all over."

"Why?"

But the dwarf's question was soon answered. Slowly, as the magmum licked the homunculus, all the way from back to front, the homunculus started to turn orange. The homunculus started to whine. Then it turned blue. It started to shriek. Then white. It burst into flames. The magmum released the homunculus, which stumbled a few steps and died.

The old man stomped his foot. The young man threw his hands in the air victoriously, and a young woman ran into the middle and kissed him.

"I am a man of my word," said the old man. "You can marry my daughter."

A well-dressed man walked into the middle of the arena, and he started passing out money to some people with big smiles on their faces. Others walked away, the disappointment of betting on the wrong monster plastered on their faces.

"Fedradin, what were those monsters?" asked Draslupp.

"Magmum and a homunculus," said Fedradin.

"That was magmum versus homunculus," announced the man in the middle. "Next battle, in five minutes, will be grint versus catdragon."

The dwarf walked up to Fedradin. "You know a lot about monsters."

"'Course I do. I'm from Narven."

"Narven! Never been there myself, would love to go sometime, though."

"Yes, but we don't let monster distributers in. Wouldn't want Narven to become Gii."

"What?" asked the dwarf in feigned confusion.

"Don't play dumb with me. I saw egg shaped bulges in your pockets, and I came to a conclusion. Am I wrong?"

"What? I..."

"Am I wrong?"

"No. I am a monster distributer. And I have two nice manticore eggs in my pocket if you're interested. Just two hundred fifty fellyers a piece."

"That's all you're carrying with you? Some monster distributer you are," scoffed Fedradin.

"Hey! If you'd really like to know I'm also carrying zaplizard eggs, catdragon eggs, and if you're interested, I'm carrying a roc egg. Though you can't battle rocs."

"You are a fool, aren't you?"

"What?"

"If I were a guard, I could now arrest for possession of all those eggs, not just the manticore eggs."

"*Are* you a guard?"

"No, I am not." Suddenly, the expression of the dwarf's face turned to pure horror. "What do you see? A guard?" asked Fedradin.

The dwarf dove behind a cart that was selling meats off to the side of the ring. The peddler's eyes widened.

"What do you-?" the peddler started to say, but the dwarf cut him off with a kick to the knees. The peddler fell to the ground. The dwarf quickly rolled on top of the peddler and knocked him out out with a blow to his head.

"He can't see me!" hissed the dwarf.

"Who?"

"The elf!" Fedradin looked back over his shoulder. Sure enough, a baffled looking elf was looking around frantically at the crowd. Finally, he shrugged and moved on.

"That's Prince Poltax!" exclaimed Fedradin.

"I know who that is!" said Breetex. "He's looking for me and Aserax!"

Chapter 16
Let the Games Begin

FEDRADIN

FEDRADIN AND THE RIDDERS retired to their rooms neither late, nor early that night. When they arrived in the Warrior Village, they found nine houses, creating a semicircle around a large field. Obviously each house was meant for one race. When they entered, there was a common room, with a fireplace and places to sit. A few men sat around the table, drinking mead, smoking tobacco and inhaling the intoxicating Stentorik stentspice, probably bought in Gii. One was holding an egg that Fedradin recognized as a manticore's.

"Wow," Fedradin said to Shah. "That guy bought something off that stupid dwarf."

The Ridders arrived at the second floor of the house, which was just a hallway with doors on the sides, after they climbed a set of stairs, twisting at a right angle at the very top. Written on the door was which team was staying there, and the Ridders figured out that each team had four rooms. They were team two and quickly found their rooms.

"'Right," said Fedradin. "Four rooms...one, two, five, seven, eight of us. Ladies, you share a room. Gentlemen, pick a roommate." After some muttered conversation, Kekk and Draslupp were sharing, Yexico and Axto were sharing, and Fedradin and Dethroid were sharing.

As everyone retired to their rooms, Fedradin said, "Kekk, Shah, Draslupp, take care of everything you have to do before tomorrow's competition before you go to sleep." A murmur of ascent went through the Ridders, and they went into their rooms. Before Fedradin's eyes could adjust to the darkness, his door was opened. He turned around.

Axto was standing in the doorway.

"What is it?" asked Fedradin.

"I wanted to check on your back," said Axto.

"My...oh, right," Fedradin had almost forgotten getting hit with a spiked club earlier in the day. "It's fine."

"Okay," said Axto, as he reached into his back pocket. "But take some of this medicine that I bought while we were in Gii. It's a potion made from a lot of the healing ingredients I use, like stranglevine berry and mandrake root."

"Axto! This must have cost a fortune!" exclaimed Fedradin, as he took the medicine.

"Yes, it cost three hundred fellyers and nine oplopecks. But if you win the competition, it'll be worth it. Just remember to apply the medicine to the wound before you fall asleep."

"Thanks, Axto, you're the best."

"Don't you forget it."

With blurred vision, he stumbled through the snow. The snow was still coming down hard enough that he couldn't see five feet in front of him, a white wall everywhere he turned. He was hardly clothed, with skin showing, a bad state to be in while battling a blizzard. He clutched a knife as hard as he could with one hand, as if that knife were his lifeline and if he let it go, he would die.

Suddenly, a large, cold gale blew up out of nowhere, its cold bite digging into his bare flesh. He cried out in pain, but obviously no one could hear him. No one would ever be able to hear him again.

He fell to his knees, then onto his face. He almost couldn't feel the snow burning his bare skin. The numbness dulled the pain.

But then a thought.

His mind bringing a picture into his head. No. Not that face.

Pure anger brought him back to his senses. He must *keep moving. He* must *keep fighting. He stood up and shook the snow off his skin. That face brought more hatred to him than any other human being had ever felt before. To lie down was to let death in. To let death win. He would not let death in. He would fight it. He would fight it by walking, by running. He would fight it with the rage in his heart, and a curse on his lips. A curse for that face.*

Ironic, wasn't it? That face would be his lifeline, not his knife. The same face that brought him to this hell. The face that destroyed his life.

He would live. He would live until he could extract revenge on that horrid face. Then he could die. Then he would die.

89

But not until then.

Fedradin woke from his dream to the sound of a horn blaring. Immediately, rage swelled up inside his chest at the sound. He leapt out of bed, sword at the ready before he realized the anger was just leftover from his incredibly realistic dream.

He looked to the right of him. Dethroid had already gotten out of bed and was dressed for the day.

"Mornin'," said Dethroid.

"Mornin'," mumbled Fedradin back as he started getting ready.

"The horn's going to be calling everyone down to the lawn in half an hour, so don't be late."

"Thanks, Dethroid."

Fedradin, Shah, Draslupp and Kekk walked down to the field together in a line, Fedradin first, Draslupp second, Shah third, Kekk fourth. When they arrived on the lawn, the some of the teams were already present. They stood by team, the four competitors standing shoulder to shoulder. Fedradin noticed something immediately. Each race had eleven teams, not three. Except for the humans. Only ten teams were present.

A group of people walked out onto the front of the lawn including Emperor Flyc, the emperor of the human; the Wrethig, the ruler of the flayers; Sir Hulten Sharpaxe, the king of the dwarves who had also been knighted; Prince Poltax, the prince of the elves; Greysvaad Moaand, the ruler of the svaadi; a yakio named King Westal, the ruler of the animal cultures; King Vivolk, the Grefturen king; Pharaoh Duztil, the pharaoh of the chultra; and finally Princess Haze, the Keshnulian Princess. The leaders lined up on opposite sides of the podium in the middle of the field. When they were in position, an overweight man jogged across the field to the podium.

"Hello warriors!" said the man, his voice probably amplified by some magical equipment. "Welcome to Gii! I hope you all have enjoyed your stay so far. I'm Lord Uslo of the Fief of Gii.

"You all are about to compete in the Gii Games." A cheer went up from the warriors. "There has never been anything like the Gii Games before. Never have these nine great nations come together for a week of intense competition. The leaders of each

90

team have been handpicked by us at Gii. You, almost four hundred warriors, will compete for the grand prize of fifty thousand fellyers and the last of the Seven Blades, Baxcanador." Everyone gasped. Probably no one had heard that Baxcanador would be a prize. "As all of you know, Baxcanador is part of a series of swords crafted by cyclopses of the Kzit Mountains. The swords have a power matched by no other blades, except each other." Fedradin knew the man was omitting something. The blades were almost too powerfull for their own good. The cyclopses designed them to be able to help the wielder of the blade accomplish his or her goals, whatever those goals may be. If an evil man took hold of one, the blade would help him do unspeakable things. This did happen, and the man who possessed a blade, Sir Rentyl, killed thousands, including all of the cyclopses who crafted the blades. Since then, no one had made contact with the cyclops race. Most thought they had all been killed off. " Whoever holds the blade at the end of the Games will have deserved the blade, since they are the strongest warrior in Haxter."

Four men started sprinting onto the field.

"You are late," Lord Uslo said, then went on, "But how do you win the blade? You all passed the first challenge, where you had to fight a troll to get across a bridge. Congratulations. That was set up, as your first of many challenges, so you and another team of a different race had to work together. We supplied you with a cream to repay you for your lost carriages and other supplies, and to heal any injuries you may receive during the Games."

They gave those items out? Axto had lied to Fedradin! Axto had tried to cheat Fedradin out of money! Anger welled up inside Fedradin. He could not *stand* disloyalty.

"You may have noticed eleven teams per race, not the three we specified. Today, we will eliminate four teams per race, and tomorrow we will eliminate another four. So, why wait? Let's get right to the Games!"

The warriors roared their approval. When Lord Uslo stepped down from the podium, men clad in wool uniforms ran into the crowd and started organizing it. When one man reached Fedradin, the man said, "There will be four events today. Each one of you will be competing in one of them. Decide on numbers, one, two, three, four for each of you, then head to the stadium down the path." The man pointed towards ten men in blue standing in a semicircle. "They'll give you directions." The man in red ran off.

Fedradin looked at his Ridders. "Let's just do it in the order we're in now," he said. They followed the path until they found themselves in front of a massive stadium, already full of spectators.

Chapter 17
Reapers

KERWAN

BIGGS WAS BROUGHT OUT by two men who looked identical to the first man Kerwan fought. One of the men was holding Biggs's scimitar and wand. Another man walked behind them with his hood up, like all the others. Only a bald head with the same tattoo on his forehead could be seen. The only thing different about this man than all the others was that he walked with a sense of leadership. He was obviously the man in charge.

"Leave Kerwan. Leave now," Biggs said in a soft but powerful voice to Kerwan who had not yet been spotted as he crouched behind a knoll, Utka at his side. One of the men holding Biggs slammed the handle of his sword into the back of Biggs's head. Biggs cried out in pain and his head slumped forward. Kerwan hoped that Biggs wasn't knocked unconscious.

"Master!" cried out Utka.

"Utka, no!" yelled out Kerwan. But it was too late. The damage had been done.

"What do we have here?" chuckled the leader. "Two apprentices." The man paused and looked around. "Where's Nirrue? Has anybody seen him?"

One of the grunts answered. "He went to get the tall one."

"Him?" said the leader, pointed a twisted finger at Kerwan. The grunt gave a confirming nod. "You there, what happened to my soldier?"

Kerwan raised his chin. "I killed him."

"You killed Nirrue?"

"Yes, I did. It was like killing a fly."

"Don't," said Biggs weakly.

"Nirrue was my second in command," said the leader with irritation creeping into his tone.

"I assume that hierarchy of whatever little band of criminals you are is *not* based on fighting skills. Am I correct?"

Again the leader chuckled, "Someone will pay for those remarks, apprentice."

"Well actually, I'm a Full Wizard, something that you wouldn't know about."

Kerwan noticed the leader's hand going to his pocket. Kerwan did the same. The leader exhaled loudly. "You're funny, wizard, and you obviously can fight. The only problem is your pride gets the better you. It will kill you one day, if not today." The leader glanced down towards Kerwan's hand reaching for his wand and said, "It looks as if you mean to fight."

In response, Kerwan pulled out his wand and said, "I'm sorry, was I being too subtle for you to pick up on?" With that, Kerwan shot a blue spell at the leader. The leader quickly pulled out his wand and blocked it with a green shield, replying with two white spells. Kerwan dropped to the ground and the spells passed over him.

In the sudden outburst, the two men holding Biggs were caught in indecision over whether to keep hold of Biggs or go for their wands and join the fight. The result was that their grip loosened and Biggs was able to thrash his way free. He twisted immediately and slammed the palm of his hand into one of the bridge of one of the grunt's nose. The grunt's nose started gushing blood, and the grunt fell to the ground. Biggs quickly dropped to his knees and with a sweep of his legs he took out the second one. Before either one could get up, Biggs stole his wand and scimitar back and quickly finished off both of the grunts with a swing of the blade.

The leader looked over to Biggs, who was pointing a wand at him.

"It's over. You've lost," said Biggs.

The leader chuckled slightly. "It does appear that way doesn't it?" The leader pointed his wand in the air. He muttered a spell and all around him the air became to shimmer. In some places, the air began to change from clear to a deep red. The red began to take shape into some form of body, and after a few seconds Kerwan could make out the hideous bodies of dune reapers. He recognized them from when he and Biggs had gone exploring in the desert.

"Dune reapers? You've really pulled out all the stops," said Kerwan.

94

"Nice to see you still have a sense of humor; nonetheless, I'm on a schedule here and I must carry on. You see, these dune reapers are under my control and can't be called off by anyone but me. They have no pity and will rip you limb from limb with no remorse." The leader was now pacing up in down in front of his dune reaper army. "I will call them off and let you off the hook for killing three of my best warriors if you give me the crystal."

"And if we kill you now?" asked Kerwan.

"I have given them the command that if anything should happen to me, they must hunt each of you down and kill you in the most painful way possible."

"I'm not giving you the crystal," said Biggs defiantly.

"Is that so?" said the leader. By this time the dune reapers were clearly visible. They walked on four legs with three long, bloody claws extending from each foot. Their backs were grotesquely muscled, and they had small faces that seemed to be hidden by their muscles. But the worst part of all was that they had no skin. With each heartbeat their muscles throbbed and pulsed and sometimes blood would dribble down, across the muscles. "Well, then there's only one more option left." The leader put down his wand and the reapers attacked.

Chapter 18
Dirtwolves

FEDRADIN

FEDRADIN WAS GEARED AND ready to go. To his right, three human warriors, to his left, the other seven. All the warriors were behind a line that stretched out in front of all of them. Across the field, seven pedestals stood, why seven? Each warrior held in his, or her, for there was a woman in the mix, hand a big, green orb. Fedradin assumed one had to place the orb on the podium to win; no instructions had been given besides to get behind the line and that they weren't allowed to use their weapons to harm each other.

As Fedradin looked across the two hundred yards long field, he wondered, *Is it really this easy?* The pedestals were just standing there. No monsters to stop the warriors, no obstacles of any sort. There had to be a catch. Uslo wouldn't make an event that was just a foot race. Would he?

"Good morning, warriors!" came a booming voice. The warriors looked up to where Emperor Flyc stood. His voice, like Uslo's, was being amplified. "Before we begin the event, you all still need to be briefed on how this first day is going to work. The humans have the field first today. Each member of your team will be competing in an event, like you. Whoever was lucky number three in your group gets to play against another race, in your case, the chultra or the svaadi. The human warriors were split up to go to those events." Number three was Shah. "Now, how do you move on? For each event, if your team wins, you earn a point. To move on in the competition, you need to be in the top seven for most points.

"To win this particular event, which is called 'Dirtwolves,' you have to put your orb on one of the pedestals. The first seven warriors to do so will earn a point. Now, I have already given you a clue..."

Dirtwolves. Dirtwolves. Dirtwolves. Wuellte. The word popped into Fedradin's head. Of course! Wuelltes! They were called dirtwolves because they prowled and hunted through the dirt as easily as a wolf. They ate anything and everything, except elves and dwarves. No one knew why. But what was known was that wuelltes attacked when they felt vibrations in the ground above, so running would be a bad idea.

"Time to start this competition. Get behind the line. It's rigged to send up a barrier right before we start that can saw off any body parts that are sticking over it, so don't false start." The warriors shuffled back, deciding losing an arm was worse than losing the game. "When you put your orb on the pedestal, you will be teleported out of the arena. If you ever want to back out of the game, throw your orb on the ground. You will automatically take a loss and get no points for this game. You will also be disqualified.

"Questions? No? Alright, in three, two, one, go!" A bright wall of red flashed up in front of them.

Unfortunately -well, fortunately for Fedradin- one warrior false-started, and the top of his boot -and possibly some of his big toe- got burned off. He jumped back in pain, but the race had begun.

Nine of the warriors started sprinting and were neck and neck. The only two who weren't sprinting were Fedradin, who was jogging along behind them, and the warrior who was hobbling his way to the pedestals because of his injured foot.

The nine warriors were about one quarter of the way across the field, when a feeling of devastation hit Fedradin. Was it all a fluke? Was the clue just a trick and Fedradin the only one suckered into believing it? Or, more likely, the only one knowledgeable enough to understand it well enough to fall for it? Fedradin started sprinting, too.

When the runners were almost halfway across, something unexpected happened. Five creatures leaped out of the ground. They were about six feet long and four feet tall with teardrop shaped, designed to help them move through the dirt -sand in the case of this field. Their heads were heavily armored with bone plates, like their backs, which ended in thick, armored tails. They stood on four legs; at the end of each was a webbed, clawed foot, perfect for digging. Fedradin recognized them, for he himself had fought one after it claimed a farmer's sheep field as its territory.

The wuelltes wreaked havoc on the front-runners. One caught a warrior by its mouth and dove back underground, Fedradin cringing at the thought of the horrors awaiting the warrior. Only one other wuelltes caught a warrior, while the other three just scattered the warriors, sending them sprawling in the sand. One warrior had made it past without hassle, though, and he started sprinting.

Bad idea, thought Fedradin.

Immediately, two wuelltes leapt out of the sand. Somehow, they both missed grabbing the warrior, instead colliding with each other, and they wound up fighting each other. The warrior ran to the pedestals and slammed the orb down. He vaporized into thin air, green mist all that was left.

Six more spots.

Fedradin had started moving forward, but even slower than last time. He had confirmed his suspicions: wuelltes were in the ground, so he wanted to tread carefully to avoid attracting the attention of the wuelltes. By the time the warrior teleported, Fedradin was at the halfway point.

Two more warriors in the middle, had got up and decided to follow suit, and they both charged. The warrior in front was the woman Fedradin had seen before. As they were running, a wuellte leapt out of the sand right in front of the two. The woman warrior in front tried to stop, but the warrior behind her pushed her right into the wuellte. The second warrior got to the pedestals and claimed a spot.

Five spots were left. Fedradin now stood where four warriors lay sprawled in the middle of the field.

The woman took out a short sword and was on her back, slashing the wuellte if it got too close. She was not able to get to her feet and wouldn't be able to keep fighting off the dirtwolf for much longer.

Three warriors close to Fedradin on the sand leapt to their feet and started running, probably because they decided to take advantage of the opportunity that three wuelltes were occupied. The only problem was that they all started running at once. Based on a hunch, Fedradin dove to the side.

Right as he did so, a wuellte leapt out of the air and grabbed one of the warriors by its leg. It sank back into the sand, taking the warrior with it. Fedradin, who was still lying on the ground, felt a rumble in the sand beneath him, and he took off running as fast as he could. So did the last warrior who was lying on the sand.

Fedradin felt the earth shake around him as the wuellte leapt out of the ground and heard the man behind him let out a cry of terror as he was dragged underground. Fedradin realized that everyone still on the field should get a point by default, as the number of warriors on the field was equal to the number of open spots.

"Attention, all warriors," said Flyc. "You must finish the game to earn a point." *Well there you have it,* thought Fedradin.

Right as Flyc said that, one of the two warriors running in front of Fedradin was taken by a wuellte. The other one finished the race, slamming down his orb. Fedradin was running full speed. He passed by the woman fighting a losing battle with the wuellte.

Can I leave her to die? Fedradin asked himself. He couldn't, so he quickly jabbed his sword through the wuellte's eye. It died without making a sound as the sword entered its brain, the body collapsing on top of the woman, who, with Fedradin's help, pushed the dirtwolf away.

"Thank you," she said, breathless.

"Don't mention it," said Fedradin. They started to run since they were so close to the pedestals. When they were ten yards away, Fedradin felt a rumble beneath his feet. He shoved the woman out of the way, twisting as he tumbled forwards, so he landed on his back, facing where he thought the wuellte would emerge from. He readied his sword. Sure enough, the wuellte leapt out of the ground. Since Fedradin was on the ground, he saw the soft underbelly of the wuellte as it was in the air. Quickly, he thrust his sword into its stomach, and it fell out of the air, right on top of Fedradin. The dirtwolf was dead.

Fedradin tried to push the dead wuellte off of him, and he was unsuccessful. He tried to squirm away. "Hey, lady! Help me!" he yelled to the woman, who was just getting up. "Help me! I helped you!"

She looked down at him and took his orb. "You're a fierce competitor. That's why I'll have to take you out of the competition." She raised his orb. No. She couldn't. She was going to smash the orb and disqualify Fedradin.

She was about to throw it at the ground, when Fedradin shot his hand out and grabbed her ankle. He pulled and she fell. His orb dropped out of her hands, but Fedradin caught it. What happened next could only be described as lucky -to Fedradin of course. The woman fell on her orb, smashing it. She vaporized in a cloud of red mist, and Fedradin left out a little laugh.

He tried to get out from under the wuellte for a few more seconds, when the man with the burned foot came hobbling to the pedestals. Fedradin guessed that since he was crippled, his feet weren't hitting the ground hard enough to alert the wuelltes.

"Hey! Can you put my orb on the pedestal! Please!" Fedradin pleaded.

The cripple looked at Fedradin. "I guess I could-" The cripple's eyes went wide. He shouted, "Dirtwolf!" And he slammed his orb down on the pedestal.

Fedradin turned and craned his neck to see over the dead wuellte. Behind him, the other four wuelltes were patrolling the field, looking for any remaining competitors. They must have seen his head, for suddenly they dove into the sand. Fedradin knew they were coming for him. He considered his options until only one made sense.

Fedradin turned to look at the pedestals. Then he felt the ground rumble. He twisted to face the pedestals, and his back erupted in pain. The ground rumbled. He twisted again, fought through the pain...

Then, Prince Fedradin threw his orb.

Chapter 19
Alone

KERWAN

THE REAPERS WERE ON Kerwan faster than he expected. When the first reaper reached him, he was caught slightly unprepared, since his warhammer wasn't drawn quite yet; it was still dangling on his back. He shot out brown spell right into the chest of the reaper and it fell to the ground twitching from the electric shock. Kerwan drew his warhammer.

Two more reapers leaped at him, almost at the same time. He smashed one with his warhammer and quickly spun to hit the second. His swung his weapon, but the reaper vanished, the weapon passing through thin air. Kerwan felt claws rake against his back. He cried out in pain, but managed to turn and blast the reaper with a purple spell. The reaper collapsed with six purple spikes sticking in its chest.

Kerwan breathed deeply and looked around. Biggs was battling a few reapers fairly successfully, and Utka was rolling around in the ground stabbing at a reaper with his pike.

Suddenly, Kerwan was knocked over by a reaper charging at him at full speed. Kerwan rolled over, but the reaper was on top of him. Kerwan had lost both his wand and his warhammer in the confusion, so he closed his eyes and swung his fist. Only, his fist didn't make connection with the jawbone of the reaper like he had intended. Instead, he felt himself holding a knife while it slid through flesh. He opened his eyes, and the bronze knife was almost fully inserted into the head of the reaper. He pulled it out, and the reaper fell onto its face, dead. In the heat of the battle Kerwan didn't think much of it. This fight wasn't over yet.

He glanced at his partners. Biggs was also getting up from a pool of blood, with a few mere scratches. Even so, just seeing the scratches on Biggs reminded Kerwan of his own injury. He felt the searing pain of his cuts come back to him and he collapsed to the ground, clutching the various scrapes, scabs, and stabs that now covered his body.

"Kerwan! Get up! We can't lose you just yet!" shouted Biggs. Kerwan started feeling the drain of energy he often felt after casting many spells, so it was even harder for him to get up. Still, he managed to do it. Kerwan stood up, putting his knife back into its sheath and collecting his wand and warhammer.

"What?" snapped Kerwan, as he rose unsteadily to his feet.

"It's Utka!" yelled Biggs.

Utka was floating in the air. It looked as if he were in a bubble tinted red. His eyes were closed and his skin was turning a sickly yellow. Kerwan looked around. The reapers were nowhere to be seen, but the leader of them was holding his wand in the air.

"Put him down," said Biggs, calmly.

"Yes, you would like that, wouldn't you?" said the leader. "You see, Utka, is that right? Yes, Utka is trapped in a magical container. Don't bother trying to break into it, because as long as I'm alive, he'll be trapped in there. Every minute he stays in the container, a little of his life is drained. Soon, he will die. The only way to get him out of that container is if you give me the crystal."

"How about if we kill you?" said Kerwan angrily.

"Then my reapers would rip you limb from limb."

"Please," pleaded Biggs, "Why do you want the crystal so bad you would kill a child?"

"Because if this crystal were to fall into the wrong hands that person would kill many, many people. The crystal is worth more than just this boy's miserable life," said the leader.

"How do we know you're not the wrong hands? Who are you anyway?" said Kerwan.

"I am leader of the cult Desert Wind. My name is Krile Wandhand. We have been preparing ourselves for the day our gods would bestow on us the power of the Rock Crystal ever since the first of our kind become the Rock Holder in the beginning. We moved out to the desert and have been waiting patiently in prayer ever since in hopes of receiving the rock crystals that rain down from the heavens."

"Oh, so you're a religious nut. There's just no reasoning with these people," said Kerwan.

"Kerwan, please. You are not helping right now," said Biggs. To Krile he said, "You'll have to excuse him, he's very uneducated." Kerwan actually had been very devoted to his studies and had learned much as Biggs's apprentice.

"Master! Look at the boy!" Kerwan exclaimed. Utka's cheek was beginning to disintegrate. Black ooze bubbled out of his face and started to eat Utka's cheek away in a ripple-like fashion, slowly, very slowly.

"By the gods...What are you doing to him, Krile?" said Biggs.

"Our gods have honored us with a little black magic, as well as our other talent," said Krile. "You should probably do something soon, otherwise Utka will be consumed by our gods. Once he dies, so will you at the hands of the reapers. The only way to end this horrific sequence is to give me the crystal."

"What can we give you instead? How about money? Food? Women?" bargained Biggs.

"Even though I would love to see you pull a woman out of your pocket right now, I have spent my entire life in prayer waiting for this day. I will do anything for that crystal."

"Are we going to fight this man, Master? Are we going to kill him?"

"No, Kerwan. You win, Krile," said Biggs, to Kerwan's surprise. "Please let the boy go. Here's the crystal." Biggs procured a brown, circular crystal, about two inches in diameter.

Kerwan heard Utka hit the ground as Biggs handed the crystal over to Krile. Krile had kept his word.

"I've been waiting my whole life for this moment," whispered Krile, as if speaking too loudly would wake him from his dream.

Biggs started talking, "Now can we-"

With no warning, Krile swung a large knife in an overhead arc straight into the back of Biggs's neck. The knife went handle-deep, protruding out the other side of Bigg's neck. Krile ripped the knife from Biggs's neck. Biggs fell to his knees, and then onto his face.

"Master! No!" shouted Kerwan. "I'll kill you!" Kerwan shouted as loud as he could. "You murderer! I'll kill you! I'll kill your family!" Kerwan's voice was becoming hoarse. "I curse you, Krile Wandhand! I curse you and your ancestors! I curse your descendants! I will kill you!" Suddenly, Kerwan's rage turned to despair. He fell to his knees next to Biggs. Kerwan lifted Biggs's head up, so he could look in his eyes. Already they were glazed over. Biggs was dead. Tears started streaming down Kerwan's face. "How could you? Why? Why?" Kerwan stuttered over the last 'why' as sobs overtook him. He buried his face into his Master's jacket. After about a moment or two, he looked up to Krile. His despair gave way to the most rage Kerwan had ever felt in his life. "He did what you asked, but you killed him." Kerwan's voice was calm. "You despicable, evil, callous man. I hope you die." Kerwan's voice began to rise in volume. "I hope you suffer! I hope you suffer my wrath!" Kerwan jumped to his feet and was now shouting. "I will kill you, Krile Wandhand! I will!" Again, rage gave way to despair. Kerwan began crying into his hands.

"It had to be done," said Krile.

"How can *that* be?" said Kerwan with enough venom in his voice to poison a river.

"According to my religion, I must kill Biggs if I am to take the crystal."

Kerwan took a deep breath. "I don't give a damn about your religion! You killed my Master; you shall die." Kerwan pulled his wand out of his pocket. Krile quickly pulled out his own wand, shooting a spell that knocked Kerwan's from his hand. With a roar of anger, Kerwan leapt forward, bronze knife in hand. He charged Krile, swinging the knife in wide, arcing patterns. Krile evaded the swings and lashed out with a fist, catching Kerwan in the side of the head. Kerwan fell backwards, landing roughly on the ground.

Krile took a step forward, pulling out a long knife. The blade glinted in the sunlight as Krile raised it overhead. He seemed ready to swing the knife and kill Kerwan, but the wizard froze. He gently lowered the blade to Kerwan's face and traced the red horseshoe birthmark with his knife, drawing blood as he pressed down gently.

Krile sheathed his knife, waved his wand, and the air shimmered behind him. When the air came back into focus, Kerwan saw hundreds of reapers and warriors -all of the warriors were dressed in the hooded robes- lined up. "On my mark they will charge and kill everything in sight. I would advise you and your...where did he go?" Kerwan looked around and found Krile was right. Utka was not there. Returning to the topic at hand, Krile said, "Wizard, I will give you five minutes to distance yourself from me."

With rage in his heart, Kerwan turned and ran, snatching up his wand on the way. As he ran through the foggy night towards no particular location, Kerwan wrapped his clothes around him tighter, his only protection from the frosty air, the temperature declining as the sun dipped below the horizon. One thought struck him as he bounded over a puddle of mud.

He was alone.

Chapter 20
The Elfish Prince

POLTAX

WHAT A FILTHY PLACE, thought Prince Poltax as he walked through the streets of Gii. *These humans have the nerve to invite all eight other races to this dump?* Prince Poltax didn't have a problem with the Gii Games themselves, he actually thought that it could be fun to see which race would win.

But the timing...So poor.

The War of Gems was raging, and the disappearance of the elfish Princess, his fiancée, just made things worse. Not that he minded her running away. He just wanted to become king of the Elfish Kingdom, but that wasn't to say that he wasn't developing feelings for his irritating fiancée...Poltax cleared his head by shaking it.

But I digress...The War of Gems... That was why he had had to come to represent the elves. His father-in-law-to-be, King Juern Sharpbow, was busy working on tactics to help find Aserax, Poltax's fiancée, and destroy the dwarves. Poltax found it interesting that Sir Hulten Sharpaxe had shown up to the competition. Either the dwarves were attempting to show the elves that they might want a truce, or that they were boasting about their confidence in victory. But if Hulten was confident, what he didn't know was that if the war weren't over soon, the elves would probably bring the chultra into the battle. Another thought popped into his head.

The Chultra Dispute could easily resurface. The elves and chultra had a close alliance, and if the truth of the Battle of Uiklo were ever discovered... *So many explosives issues. And these Games are a spark.*

As Prince Poltax rounded a corner, he saw an illegal monster battle in progress. What disgusted him most were the guards betting on it. He stood for a minute to watch it. What appeared to be a flaming, small person with claws was fighting a blob of clay with wings and appendages. Poltax didn't know much about monsters. The battle raged for a few minutes until the flaming

106

thing managed to get the upper hand on the clay thing and immolated its opponent by...licking its back? Poltax saw a young man and a woman embracing in the middle of the ring. Prince Poltax was just about to leave the scene when he caught a glimpse of a dwarf. A dwarf with a familiar face. Poltax looked around more intently, but he didn't see the dwarf. The only interesting thing was the man standing by a meat stand, looking at it with much interest, with no peddler. Prince Poltax paused, shrugged and decided to keep walking. If he continued dawdling he would be late.

He was on his way to an LNR meeting. It was to be one of the first.

Prince Poltax arrived at the Noble Passage. Two guards stood in front of the door. One of the guards carried a pike and the other had a dangerous looking cur on a leash. The guards recognized him and shifted to the side to give him room to pass. Prince Poltax passed into the tunnel and gasped. Despite his four-foot stature, Prince Poltax was extremely claustrophobic.

The elfish Prince took a deep breath and started walking. He tried to look at the ground and not the walls that seemed to be closing in fast...very fast...too fast. Poltax thrashed out to keep the wall at bay, but came into contact with nothing.

It's all in my head, he assured himself. *I'll get through this.* He kept walking, focusing on that light at the end of the tunnel. Every step he took it got bigger. *Focus on the light. Look at nothing but the light.* The light was reassuring. The light was always there...

Before Poltax knew it, he was out of the tunnel.

Now, Poltax was at the gate of the castle. The sixteen guards stood in front of it. He was recognized just like at the front of the tunnel. They moved to the side and opened the gate.

"Enter the castle, third room on your left," said one of the guards as Poltax passed. Poltax nodded to the guard and walked up the stone pathway to the heavy, oak, castle doors. Poltax pushed the door open -with great difficulty- and slipped inside.

The castle, unlike the rest of Gii, was very nice. Woolen rugs dyed in expensive purple dye covered the walkways. He knew the dye was derived from rare, murex sea snails, so he was very impressed, considering Gii was not too close the oceans. Crystal chandeliers hung from the ceilings and the whole place was crawling with servants wearing brilliant, white robes. Prince Poltax passed two doors and entered into the third. Inside, a round table had been set up with nine chairs surrounding it. Emperor Flyc was already seated, Lord Cienko of Borave standing next to him, the Wrethig sitting near them, Pharaoh Duztil and Sir Hulten Sharpaxe also present. The Prince seated himself at the table as far away from Sir Hulten Sharpaxe as he could. If Hulten got the idea to slide a knife in between Poltax's ribs, Poltax wasn't going to be an easy target.

He wound up sitting across from the Wrethig. Prince Poltax immediately averted his eyes from the Wrethig. Flayers were disgusting.

"Prince," said the Wrethig, in his gurgling voice.

Poltax had no choice but to meet the eyes of the Wrethig. "Wrethig," said Poltax, as greeting. The Wrethig had a large purple head that resembled an octopus. Coming out of his chin and cheekbones, large tentacles protruded, about seven or eight of them. The tentacles dangled down onto his darker purple shirt, soaking it with slime. His five beady, black eyes were all gathered near the center of his face, and underneath them, there was no nose, just one hole. On its throat, a small slit passed for a mouth. Poltax had learned recently that some flayers had cut themselves there so they could speak Leaguespeak. Alone, flayers spoke their own separate language that consisted of grunts, clicks and gestures (mostly with their eyes). None of that required a mouth. Flayers were one of the three races in the LNR that didn't speak any dialect of Commonspeak. Svaadi and chultra were the other two.

By now, the rest of the rulers had arrived, Greysvaad Moaand, King Westal, Ambassador Vivolk, and Prince Haze. When Poltax spotted Princess Haze, he was taken aback, just like always. No matter how many times Poltax saw Haze, Poltax was struck by her beauty. Haze had long, flowing blond hair. Pining it back was a sparkling diamond tiara. On her face, two perfectly sized and spaced, brilliant blue eyes tore a hole through Poltax's soul. She sat down in her spotless white tunic. Poltax forced his eyes away from examining her perfect figure. He knew that every single celestial had the same affect. Even males celestials.

Anyways, he was an engaged elf, even if his finaceé was on the run with another man. Maybe he wasn't as tied down as he thought... He pulled away from the idea. Anyway, celestial beings were practically gods. They had come to Haxter in an attempt to keep peace. In fact, the LNR had been their idea.

"Since we're all here, why don't we get started?" said Flyc. "We have a lot to discuss today, starting with the disputes between Borave and the Grefture Kingdom over Lake Oxler. Lord Cienko, would you like to..."

But Poltax wasn't listening; his eyes drifted back to Haze, where they stayed for a long time.

Chapter 21
The Urchin

FOUR YEARS PREVIOUSLY

STREET URCHIN

HE WAS AWAKENED BY the smell of food. Not just any food, but meat. By the smell of it, it was probably venison. The spices, even some stentspice, mixed with the sizzling meat, and the aroma wafted up from the kitchen, his mouth watering. What he wouldn't give for a piece of meat like that. As he fantasized about the food, he smelled something different. He sniffed the air. Sweet bread. He almost cried. He was so hungry, since he had been living off of the condensation off the wall and insects that happened to wander passed him for a few weeks.

It all happened a couple weeks ago. He had been a happy urchin of about twelve years old, living in a room in the castle of the capital Bal-gastar that no one knew existed. In the ceiling of his small room, there was a hole that he could climb through to the roof. By day he climbed the roof of the castle, watching busy people pass below.

Occasionally a girl, Sgire, would climb the wall of the castle to visit him, maybe bring him a roll of stale bread or rotten apple she had managed to pilfer from the kitchen on her way up. Sgire was about his age and had taken a liking to him after she noticed him escape an angry cook by climbing the wall of the castle. Since then, they had a special relationship, of love, but not of the passionate kind, a more brother-sister type. She was always there to look after him.

A couple months ago, Sgire was taken in as a ward by her aunt in the countryside. She was to marry some landowner's son. When she left him, he realized just how dependant he was on the food she got for him. He began to starve, never quite mustering up the courage to steal from the kitchen, traumatized after the angry cook incident.

His moral conscience faltered though, when his stomach began to swell and throb. He had seen enough beggars to surmise that he was starving. It wasn't a shocking revalation.

He started to look for a quick way in and out of the kitchen. A passage so that he could rush in, grab a handful of whatever they were cooking up for the royals and nobles and leave. As he was trying to solve his dilemma, he remembered something from his last winter. Heat always came from the lower right corner in his tiny room. When he neared this corner, he realized, he could often smell the food the kitchens were cooking in more clarity than elsewhere in the room. He assumed that this was one of the tunnels that took the smoke from the fires out of the building.

The urchin began chipping away a hole in the wall, feasting on mice and insects he caught as he worked. When he had created a hole big enough to look through, he saw that his plan would work. He could shimmy down the opening and land in the fireplace that was used to cook stew. From his position he could see the stone stoves. With renewed faith, the urchin began chipping away in earnest for the next fortnight. Finally, he had a hole big enough to climb through.

The urchin waited until midnight, when the cooks finally packed up and left the kitchens for their beds. As they left, the cooks extinguished the fire, but the urchin knew better than to leap onto hot stones where the fire had been blazing not three minutes ago. He waited for another ten minutes, and then spit onto the stones to test the heat. His spittle landed on the stones, but didn't evaporate immediately, so the urchin deemed it safe to jump.

When he landed, the stones were still hot, but not so hot the skin on his feet got burned. He yelped and jumped forward to the cooler floor. He landed face first on the ground, so he didn't see the food immediately, but when he did he was amazed. He gasped in wonder at all the food left about. Altogether, the food was the best thing he had ever seen in his life.

He rushed over to the meat first. Pieces of chicken and cow lay scattered all over the stovetop. He started cramming the food into his mouth eating as fast as he could, only stopping to spit out bones. When he finished, he glanced over at the vegetables. Cabbages, turnips, carrots, spinach. He started gobbling up the food as if it were the last thing he would ever eat. But while in the middle of wolfing down an artichoke, he felt his stomach cramp. He bent over on the floor and started vomiting; however, he was barely finished throwing up before he sprinted towards the desserts sitting on another table. He began feasting on custard, almond pudding and bread pudding. As he finished and started eyeing up sweet bread and bread rolls, he heard a voice. He listening more intensely and heard the person, a woman, was muttering to herself. More importantly the voice was getting closer. The urchin sprinted to the water tub, drank deeply and ran to the bread. He started stuffing the bread into his mouth and rags he called clothes. When he started hobbling towards the fireplace, the woman entered the kitchen. As soon as she saw the mess in kitchen she let out a cry.

"Oh, no..." she said. She wailed when she saw what was left of the food she had labored to make. She stepped forward into the room and saw the urchin making his way to the fireplace. "What are you doing in here?" she cried. His mouth too full of bread rolls to even come up with a pitiful excuse, the urchin reached the fireplace and started to jump up and down, desperately trying to grab an edge of the hole he created.

The woman rushed forward to grab the urchin, but he noticed her coming and slipped under her flailing arms. Then woman turned around and started screaming, "Somebody! Anybody! There's a child in the kitchen!" Suddenly, the urchin felt pure rage. Who was she to stop him from getting some food? Would she let a little boy starve to death just because she was too lazy to bake some more bread rolls? "Help! I think it's sick!" It? What was he, an animal? Suddenly, his hands were raised, arms outstretched. Both palms faced directly at the woman. The urchin didn't even know what he was doing. The raising of his hands was almost an involuntary reflex to the rage he felt inside of him. "Help! Anyone! I need help!" Why wouldn't she just shut up! Her latest outburst sent pure anger pulsing through his veins. Before he knew what was happening, there was a blue flash of light, and he felt energy rush to the end of his fingers. He closed his eyes since the light was so bright, but when he reopened them, the woman was crumpled on the floor.

"Oh, no," he murmured. The urchin ran over and quickly took the woman's pulse. When he put his fingers to her wrist though, there was nothing. Not one beat. "No!" he yelled. The woman was dead. What had he done? Sure he had been mad at the woman, but he never meant to kill her! Or had he?

Suddenly, the urchin heard footsteps outside and a distant voice he thought he heard say, "Did you hear that?" Even with his conscience screaming at him to stay by her body and take responsibility, he knew that the magistrate would never take pity, or even listen to an urchin's side of a story. If he stayed a second longer, he was doomed to be hanged or flogged. Despite what he knew was right, Roger ran for the hole in the chimney.

Chapter 22
Quivel

FEDRADIN

AS FEDRADIN THREW HIS orb, he felt as if he were the orb, sailing through the air towards that pedestal, all hopes and dreams riding on whether or not it would land. If it missed, it, like Fedradin's hopes, would be shattered on the ground in beautiful green shards.

Then he heard the sounds of the dirtwolves. He heard them rip through the soil as they raced to be the first to tear into Fedradin's flesh. Fedradin closed his eyes. What would come first? Would the dirtwolves rip him open and eat him before he was even dead? Would his orb land on the pedestal and earn his team a point? Or would his orb miss the pedestal completely and doom him and his team to lose the competition by disqualifying him?

Suddenly, he felt a tug. Was this the beginnings of the dirtwolf ripping him apart? But then he realized he felt the tug everywhere, not in just one singular location. The tugging sensation grew stronger and stronger until it stopped suddenly. Fedradin opened his eyes. With a quick glance he knew that his orb had beaten the dirtwolf.

He was in a small room with four other people. One of them was the man whose boot was burned at the top. He was being nursed by a few Scholars for it appeared that his big toe had been burned halfway off. Fedradin looked around again and noticed that these were the warriors who had placed their orbs on the pedestals. Fedradin was one of the winners. He had scored a point for his team.

"What took ya so long? Ya figg'red out what the tournament was gonna be like, din't ya? You was walkn' real slow." called a man. Fedradin recognized him as the first man to score and also as one of the men who had been late for the starting ceremony.

"I was tricked by that vixen," Fedradin answered calmly.

"Jlope trick'd ya? Yep, she untrus'wor'y, ta say the leas'."

"You know her?"

"Trained in the same school 's her." The man reached out with his hand.

"Name's Quivel."

"Prince Fedradin Quickblade of Narven." Fedradin shook Quivel's hand.

"Narven, eh?" Quivel scoffed.

"What?" demanded Fedradin, now angry. "You have something against Narven?"

"Ya know, this's a *warr'r* comp'tition. N' you're f'om Narven."

"I'm still not sensing the problem," said Fedradin, rising to his feet.

"Look, Prince. I'm f'om Swenvip. One a the best mil'tary fiefs. Ya f'om Narven. Go stu'y some monsters." Quivel also stood up.

"You think since you're from Swenvip and I'm from Narven you can beat me?"

"Well, I did 'n that com'titon jus' now." Fedradin lost his compusure and threw a hard puch. Quivel got his arms up, but not quite soon enough, and Fedradin's blow still caught a piece of his cheekbone. Quivel stumbled back and hit the wall. He looked up in time to see Fedradin's foot collide with his chest. Fedradin felt a rib or two break. Despite the pain, while Fedradin's leg drew backward, Quivel swung his fist out. Fedradin pulled his fists into a protective covering and parried Quivel's blow. A few more blows came, but Fedradin blocked them all. Then a pause. His forearms hurt, so he took them down. When he emerged, he saw something he dreaded would happen. Quivel had taken out a weapon: a sharp steel dagger.

"Die, you Narvish scum!" seethed Quivel. Until this point, the other people in the room were mesmerized by the fight, but doing nothing. Now that the fight had escalated to weapons, one of the other warriors took action. He grabbed Quivel and put him in a headlock. Quivel squirmed and stabbed at the warrior's forearm. The blade sliced the inside of the man's arm, and blood started streaming from the wound. The warrior released Quivel and fell back into the wall with a cry of pain.

Seizing the moment when Quivel was distracted and looking at the fallen warrior, Fedradin punched Quivel as hard as he

115

could in the nose. In that moment, everyone in the room could hear a sickening bone snapping noise as Quivel's nose broke. He shouted a curse and dropped to the floor as blood began streaming out of his nose.

"What's going on?" came a voice. Fedradin felt himself being grabbed, and he didn't put up a fight. He was going to have to answer for the two men lying on the floor with serious injuries, and he wanted to be on the guard's good side by not resisting arrest. Fedradin was shoved to the ground mercilessly. He looked up and saw four armed guards with crossbows. One of the Scholars was gone. He must have called the guards.

"There was a big fight," answered Fedradin truthfully.

"No damn. How stupid do you think I am?"

A few short moments later, Fedradin felt himself being dragged out of the room. As he walked along, he passed a room, which door was ajar. Inside, he glanced all the other five other warriors that he thought had been eaten by the dirtwolves. It appeared that they all were fine. Fedradin deduced that the dirtwolves were fake dummies like the training one's he used in his training facility. He also caught a glance of the woman, Jlope, who had accidentally disqualified herself trying to explain her complicated situation to a referee who was trying to escort her out. Eventually, Fedradin was shoved into another room. There stood Lord Uslo.

"Prince Fedradin, what do we have here?" said the king.

"Where are the other two?" asked Fedradin without answering the original question. He did not want to be under interrogation alone.

"Being treated by Scholars. One of them has *knife* wounds. Care to tell me anything about that?"

"Quivel stabbed that man in the arm. That man had put Quivel into a headlock when Quivel came at me with a knife. That man probably saved my life."

"Quivel has a broken nose. How did that occur?"

"After the man who got stabbed fell down, I disabled Quivel by punching him in the nose."

"So you were involved in the fight."

"Yes."

"And did you start the fight?"

"What do you mean by that?"

"Who threw the first punch?" Lord Uslo said, leaning forward.

"I did." Fedradin did not back down.

"At least you're honest," murmured Uslo. "Why did you do it?"

"He insulted me and my homeland, Narven."

"And that gave you the right to hit him?"

"If I hadn't, he would've hit me."

"For insulting *his* homeland?"

"Probably. I was about to."

"What can you say to stop me from throwing you and your team out of this competition?"

"Well, nothing about me personally. But imagine this: how will the other races see us if they know we've had this altercation?" Lord Uslo opened his mouth but didn't utter a sound for a moment or two, so Fedradin continued in a quieter tone. "They'll see us as weak, unable to cooperate. In some races, maybe the flayers and svaadi, they might seize this opportunity to attack us. They might not succeed, but think of the consequences. The LNR would crumble. Wars would break out all across Haxter. Some of the races would truce with each other, eventually forming two sides. Goblins, giants, orcs, kobolds, medusas, yaun, golems, djinns, azzets, Salamanders from the Plane of Fire, trolls, ogres, Formiant, loxon, bugbears, hobogoblins, elementals, sprites, the undead, werebeings, and more would all join in. We already have a war right now my lord, do you want to be singlehandedly responsible for starting another?"

Uslo thought for a moment. "You make a convincing case, Prince. I don't know how much of that is true and how much you fabricated, but I'll cut you a deal. The three of you, you, Quivel, and Velk, will have a little competition at the end of the day. I'll pick what game you will play. The winner gets to keep the point you won at this game." Lord Uslo began walking out the door. "Good luck, Prince Fedradin. Despite my best intentions I have taken a liking to you."

Chapter 23
The Chultra Pharaoh

FEDRADIN

FEDRADIN WALKED OUT OF the room in a daze. Lord Uslo had practically let him off the hook. Fedradin could easily have been disqualified or worse. Maybe his completely fabricated story had scared Uslo slightly. Was Uslo really that gullible? Maybe Uslo was just a little on edge. After all, many people were criticizing the Games, saying they were going to push the LNR over the edge. He had already taken enough criticism dealing with people who claimed he had escaladed the War of Gems. Didn't they realize that was obviously because the elfish princess had run off with a dwarfish Gruel? Little did anyone know that they were right here in Gii.

Fedradin couldn't believe that the dwarf had told Fedradin about his situation. The dwarf was very trusting. If Fedradin had turned and shouted to Prince Poltax, he would have received a fairly substantial reward. But in retrospect, Fedradin could see why the dwarf had done it. Fedradin had been shocked by the dwarf and not said anything. Possibly, Fedradin *would* have called attention to Breetex if the dwarf hadn't opened up. When Breetex did, Fedradin felt bad for him. Breetex was in a bad situation, and Fedradin had decided to show some pity for him. No one had shown Fedradin pity as a child.

Fedradin reached his seat in the stadium. The crippled man sat nearby. Fedradin noticed the man's foot in a splint.

"Will you be able to compete in the next game?" asked Fedradin.

The cripple glanced over at Fedradin and realized he was being spoken to. "I hope so. I'm going to have a Scholar look at it tonight and try some of that cream, so I'll probably have a fixed toe by tomorrow."

"Hopefully they'll be able to wait for 'go.'"

"Really? I false-start once. Once! In my entire life, and it happens to be while a wall of fire is in front of me."

"Better than a real wall," said Fedradin. The cripple chuckled.

"Name's Lider," said the cripple and he stuck out his hand.

"Prince Fedradin Quickblade of Narven," said Fedradin. He reached out to take Lider's hand.

"Wait!" said Lider, jokingly. "If you shake my hand, will you punch me in the face?"

Fedradin laughed. "Not unless you insult my fief."

Lider cocked his head. "Really? It irritates you *that* much?" Fedradin gave a half-hearted shrug. "To each his own, I guess." While they talked, the dirtwolves changed into bugbears. Workers began to assemble the pit into a different game, removing the pedestals and placing new equipment down.

"Ladies and gentlemen," came the booming voice of Emperor Flyc. Fedradin glanced around and saw that more people had arrived for this game than for his. "Allow me to introduce the next game: Bugbear Ball." Flyc went on to explain that the object of the game was to be one of the seven to steal a ball from seven beasts that each guarded one. Fedradin had only seen bugbears in his book and made replicas of with his dummies. Granted these were replicas, just like the wuelltes, but they sure felt real. Each one was a massive hulk, covered in fur. Their heads resembled that of a bear with large teeth hanging out of their mouths. Each foot and hand was clawed at the toes or fingers and they each carried a large spike club and wooden shield.

He looked down to the warriors, all lined up. In this line, there were no women. All the men were clad in steel armor and holding large weapons, shouting battle cries and flexing, except for one. Draslupp was dressed in light leather armor. He had a medium-sized quiver on his back, a bow in his right hand and a knife in its sheath on his waist. He was calmly examining his nails.

Emperor Flyc finished his spiel, "On your marks, get set, go!"

Draslupp acted surprised and leapt into the battle later than the other warriors. It was then that he vanished. When that happened there was an uproar from the crowd.

"No wizards!" yelled a man a few rows back and to the left of Fedradin.

Draslupp reappeared just to make an obscene gesture directed at the man. This caused the crowd to get even angrier. Flyc, watching this event come apart at the seams, stepped up quickly.

"Ladies and gentlemen, quiet, if you please. That boy is not a wizard. He is a Domer. He is not cheating; he is well within the rules. So please be quiet and let's get back to the Games." The warriors had frozen on the battlefield. "Go on, get on with it," announced Flyc, somewhat angrily.

Slowly the warriors began moving again. Fedradin counted the warriors and counted ten of them. Where was Draslupp? One of the warriors charged the circle of bearbugs. The bearbug to which he was closest pulled its club back and swung; the spiked club making contact with the man's helm. Suddenly, Draslupp appeared behind the bearbug. He tapped it on the shoulder and it spun around. Before it could react, Draslupp swung his dagger into the neck of the bearbug. The bearbug yelped in pain and collapsed to the ground. Draslupp bent down and picked up the ball. Instantly, he vanished in puff of green smoke.

That was quick. Later on in the competition, three other teams made it through and scored a point.

The next competition was with Shah. It was the team battle against the chultra. To introduce the event, Emperor Flyc and Pharaoh Duztil stepped up on their stage near the top of the stadium. The crowd stopped talking when the two leaders stepped up, probably because of Duztil. He always made an impression.

A chultra in itself was incredible. They resembled large, bipedal cats. Their red-orange fur varied in hue depending on age, the older the chultra the darker the fur. Coming off of their noses, three bones stuck out in diagonal slants on each side. The most stunning part of a chultra was on their backs, where a large, spiked turtle shell covered the length of their back, protecting them. Pharaoh Duztil had these characteristics, but what he always wore made him even more memorable. Chultra were adroit miners, so they dug up many minerals like gold, emeralds, diamonds and many other rarities. Duztil wore a golden helmet with a sapphire embedded in the center. All around the helmet, tiny diamonds were pressed into it so the headdress sparkled when exposed to the sun. His nose bones were covered with gold leaf and he wore a solid gold chestplate, streaked with emerald lines. Silver shoulder pads covered his shoulders. Duztil wore no shoes, just like the rest of the chultra race. The most stunning feature was his staff. A long wooden pole, covered with gold leaf and embedded with various crystals like rubies, emeralds, sapphires, and so on, constituted the staff. At the top, am enormous diamond was attached.

Flyc began giving a similar speech he had given at Fedradin's and Draslupp's Games. Draslupp was sitting next to Fedradin, getting dirty looks from warriors sitting nearby. He was not popular with the other warriors.

As Flyc talked, after every sentence, Pharaoh Duztil repeated what Flyc said in the Tree Tongue of the chultra. Pharaoh Duztil had an odd accent; it sounded fuzzy and slightly muted, like someone was covering his mouth with their hand. As they talked, giants helped push rock formations out onto the field. Wizards helped levitate boulders and debris.

The main gist of what Flyc was trying to say was that this game would involve the warriors riding hippogriffs. They were given a wooden club each, and the goal was to knock all the players off their hippogriffs. The first race to eliminate the other race would win. All the teams playing for that race would earn a point. The rock formations the giants had pushed formed obstacles for the competitors to fly around.

"Without further ado, let the game begin!" Out from the two ends of the stadium, five humans and five chultra emerged riding hippogriffs. Fedradin noticed Shah flying around on the outside of the group of humans. She had a slightly upset expression on her face. Fedradin wondered why.

SHAH

Immediately, the chultra split up. Two of the chultra went down the sides of the battlefield, while three went down the middle. The humans were different. Four of them were gathered in a tight group in the middle. But Shah was not in the group of humans. She was speeding down the right side of the field towards a chultra. As soon as they were about to crash into each other,

121

Shah, riding her hippogriff, dove under the chultra's hippogriff. After she passed under him, she looped upside down and went over him, so she wound up in front of chultra's hippogriff. The chultra didn't react soon enough, and Shah hit him across the face with her wooden club. He cried out in pain and fell off his hippogriff, landing roughly in the sand below.

Shah turned her hippogriff towards the group of humans. It wasn't pretty. The chultra descended on them like vultures on a carcass. Shah couldn't see very clearly, but after the commotion stopped, all of the humans had been knocked off their hippogriffs, but they had only taken out one chultra with them. Shah rolled her eyes.

One against three. Maybe if they get a few more chultra it will be a fair fight.

Shah urged her hippogriff towards the chultra. After their success, they tried their split-up technique again. One went down the middle as two came down the sides. Shah sped toward the chultra in the center. In between Shah and the chultra was a rock arc. Closer to the chultra, there was a large floating boulder. With this in mind, Shah formulated a plan. She accelerated. Right as Shah approached the rock arc, she leapt off her hippogriff, so she landed on the top of the arc. At that particular moment, the chultra's view was obstructed by the boulder as he went under it. Immediately, Shah flattened herself on the rock arc.

The chultra approached the arc. Suddenly, Shah's hippogriff flew out from under it, almost hitting him. As the hippogriff fluttered in front of him, he turned his head away, to protect his face from its talons. When he turned his eyes back towards the arc, all he saw was a wooden club coming down on his head. The chultra let out a squeal and fell off his hippogriff. Quickly, Shah jumped onto the back of his hippogriff from atop her rock arc. Unfortunately, the hippogriff was alarmed at having someone land on its back, and began to try to buck her off. As she was desperately trying to stay on the hippogriff, another chultra descended on her. The chultra pulled up beside her and drew back his club. Shah recognized this as an opportunity to escape her frightened hippogriff. She pushed off the side of the hippogriff and flung herself at the new chultra's hippogriff. The chultra swung his club and tried to pull away, as Shah flew through the air towards him. Shah caught his blow on her wooden club, and just managed to get her knee and her free hand on the chultra's hippogriff, as hers flew away. The chultra, trying to gain control of his hippogriff, that was falling because of Shah's extra weight towards a large mass of rock, about twenty yards long, and three yards wide, didn't notice that Shah was still grabbing the hippogriff. Shah swung herself onto the back of the hippogriff, behind the chultra. He looked back just in time to see her smash her elbow into his cheek. The chultra fell off the hippogriff and narrowly missed hitting the mass of rock below as he plummeted out of the sky.

Shah looked away from the falling chultra and towards her falling hippogriff. With the weight of the chultra gone, the hippogriff could try to regain control of its flight path. Sadly, Shah realized, was that it was to late. The hippogriff was going to splatter on the rocks, and by default, Shah, too. Shah waited until she was very close to the rock before she leapt into the air, off the back of her hippogriff. Sure enough, the hippogriff hadn't been able to get out of the collision course, and met a gory demise on the mass of rock below. Shah landed ungracefully on the mass of rock, but had to look away. She was a fearless warrior, but why did the hippogriff have to die? It had done nothing wrong.

Suddenly, the sound of paws hitting rock came from behind her. Shah spun quickly. Standing behind her was a chultra she had seen once before.

"Sapplezul. What...what are you doing here?" asked Shah.

"I could ask the same of you," said Sapplezul.

"If you did, I would tell you Fedradin picked me to compete with him."

"Interesting. At least *I* was picked by Gii directly, not through some wimpy prince."

"I bet I could still beat your furry ass."

"Bring it on, *Shah*."

With that, Sapplezul ran forward, club in hand. Shah did the same, but was less aggressive with her charge than Sapplezul. In the moment before they clashed, Shah had a sudden flashback.

A young girl, wearing tattered clothing, walked slowly down the sidewalk in the dead of night. The debris tattered street was only

123

lit by the small amounts of distorted moonlight penetrating the thick layer of clouds. She was weary and exhausted; her only motive not to just collapse on the streets was the hope for a savior.

The young Shah and just narrowly escaped the boat that had been sunk by a chultra dromond. All of Shah's family had been on that xebec when it sunk, her father, Frem, her mother, and sisters. Well, there was still her bastard half-brother Fern. He was back on Tide Isle. But Shah had never really liked him. Only Shah had made it out alive. The worst part was emerging from the water and crawling towards the beach, only to find the bloated corpse of her younger sister washed up, the eyes eaten by fish. She had cried for hours, until night came, when she decided she should probably continue walking. Her sister was never coming back to life.

When she arrived in a village, she was relieved. Maybe someone could help her. But walking through the streets, she realized that those dreams were soon to be crushed. Blood stained everything. Not just human blood. Other blood too. Corpses, human and chultra, were piled up on street corners. Examining the piles, Shah saw the horrid wounds that had killed almost every single person that now helped constitute the disturbing piles. Arrows to the head, gashes in the neck or chest, disemboweled corpses, even some without heads. These were all the wounds that had been delved out. Shah retched, but she produced nothing but bile, since she had had nothing to eat for days now. The ship had been in bad condition already coming into the port. They had barely survived the pirate attack.

The worst part was that it wasn't only warriors, human or chultra. Civilian bodies were piled with the warriors. Men, women, children, it made no matter, they were all dead. Shah had to look away when she saw a baby in one of the piles.

Shah, only twelve at the time, understood there was a large battle. That must have been why the chultra navy attacked a merchant ship. Then again, they had killed many civilians in the town. With a little more research, Shah figured out that this was the trading post town, Uiklo, which was on the border of the Biztil Rainforest and the Cientile Plains. Uiklo was a human city, a trading post between svaadi, flayers, chultra, and humans.

Spice Merchants from the land of Stent came across the Trading Seas to Uiklo to barter their stentspice, which was always high in demand. Westlanders and Jade Islanders sold their exotic silks, fruits, skins and spices.

She wandered the streets for a long time, until her knees were ready to buckle. But before that happened, a body of a chultra stirred on one of the piles. She initially jumped back in shock, but soon advanced to investigate.

The chultra who was stirring had a gash on his chest. His armor was in ruins, and Shah saw that a piece of debris had been lodged in his shoulder. Shah pulled him out of the pile of bodies and started tending to his wounds. After a while, she was able to revive him.

The two quickly became friends. He taught her how to fight and she helped him find food to eat. The friendship was good until the Human Empire came to seize the town back. Sapplezul believed that Shah had summoned them to come and kill him. The Empire found Shah and her chultra friend, and they took Sapplezul into the woods. Shah thought they had killed him. She found out later the chultra attacked Uiklo after they caught a human poaching in the Sacred Grove of the chultra.

Now, Shah was at the Gii Games, facing off against her former childhood friend, currently, her enemy.

Shah and Sapplezul clashed. Shah swung her club at Sapplezul, but he easily parried her blow. Sapplezul pulled his club back, and Shah pulled her club into a position where she could block his blow. Sapplezul swung and Shah's club was there to stop it. Sapplezul's club bounced off Shah's, and Sapplezul almost lost control of it. While he bobbled his club, Shah swung her club. Sapplezul saw it coming and turned so that her club hit his shell. Shah hit one of his spikes, and her club chipped on it. Shah was slightly confused for a millisecond and froze. This was enough time for Sapplezul to spin around and swing his club. Shah couldn't bring her club back to where she could block it, so she turned and took the blow on her shoulder. Shah stumbled back after the club struck her, but the pain wasn't unbearable. Still, she couldn't help collasping. Sapplezul walked over to her and prepared to roll her off the rock ledge. Before he could do that,

125

though, Shah swiped outwards with her legs and tripped Sapplezul. The chultra fell to the ground, and Shah pounced on top of him. She began furiously beating his head with her club until he was able to grab her club and pull it away from her. Shah, left unarmed now, began to beat him with both her fists. This time she spared him though, and she beat his stomach instead. Sapplezul dropped both the clubs, needing free hands to attempt to stop the beatings. He finally was able to get his hands on her wrists and threw her off of him. Shah rolled to her feet, but not before swiping both the clubs out from under the chultra.

Sapplezul got to his feet to find Shah standing in front of him with both clubs. Sapplezul put his hands in the air. It was now that the blood started to dribble down his face. Sapplezul started backing up.

"You win," he said.

"It appears I have," said Shah.

"I'll give it to you, Shah, that was some great fighting," said Sapplezul, still backing up. "You beat me."

"If I beat you so bad, why don't you jump off the edge and end this?"

"Alright, I will." With that, Sapplezul fell backwards off the edge, in a spread eagle form. Shah watched him fall as a cheer went up from the humans watching the game. But was that a wink she saw? Shah tore her eyes away from Sapplezul's descent and threw her hand in the air victoriously, facing the crowds. The humans cheered louder. Shah pranced around the rock, enjoying her moment of victory. Suddenly, the crowd went quiet. Shah felt a breeze on her back. Shah spun around to see Sapplezul hovering in the air on a hippogriff. Sapplezul urged the hippogriff forward, and before Shah could do anything, it planted its talons into Shah's chest, pushed, and sent her flying. Shah crashed to the ground. She got to her feet and put up both clubs. When the hippogriff reached her, she lashed out with the clubs, but this only angered the hippogriff, and it attacked her more furiously. Shah fell to the ground, and she put her hands over her face to protect herself from the flying talons. The hippogriff, with Sapplezul's coaxing, started to roll Shah towards the edge of the rock. Shah realized this and used one hand to try to gain some purchase on the rock face. Shah kept clawing at the rock until she felt herself drop. Shah took her hands away from her face and looked straight into the air to see Sapplezul's smug face looking down on her. This image lasted only a few seconds before Shah found herself in a room, surrounded by the other humans, knocked unconscious from the hitting the sand.

Chapter 24
The Switch

FLYC

EMPEROR FLYC STEPPED OUT of the stadium. A Game had just ended and he had some time to himself before the next one. He pulled a pipe out of his jacket that he had bought in Gii that morning. Flyc looked around him, and seeing no one, lit the pipe with a spark from his fingertips. That was the real reason why he had been secretive.

As he smoked his pipe, he reached down his shirt and pulled out an object that dangled near his breast. A nervous habit. But it was still there. He leaned back against the stadium, enjoying this moment to himself.

"There he is," whispered Frin, pointing to Emperor Flyc, who was leaning back on a wall, smoking what appeared to be a pipe. Oxlo and Tawassa were behind him, lying in the shrubbery like Frin. Tawassa held a bag big enough for a head. "Let's move in."

Frin held up three fingers, and then two, and then one, and then he put his hand down. The three men rushed forwards. Tawassa swung the bag over Flyc's head. Oxlo knocked the pipe from Flyc's hand and pulled his arms roughly behind his back. Frin put a hand over Flyc's mouth to muffle any potential screams. The three men forced Flyc to his knees, and Tawassa pulled out a knife.

"I regret doing this to you," said Tawassa. "You have been a great Emperor. It is a shame people will have to remember you as the worst." Tawassa swung his knife into Flyc's belly. Flyc flopped forwards, and soon, Frin felt Flyc stop breathing. He pulled his hand away from Flyc's mouth. Oxlo released Flyc's hands and Tawassa pulled the knife from Flyc's stomach. Flyc fell over, onto his face.

"He's dead," whispered Oxlo.

Frin hoisted the body Flyc onto his shoulders. "We need to go." The three men quickly ran off into the forest, all that remained was some blood and the signs of a scuffle in the dirt.

Chapter 25
Cliffs

FEDRADIN

THE LAST HUMAN EVENT of the day, other than Fedradin's extra competition, was Kekk's. Shah joined Fedradin and Draslupp as the pit was rearranged. Shah sat down next to Fedradin.

"What happened out there, Shah? You looked upset coming out, didn't go along with the strategy, and then you had some sort of discussion with that chultra on the rocks. What went wrong?" Shah didn't say anything. She just gazed out at the rock face that rose from the ground as the stadium lowered. "Shah?"

"It's because I'm a woman, okay? Those men wouldn't listen to a thing I said! I'm the only woman in this whole damn competition! People treat me like a joke! They think you only picked me because they think you're trying to...you know."

"There's another woman. I competed with her," avoiding responding to Shah's last statement.

"She was disqualified, Fedradin."

"Really?"

"No, I'm making it up!" exclaimed Shah, sarcastically.

"I still don't understand why you're so mad at me..."

"Is it true?" asked Shah.

"Is what true?" asked Fedradin.

"You know what. Is that why you picked me? Is this all because I kissed you?"

"Shah, please, calm down. You know we had that whole competition to decide who would compete. You won second place, Shah."

"Maybe you treated me easier because you want me."

"No, Shah. You're being crazy. Slow down and listen to yourself. You are just my student, and that's all you will ever be. And, besides, you are about to move away!"

Shah took a deep breath. "Sorry. I just don't like getting treated differently because I'm a woman."

"It's okay, Shah. Now, can you please tell me about this chultra?"

"Sure." Shah told Fedradin all about her voyage on her father's boat, how it had sunk, her sister, Sapplezul emerging from the pile of bodies, them becoming friends, and finally how the Emperor's troops had come to investigate what had happened.

"Why hasn't this event started yet?" wondered Draslupp aloud, for they had been sitting in the stadium for a long time, but Kekk's event hadn't begun yet.

Fedradin nodded, agreeing that, indeed, it had been a while. A few more confused moments passed. Finally Lord Uslo stepped up onto the platform Fyc had previously been using.

"Ladies and gentlemen, sorry for the delay. It appears that Emperor Flyc has urgent business to attend to. So, without further ado, I give to you 'Cliffs of Despair!'" Lord Uslo explained that the goal of the game was to reach the top of the cliffs without falling off. Other players were not allowed to use their weapons to knock other players off. Fedradin thought that it seemed simple until he noticed something wasn't right with the air in one place on the rock face. Fedradin pulled out a spyglass he kept in his pouch and looked closer at the air. Fedradin could now see more clearly, and he knew what was going on.

Husfers. Husfers had some chameleon-like characteristics. They could blend into their surrounding. Their feet and tails were also designed like chameleon feet and tails to grab rocks on cliffs. A big difference though was the scale; the husfer was the size of a human. On certain places of their bodies -knees caps, chest, and forehead— bone had become extra thick to protect them from scraping the sides of cliffs. Fedradin also recalled that they had been designed to protect Bal-gastar's flank, since it had been built near a cliff, by James of Dire, the leader of Thunderflash.

This is going to be one tough challenge, thought Fedradin.

The competitors stepped out to the base of the cliff. Fedradin saw Kekk decked out in a helmet and boiled leather armor. He carried a short sword in a sheath on his waist. The rest of the warriors were all men and they were wearing the same things that Kekk was.

"Go!" shouted Uslo. The men ran forward and started scaling the cliff face. Fedradin saw Kekk take the lead.

130

"I'm glad I'm not doing this event," said Draslupp.

"Why?" asked Fedradin.

"I'm afraid of heights."

KEKK

His right hand tightly gripped a rock that jutted out from the cliff. He swung his left hand up in the air and grabbed the edge of a small crevasse in the rock face with four fingers. Kekk looked up. A ledge where he could catch his breath was just above him. Kekk pulled his left leg off a foothold, raised it so it was at a ninety-degree angle to him, and wedged it into the same crevasse his left hand was in. Kekk looked at the rock face and found what he was looking for: another foothold. Slowly, he pulled his right knee up high until his right foot could get a purchase on the foothold. He had just felt the hold with his toe when his left foot slipped out of the crevasse. Kekk knew what he had to do. Before his left leg could pull him off balance, Kekk sprang upwards off the rocks. It was a risk, but it paid off when Kekk grabbed the ledge above him with both hands. Kekk tried to gain some purchase on it, but couldn't, because a layer of dirt covered the ledge. Kekk began sliding off the edge of the ledge. If he didn't do something soon, he would fall to his death.

But Kekk was no idiot. He had climbed cliffs all the time when he was little to get bird eggs to eat. When he had gone climbing then, he had taken a hooking tool to grab edges of ledges, like this. He didn't have one of those now, but he knew what to do. Kekk took his left hand off of the ledge, while grabbing it with his right hand. He began sliding backwards faster, his right hand virtually ineffective at slowing him. Kekk pulled out his dagger and stabbed it into the layer of dirt covering the rock. He didn't stop until he felt the blade collide with the stone. The knife's blade was completely buried in the dirt. He grabbed the handle with both hands and started to feel for a foothold with his feet. Then, two things happened simultaneously. Kekk found a foothold for his right foot, and his knife pulled out of the dirt. Again, Kekk leapt for the ledge, and this time he was able to get a knee on top of it. Kekk pulled himself up and collapsed in a heap, breathing heavily.

As Kekk leaned against the cliff and waited for his adrenaline to wear off, he began to feel a different experience, pain. As he looked closer, he found the source of it, his ring finger on his right hand. The finger was bleeding fairly badly; he assumed that he had stabbed himself while trying to get his knife in the ledge. Kekk looked closer and saw that he could see the bone in his finger, so he pulled a piece of fabric off the shirt underneath his armor. He wrapped it around his finger and tied a knot. That would have to do.

Kekk looked up to the top of the cliff, which was probably a total of fifty yards tall. He had around another thirty-five yards to go.

Kekk heard a noise behind him, the sound of footsteps. He spun around, crouching slightly. That decision saved his life. A man, one of the other competitors, behind him had swung his broadsword at Kekk. Kekk had managed to duck the blade by crouching. The blade struck the side of the cliff. Quickly, before the man had a chance to pull it back and swing, Kekk kicked him in the chest and sent him reeling off the edge of the cliff.

Kekk found another ledge, probably another twenty yards higher than where he was standing. He jumped onto the cliff wall and began to scale it. Right hand, left hand, right foot, left foot. He repeated this process many times.

Kekk was just about to heft himself onto the ledge when he heard a noise, something entirely different from the sound of a footstep. It was a hissing noise of sorts. Kekk noticed that it was coming from his right. He turned his head in that direction and saw that the air around the noise was shimmering unnaturally. He prepared to move sideways to investigate, when suddenly a monster appeared. It had sharp teeth, two protruding horns coming out of its head, a long tail that was grasping a rock, some bone plates on it, and two feet the stuck onto the rock. It growled and swung its body at Kekk by taking its feet off the rocks and using its tail to hold on.

When it got close to Kekk, he let go of the cliff. Right as it passed over him, Kekk grabbed it around the stomach. He swung his legs into the air and wrapped them around its stomach, too. The husfer was confused at first, but eventually realized where Kekk was. It began to twist from side to side in attempt to shake

Kekk off. Kekk knew he was in trouble, so when the husfer stopped shaking, he grabbed his sword out of its sheath.

The husfer reached with both hand towards Kekk and tried to pry him off. Kekk felt himself slipping off the husfer as it pushed, so he slashed with his sword and cut one of the husfer's arms off. It roared in pain, and with its intact arm it started to claw at Kekk. After a few seconds, the husfer had torn through the leather on Kekk's left arm. Then it started to rip into Kekk's open flesh. The pain was almost unbearable, and Kekk knew he needed to do something or otherwise he would have to let go. Then, in one swift, upwards arc, Kekk slashed off the end of the husfer's tail. It was then that the two started to fall.

As they did so, the husfer put its one arm and two legs around Kekk, as if to protect him. Kekk knew better. The husfer knew it was going to die, so it was taking out a predator with it.

Kekk had seconds to do something. He knew that if he struggled, he would get nowhere. He remembered Fedradin's lesson on this. Husfers had what some people called a "hug of death." Kekk took his sword and shoved it through the creature's skull. The ground was approaching fast. Kekk shoved the limp limbs of the dead husfer aside and lunged for the cliff.

His left hand grabbed a good handhold, but he was falling too fast, and the speed of his descent ripped his arm out of his socket. He held on for a few milliseconds in agonizing pain. The longer he held on, the softer his landing would be. Finally, he couldn't take the pain, and he dropped off the cliff and landed on his back.

As the crowds melted into a room while he teleported, Kekk thought, *I failed my team.*

Chapter 26
Bluesvaad

BREETEX

BREETEX WAS HAVING A bad day. He hadn't made a sale all day and soon he wouldn't be able to sell the rest of his manticore eggs, for they were about to hatch. His flashdog puppy had begun to teeth and was gnawing on Breetex's arm from inside his coat. Luckily, the poison glands in its mouth weren't fully developed yet, so all it left was an unpleasant stinging feeling. His zaplizard eggs were emitting shocks, which meant they were almost ready to hatch. When they hatched, no one would buy them. Worst of all, Aserax was mad at him. He figured she was probably on to him selling monsters, but what choice did he have? He was a poor, fugitive dwarf with no other means of making money.

"Please! How about only six fellyers!" cried Breetex, who was now clinging to the arm of a passing man.

"Unhand me, dwarf!" shouted the man as he tried to pull Breetex off of him.

"One fellyer! Six oplopecks!" Tears were streaming down Breetex's face. If he didn't make a sale he would probably be fired...or worse. Breetex's grip was slipping. Soon the man would get away.

"Please dwarf! I have no interest in monster battles! I simply want to watch the Games!"

"Please! My job is at stake. Just buy something! You can just kill it!" Breetex was now being dragged along on the cobblestone streets. He looked around and saw people staring.

Suddenly, he felt a hand grab him. It was a large hand, larger than a human's. Strangely, this was comforting to Breetex because now he knew that it wasn't a guard. He squirmed around, but he wasn't going anywhere.

"What are you doing, little dwarf?" came a low, gruff voice. Breetex wriggled until he was in a position where he could see his assailant's face. When he got there, he looked up into what looked like a blue toad's face. He recognized it as a bluesvaad, the biggest of the svaadi. Red, green, and yellow svaad made up the lower rankings, and Greysvaad was a term given to the leader of the svaadi race.

Breetex decided to try to act nonchalant. "Trying to make a living. How about you?"

"Right now I'm busy catching illegal monster distributers, who assault innocent bystanders," said the bluesvaad in garbled Leaguespeak. The bluesvaad spit on Breetex's face, who wiped it off with his shoulder.

"What gives you the right to do that? Are you a guard?" asked Breetex.

"No, but I can crush you like the worthless bug you are."

"What challenge is that to you?" asked Breetex. "Why don't you put me down so we can fight with honor."

"As you wish." The bluesvaad dropped Breetex five feet, which from a dwarf's perspective, was very high. Breetex landed on his back, hard on the cobblestone street. He opened his eyes to see the bluesvaad pulling its fist back. He closed his eyes again, bracing himself for the pain.

"Stop." Came a voice. A familiar voice. It wasn't pleading, asking, groveling nor ordering, commanding, or decreeing. It carried no desperation, nor sense of authority. It simply was, as one would talk about the weather or a sporting event. Breetex recognized that voice as it spoke again. "Why would you hurt that dwarf?"

By now, the bluesvaad had dropped its fist to its side. "The dwarf was chasing a man, trying to sell him monsters."

"Does that concern you?" asked the voice again.

"Not exactly, but..."

"Then here's a few fellyers. Go find something that does." The sound of coins bouncing on pavement. The bluesvaad bent down nervously to pick them up, and he left in a hurry.

Breetex got to his feet. When he did, he found himself standing in front of the same man who had approached him after the magmum against homunculus battle, when Breetex had dived behind a cart to avoid being seen by Prince Poltax.

"Are you alright?" asked the man.

"Yes..yes I'm fine, thank you," Breetex said.

"Dwarf, you need to learn to stay out of trouble."

"Breetex is the name."

"My name is Prince Fedradin Quickblade of Narven."

"That's quite a title," said Breetex.

"Why thank you."

A peddler pushed a cart full of opium in between the man and dwarf. When he passed Fedradin said, "Isn't he worried about getting caught by the guards with his drugs just sitting on his cart in plain view? I haven't been in the city very long."

"Nor have I. I arrived no more than a few days before the competition was to start."

"What brought you to the city?" asked Fedradin, alluding to the fact that Breetex was a fugitive. Breetex's face turned red and he rubbed his palms together. Fedradin decided not to push the conversation.

"I...um...I...my contract expired and I decided to earn a little extra cash."

"So you're trained to fight?"

"Yes, I fight in the dwarfish army."

"So how come you couldn't escape from that bluesvaad?"

"I...prefer that people don't know of my military experience."

"Interesting...I should be off now, but if you need anything, feel free to visit the Warrior's Village."

"Thank you. I appreciate it."

Chapter 27
Possessed Sheep

FLYC

FLYC WAS STILL ALIVE, but just barely. He had stopped his breathing for just long enough to make the men believe he was dead and take the knife out of his stomach. Still, the knife wound was bleeding very badly. Flyc didn't have much longer.

When the men had carried him into the woods, they traveled for around fifteen minutes, before Flyc felt a tingling sensation. Through the bag on his head, Flyc saw a purple light. A few minutes later, the men came to a cave. Flyc sensed that they had entered as the temperature and light changed.

That was all Flyc remembered for a while as the entire world went black.

THE MASTER

There it was. Large, blue, glowing, pulsing, slimy. The Heart was disgusting.

The Master walked closer to it and ran his red hand down one of its veins. It was beautiful in its own way; contained inside its grotesque appearance was an unfathomly vast amount of power. It was like him in a way. The Master looked around the room at the tendrils of blue goo that snaked out across the floor. It was hungry. It was getting bigger. It was getting more powerful.

As the Master paced the floor impatiently, he heard a sheep bleat from the opening of the large cave in which he stood. The Master looked up. This was no ordinary sheep.

Pieces of its wool were ripped out of its skin. In those bare patches, a blue crust, something that looked like lichen, spread outwards at a slow pace. On its head, the blue crust enveloped it like a mask. It some places, the crust dangled from its face, revealing pieces of the sheep's skull and brain underneath. One of its eyes was visible, but it was disconnected from the socket and hanging limply, attached by some sort of bloody string which had emerged from somewhere in the sheep's head.

As it walked, one of its legs buckled. The sheep fell to the ground, and thrashed about in pain. It could no longer move.

The Master watched in absolute wonder as the tendrils on the floor, protruding from the Heart, started to move towards the sheep, slower at first, but speeding up. As they reached the sheep, the tendrils wrapped around its appendages and started pulling. The sheep began to move across the stone floor of the cave in the direction of the Heart.

The sheep let out a loud whimper. It appeared that it had temporarily won some control over its body and had realized the horror of the situation. This only lasted a few seconds before the crust took over its brain once more, and the sheep grew quiet.

By now, the sheep had reached the Heart. It began disappearing bit-by-bit into the unfathomable depths of the Heart, never to be seen again. Soon, all that was left was its head. It let out one last bleat and vanished completely.

The Master resumed pacing, but it was not a long wait until the three men showed up at the cave. The Master looked up and saw that Frin was carrying another man with had a bag over his head on his shoulder.

"Who do we have here?" asked the Master.

"Emperor Flyc the Third of Bal-gastar, Master," said Frin.

"And I am to replace him?" asked the Master.

"Yes, Master. I will have the Heart transfer his looks to your body. I will see if I can also transfer some of his memories to you," said Frin.

The Master merely nodded, not particularly interested by Frin. The Master pulled the bag from Flyc's head. The emperor's eyes were closed and his mouth was slightly open. The Master stroked the side of Flyc's head, but as he was about to lift his hand, he felt a pulse.

"This man's still alive!" shouted the Master. His lifted his hand and slapped the man in the face with an open palm. Flyc's eyes shot open, and Flyc put out his arm, palm facing the Master. "No, you don't," said the Master, who grabbed Flyc by the shirt and flung him across the room.

Flyc landed in a heap, and he didn't have the strength to get up. He turned over and once again pointed his palm the Master. The Master quickly waved his own palm, and the arm that Flyc was holding out bent at a horrific angle. Flyc yelled out in pain, and the Master silenced him by smashing a rock, that appeared out of nowhere, into Flyc's head.

The Master ran over to Flyc's body and pulled out what appeared to be a piece of jewelry from inside Flyc's shirt. He held it up to the Minions and exclaimed, "You fools! You've captured the Sage of Fire!"

Chapter 28
Cages

FEDRADIN

FEDRADIN HAD CRUNCHED THE numbers. Quivel, Velk and Kekk had recovered. Lider had sadly not managed to recover from his foot injury. His team had no one to replace him, so they were automatically disqualified. Jlope's team had brought an extra person to the competition, so they could replace her, and therefore remained in the competition. That left three teams for disqualifications. The second team of humans had beaten the svaadi. With some statistics Fedradin had gathered from an official, he found that four teams had but one point, including Fedradin's team, since they had not counted his win in 'Dirtwolves' after the fight. Velk's team and Quivel's team were also in the one point category, their win during Dirtwolves not counted either. Fedradin had also learned that only the winner of the event he was about to play would get the point; therefore, whoever won the event he was about to play would not be disqualified. The rest of the races had played their Games.

Fedradin was standing in a cage. Literally. A cage, cubic in shape, around twenty feet by twenty feet by ten feet, covered with metal bars and a dirt floor. He was standing in the center of a stadium, two other identical cages on either sides of him. Velk stood inside one, Quivel in the other.

Flyc, who claimed he had returned from some "urgent business," had just given out the instructions for the game. Real monsters, he emphasized, not dummies, would be teleported into the cages, the same monsters in each cage. Once the monster was dead, the competitor would wait for his opponents to finish. Each competitor had a headband wrapped around their heads. If a competitor ever needed to be removed from the cage, they were to rip off the headband and be disqualified.

A six-legged weasel-like creature, around the size of a medium-sized dog, appeared next to Fedradin. Its yellow fur was matted down with dirt, sweat and blood. It had two glowing eyes and a gaping maw with razor sharp teeth.

An aurvorax, thought Fedradin. Aurvoraxes lived in any alpine regions and dug out lairs in the rocks.

The aurvorax snarled and leapt at Fedradin. Fedradin easily dodged the jump and slashed out with his sword. The blade cut into the side of the aurvorax, which merely snarled more ferociously. Fedradin stabbed at it again with his sword. The aurvorax rolled to the side and pounced at Fedradin. The aurvorax hit Fedradin in his side, and the two of them crashed to the ground. The aurvorax slashed Fedradin with his paw. Luckily, the claws didn't make it through Fedradin's armor. Quickly, Fedradin brought the handle of his sword into the side of the aurvorax's head. The beast fell off Fedradin, and Fedradin jumped to his feet. Fedradin kicked the aurvorax under the chin. The aurvorax stumbled back a few feet, and, before it could react, Fedradin stabbed it through the eye with a quick lunge. The aurvorax collapsed in a heap and after a few short seconds, disappeared.

Fedradin looked at his competitors. Fedradin caught a glimpse of Quivel's aurvorax disappear. He turned to look at Velk, but there was nothing to see. He had killed his monster as well. All three competitors had successfully made it through the first round mostly unharmed.

"It appears it is time to up the ante," said Flyc.

As soon as Flyc finished, another monster appeared in front of Fedradin. The monster looked like a large baboon, with cobalt fur. Two large tufts of hair stuck out from either side of its head, and a long, hairless tail protruded from his rear. It had a large mouth full of long, pointed teeth. Blood and dirt matted its fur, and the beast stood about ten feet tall.

A julamus. I haven't seen one of these in a while, thought Fedradin. Julamuses lived out in the tropical regions, near the Biztil Rainforest and the Cientile Plains.

The julamus roared and slashed out with its claws. Fedradin leaned to the side and dodged the slashes. Fedradin returned the attack and stabbed his sword into the julamus's side. The julamus yelped and leapt backwards, the sword still stuck in its hide. Fedradin tried to hold on to the pommel, but the sword was pulled from his grasp. It seemed the julamus was unaware of the sword sticking out of its side.

141

Fedradin was facing the julamus, unarmed. The monster roared at Fedradin. It may not have been aware of why Fedradin was disarmed, but it knew Fedradin was. The julamus was going to enjoy its kill.

The julamus pounced and flew through the air towards Fedradin. Fedradin jumped to the side to avoid the monster. Fedradin narrowly avoided the julamus, and it landed on the spot where Fedradin had been standing, flailing its arms and biting. It looked for Fedradin, and it found him standing, not four feet away. The julamus pounced once again, and Fedradin once again eluded the julamus by jumping to the side. This pattern repeated once more before Fedradin could formulate a plan.

As the julamus searched for Fedradin, Fedradin walked backwards until his back was pressing against the bars of the cage he was in. When the julamus found him, it pounced as it always had. Fedradin sidestepped the flying julamus as it crashed, headfirst into the bars of the cage. Dazed, it fell to the floor of the cage. Quickly, Fedradin pulled his sword from its hide, and with a quick motion, Fedradin slit the julamus's throat. The body of the julamus instantly disappeared.

Fedradin stood up and looked at his opponents. Quivel was still fighting the julamus, but he was clearly winning. Velk was also fighting the monster, but he was on the losing side, fending off the monster, but taking severe hits.

Finally, both won the battle, but Velk was barely on his feet.

"Get ready for challenge number three," said Flyc.

As Flyc spoke, a vile creature appeared in front of Fedradin. A beast, standing about seven feet tall, roared. But the roar did not just come from one head. Instead, it emanated from two. Each head was equally disgusting, with a large nose and mouth. Two large teeth stuck upwards from the mouth of each head, and the small eyes were crisscrossed. The beast had two muscular arms, one grasping a wooden club.

An ettin, thought Fedradin. Ettins lived in between forests and mountains, where they often lived with a few other ettin.

The ettin swung its club at Fedradin, who ducked the blow. Fedradin slashed out with his sword, and he cut from the right shoulder of the ettin, all the way down to its left hip.

142

The ettin roared in agony, and started swinging its club wildly. Fedradin backed away from it, but it didn't seem to notice and kept swinging its club at a nonexistent foe. Out of the corner of his eye, Fedradin noticed a red smoke appear in Velk's cage. The ettin in Velk's cage threw his arms in the air victoriously. Velk had been defeated.

The ettin in Fedradin's cage finally came to its senses, and started walking towards Fedradin, menacingly. Fedradin charged, blocked the club with his sword and promptly chopped off the ettin's left head. The right head didn't seem to feel any pain and kept walking. However, without the left head, the left side of the ettin's body ceased to work. The ettin fell to the ground, because it couldn't move its left leg. It strugged fruitlessly on the ground, and Fedradin walked over and chopped off the right head of the ettin, ending its pitiful struggle. It was finally dead.

Quivel had also finished with his battle, but he had taken a club to the side of the head, and was walking around dazed.

"It is time for a greater challenge, one neither of you may finish!" said Flyc.

Suddenly, a large behemoth appeared in front of Fedradin. It looked reptilian, much like a dragon, except it didn't have wings and was much smaller. It had three heads, all connected to its small body by long necks. It stood on all fours, and had a tail with a spike on the end. It let out a loud roar.

Now this is a challenge! Thought Fedradin. This monster, of course, was a hydra.

Chapter 29
Abominations

VASIRD

IT SEEMED AS NORMAL a day as any other when Vasird awoke. The sun was out in the town of Haneou, and already people were bustling around in the streets.

Vasird lived in a manse right in the middle of town. He was an older, yet active man, so retiring in the countryside in a large estate seemed like what he would want to do. But he had always preferred the bustling city streets to the boredom of the country.

As Vasird rose from his bed, he felt different. He almost felt shorter. He began to feel an itching sensation in his arm.

Vasird did not like change, not one little bit, and he immediately called for his servant. His servant came running to the room, and entered through the door. Vasird turned to face his servant, and on his servant's face was a look of shock. And that look of shock would be permanent for his servant turned to stone.

"No!" shouted out Vasird. His servant couldn't possibly be dead. He just couldn't! The itching in his arm became a burning, and Vasird collapsed to the floor. He grabbed the part of his arm that was burning, and Vasird felt a bump. A throbbing bump. A growing bump.

The pain grew worse as he felt something trying to push its way out of his arm. That was when he felt the same itching sensation in his other arm. He stumbled out into the streets in only undergarments, and the cold bit into his bare flesh.

The pain grew unbearable and Vasird started screaming. People began looking at him, but if any met his gaze, they turned to stone. As he stumbled through the streets, a wing erupted from one arm, the arm in which he had first felt the itching sensation. A few seconds later, a wing erupted from his other arm. Wings! Vasird couldn't have *wings*!

People started yelling for the guards in the streets.

Vasird felt his mouth start to contort, grow, change until a beak replaced his mouth. He fell to the ground screaming in a horrid, bird-like screech, as his nails turned into claws.

People started to flee the scene as the guards showed up.

More human arms with claws started to erupt from everywhere on his body. Suddenly, he felt a tail sneak its way out of his rear, and tail like that of a mouse, hairless.

He felt the hands of the guards on him, and he closed his eyes. He didn't want to turn any of the guards into stone. As the guards lifted him, he felt fur start to grow out of his body all over him until he was completely covered.

The guards tied his hands together and shoved his head into a bag. As that process was going on, he felt more eyes pop out of his forehead and cheeks. When the last eye broke the surface of his skin, all the sensations that had been tormenting him ceased. His transformation was complete.

IRROTHURE

It was a warm day. One of the first of its kind of the new spring. A pleasant breeze passed through the trees, rustling the newly formed leaves. It was one of those days when one could simply sit and stare off into space, just enjoying their surroundings. Unfortunately, there was work to be done. For the umpteenth time, he placed the log of wood, vertically, on his cutting stump. A large gray dog was lying down off to his side, watching with a minimal amount of interest. He pulled his trusty axe, dulling from a long day's work, up to his shoulder and brought it down on the log of wood, directly in the middle. The two halves fell apart, almost identical in shape. Irrothure wiped the sweat from his brow as he dropped his axe and grabbed the two halves of the log of wood, flinging them into a large pile with similarly shaped wood. Looking back, he saw that he had chopped all the logs he had hoped to for firewood, so he picked up his axe and swung it so that it embedded itself in the stump, with a satisfying "thunk."

He started walking towards his wooden cabin, a small cabin with one room, meant only for him. Irrothure had never been one for relationships or human interaction. And the last time he had tried it, it hadn't worked out too well. He liked living by himself, with his dog, Kuine, where no one could bother him. He could do what he wanted and when he wanted to do it, and the only way for him to achieve that was to move to the Mendelgar Forest, away from Gii and the dwarves and elves.

He had built the cabin with his own hands, everything from the walls to the small amounts of furnishing inside. He had chopped down the trees around his cabin to create the glade he called home, and he hunted or trapped everything he ate.

"C'mere, boy," he called to his dog, snapping his fingers. The dog lifted its head lazily, its eyes staring at Irrothure, as if accusing the man of committing a crime. Still, the dog did not make a move to get up. "Kuine, come boy," said Irrothure. The dog rolled over and faced away from Irrothure, who began to get angry. "Kuine, come," demanded Irrothure. The dog barked in annoyance at Irrothure's insistence on him moving.

Irrothure was more than irritated. Kuine, the runt, was suddenly too good to come to Irrothure? Kuine had been abandoned, and Irrothure took him in and nourished the dog back to good health. All Irrothure asked for in return was that the dog obey him.

Irrothure marched over to the dog and grabbed it by the leather strip that constituted its collar. Irrothure pulled on the collar, in attempt to get Kuine to stand up. As the collar started to press against Kuine's neck, the dog's head snapped around, and it sank its fangs into Irrothure's hand. Irrothure yelped, alarmed, for his dog had never hurt him before. Irrothure became even angrier.

Suddenly, he felt a transformation coming on. He felt his body growing, his arms getting bigger and more muscular. His teeth grew into fangs and spikes stuck out from his back. He roared out, an angry roar. And that was when Irrothure blacked out.

COID

His wrists bled from the abrasion of the ropes on his skin. The fresh scabs on his back cracked open and blood trickled down his back every time he bent over. His arms felt limp and useless, but he still had to find strength to finish his duties, lest the whip of the slave driver bite into his already marred back.

Coid was awoken the usual way. Kicked out of his pitiful straw bed, and whipped when he didn't stand up fast enough. Coid held back a cry of anguish, but he wasn't entirely successful, and a pitiful murmur found its way through his tightly closed lips. But he knew the slave driver had no pity for the slaves, and would whip Coid again if he did not get to his feet. When he did so, he noticed that he was a few inches taller than the slave driver, strange, for every other day Coid had been much shorter. The driver took no notice, and he began walking down the line of slaves, kicking them out of their straw piles and whipping them if they weren't quick enough. Coid saw the driver's short sword in its scabbard by the driver's side. He felt tempted to attempt to take it and use it to kill the driver, but when another slave had tried that before, they had wound up with no head.

Eventually, Coid, and the other 'barbarians' from Mystike walked to where they would be working that day, transporting stone blocks from the mines to the unfinished cathedral that was to be built in Histam. He knew he was supposed to be free. All the slaves were. It had been abolished by the LNR. But the Grandlear was protecting this operation, because they were building a cathedral. No one dared accuse the Grandlear of a sin, despite how terribly he was sinning.

Like usual, Coid walked over to a stone block and got his hand under it to heft it onto his shoulder. As he mustered the strength to do so, he fell to the ground clutching his head. He had a pounding pain in the sides of his head, and pain that felt like something was trying to find its way out of his head.

"Slave! Get up and work!" shouted the driver.

Coid couldn't reply, as the pain grew worse and an itching sensation started to cover his body. He screamed out.

"I will have you flogged to death, you slave! Do your work!" the driver yelled right into Coid's ear.

Suddenly, the pain in Coid's head disappeared as he felt two things grow out of his head. They felt like...horns? Coid looked at the driver, whose eyes were now wide in terror. Only for a second, for the driver began to whip Coid mercilessly. The whip first found its mark on Coid's arm, but he felt little pain. He looked at his arm to see it covered with what appeared to be buffalo hide.

"Guards! Guards!" shouted the driver as he whipped and whipped. No matter where they hit Coid, Coid felt no pain. Still, it was annoying.

Coid looked at the whip, and suddenly, what looked like a red beam flew out of Coid's right eye and burned the whip into two separate pieces. The driver's pleas for help grew louder and more desperate, so Coid threw his fist at the driver's head. As his fist connected, it kept going and came out the other side of the driver's head. Coid retracted his fist, in absolute horror at what he'd done. The slave driver collapsed, dead.

The guards came running, so Coid ran, too. Away from them. Far, far away. But instead of running, Coid stopped feeling the ground underneath his feet. He heard the guards yelling and screaming, but their voices were quieting as he rose higher and higher into the air. Coid was flying.

Chapter 30
The Hydra

FEDRADIN

HOW DOES ONE FIGHT a hydra? It was a question that had been debated -mostly in Narven— for years. Does one try to cut off all its heads and seal the neck stumps with acid or fire before it can regenerate heads? Does one attempt to stab its heart? Does one simply flee?

Normally, Fedradin never chose the last option, and this time it wasn't any different -especially with him trapped in a cage. He had never felt so helpless in his life, standing in a small cage fighting a full-grown hydra.

He decided to try the first option. In his pouch, there were a few bottles of acid. The hydra already had two heads, all with poisonous fangs hungering for his flesh.

Fedradin swung with his sword and easily chopped off one of the heads. Quickly, Fedradin threw a bottle of acid at the stump. The bottle was on a collision course for the bleeding stump, when the hydra swung its tail, knocking the bottle out of its flight path. The bottle sprayed acid everywhere, but it wasn't enough to seal the neck stump. Two more hydra heads grew from the stump.

The hydra was angry now, and its three heads tried to bite Fedradin. Fedradin swung his sword and jumped to the side, narrowly missing getting bitten by one of the heads. His sword connected with the neck of one of the hydra heads, so Fedradin threw another bottle of acid. Again, the hydra prevented the bottle from reaching the neck stump, this time by using one of its heads to block the bottle. The bottle ricocheted off the head of the hydra and exploded on the ground.

As two heads sprouted from the neck stump of the hydra, Fedradin gave up on his strategy. The head count was up to four now, and Fedradin didn't want to have to deal with any more heads.

His wish didn't come true, as another head came towards him. Without thinking, he chopped it off. Two more heads sprouted out of the neck stump.

Fedradin knew he would have to stab the hydra's heart. The only problem was the suicidal heads. Whenever he tried to stab the heart, the hydra would throw a head in the way of the blade. He tried several times, and when he finished, there were nine or ten heads all wanting to kill him.

Then, an epiphany.

Fedradin started running circles around the hydra, poking it with his sword. All the heads tried to follow him, and after he had run around the creature maybe six or seven times, the heads became tangled. As the heads tried to untangle themselves, Fedradin ran forward and stabbed the hydra through the heart. The beast collapsed, dead.

Fedradin looked over at Quivel's cage, but it wasn't pretty. The hydra was ripping into Quivel's dead body, tearing him to shreds as it feasted. It appeared that Quivel had had too much pride to back out of the competition by pulling off his headband.

Fedradin didn't care though. Fedradin would be advancing to the next round.

Chapter 31
Across The Sea

TRUMBELL

HIS BEARD NEEDED TRIMMING. That was all he could think about as the winds whipped it back into his face. Trumbell stood on Dragonsback Ridge, a line of mountains so bare and out of place in the thick, dangerous forests of Qassar, that it seemed it could be seen for miles. The spear in his right hand itched for battle. He could sense it as he examined its fine, obsidian point. It hadn't had blood in a while. Hopefully it would get some soon. The sun began to set on the expanding forest in front of him, Illusion Lake shining a deep red to mimick the sky.

"Night falls, sire," said a man next to him.

"I'm not blind, Joloak."

"I'm sure you're not. Your sanity is for what I worry."

"Smoke was seen yesterday and the day before and -"

"That may be, sire, but *night falls*. No man has survived the night. Once the gates close and the gods know they will, at dusk, just like every night, the poor, pitiful souls left in the forests will never be seen again."

"I know the legends. Tales do not frighten me."

"Tales? Koip's disappearance? Mynn's corpse?"

"Stupid men. Careless deaths."

"Stupid and careless because they did not heed the words of their squires and return to the gates before they close."

"Go if you want, Joloak. I stay here."

"We cannot afford to lose good men like you. We haven't received reinforcements in months! Please, do not be stupid."

"Maybe I'm stupid, but at least I'm not careless."

FENDER

"It's dusk."

"I can see that!"

"Why have we not shut the gate?"

It was pitch black now, and nothing could be seen in the darkness beyond.

"Because I'm stalling."

"For Trumbell and Joloak at Dragonsback? To come back to Sequo in the pitch black is a suicide mission!" said Gent.

"What are our lives without hope?" Fender, the viceroy, sighed, waited a moment. "Shut the gates!" commanded Fender. Armor clad soldiers walked forwards, grabbed the gilded handles on the gates and began to shut them.

"Wait!" came a wailing voice.

"What is this? Does he mean to wake the dead?" said Gent.

Fender ignored him. "It's Joloak! Halt! Leave the gates open!" The soldiers froze, and Joloak came sprinting inside. "Where's Trumbell?"

Winded, all Joloak could do was look up and shake his head.

ASH

Far away from Qassar, in the land of Stentor, there was bugling. The horns pierced the anxious palace of Stent, letting every soldier know of the orcish victory.

"What can these damn orcs possibly want?" shouted Ash, a fat man who paced the battlements, running his hand up and down the hilt of his sword.

"Our spices, I presume," replied Sir Fane, who was sharpening his sword on a whetstone. A knight's bond of considerable length dangled from his swordbelt.

"What do bloody *orcs* want with our stentspice? I don't see any ships with which they could trade it."

"Maybe the value of the spice is the value *we* put on it," said Fane wisely as he tested the sharpened sword on his thumb, drawing a drop of blood.

"The hell does that mean?" said Ash, as he peered through a spyglass in the direction of the horn.

"It *means*," said Fane, rising to his feet, "that if the orcs steal our spices, we're going to need to get them back. On another note, it seems we have a message" Fane reached out a hand, and a pigeon landed ungracefully in his palm. "It's from Welnn."

"The spicetown? In the middle of the desert?"

"That's the only Welnn I know. Look, it has Lord Danni's seal."

"I'm surprised the orcs didn't shoot it down."

"I'm not. Take a look." Ash peered at the letter.

"It's written in Orc."

"It was sent by the orcs. Hence the language. Lucky for you, I picked up some Orc before I came here from the mainland. Stentor's full of orcs. It's a usefull skill." Ash, irritated by Fane's comments, returned to looking at the barren desert.

"Orcs attack in the night. There's no danger for another couple hours," said Fane, noticing Ash.

"Shut up and translate the letter."

"I did. They've taken Welnn. Everyone inside is dead, including Lord Danni, and they've begun stealing our spices. It's even signed by F'ntok, who I assume is their chieftain."

"Why would they send us a letter? Shouldn't they want to keep such a thing a secret?"

The horn bugled once more, loud and clear. "Because stealth is what they're going for."

Ash ignored him. "We attack in the morning!" he cried. "The orcs have taken Welnn!" There was a roar from the soldiers and knights.

"What are you doing?" cried Fane.

"I took an oath to protect the Spice when I became the Spice Sultan. It is my duty to stop the orcs from doing just this." Then, to his army. "Don't bother to polish your armor or clean your swords! Tomorrow they dirty themselves with blood!"

DUNLOCK

Not terribly far away, in the land of Corsair, the treasury grew smaller by the day. The unsold slaves filled the streets, brigging the city of Gusar to a standstill. King Dunlock looked out the window of his solar to see them gathered at his gate, in protest. The slaves were a mix of humans, orcs, a few chultra and flayers, and more.

"Damn the LNR! Damn the Haxtish! Damn them all!" roared Dunlock. "What are we supposed to do? Where are we supposed to sell our slaves?" The abolition of slavery in Haxter had destroyed the Corsairian slave-based economy, towns such as Slaveport no longer opening their ports to his slavers, which defeated the purpose of the town, in his opinion.

"We could sell them in Stentor or Mazlek or Shang-Li or Osup," suggested Kolan, Dunlock's Scholar.

"Fool," scoffed the Corsair King. "We *capture* our slaves from Stentor or Mazlek or Shang-Li or Osup."

"We could...we could sail the Silver Sea. Look for another port?"

"Another outlandish idea. You know haow many captains have tried to cross the Silver Sea. Berlock the Bold, Curlock the Curious. They never returned."

"They were your kin..." murmured Kolan.

"Yes, Kolan. Thank you. I almost forgot."

"The Sant?" suggested Kolan.

"Half a world a way. Also, they abolished slavery a hundred years ago."

"Sorry," said Kolan, as he moved to join Dunlock at the window. "What if we...no, it's a bad idea."

"Can't possibly be worse than your past three," said Dunlock. "Spit it out."

"What...what if we...we let the slaves *win* their freedom, since we can't sell them," stammered Kolan.

"Meaning...?" asked Dunlock, beseeching Kolan to continue.

"Look out there."

"On the streets? With the slaves that want to rip me limb from limb?"

"Precisely," said Kolan with newfound confidence.

"Why would I want to free them?"

"Because they will give you an army. They will give you redemption."

Chapter 32

A Small Favor

FEDRADIN

THE RIDDERS HAD MOVED up in the competition. All of the Ridders wanted to go out and celebrate in Gii, but the moment they arrived at their rooms in the Warrior Village, each one fell asleep almost immediately. Except Fedradin. No matter how hard he tried, he just kept staring at the cracked ceiling.

Midnight came and went, and with no sleep to show for it, Fedradin lifted himself out of his cot and wandered down the stairs to the common room. He sat down in one of the chairs and stared into the embers of the dying fire. He sat there for an amount of time, he didn't know how long, for the soothing heat from the embers put him into a dream-like trance. He must have fallen asleep at some point, for he awoken suddenly.

Fedradin felt a small, inhuman hand on his shoulder. It shook him slightly, trying to gently rouse him. Obviously, the being had not realized Fedradin was already awake.

Fedradin evaluated his options: either this creature meant no harm and was being considerate by trying not to jolt him awake, or it was trying to stir him quietly so no one would be alarmed.

Fedradin, always paranoid, decided not to take any chances. He quickly spun around, grabbed the arm of the being and flipped it over his head. It landed on a cushioned chair nearby, making too little noise to wake anyone in the house. Fedradin pulled out his knife and pushed it up against the being's throat before he could identify it. When his eyes adjusted to the dark, Fedradin realized it was only the dwarf he had seen twice in Gii earlier. It also happened to be the dwarf that was being hunted by two races.

"Breetex?"

"Yes. Would you mind taking the knife off my neck?"

"'Right...of course...'" said a nonplussed Fedradin, taking his blade away from the dwarf's neck. "Why are you here?"

"They've found me...they know I'm here..." said Breetex. "Poltax sent out some elves to find me - I only just escaped."

"And you want me to harbor you?"

"You offered, didn't you? At the monster battle?"

"I wasn't really offering you shelter, it was more like if you wanted money, or food, or..."

"Please, Fedradin. They'll kill me if they catch me!"

"They'll kill me if they catch me with you."

"Just harbor me until the Games are over. Please. Then we'll leave."

"Excuse me, *we*?"

"What, I'm supposed to abandon my own lover, the reason the elves are hunting me?"

"Breetex, you can't ask this much of me right now. Why can't I give you a couple fellyers and have you leave me alone?"

"Haven't you noticed? Patrols, sentries, doubling of the guards, even elfish soldiers are everywhere, all because of me!"

Fedradin put his hand on his forehead, thinking of his options. "I'll make you a deal, Breetex. You really shouldn't have told me about being a fugitive. That was quite idiotic. Almost every normal person would turn you in right now for the reward, and I'm not saying I'm not tempted. Still, I can't bring myself to do that, because I've taken a liking to you. So what I'll do is let you and Aserax stay in one of our rooms, *but*," said Fedradin, exaggerating the word, "If either of you so much as looks out the window, I will sell you both to the elves without a second thought."

"Thank you, thank you, thank you, thank you *so* much!" said Breetex, hugging Fedradin's leg. "You are a kind man!"

"Please, stop," said Fedradin. "or I'll tie you to a tree and let the elves throw darts at you."

"Aserax, come here! We can stay!" said Breetex. A beautiful she-elf came darting out from behind a chair.

"Thank you! Thank you a thousand times!" said Aserax.

"Both of you, enough with the thanks. I realize how important this is for you. If we all make it through this week and alive and not incarcerated, you owe me everything. Now, follow me, and I'll find a place to hide you."

Fedradin crept up the stairs with the two four feet high beings behind him. They walked down the hallway to Fedradin's room and entered it, very quietly, as to not wake Dethroid.

"What the hell, Fedradin?" Dethroid was awake and sitting on his bed. "Dwarves? Elves?"

"Actually one dwarf and one elf," piped up Aserax.

"Shut, up," said Fedradin.

"Why are you bringing them here? We're going to get into so much trouble!"

He knows they're fugitives! "Well no one knows they're here..."

"Dwarves and elves in a human house? Preposterous!"

Fedradin resisted sighing in relief. "If we tell no one else, we can hide them in the closet and no one with know."

"Are you sure Fedradin? I mean can you really be...wait, wasn't that dwarf at the monster battle?"

"Yes, he was selling monsters there."

"I knew it!" hissed Aserax, hitting Breetex in the arm.

Dethroid raised an eyebrow, "And why do we have to keep them? Are the guards onto Breetex's monster dealings in the city?"

"Yes," said Fedradin, fabricating a story. "And I owe him some money because I bought a manticore egg but I didn't pay him fully."

"That doesn't seem like you, Fedradin, but I guess I have to trust you. The dwarves can stay in our closet."

"I'm an elf!" exclaimed Aserax.

"What, so being a dwarf is a bad thing?" asked Breetex, indignant.

"Well, no, but I'm not a dwarf, I'm an elf."

"And you can't resist correcting people every time they call you a dwarf?"

"How would you feel if someone called you a gnome?"

"Oh, so the equivalent of an elf being a dwarf is a dwarf being a gnome?"

"I just randomly picked a race-"

"But why didn't you pick an elf?"

"Well..."

"Oh, I see, I'm supposed to be honored at the thought of being an elf."

"I wasn't going to say that..."

"What were you going to say?" inquired Breetex.

"I was going to say elf, but I didn't want to hear you say that you hate my race and don't like the thought of being an elf."

"Do you hate my race?"

"No."

"Why would you think I hate yours?"

"*Do* you hate elves?"

"Of course not! You're an elf, and I love you."

Chapter 33
By the Lake

FEDRADIN

"FOUR TEAMS FROM EACH race have been eliminated," announced Uslo. "Today, we get rid of another four. Humans began our Games yesterday, so today, humans are moved to the end of the rotation. First up will be dwarves, so all dwarfish warriors should report to the stadium for further instruction. Each race's Games should only take an hour, and there will not be any inter-race competition today. Please report to the stadium on time. Now, let the Games begin!"

The dwarfish warriors began shuffling down the path towards the stadium. Most, if not all, of the dwarves wore metal armor upon chainmail, beautifully crafted, with axes or broadswords hanging at their sides. Many had beards, some braided, some dyed, of varying lengths and color. Fedradin recalled the Breetex had no beard, just some stubble on his chin.

He turned to talk with his Ridders, but they had already left for Gii. Fedradin, too tired with bringing in fugitive creatures to go to the markets of Gii, decided to go somewhere quiet, so he made up his mind to go to the shores of Lake Gii. He walked up to a guard and asked for directions, and off he went.

It wasn't a short walk, nor a long one, and Fedradin enjoyed it the entire way, for it was a pleasant day: warm, with a nice breeze. When he arrived at the large lake's shore, he lied down in the grass and simply lay there, not closing his eyes for fear of falling asleep. But the grass was so soft, and he was so tired. As the waves lapped gently at the sandy shore, and the breeze lulled him into a haze, Fedradin closed his eyes.

'Beware', came a voice. 'Beware. Your journey has begun.' Around him, a blizzard raged but he didn't feel the cold. 'You will be betrayed, by the men you hold most dear.' From the snow emerged two yaks. They turned to face each other and charged. When they collided, the two creatures became one. 'The merging yak.' The snow continued to fall, but in one place it revealed an

invisible figure. 'The invisible relative.' An icicle fell from the sky, wrapped in a patchwork coat. 'The patched icicle.' A featureless man walked forwards, holding a key. 'The grim gatekeeper.' A tree pushing a cartful of...something...came forwards. 'The bargaining plant.' A small child appeared, a wick of flame in between its fingers. 'The magic orphan.' The six figures turned to look at Fedradin. 'Trust none of them. Each one will betray you.' At once, all six charged.

He jolted awake, heart pounding. He looked up at the sky, trying to figure out the time. After some quick calculations, Fedradin had plenty of time.

Still, it was scary to think that he had just lost three hours of daylight, so Fedradin got to his feet and began walking around. He watched trout leap out of the lake for bugs, he watched ants scuttle about their business in the grass, he even watched a salamander slither its way across the sand into the lake. When he started to grow restless from lack of activity, a voice called out from behind him.

"Fedradin! I've been looking for you." Fedradin recognized the voice as that of Axto.

"What do you want, Axto?" said Fedradin coldly, without turning around.

"I want to apologize."

"For what?" asked Fedradin, who knew very well what.

"You know what. I tried to cheat you out of a lot of money, and I sincerely apologize for my actions."

"I just don't understand. I trusted you and you went behind my back."

"Look, I don't think I ever told you, but I have a wife, and now we have a baby on the way. I've been training as a Ridder, but I don't make much money that way, only from my shares of the Riddings. We need money to raise the baby, and as much as I didn't want to have to cheat you, I had to. For my baby! I'm going to be a father, Fedradin, I don't want to mess things up."

Fedradin turned to face Axto. "You're not a bad person, Axto. You should have told me about your situation earlier. I can promise you a bit of the prize money if we win."

"Thank you, Fedradin!"

"My only request, no more trickery. I want you to be honest from here on out."

"Yes, of course!"

"Now, shoo. Can't a man get a little privacy every once in a while?"

Chapter 34
Six Inches To Death

FEDRADIN

THE TIME HAD COME. Fedradin had not been late to his competition, in fact, he had been early. He was standing in a room, similar to the one he had been in when he had gotten into a fight with Quivel. All twenty-eight human competitors were present in the room, each wearing any and all possible armor needed for the competition. Fedradin had only come in his chainmail, but he had brought his shield with him to these Games unlike the day before. It was a simple shield, wooden with a metal rim, and a leather covering. It was slashed and torn from heavy usage. Fedradin had strapped the shield to his back. He also had his pouch, sword, and knife.

"Human competitors!" announced Uslo from the front of the room. "To whittle down the amount of competitors, today will just be disqualifications among the humans again. There will be four rounds, and for each round, we will pair off everyone from your team with another person from a different team. Similar to yesterday, each victory in a random Game of our choosing is worth a point, and the team with the least amount of points is disqualified."

The Games began. Draslupp scored, and so did Kekk. Shah, unfortunately, did not. Draslupp was the first to get passed a sphinx, and Kekk, who, thanks to Dethroid and Axto, had made a full recovery, won his fight against his opponent by throwing his opponent off the wall on which they were battling with fists. Shah, however, lost to her opponent in the speed test of who could kill all the different types of Elemental Salamanders fastest.

Finally, it was Fedradin's turn. He stepped into the stadium and looked around, to find that it was practically deserted. A few humans had stayed to watch the final disqualifications, but that was it.

Fedradin looked out at the field to see a cage full of dranes. The creatures looked like small dragons, with two legs and a long tail. Two small arms, on which they usually ran, stuck out from what constituted their shoulders. Some were green, some were black, some were blue. Some had horns, some had none. Suddenly, trees appeared around Fedradin. It felt as though he was in a forest.

"Competitors!" came the voice of Uslo. "You will be facing an army of angry dranes. They are simulation dranes, so you cannot die. But, whoever can last longer in the stadium without having to be pulled out of the Game wins." Fedradin heard the cage door clang open, since he could no longer see it. "Good luck."

Fedradin began sprinting for a tree, since dranes could not climb. He leapt at the tree, grabbing a branch and pulling himself on top of it, right as a drane lunged at Fedradin, biting thin air. Fedradin began to climb higher and faster, away from the gathering dranes below. When Fedradin decided that he was high enough, he glanced over at the other treetops. He saw his opponent very close by him, in a tree as well. Fedradin immediately had an idea. He reached down into his pouch and pulled out a small, leather bag. He pulled back his arm, and he threw the bag all the way into his opponent's tree.

As soon as the bag hit the tree, fire immediately took hold of the one. It quickly spread, and the warrior in the tree leapt off the side. The warrior wasn't too far up and would probably survive the fall.

Dethroid was right, thought Fedradin, *Fire is always useful*.

After a few seconds, when Fedradin wasn't taken out of the battle in victory, he knew that his opponent had survived and had not been eliminated.

I may stand corrected, thought Fedradin, as the fire began to spread through the forest, towards him. He glanced at the ground, but the dranes were persistent, and even with a fire raging, they were still busy clawing at the tree trunk, trying to topple the tree.

As the fire grew nearer, Fedradin looked another tree nearby. It was slightly shorter, and he might be able to escape from the flaming trees if he got onto it. Fedradin began to look for ways to do so.

The tree he was targeting was behind one he clung to, so he had to rotate around it to get a good angle at the other tree. Fedradin sized up the jump, making sure he had sturdy and balanced footing. As he prepared for his leap, he suddenly had a change of heart, and he decided he didn't want to risk the jump. But as he stepped back from the branch, he felt flames lick across his back, the stimulis he needed to leep off the branch.

As he flew through the air, he saw the branch he wanted to grab fly quickly out of his reach. He flailed out his arms and found himself with another tree limb in his left hand; however, as he continued to fall, he snapped the branch. The ground was getting closer, faster, and he knew he only had one more chance to stop his fall. He thrust out with his right hand, grabbing a nice, thick branch. There was no way it would snap. The same wasn't true of his arm. He had to do something to avoid dislocating it. He decided to swing around the branch, so he twisted his right hand and made a full rotation around the branch before being able to grab the branch with his left hand and come to a stop. Fedradin hung there for a moment and looked down. He let go of the branch, fell about six inches and hit the forest floor. He had been six inches from death.

Fedradin felt the heat of the raging inferno on his face as he tried to orient himself. He had no idea which way the dranes were, so he started running away from the fire. He hadn't got very far when he heard what sounded like a cross between a growl and a hiss coming from behind him. Fedradin twisted around to see a purple drane with horns charging him from behind. He pulled out his shield quickly and caught the horns of the drane in his shield. The horns bounced off, and Fedradin quickly finished off the drane with a quick slash to its side. He put his shield back on his back.

The heat started to grow more intense as the fire spread throughout the forest. Fedradin sped up, not wanting to be cooked like a chicken.

As he continued to run, he realized something. Everything in the woods: the dranes and his opponent would be driven out towards him by the fire. Fedradin looked behind him over his shoulder to see about thirty drane running towards him as well as his opponent. His opponent was almost next to Fedradin, but Fedradin was a little farther ahead. The two kept running for a long time, neither one daring to stop, when Fedradin tripped.

He soared through the air, but tried to land on his feet. As he hit the forest floor, his ankle rolled and he fell to the ground in pain. He saw his opponent laugh and run away.

Fedradin got to his feet and started hobbling in the direction of his opponent. He heard the fire crackle as it burned its way through the forest, and he heard the hiss/growl of the dranes as they grew nearer.

His sprained ankle wasn't as bad as it could have been, and would probably be fine given a good night's rest, but his ankle hurt to walk on, and he could not run very far before the pain grew agonizingly brutal, and he had to stop.

Eventually, Fedradin knew he had to give up running. He had to fight the army of dranes behind him. He could hear the claws tearing up the dead leaves on the ground, but suddenly the sound stopped. He had a millisecond to react, and luckily, he knew what was happening.

Fedradin crouched and in the process, twisted one hundred eighty degrees. He also had pulled his sword from its scabbard, swinging in the direction he was turning. He also moved his hand toward his shield. He preformed these actions because the drane behind him had just leapt towards him.

The results: his sword collided with the ankle of a drane as it jumped over him. The drane's flight path was disturbed, and the monster fell out of the air to the side of Fedradin. He pulled his shield off his back and turned to face the monster that was attacking him. As he turned, he caught a glimpse of many more dranes coming in fast from behind him.

He faced the drane scrambling to its feet and chopped off its head. Once more, Fedradin turned with his shield up, braced against his forearm. He felt a drane collide with his shield, hard, very hard. The force was enough to push Fedradin back a good foot or so. He came out from behind his shield, swinging his sword. It collided with a dazed drane at one of its hip joints. The drane recoiled, this time letting out a full-blown roar. Fedradin quickly slashed again, this time, hitting it across the stomach. Its stomach came apart, spilling guts everywhere.

He took a deep breath and plowed on with the battle. Two dranes stood ahead coming at him from both sides. Fedradin, not unfamiliar with this common predatorial tactic, knew what to do.

He jogged forward, not towards any particular drane. When they were both within stabbing range, Fedradin feinted with his sword at the drane on the right. The drane let out what sounded like a shriek of terror and dropped to the ground, rolling away from Fedradin's sword.

As the drane made elaborate attempts to avoid the blade, Fedradin, without looking at it, bludgeoned the drane on the left across the head with his shield. The drane stumbled away, and Fedradin charged forward, grabbing the drane, one hand under its underbelly, one hand over its back. When it realized Fedradin had picked it up a few seconds later, a slow realization because it was still extremely dizzy from the blow to its head, it started flailing around, trying to scratch and bite Fedradin. But Fedradin was already where he wanted to be. A large oak tree, not yet on fire, stood in front of him, not three feet away. He threw the drane into the side of the tree. Without missing a beat, Fedradin stabbed the drane through the heart before it could fall to the ground, pinning it to the tree.

The drane behind Fedradin must have been pursuing him, for he again heard the same sound of claws on dead leaves. Fedradin quickly pulled out his sword from the dead drane. The carcass fell to the ground. Fedradin decided he didn't have enough time to turn around, so he made a desperate move. Fedradin leapt into the air, grabbing a tree branch. He pulled his legs up as far up the tree as he could. He heard the drane ram the tree, so Fedradin sprung off the tree, pushing as hard as he could off the trunk with his legs. He expected to land behind the drane and then chop its head off. What actually happened was quite unexpected.

Chapter 35
Quynn

QUYNN

STUPID JOUSTING TOURNAMENT, THOUGHT Quynn from his bed in the hospital wing. *If only I hadn't gone.*

It hadn't even been his fault. When he heard about the jousting tournament, he thought he could make some extra money, so he had applied to be the squire to one of the jousters. He got accepted, so of course he had been very happy.

When he arrived at the tournament, right outside the city of Narven, he went to the tent of his assigned jouster, whose name was Monteletok. He entered the tent, and helped Monteletok get dressed, saddled and so forth. Thus far, everything was going well.

The two went out of the tent, and Monteletok began jousting. Monteletok got to the semi-finals. That was when the accident happened. Quynn was watching from the side, leaning against one of the fences that separated the crowds from the jousting arena. Monteletok was taking a warm-up run down the field, when his horse was frightened by something. It started running around crazily in the jousting arena, and it was all Monteletok could do to hold on the horse with one hand. The other hand was holding the jousting spear.

As Monteletok grew nearer to Quynn, Monteletok's horse started brushing against the fence Quynn was leaning on. Quynn didn't see the problem until it literally hit him. Monteletok's jousting spear was not in Monteletok's control at all, and when the horse passed by Quynn, the spear hit Quynn in the shoulder, going almost completely through it and dislocated his arm. Now, he was in Narven, in the Wing, where the Scholars trained in medicine at the Floating Chapel tried to fix him up. Quynn had been lying in the bed for weeks now.

One day, a redheaded wizard by the name of Misk was admitted to the Wing. It was the most exciting thing to happen to Quynn in all the time he was bedridden; however, it brought back something that he had forgotten about entirely. He was Biggs's apprentice, but he couldn't receive the training he needed because of his injury!

Misk was unconscious when he was brought in. Quynn spent his days staring at Misk, until Misk woke up suddenly. It was quite abrupt: one second Misk was not moving at all, the next he was sitting straight up in bed, eyes wide-open. Quynn pretended he didn't notice, but it was hard since Misk was staring at him, with different colored eyes.

Misk sat there for the rest of the day, while a few Scholars tended to him. From what he heard from their conversations, Quynn knew that the Scholars were not planning to discharge Misk from the Wing; however, the next morning, when Quynn woke up, Misk was gone.

Chapter 36
An Unexpected Happening

FEDRADIN

FEDRADIN FLEW THOUGH THE air, his sprained ankle tucked up against his quad to avoid hurting it in the landing. As he braced his good leg for landing, he looked for the drane, but he couldn't see it. Until its head poked out in front of him. That was when he saw that he was going to land on it. Quickly, he leaned back. In part to try to avoid the drane, but also if he landed on the drane he wanted to hit his buttocks. As he hoped for option one, avoiding the drane entirely, he felt himself collide with the drane's back. Option two it was then.

He started falling off the back of the drane fast, so, to stop himself from falling off and injuring his head, he threw his arm around the drane's neck. It hissed and bit into his forearm. He pulled his arm away from its mouth, before remembering dranes were not poisonous. As he stopped sliding, Fedradin went for the kill. Fedradin pulled out his dagger with his shieldarm and swung it at the drane's head, but it jerked in a strange way and Fedradin missed, hitting its left shoulder. It hissed in pain and started running, swerving to the right. Fedradin pulled himself up using the knife as a handhold. As the drane picked up speed, he positioned himself as if he were riding a horse.

Apparently, Fedradin was riding a drane.

'Right. I'm on its back, thought Fedradin. *How do I steer this thing?* Fedradin thought back to how it swerved to the right when he stabbed it in the left shoulder. Would the opposite be true? He decided to test his current theory by pulling out his dagger, which currently was hilt deep in its left shoulder, and stabbing its right shoulder, only about two inches in, with his sword. The drane hissed in pain and swerved to the left. Fedradin pushed his sword farther into its right side, and it swerved even farther to the left.

Fedradin realized that the drane was running towards the fire that was spreading rapidly. He pulled out his sword but it was still deadest on charging into the blazing inferno. Fedradin wanted to turn around, and looked back to see about twenty-five

169

or so dranes standing menacingly. Then, one by one, they started to charge at Fedradin and his drane mount. Fedradin was trapped between a fire and a horde of angry dranes. Both were approaching rapidly.

He decided the best way to do this would be to go straight into the fire. He put his dagger and his sword into the sides of the drane and it leapt forward, going straight. His drane's acceleration had startled the other creatures, and they started to run faster after him. His urged his drane on into the flaming forest. The goal was to lose the angry beasts and then loop around towards his human opponent.

This plan was working until the forest started coming down around Fedradin. A large, flaming branch came tumbling off a tree towards him. He pushed his sword farther into the drane's side and it swerved to the left. The branch slammed into the ground not four feet from Fedradin.

As he glanced backwards and saw no pursuing dranes, Fedradin dug his dagger, all the way up to its hilt, into the drane's side. The drane cried out in agony and pulled to the right so much that it started to turn around. Fedradin gently eased his dagger out of the drane's side when it made a full turn. He was now going straight out of the woods, hopefully towards his opponent.

All seemed fine, until he heard a loud crack. He looked up to see a gigantic branch crashing through the treetops, pulling other flaming branches down beside it. Fedradin's drane saw the branch coming down, too, and started to accelerate. The two, the drane and branch, were getting closer together, but Fedradin could not tell which one would win the race. And he was not willing to take the chance. He shoved his sword deeper in the drane's shoulder, but it didn't budge. Fedradin kept pushing his sword into its shoulder, but it seemed to have no effect. The drane had gotten used to the pain and was simply running for its life.

Fedradin looked at the branch, and it appeared to him that it would come down slightly before his drane. Fedradin needed to figure out an evasive maneuver, but it had to be something besides turning away from the branch.

As he thought, the branch kept knocking smaller branches off the flaming trees. A few of these burning branches fell towards him, so Fedradin left his dagger in the drane's shoulder, and put up his shield to protect himself. As they hit his leather shield and ricocheted off of it, the leather ignited. Fedradin tried to exitinguish it, but it was a fruitless endeavor. Then he got an idea.

As the large branch crashed down in front of him, Fedradin shoved his flaming shield underneath the belly of the drane. The drane leapt into the air, clearing the burning branch by a good foot and a half.

After a couple more yards, Fedradin had cleared the burning part of the woods and was running towards where his opponent was. The other dranes had followed Fedradin into the woods, and they were nowhere to be seen. Fedradin's plan had worked.

He rode around the woods, with no control over his drane. Finally he saw his opponent, and the drane did, too. The drane was very stupid, and it assumed that Fedradin's opponent had caused it all the pain that Fedradin had. It started running at an alarming rate, so Fedradin jumped off his drane. It continued running until it had caught up with Fedradin's opponent. The drane tackled the warrior and began to attack viciously. Soon, Fedradin felt himself get teleported out of the arena a victor.

Fedradin's team moved to the next round with points to spare. He had retrieved his sword and dagger from the arena, and he had managed to put out the fire on his shield, but it was very damaged.

In the next round, all of the Ridders won their competitions. Fedradin got lucky with his hurt ankle, for his competition required him to ride something a little less dangerous than a drane, the common horse.

Fedradin lost his next competiton because of his sprained ankle. The rest of the Ridders won their competitions, so they moved on to the next round.

For the last round, both Fedradin and Shah lost their competitions, Fedradin again lost due to his injured foot. Shah merely made a mistake, losing her the game. It was close, but the Ridders advanced to the finals of the competitions, even with a low score.

Chapter 37
The Prisoner

IT HAD BEEN A successful heist. They had captured the man the Master had requested. He would be pleased, or at least slightly forgive them for losing the baby. The Minions were gathered around their prisoner, who was struggling fruitlessly against his binds. He was bound to a table in the center of a stone room.

Frin turned and walked to a shackled monster in the corner of the room. Its hands were chained together, so tight that its wrists were rubbed raw, bleeding with every slight hand motion. Around its neck was an iron collar, chained to a metal bar protruding from the wall. The collar was not as tight as the handcuffs, for the Minions needed the monster to talk. Its feet were chained together, with an attached metal ball at the end. Near the monster, a crystal sat. The monster stared wistfully at the crystal, as a beggar does a fresh loaf of bread.

It was a bluish-grey monster, hairless, and about three feet in height. It was bipedal, with two arms, though at the moment it sat against the wall. It looked like a toddler, with two large eyes in the normal position, and an additional eye centered between the two eyes. Ribs stuck out the skinny monster's stomach, so much so that every detail of the ribs was visible.

"Djinn!" shouted Frin, striking it across the cheek with his hand. "Connect me with my Master!"

"As you wish," murmured the djinn. It closed its eyes, squeezing them tightly closed. When he opened his eyes again, they were red.

"Master," said Frin, "we have captured the man you requested."

"Good," said the djinn in the Master's voice, "Now I wish you to torture this man until he tells you everything he knows about this operation to which he belongs."

"As you wish, Master," said Frin, bowing slightly. The dijinn collapsed to the ground, but his eyes were back to normal. Frin turned to walk back to the prisoner.

"M'lord," said the djinn.

172

Frin stopped, but did not turn around. "What, djinn?"

"Could I bother you for some food? I haven't been fed in weeks. I'm afraid I will die soon without some sustenance of some sort..."

"Do I look like an innkeep to you?" asked Frin, turning around.

"No, my lord, but I am starv-"

"Enough! You are my prisoner and you will keep quiet until I ask you to speak!"

The djinn looked up at Frin, all three eyes betraying the djinn's anger. "You are making a more powerful enemy than you could possibly know."

"Am I now?" asked Frin. Those were the last word the djinn would ever hear. With a quick motion, Frin leapt forward, snapping the djinn's neck.

"What did you do that for?" shouted Tawassa.

"We'll get another one. It's not that hard to capture them."

"Speak for yourself! Do you summon that djinn? No! I summoned us a tenth ring djinn! Have you ever done sorcery? It's not very easy."

"Shut up, Tawassa. How about this? You get to go first torturing the prisoner."

The prisoner starting shouting into the gag that was in his mouth.

"Oh, we can take that out now," said Frin. "You're going to talk. You're going to talk a lot."

Chapter 38
The Race Against Races

FEDRADIN

AXTO HAD HEALED FEDRADIN'S foot as well as he could. Axto had put Fedradin's foot into a splint for the night and by morning, Fedradin hardly felt any pain in his foot as he moved around.

Breetex and Aserax had remained loyal to Fedradin and stayed in the closet. They had been given some food and drink and told to stay in the closet for the next day.

In the morning, Fedradin and his Ridders dressed in armor and came out to the field. Only three teams per race showed up, because the other eight teams per race had been disqualified the day before.

"Good morning finalists!" came the voice of Uslo from his podium in the center of the field. "Today, we have a special Game scheduled. It will take place outside the stadium, and it is a ten-mile race across a variety of terrains filled with many challenges. You will not be competing against the other races directly today, but they will be present during the race. Once a team's last warrior crosses the finish line, the team is considered finished. The team from each race that finishes first will continue to the next round." The warriors murmured their approval. "Now let's begin. All warriors to the starting line!"

Fedradin and his Ridders stood with all the other teams on the starting line. Most teams had shed their armor, the Ridders included. Fedradin was down to just his leather armor. The rest of the Ridders had followed suit, except Kekk, who wore his chainmail.

Ahead of them stretched the woods, as far as Fedradin could see. Far to the sides, a dull red light projection, similar in appearance to the one in 'Dirtwolves', marked the boundaries. Twenty horses, saddled up, were tethered to posts in front of the warriors. The warriors jostled for position to try to get a good angle on the horses.

"On your marks! Get set. Go!" yelled Uslo. The warriors rushed forwards towards the horses. Fedradin was not running as fast as he could, due to the slight pain in his foot. Two warriors were in front of him: a human and a satyr. The human leapt for the horse and landed on the saddle, pulling out a blade to cut the tether. The horse reared up, stopping the human from slashing the tether with his sword.

The satyr didn't realize that the tether was still on, so it jumped into the air as the horse reared, tackling the human off the horse, flying off it himself, leaving it open for Fedradin, who saddled the horse gently, so as not to startle it. He slashed the tether with his sword, and urged the horse forward with the reigns. The horse jumped forward and started trotting. As it started moving, Fedradin glanced behind him to see a halfling throw itself at Fedradin's horse, missing by inches.

Fedradin turned back. He saw two other humans, a chultra, a svaad, and a beaverio all on horses and slightly ahead of him, plus a centaur, who was not in need of a horse. Fedradin urged his horse on and it began to gain on his other competitors.

He had rode about a mile, but not quite, when he was attacked. He was riding along when his horse fell on its side suddenly. Fedradin barely dove to the side to avoid being crushed by the horse. He looked at it, and it was dead, with a large gash down its side.

Fedradin jumped to his feet, pulling out his sword and shield. He looked around for his assailant, but he couldn't see anything, until a dark shape flew out of the bushes.

Fedradin got his shield in front of him right as the shape got near. It collided with the shield, knocking Fedradin backwards a few feet. Fedradin put his shield down and swung out with his sword, but the dark shape had leapt away. The shape came to a stop farther in front of Fedradin and that was when he got a good look at it.

It stood about five feet high, dark purple in color. It looked similar to a monkey, with metal loops punctured through its large ears. Its eyes had no pupils; they were just a solid black. Spikes stuck out of its skin and through the rags it wore over its chest. An enormous blade protruded from its right hand. It was an aptly named a slash ape.

The slash ape ran forward, swinging its gigantic weapon. The blade was so big and heavy that its whole body rotated three hundred sixty degrees as it swung. Fedradin barely ducked the giant blade and slashed outward with his sword. The sword cut across the outward facing back of the slash ape, Fedradin taking advantage of its exposing swing.

The slash ape roared in anger as it finished its rotation, the blade falling to the ground, but still moving in its circular path. It flicked up when it finished the rotation, Fedradin rolling to the side to avoid injury. As Fedradin jumped to his feet, the slash ape swung again. Fedradin threw himself backwards, and the slash ape's blade passed a few inches in front of his throat. Fedradin landed on a branch, and he got an idea. As the slash ape approached him, Fedradin picked up the branch and hurled it at the slash ape. The slash ape saw the branch coming and swung its blade, which severed the branch in half. As it cut the branch in half, Fedradin jumped at the slash ape, kicking it in the chest. The slash ape collapsed to the ground, and Fedradin stabbed it through the eye with his sword before it could get back up.

Fedradin dusted himself off and looked around. He didn't see anyone else, but he did see another horse, dead, with the same injury his horse had. Fedradin ran forwards and he saw the rest of the horses lying to the side, as well as the centaur. Somehow, it was still alive, and Scholars were attending to it.

Fedradin kept running. A horse with a flayer rider passed him, but the horse was intercepted and killed by a slash ape, and the flayer began to scuffle with the slash ape. Fedradin just kept running and running, until he arrived at a body of water.

He could see the end of the body of water and where the land began on the other side, how far away, he couldn't guess. To the side of the water were many canoes and rowboats, many of which were in a state of disrepair. Already, a human was paddling his way across in a canoe and he was about a quarter of the way across. Another human was pulling away from shore in a rowboat. A beaverio was examining the boats and a svaad was pacing in front of the lake, as if preparing to attempt something. The chultra must have still been in the woods with the slash ape.

Svaadi were capable of running across water without sinking in by running fast and in a certain way. Fedradin knew this, so he called out to the svaad.

"Excuse me! Svaad!" said Fedradin.

The svaad turned around to face Fedradin, "Yes, human?"

Oh, good. He speaks Common. "Is there any way I can get a ride on your back across the lake?"

"What's the matter with the boats?"

"Can't you see? They're broken."

"Some. Not all."

"Please, svaad. We aren't competing with each other."

"I know that, but..."

"Why not?"

"You'll slow me down."

"Only a little. How about I make you a deal. As soon as we get to the end of the lake I'll help you get to the finish line."

The svaad thought for a moment. "I can handle myself."

"Two swords are better than one."

This gave the svaad pause. "Alright, I guess. Hop on."

Fedradin jumped onto the back of the svaad, and it started to run towards the lake. As soon as it touched the water, its legs shot out to the side, widening its stance. Its feet merely skimmed the water as before it pulled them back up and around. The way it ran reminded Fedradin of a basilisk lizard he had once seen run across the water.

The two were flying over the water, Fedradin's elbow around the svaad's neck and his legs wrapped around the svaad's back. They grew close to the first human in the rowboat, who shouted out in fright at the sight of what appeared to be a grown man riding a man-sized frog as it skipped across the lake. They kept going as they passed the human in the canoe. They got so close to him boat that the wake from the svaad capsized the canoe and the warrior was sent tumbling in. Fedradin didn't look back.

The two arrived at the other side of the lake uneventfully a few minutes later. As soon as the svaad stepped off the lake, it collapsed in a heap on the sand. For a moment, Fedradin thought to leave the svaad panting on the beach and continue with the race, but decided against it since he was in the lead, so he waited for a moment beside the exhausted svaad.

"Are you alright?" asked Fedradin.

The svaad looked up to make eye contact with Fedradin. "Yes." The svaad got to its feet. "Which way are we going?"

Fedradin was confused for a moment, but he turned around and saw that the path split up into two different directions, right and left. The path on the right was at a steep, upwards incline and the path on the left was at a gentle, sloping downwards path into the woods. "I think we should take the one on the left so we don't have to walk uphill."

The svaad, still exhausted from its run across the lake, agreed with Fedradin.

The odd pair began making their downwards descent. The two walked for a while, maybe a half an hour, when the path became noticeably steeper. The trees began to thin, so much so that Fedradin was able to see that he and the svaad were walking down towards a gorge with a large river running quickly through the middle of it. Fedradin saw a tree trunk that hung haphazardly across the river, and it appeared to be the only way across. There was a small beach on either side of the river, each end of the tree trunk anchored on one side or the other. After the beach, on the side closest to Fedradin, the woods kept going, but on the other side, cliffs jutted out into the water.

Fedradin sighed and continued walking down the path. The walk to the river's edge took about another hour or so and it passed uneventfully. When they arrived at the river, they saw that it was about twenty feet across, and the log covered that entire distance. Fedradin saw that the log was soaking wet, covered in water by the spray from the river.

The svaad climbed onto the log first, its suction cup covered hands grasping the log with ease. It began slithering up the log, inch by inch, with a movement almost as strange as the one it used to run on water. When the svaad was about five feet away from the riverbank, Fedradin clambered onto the log, grasping it with his arms. Fedradin used his feet to push himself across the log, but this process was slow. He was only about three feet of the way across the river while the svaad was about fifteen. Fedradin was about to call out to ask the svaad if he could grab its ankles to hitch a ride, when they were attacked.

A bellowed roar sounded from upriver, and Fedradin looked up to see what was happening. What looked like a seal had poked its head above the water, but it had one major difference. There was a stone on its head, perfectly circular from most likely much grinding. The stone was sharp all the way around its circumference, with bloodstains in a few spots. The stone was clamped to the seal's head by mandibles protruding from above its eyes, the mandibles each grasping a side of the stone. The stone began to rotate in a circle, picking up speed as it went. Fedradin knew that an organ in between the mandibles helped to turn the wheel faster and faster. Fedradin recognized this creature as a razor seal.

When the stone became just a blur, the seal dove underwater again, moving towards the warriors. All the while as the stone had been spinning up, the svaad had been moving towards the other bank, not paying any mind to the angry razor seal. Fedradin had been frozen in place, too scared to move, since the situation was new to him. He began to move towards the opposite bank, but it was to no avail as he moved too slowly to beat the razor seal. The razor seal's stone cut through the trunk in between Fedradin and the svaad. Fedradin's trunk crashed into the river, the water spashing up and soaking him. The tree trunk began floating downstream; however, the ends of the truck were stuck in the sand on either sand of the river, so they began to drift in an arc, going towards the side of the bank on which their log's endpoints were anchored.

Fedradin remained frozen on his trunk, trying to decide what to do, when the razor seal turned around for a second attack. It focused on Fedradin, since the svaad had already crossed the river onto the other bank. The razor seal truncated the top of the log, where Fedradin desperately clung. The trunk began floating away from the svaad, who stood on the other side of the river, at a rapid pace. Fedradin realized what the razor seal was trying to do. Fedradin was now vulnerable, sitting on a segment of a tree trunk, floating down a whitewater stretch of a river filled with jagged rocks, towards a moss covered cliff. The razor seal was going to cut the wood again, but this time it would slice Fedradin in half as well as the log. Fedradin decided on what he had to do. He had to reach the cliff and climb it onto land.

He saw that the razor seal had turned to make its final attack. However, it had to fight against the current to reach him, and Fedradin could use the current to his advantage to reach the cliff. He put his legs into the water and began kicking to try to reach the cliff even faster. He kicked and kicked until he decided he was close enough to the cliff. Fedradin lifted his legs onto the log to prepare to jump. As he prepared, he heard the sound of the razor seal's stone cutting into the back of his log. Fedradin needed to jump immediately.

He pushed off the log with feet, soaring into the air. The forward momentum he gathered on his trunk slammed him into the cliff, but he was able to get two good handholds and one foothold before he bounced back off the cliff. He heard the razor seal and the tree trunk collide with the cliff, the razor seal's stone cutting the trunk in half and cutting into the cliff face, spraying wood and stone debris everywhere. The razor seal bellowed in frustration and dove beneath the surface again, hunting for its next victim.

Fedradin looked up the cliff face, for he now faced the task of climbing it. The top was about six feet up, but it was mossy and slick. Fedradin had to be very careful in climbing it. He slowly made his way up the cliff, but arrived at the top of it uneventfully. He looked around, but his svaadi friend was nowhere to be seen. Fedradin shrugged and continued walking.

It was another walk through the woods, during which Fedradin checked his sword, shield and dagger. None of them had fallen off him during the excitement with the razor seal. The walk took him about half an hour, and he jogged a small portion of it, not sure of his competition and where they were in the race with relation to him.

He arrived at a strange place, one like he had only seen once before at the Floating Mountains of Quoll when he visited the Chapel.

Chapter 39
Floating Mountains, Giant Eagles

FEDRADIN

THE MOUNTAINS STRETCHED OUT in front of Fedradin, but they did not attach to the ground. They were about the size of a turret of a castle each, and they floated from a range of one hundred yards in the air to fifty yards in the air. They looked like miniature mountains, covered in rocks, dirt and a few small trees. At the bottom, they came to a point. Fedradin was elevated at about seventy-five yards above the forest now, standing at the edge of a cliff. Fedradin could make out the red barrier running along around the sides of the floating mountains. It looked as if the barriers had expanded during the course of the race.

Fedradin could make out a figure already on the mountains, but it was too far away for Fedradin recognize which race it was. The svaad had not yet arrived. Fedradin assumed that the svaad was walking slower because it was more exhausted than Fedradin, after running across a lake.

A beaverio emerged from the woods right as Fedradin prepared to jump to a mountain about five feet away from the cliff. Fedradin took a running start and leapt over the cliff, landing on the mountain. He walked to the edge of the mountain and saw two possible paths. There was a closer, higher mountain on the right and on the left, a farther, lower mountain. He opted for the one on the right, deciding it would be easier to navigate the maze of mountains from a higher vantage point.

Fedradin took a running start and threw himself at the mountain on the right. He landed on the side of it, where it slanted downwards towards its point. Fedradin started to slide down the slope of the mountain, spraying dirt chunks and pebbles into the forest below. Fedradin dug his hands into the side of the mountain, but the action barely slowed him down. He kept trying to slow himself down to no avail, until finally he saw a small sapling clinging desperately to the side of the mountain. Fedradin lunged for it, grabbing in around its small trunk. Its roots began to tear out of the side of the mountain, but by then Fedradin had been able to use the sapling to propel himself onto the top of the mountain.

When he climbed to its pitiful summit, he looked around, trying to find a mountain close enough for him to jump to. Fedradin located a mountain, about thirty feet away, but twenty feet down. The mountain had a large tree on it and some of the tree's roots dangled off to the side. Fedradin decided to risk the jump. He had always been a risk taker, and hopefully, if he missed the jump, he would be teleported out of the race before he was splattered on the forest floor far below.

Fedradin took a running head start one more time. He hit the edge of the mountain he was on, and he launched himself into the air as high and far as he could. Fedradin soared through the air in the direction of the mountain. All seemed well until he started losing momentum and gravity started kicking in. He dropped harshly out of his flight path and fell. Fedradin had no idea if he was going to hit the mountain, even the sloped dirt part, but he knew it was going to be close. Fedradin slammed into the sloping part of the mountain, just barely grabbing a root before sliding back down the mountain. As he dangled in midair, the root began to pull out of the ground, the dirt that it loosed hitting Fedradin in the face. As he dangled, the minutes started to go by. The root continued to pull off the mountain, and the strain on Fedradin's arms caused them to start to burn. Just as he started to feel unsure about how long he could hold onto the root for, something amazing happened.

An eagle's call, loud and close. The sound of winds swishing through air and the wind on his back. He turned his head to see a bird, identical to an eagle in every way, except that it was about twenty times larger. This gigantic bird put its talons around Fedradin's chest and ripped him from the root was clinging to. Fedradin knew that he was being carried off by a roc.

The roc began flying in the direction in which Fedradin wanted to go, but Fedradin knew that it wasn't trying to help him out. The roc was going to feed him to its newborns; however, he knew better than to try to free himself from the roc's grip, for he was very high in the air, and the roc was still climbing in elevation.

After about a five-minute flight, the floating mountains ended, and real mountains began. The roc started to descend into the mountains. It grew so low that Fedradin saw what it was trying to do. Another warrior, a human, was running along a mountain path, and the roc was trying to catch him. The roc was successful, and it grabbed the human with its talons. The human beat furiously with his fists on the talons, for he had lost his sword when the roc had picked him up, but it was to no avail.

The roc flew into the mountains again and finally landed at the top of one in a pile of trees, its nest. Inside, a few young rocs, larger than a fully-grown human, stumbled around, just figuring out the mechanics of their bodies.

The larger roc deposited the two warriors into its nest, before flying off again to find more food for its hatchlings. As soon as they saw the food drop into their nest, the hatchlings started moving towards Fedradin and the other warrior. Fedradin glanced over the edge of the side of the nest. The mountain dropped off into a steep slope, not steep enough to be considered a cliff, but steep enough to be an obstacle. Fedradin thought about jumping, but he would probably fall and roll down the hillside, breaking bones all over his body.

The hatchlings had approached Fedradin and the other warrior. Fedradin pulled out his shield and battered the birds away, hitting them with his shield. They squawked and squawked and ran away. As they ran and cowered in a corner of a nest, Fedradin looked for something he might use to act as a sled to carry him to the bottom of the hill. As he searched, Fedradin caught his foot on a branch that helped make up the bottom of the nest. Fedradin fell on the ground, pulling the branch with him as he did so. When Fedradin stood back up, he looked at where he had pulled the branch from. The branch had been covering some sort of hidden compartment in the nest, and inside Fedradin saw about five roc eggs.

Fedradin heard an eagle call in the distance, and he looked up to see the roc approaching from far away, carrying two more warriors in its talons. Fedradin knew he had to act fast to escape the roc's nest. Fedradin pulled an egg up and out of the compartment. He pulled out his dagger, and he began to cut the eggshell in the shape of a sled. As soon as he finished making the cut, Fedradin kicked his foot into the area surrounding the shape he had just cut. The egg imploded, sending out all the gunk and goo that was associated with eggs, as well as a partially formed baby roc. Fedradin tore his sled from the rest of the remains of the egg, and he ran over to the side of the nest.

Fedradin checked the thickness of the eggshell. It was about a foot thick, maybe less, but hard and firm. Fedradin turned to see the roc coming closer to the nest, so he knew he had to act immediately.

"What are you doing?" asked the other warrior.

"Follow my lead!" shouted Fedradin as he threw himself off the side of the nest. He landed on the cliff with the eggshell underneath him. He didn't hear it snap, but he heard it groan under his weight.

Fedradin began to pick up speed going down the slope, the rocks scraping away layers of the eggshell. The shell was holding up until about three quarters of the way down the slope, when Fedradin hit a rock that sent him and the eggshell sled flying into the air. When he landed on the ground, the shell broke into two pieces. Fedradin fell off the shell and started rolling down the hill. Eventually, he managed to dig his heels into the ground and stop his descent. When he did, Fedradin was already at the bottom of the slope.

Fedradin picked himself up and began running away from the roc's nest, up the mountain path. He looked back occasionally, but the roc didn't pursue him because it was busy feeding the warriors in the nest to its newborns.

The rest of the race passed uneventfully for Fedradin. He ran the rest of the way to the finish line, through the mountains, through the woods and paddled across another, smaller lake. When he arrived at the finish line, he was greeted by the human in the rowboat he had seen earlier, and the svaad who had helped him out earlier.

As Fedradin waited for the rest of his team to finish, two human warriors joined the human in the rowboat. Fedradin knew if their team was complete, he would be eliminated. Shah and Kekk finished. It all came down to Draslupp. A man turned the path and ran up the road. The other human team started cheering, so Fedradin knew the man on the road was the last warrior.

Fedradin's heart fell. Until the man tripped. Draslupp appeared, smiling. He finished the race laughing. As soon as he finished, Fedradin pushed him to the ground. "Don't ever do that again!"

"I won't, I promise," said Draslupp, but in a tone that made Fedradin think otherwise. "By the way, nice tactics with the razor seal."

"You saw that?"

"I saw everything."

Chapter 40
Curiosity Killed the Elf

BREETEX

BREETEX AND ASERAX HAD been cooped up in Fedradin's room a while, how long they didn't really know. The two had grown bored and hungry, waiting for Fedradin to give them scraps of food as they sat in the closet.

When Fedradin did show up, he simply tossed some scraps into the closet and then slammed the door. They weren't great conditions, but Breetex thanked the gods he wasn't facing the same conditions in an elfish prison.

ASERAX

Aserax was not the type of elf who could be stored away in a closet for days at a time. In fact, there were no types of elves who could be stored in a closet. They were a naturally active and exploratory race, and when day four of the Gii Games came around, Aserax was ready to burst.

When Fedradin and Dethroid had both left the room, Aserax decided she could not stay put in the closet for another second. She saw that Breetex had fallen asleep; it seemed his body had forgotten what time of day it was, and when he should be sleeping. It was hard to tell when no sunlight entered the closet, and it remained dark all day.

Aserax cracked open the closet door slightly, determined to at least get a bite to eat. She and Breetex had not had much food. She saw no one in the room, so Aserax pushed the door open slightly more, and she slipped out of the closet. As soon as she exited, her eyes started to water, hurt by the sudden exposure to sunlight coming through the window.

As soon as her eyes were adjusted to the sunlight, Aserax walked over to the window. She stood on the tips of her toes to peer over its edge. Outside, the remaining team per race stood on the field in front of Uslo, as usual. Aserax watched the warriors until Uslo finished his speech and the warriors marched to the stadium. Aserax ducked back down beneath the window.

She paced around the room for a while, exploring every inch of it. Still, the room was small, and after a few moments, Aserax became bored. She moved to the door of the room, opened it and crept out of the room. She walked down the stairs to the common room, on the hunt for food.

POLTAX

Prince Poltax had been caught in a meeting with an elfish soldier about the war, even though he wasn't the king. When he finally escaped the meeting, he had rushed out to the field to congratulate the teams of elves competing to represent his race and wish them good luck. Prince Poltax was slightly too late, and when he arrived at the field, it was deserted. Prince Poltax knew where everyone was: at the stadium. He started to walk in that direction, when a flash of movement caught his eye.

BREETEX

Breetex's eyes opened. He had been woken up from the light streaming in from the window. Breetex jumped to his feet. Aserax was gone. And the closet door was open.

Breetex walked out of the closet, looking for Aserax. She was nowhere to be found in the room. Breetex saw to his horror that the door out to the hallway was ajar.

ASERAX

Aserax found no food in the common room. She almost decided to give up and turn around, but hunger drove her on. Aserax opened the door to the field, a little faster than she had with the other doors. She was about to step outside, when she saw Prince Poltax standing in the middle of the field, his head turned away from her. She closed the door quickly and ran back up the stairs, colliding with Breetex on the middle of the stairs.

POLTAX

Prince Poltax flung open the door, sword drawn out and at the ready. He was looking around the common room of the house, when he caught a glimpse of motion at the top of the stairs, near where it had a sharp twist.

The prince charged towards the motion, bounding up the stairs. *Am I crazy?* he wondered. *She wouldn't be here would she?* Still, he had seen the lousy dwarf she had run off with in Gii earlier, the one she had left Poltax for.

BREETEX

Breetex grabbed Aserax and threw her up the stairs as he heard the door open. Breetex followed her by hurling his small body to the top of the stairs. A few short seconds later, he heard someone beginning to climb the flight of steps. The staircase had a curve at the top of them, so he and Aserax were blocked from view temporarily. Aserax lay dazed on the floor, so he put her over his shoulder and ran into a nearby room. He quickly closed the door behind them, but quietly.

"Under the bed!" he hissed. Aserax crawled under the bed, Breetex right behind her.

ASERAX

The door to the room they were in slammed open. Aserax saw the legs of Prince Poltax enter the room. He stayed there for a few moments, before shutting the door.

Aserax crawled out from under the bed, following Breetex.

"We have to leave," said Breetex.

"What? Why? He didn't see us," said Aserax.

"Merely a cursory glance. He'll be back when he doesn't find us in any other room."

"What should we do?" asked Aserax.

Breetex looked around for a second or two. "The window! We'll jump out the window." Breetex walked over to the window and tried to pry it open. No matter how hard he pulled, the window wouldn't budge.

"Aserax," he whispered, "Can you give me a hand with this?" Aserax walked over to the window and pulled up on the window as Breetex pulled also. The window remained shut. "Probably decorative," said Breetex. The dwarf thought for a second. "Aserax, I need you to get ready to jump."

"You're not going to break the glass-"

"Yes I am. As soon as I do so, Poltax will rush into this room, where I will subdue him as you escape through the window."

"Why can't we stay here?"

"I'm not exactly confident about hiding underneath the bed."

POLTAX

Prince Poltax slammed open another door to another room, searching for his fiancée and her dwarfish paramour. So far, he had not found them, but then again he had not looked very hard. If he couldn't find them with a quick glance into each room, he would have to look harder, and then if his searches still proved fruitless, he would call in the elfish army. He was in Gii, that dwarf, and Poltax would have his head yet.

Poltax stopped. Was he being paranoid? Was he chasing a mere cat or mouse? Calling in the army over nothing would destroy his political standing. He turned to exit the house, when he heard glass shatter.

BREETEX

"Go!" yelled Breetex, practically defenestrating Aserax as he helped her through the window. As soon as she was fully out the window, and on her way to the ground, the door to the room Breetex was standing in swung open. Out in the hallway stood Prince Poltax, sword raised.

"You," hissed Poltax angrily. Breetex pulled out a hatchet strapped to his leg. He felt he did not need the battleaxe strapped on his back.

"Me," said Breetex, slowly backing towards the window.

"What have you done with my wife?" growled Prince Poltax.

"She's not your wife anymore, Poltax." Poltax let out a roar of anger and charged Breetex, swinging his sword when he got close. Breetex swung his hatchet and parried the sword. "She was never your wife."

Poltax swung overhand at Breetex, who rolled to the side to successfully avoid the blow. Poltax roared again and swung his blade once more. Breetex dodged the blade with ease. This pattern repeated itself many times, until finally Poltax's anger bubbled over. "I loved her, you dwarfish bastard!" Poltax swung his blade again, horizontally this time, and Breetex ducked underneath it.

"I can tell you one thing, Poltax. She never loved you back."

ASERAX

Aserax heard her fiancée and her lover fighting in the upstairs room. Aserax had landed on her feet on the grass near the house without a problem. Elves were a nimble race, so it was never a problem for her. But she was a bit worried about Breetex.

Aserax heard the two throw insults at each other as they continued to fight, which scared Aserax. The conflict would not help the War of Gems.

POLTAX

Poltax had never felt so much anger in his life, which probably affected his fighting. The dwarf that ruined his life danced around in front of him, taunting him about his fianceé. Poltax had never wanted anything more in his life than to chop off the dwarf's head, but he couldn't seem to do it. Every time his blade would approach the dwarf, the dwarf would magically avoid it. Poltax was about to give up the fight and call for some elfish soldiers, when the fight had an interesting development.

BREETEX

Breetex decided that he was done fighting Poltax. It had been fun battling Aserax's betrothed, but he needed to flee before someone was alerted by the noise of the fight.

Breetex needed to subdue Poltax. The task was marginally easier because Poltax had become angry. As Poltax took another clumsy swing at Breetex, Breetex disarmed Poltax by avoiding the blade and slamming the handle of his hatchet into the guard on Poltax's sword. As Poltax dropped his sword, Breetex knocked out the Prince by hitting the handle of his hatchet into Poltax's head. The elfish prince collapsed to the ground, unconscious. Quickly, Breetex turned around and leapt out the window, landing ungracefully on his back.

"Are you alright?" asked Aserax, sounding quite unconcerned.

"Yes, I'm fine, thank you. It wasn't that far a fall. Now, we have to leave town, find somewhere to hide. As soon as Poltax regains consciousness-"

"You knocked out Poltax?"

"Oh, yes. He should be fine, no permanent damage. Anyway, we need to leave now, Poltax will be back to search the house, all the houses in fact. Maybe we can find another town, or..."

"Breetex, we can't live like this, migrating around from place to place, *I* can't live like this!"

"I know, Aserax, I know."

Chapter 41

Black Arrow

IT WAS AMAZING HOW long the prisoner had been able to resist talking. However, with three Minions torturing him, he finally started telling them everything. It had taken a few days, and it had required Oxlo to go back and capture the prisoner's son, but the results were worth it.

The prisoner was a senior member of Thunderflash, so knew everything. He told them all the tricks, traps, defenses and any other means of keeping the precious Demon Callers hidden. Of course, after they interrogated him, they had to kill him and his son, which was unfortunate, but had to be done.

After they had finished, Frin had Tawassa summon another spirit. This one happened to be a sixth ring genie. It wasn't as strong as the djinn they had had before, but it worked just as well to communicate with the Master. When they were able finally wrestle the genie into all the various shackles they had, they contacted the Master.

"Was the interrogation successful?" demanded the Master.

"Yes, Master," answered Frin.

"What did he tell us?"

"Everything, Master. Finding the Demon Callers now will be as easy as taking candy from a baby," said Frin.

"So what shall we do about the foreseen one?"

"The baby?" asked Tawassa.

"He once was the baby, but now I believe he is about to win the Gii Games."

"We can't let him beat us to the Demon Callers!" exclaimed Tawassa.

"Of course he will beat us to the Demon Callers. He is foreseen to do so!" said Oxlo, speaking up.

"The prophecy could have never seen us capture the man we just tortured," said Frin.

"Or it could have foreseen exactly that!" said Oxlo.

"I don't give a damn about the prophecy," announced the Master through the genie. "I have waited nigh on twenty years for this man to do something, and I have grown very impatient."

"I don't agree with you, but you are my Master," said Oxlo.

"What do you want us to do? Kill the man?" asked Tawassa.

"You morons have proved to be ineffective at killing this particular person, even when he was a baby. I want Black Arrow on this case," said the Master.

"You want us to hire her to kill that baby Fedradin?" asked Tawassa.

"No, I want you to invite her to tea!" exclaimed the Master sarcastically. "Find Black Arrow and have her kill this man. I don't want this man, this waste of time, around for much longer."

A few hours later, the Minions were at the liar of Black Arrow. It was a dark cave in the middle of the Mendelgar Forest. The Minions approached the cave with slight trepidation. Black Arrow was a ferocious creature that could strike fear in the heart of any creature on Haxter. However, most of the creatures alive on Haxter did not remember Black Arrow. They would soon be reminded.

The Minions entered the cave, which was carved into the side of a hill. Inside, a massive chamber lay before the Minions, and in the center of it, a large spider web was built inside a square, stone frame. Upon that web was a black cocoon, and the Minions all knew what was inside it.

Frin walked forward, hesitation and regret in every step. He let out a long breath, and rapped on the side of the cocoon, before jumping backwards, covering his head with his arms.

The cocoon began to transform. It seemed to melt down to black ooze, which started to form a figure. It built upon itself, forming the shape of a woman. When the outline of the woman was complete, the ooze changed color, giving it the appearance of an attractive, blond haired woman, wearing a skintight black suit that appeared to be the ooze, but slightly hardened. A black quiver appeared on her back, full of black arrows, as a black bow appeared in her right hand.

"Sages," said Black Arrow. "Why do you disturb my rest?"

"We have need of you once again, Black Arrow," said Frin.

"What for?" asked Black Arrow.

"We need you to kill someone who has been getting in our way."

"Who is this person?"

"'Tis Prince Fedradin Quickblade of Narven."

"Ah, yes. I have seen this man in my visions. He seems like a good man."

"Nonetheless, in our way," said Frin.

"You want me to kill him?" asked Black Arrow.

"Yes."

Black Arrow thought for a moment. "No."

"No?" shouted Oxlo. "After all we've done for you?"

Black Arrow scoffed. "You have done next to nothing for me."

"Have you forgotten us saving you? Has that slipped your mind?"

Black Arrow turned away. "It has not."

"Then do us one more favor. Please."

Black Arrow turned back. "Fine. I will help you once more."

"Thank you, Black Arrow."

"But, if you dare to disturb me from my much needed rest, I swear to you, Sage, you will not live to see another day."

Chapter 42
Champions' Feast

FEDRADIN

WITH ONLY NINE WARRIORS left competing for the title of the Greatest Warrior in Haxter, Uslo had invited the remaining warriors to a feast in the castle. The warriors were even allowed to use the Noble Passage.

Uslo had only invited the warrior from each team who would be competing the next day and representing his race. The warriors were the following: Nesmer, the elf; Zocatrar, the dwarf; Ontlaar, the svaad who had helped Fedradin cross the lake; Bafflagen, the flayer; Folpik, the half-celestial who represented the Keshnul race; Sapplezul, the chultra; Thrasp, the centaur representing the Grefture race; and finally, Yuntile, the yakio representing the animal cultures race with whom Fedradin had crossed the troll infested bridge.

A few warriors were already present at the castle. Sapplezul was already sitting at the table, along with Nesmer and Folpik. Fedradin sat down at the table, nodding to each warrior, most nodded back. The exception, Nesmer. Still, Fedradin took a seat next to the elf, not wanting to be near Sapplezul, Shah's enemy.

The LNR meeting was still going on down the hall from the dining room, and Fedradin could hear snippets of the conversation. It sounded as if they were arguing over the actions to take against a band of goblins heading near Borave, headed by, what sounded like 'a man with horns.'

Uslo was not actually present in the meeting room, but he was skulking around the hallway, making sure no fights erupted in either the dining room or the meeting room.

During this time, Bafflagen, Ontlaar, Thrasp, Yuntile, and Zocatrar showed up. Bafflagen did not have the slit in his neck to be able to speak Common, so Fedradin would not be able to talk to Bafflagen.

Finally Uslo moved away from the meeting of the LNR. He took his place at the head of the table. The table was set with plates, inlaid with various metals and gems. Polished silverware lay to the side of the plates.

"Warriors! Only nine of you remain. From almost four hundred to nine," said Uslo, shaking his head. "I can't believe it. You are the best warriors in your races. Tomorrow, we will eliminate six races, but tonight we feast!"

Servants came out from the kitchen, placing bowls of chowder at each place setting. There wasn't much talking, mostly awkward silence since the warriors knew they would be fighting each other the next day.

They continued to feast, on fresh trout caught in Lake Gii, delicious venison hunted down in the woods of Mendelgar, rare fruits and berries, truffles, lobster, and many other delicious items. Wine and stentspice flooded the food along, livening up the warriors.

When they were about to bring dessert, the LNR meeting disbanded. Fedradin looked down the hallway to see the leaders of the nine races. As he looked he saw Prince Poltax, and Prince Poltax saw him.

"You!" shouted Poltax, drawing his sword and running forward. Fedradin looked to Uslo, who appeared just as confused as Fedradin. Fedradin went to draw his sword, but his scabbard wasn't at his side as it usually was.

"Looking for something?" taunted Nesmer, holding Fedradin's scabbard in his left hand. Fedradin made to try to snatch it back from the elf, but Nesmer pulled the scabbard back and drew his own sword, holding it menacingly. "I wouldn't advise that."

By now, Poltax had entered the dining room. Fedradin had left his knife at his room, thinking his sword was enough defense. Besides, if he had brought it, Nesmer would have probably swiped it as well.

Fedradin saw that Poltax meant to stab him with the sword, so Fedradin quickly pulled the silver tray out from under a roasted turkey. He used the tray as a makeshift shield, deflecting Poltax's sword.

Before the Prince Poltax could swing again, he was tackled by Sapplezul. The chultra kicked Poltax's sword to the side.

"Thank you, Sapp-" began Fedradin, who was cut off by the feeling of a sword on his neck.

"Drop your weapons or I slit his neck," said Nesmer.

"What the hell are you doing, Nesmer?" yelled Uslo. "You're disqualified if you don't drop your sword this instant."

Nesmer let out a long breath, before saying, "I'm sorry, Prince Poltax." Nesmer dropped his sword away from Fedradin's neck.

"Now I want to know what the hell you elves think you're getting at," demanded Uslo. By now, the leaders of the races had arrived on the scene.

"That human!" yelled Poltax, still on the floor. Poltax stood up. "He was harboring the elfish Princess and her dwarfish lover!"

"Greul Breetex?" exclaimed Sir Hulten Sharpaxe.

"I have done no such thing!" said Fedradin, remaining calm on the outside. On the inside, Fedradin cursed the elf and the dwarf and his bad luck.

"I saw them both in the human house. The dwarf knocked me out with his hatchet!" said Poltax.

"I'm sure Breetex would do no such thing," said Hulten, facing Poltax.

"He already ran away with my bride! What are the limits to his madness?" demanded Poltax.

"I still refuse to believe that," said Hulten stubbornly.

"Then where is your Greul now?" shouted Poltax.

"On a military mission," said Hulten.

"Against my people? Surely you wouldn't tell me that information," said Poltax.

"Of course not against the elves," said Hulten.

"Against who then?" demanded Poltax.

"Why the...goblins of course."

"Lies! All lies!" shouted Poltax. "I want to search the human house and find these two cowering in a corner somewhere to show you that I am right!"

"You won't find anything in the human house," said Fedradin.

"You're bluffing," said Poltax. "Do I have permission to search the human house?" The question was directed at Flyc.

"Of course. Fedradin would not do something as horrid as harbor fugitives." *Was that a smile?*

"Lord Uslo?" said Poltax.

"I...well, I agree with the Emperor, of course," said Uslo, hesitantly. "I trust Fedradin."

"It's decided then," said Poltax, sticking his chin out at Hulten.

Minutes later, Poltax, Hulten, Uslo, Flyc, Fedradin, Nesmer, a small band of armed elves, the remaining warriors, and the leaders of the races were outside the human house.

"I will be out with the head of Breetex in a few short minutes," announced Poltax. He, Nesmer, and the band of elves entered the house.

POLTAX

"Where are you?" said Poltax as he searched the house. He walked to the common room, flipping the furniture, checking the chimney, and looking in all the corners. When his searches turned up fruitless, Poltax sent Nesmer outside to circle the house to make sure the two didn't escape like last time.

He and his band of elves made their way up the stairs. He split them up to search the rooms, as he began looking for the two himself.

FEDRADIN

Poltax exited the house a few minutes later, frustration showing on his red face.

"Couldn't find what wasn't there?" asked Fedradin.

"This doesn't concern you, Prince," said Poltax.

"Then who does it concern?" asked Fedradin. "You just tore apart my room looking for the two fugitives you accused me of harboring."

"Shut up," said Poltax. "This is about Hulten and me."

"Is it now? Well, it seems that I have won this little dispute," said Hulten. "You have been unable to procure any evidence to whether or not my Greul has run off with your bride."

"But the hole in the window! That was how they escaped!" exclaimed Poltax.

"Really?" said Fedradin. "For I seem to recall breaking that window as I practiced with my sword." Fedradin flashed a smile at Poltax. "You must try harder than that to try to get me out of this competition. I know you're just worried I'm going to beat Nesmer."

Chapter 43

Across The Sea

FENDER

"IT'S THE DARK THAT gets 'em," said Fender to Joloak, staring out into the night.

"Would you let a man in if he returned to the gate after dark?" asked Joloak.

"I would," said Fender, "but alas, we haven't yet had that problem."

"Then why do we have a gate?"

"The same reason that none of these men return."

"The dark?"

"What *lurks* in the dark. There are some sinister forces hiding in these woods."

"Do you think we'll ever find Trumbell?"

"Sure, we usually find 'em."

"I mean *alive*."

"If we're to learn anything from the past—"

"Do you have no hope?" said Joloak. "All I want is something to cling to, some shred of possibility, but you have to take that away from me."

"I'm just being realistic..."

"I don't want realism! I want Trumbell back!" With that, Joloak turned and left Fender to stare off into the woods, contemplating if it were at all possible for somewhere, Trumbell to be alive and fending for himself in the deadly dark.

FANE

"Any man who comes out of this battle without orcish blood on his blade will have his head on a spike by morning!" shouted Fane, as he drew his own sword. He and his army behind him, sitting astride horses, all drew their weapons and raised their shields. Fane glanced back, to see the armor of his three hundred men catching the noonday sun. He turned to the fortress, to see the orcish archers taking positions on the battlements. "Let us show these orcs whose land this is! For the Spice Sultan! For stentspice! For Stentor! Charge!" With those words, Fane spurred his horse into action, sword outstretched, as the battlecries of his men swirled up around him.

Sir Fane lowered his blade and raised his shield, as the storm of orcish arrows rained down on him and his men. He braced himselves as the arrows imbedded themselves on his shield, with loud thumps.

His men surged up around him, some falling to the arrows, as orcish foot soldiers poured out of the gates of Welnn, their hallmarked dual-handed black blades gleaming. Orcs riding wargs appeared next, bounding across the sand. Their repulsive faces with squashed noses and large ears and black beady eyes, were visible through the visors of their light armor. The arrows ceased as the two forces met on the hot sands.

The orcs smashed against Fane's vanguard, but to no avail. The green blood of the orcs' was spilled and soaked the battlefield. Until a horse fell. The horse of Sir Tune, the captain of the vanguard, was stabbed through the heart by an orc. Sir Tune was flung from his mount and to the wet, green sand. The orcs descended on him like flies, ripping him to shreds before he could let out a cry of pain.

Fane fought back as the orcs surged forwards, slashing down orcs left and right, but his success wasn't matched with the other soldiers, as the green sand was colored with red. A warg, which had lost its rider, tore through the men, leaving a swath of the dead and dying in its wake.

Pain ripped through his arm as an arrow struck him in the left shoulder. Fane toppled off the back of his horse, crashing to the wet sand. His horse was quickly felled by orcs, and it collapsed. Fane had to shuffe back, his shoulder crying in protest, to avoid being crushed. An orc leapt over the horse, swinging an overhand blow at Fane, who was barley able to deflect the blade with his own. The orc lashed a kick out at Fane's sword hand, knocking the weapon away. It then pulled its sword back and prepared another attack.

Sir Fane closed his eyes and braced himself. A twang of a bow, a thud, a cry. No death. The knight opened his eyes to reveal the orc, an arrow buried in its neck, dead on top of his horse. Fane looked behind him to see a squad of archers, only one of whom still had his horse.

"Thank you," croaked Fane. The man on the horse quickly nocked another arrow on his bow, pulled back the bowstring, and loosed the arrow at an orc, which had made it over Fane's dead mount. The creature fell backwards, dead, with an arrow inbedded in his heart.

"You're welcome," said the man coolly, then to his men, "take out the orcs on the wall." The archers aimed their bows and fired. A few seconds later, dead orcs tumbled down from the battlements on the fortress wall. "Only the vanguard pushed to the castle." Fane, who had been watching the orcs fall, turned his head back to the archer in surprise.

"What?"

"Those orcish archers have been holding the rest of the army back." There was a loud battlecry, and men came charging by Fane, the sounds of metal-on-metal and cries of pain resounding through the battlefield.

"What's your name?" asked Fane.

"Hunnex," said the archer.

"Who do you serve? The Spice Sultan?" Hunnex loosed yet another arrow. Fane didn't have to turn to know he'd killed an orc.

"I serve no one. I am from the Orcslayer Guild in the Desert of Spice."

"Are you coinswords?"

"If anything, we'd be coin*bows*, but no. We slay orcs, so here we are."

"Well, I can't thank you enough. But, to put myself more into your debt, how good of a medic are you?"

DUNLOCK

Redemption came on the wings of a pigeon, not at the hands of his slaves. King Dunlock had been weighing Kolan's proposition, but was interrupted by one bird. A scrawny bird, fluttering against the sea breeze, carrying with it a small, handwritten note that would forever alter the course of the Corsair Kingdom.

"Do we know who this is from?" said Dunlock, accepting the note from the pigeonkeep. The pigeon bearing the letter had died of exhaustion upon arriving at Gusar's pigeonpen.

"No, Your Grace. Your eyes will be the first to look upon this note."

Dunlock grunted and unfolded the parchment. He squinted at the words, before beckoning for Kolan, his Scholar, to read the note. "It's too small," he complained, to avoid revealing his illiteracy. Kolan took the note.

"It is small, Your Grace, very small and hard to read—"

"Shut up and read," snapped Dunlock.

"Certainly, Your Grace." Kolan took the letter and cleared his throat. "It has the seal of King Grent."

"King Grent?" said Dunlock. "Of...Creopolis?"

"Yes."

"Well, what does it say?"

"My apologies, your Grace. It reads, '*To King Dunlock Searider, ruler of the Corsair Kingdom. King Grent of Creopolis would like to propose an alliance. An alliance to end the rule of the LNR. For years Creopolis has been imprisoned by the Human Empire of Haxter, unable to break free of their clutches. With help from the Corsair Kingdom, Creopolis could escape and bring back slavery to Haxter. Details of the plan will not be discussed, in case this letter is intercepted. Please write back soon with your answer.*' It's signed by King Grent."

"The day we let a dot of wax and a scribbled name verify the authenticity of something is a sad day. I want to meet face-to-face with this King Grent."

GRENT

King Grent received work back from the Corsairs sooner than he expected. However, the answer he received he did.

"He said yes," whispered Grent, as he read the letter.

"Well... that's great!" said Treo, one of Grent's advisors.

"Yes. It is," said Grent, with an unfitting tone.

"What?" asked Treo, "What's wrong? You sound upset."

"He wants to meet with me. Face-to-face." Grent looked to Treo.

"Well..." said Treo. "I guess we need to get you to Gusar."

Chapter 44
The Final Game

FEDRADIN

FEDRADIN ARRIVED AT THE field. Today, Shah, Draslupp, and Kekk stood off to the side. Fedradin would be advancing alone to the finals of the tournament, he himself representing the entire human race. No pressure.

"In the last Game of the Gii Games, you, the warriors will compete in a series of challenges," announced Uslo. "Those completing the challenges will continue, the ones failing will be eliminated. The last two warriors will face each other in one final fight."

The first few challenges passed uneventfully for Fedradin. In the first he defeated a dire elk, everyone but Folpik doing the same. In the second, everyone passed the test of slaying a pack of kobolds. The third was a bit trickier, the warriors had to free a captive from the grasp of a minotaur. Thrasp's captive was torn to shreds in the battle, and Yuntile was defeated when he was cut in two by the monster. Luckily for him, it was a simulation.

"The final six," came the voice of Uslo. "Time for things to get harder." Orcs appeared on the field, behind them six chests. A Stentorik man stood even farther back, holding a cutlass. "The goal of this Game is to deliver one chest of stentspice to the Stentorik, without being defeated by the orcs. Without further ado, go!"

Already tired from the three previous events, Fedradin hefted his sword with difficulty, as the first of many orcs came whirling by, black blade in hand. Fedradin met the orc's weapon with his own, just in time. He returned the blow with a clumsy swing, which the orc easily avoided. The orc lashed out once more, and Fedradin used his shield to batter it away. He took a step forward and feinted a swing. The orc leapt to the side, and Fedradin smashed it on the head with his shield. Dazed, it reeled away, but soon lost its head to Fedradin's sword.

Sapplezul had already made it to the chests. Fedradin redoubled his efforts and pushed his way into the horde of orcs.

Once he got into a rhythm, he was cutting down orcs left and right, and soon found himself at the chests. Nesmer and Bafflagen had also made it there. Fedradin began to pull his chest, when out of the crown came an orc on a warg.

The wolf-like creature landed in between the three warriors, scattering them. Fedradin's blade gashed its side, and it turned to snap at him. At the same time, Bafflagen launched himself at the warg-rider, knocking him from the beast. Nesmer quickly finished the warg with a slice to the neck. The three warriors looked to each other.

"Teamwork," muttered Fedradin, who spun to stab an orc, which had been creeping up on him. They all grabbed their chests and pulled them towards the Stentorik, one hand pulling, the other slashing.

Two orcs attacked Fedradin at once. He blocked their blows, finding no time to launch his own, losing ground all the while. Suddenly, one of the orcs' blades made contact with his hilt, sending the sword spinning from his grip. The orcs approached, but with a feat of strength, Fedradin saved himself by hurling the chest and taking out both orcs at once. The heavy, wooden object caught one in the head, the other in the chest, sending splinters flying. He grabbed his sword and finished them off.

The final pull to the Stentorik man was difficult, but he pushed through, leaving a trail of dead orcs in his wake. Nesmer, Sapplezul, and Bafflagen were already there. Fedradin watched and saw Yuntile fall prey to a warg-rider and Zocatrar felled when five orcs attacked him at once. Ontlaar, the last one on the field, was swarmed with orcs and soon overrun. Of course, Yuntile, Zocatrar, and Ontlaar were fine, the simulation orcs doing no damage.

The next event, where three greatbears were released among the warriors, left Bafflagen behind.

The field was split up into three sections for the next event, a nemean lion and a whip placed in each. "The first two warriors to defeat their nemean lion advance to the final round. If two warriors don't beat the lions, then the ones surviving the longest will advance."

Fedradin walked towards one of lions, ready to fight. Walls around him stopped him from seeing his fellow warriors fight. He knew that the hide of nemean was impenetrable to nearly everything, his sword included. His only option was to aim for its eyes.

Fedradin approached cautiously, sword leveled, shield up. The lion growled and turned to face him. Fedradin charged, but was batted away by a paw before he could get anywhere close. He tried again. The lion knocked him down once more. He managed to swing, but the weapon bounced uselessly off the lion's hide.

Fedradin retreated, but the lion advanced, pouncing. Fedradin rolled to the side, avoided the beast as it came crashing to the ground. Fedradin, to the side of the lion, jumped on top of it, grabbing a fistful of hair to avoid falling off. He swung his sword, once, twice, thrice, but it did nothing. Still, it irritated the lion, which bucked and sent Fedradin tumbling off. Fedradin hit the sand, landing not a foot away from the whip.

A thought struck him. Why were the warriors separated? Why was there a whip? There was a way to defeat the nemean lions and it involved the whip. This challenge wasn't about strength or endurance. This challenge was a puzzle, a test of intellect. It was also a puzzle Fedradin had just solved. Fedradin sheathed his sword and snatched up the whip. He knew what he had to do.

He cracked the whip as the lion approached. It snarled as it stalked forwards. Fedradin charged, ducking the lion's paw, vaulting onto the lion's back. The beast bucked once more, but Fedradin threw the whip around its neck, grabbing each end with a hand. The lion reared, and Fedradin tightened the whip. The lion continued to thrash about, and Fedradin continued to tighten, until the lion collapsed. Fedradin leapt off his back to avoid being crushed. To make sure it was dead, he thrust his sword through its eye.

Neither Nesmer nor Sapplezul could figure out how to kill the lion. Sapplezul was defeated, and Nesmer claimed the second spot by default. As a consolation prize, Sapplezul was awarded with a small, jade monkey from the Westlands.

"Tomorrow," announced Uslo. "The human, Fedradin, will face the elf, Nesmer."

Chapter 45

Abominations

VASIRD

VASIRD WAS AT THE gallows, with a bag that used to carry potatoes over his head. He was no longer human, didn't even resemble what he had been before his change. The entire town of Haneou had turned out for his public hanging, all of them outraged, throwing various items at him. He had no idea what they were throwing, but he did know that when the items hit him, they could draw blood.

Someone was announcing his crime to the public, but since his ears had become deformed during his transition, he had no idea what the man, or perhaps woman, was saying. What he could feel, though, was the noose slid over his neck. He thrashed around helplessly, but his hands and feet were tied. He felt the plank he was standing on come out from under him.

As he fell to his doom, he closed his eyes. An hour ago he had been a normal human.

IRROTHURE

Irrothure held the body of his dead dog. Its head lolled back and forth on its broken neck. He was no longer in the form of the giant beast that had killed Kuine, his dog, but he knew he hated the beast. He hated whoever turned him into that beast. Worst of all, Irrothure hated himself.

All Irrothure had was his dog. Without Kuine, Irrothure decided that his life was unbearable. He had loved Kuine like a son. He had already killed his real son. Why did he have to keep killing things he loved? Alcohol wasn't a factor this time, it was something else. Whatever that something else was, Irrothure knew he hated it. He would find this evil force and he would do to the force what he did to his dog.

Irrothure looked up from his dead dog. He stared at the moon, and howled, much like a wolf. With that, he began to transform into the horrid beast that had already done the most damage it could possibly do to Irrothure.

COID

Whatever the force was that had transformed Coid into what he was now, Coid wanted to thank it. No, thanks wouldn't be enough.

The goblins bustled around before him. The small, scaly, ugly things bending to his ever will. He was lying on a bed of silk, two goblins on either side of him fanning him with large, palm leaves. Another goblin slowly fed him purple grapes from a large bunch.

With his new powers, taking over the goblin den had been the easiest thing he had ever done, which didn't exactly say much, since he had been a slave all his life. He had a plan in mind, though. He didn't just kill things for no reason. Coid would become King of the Goblins. He would take his goblin army and free all the slaves from Histam, and afterwards, he would destroy as many Boravians as he could. He had lived a hard enough life before he was granted these new powers, and it was time for his revenge.

Chapter 46
One Final Battle

FEDRADIN

FEDRADIN STOOD ON THE field, facing Nesmer. The winner of the Gii Games would be decided by one final battle.

His heart had been beating fast all day, and he had barely gotten any sleep the past night. The nerves were starting to get to him today, as well as the fatigue from the past competitons.

They would use their real weapons, and Uslo declared that the winner would be the warrior who forced their opponent to surrender. At any point, Uslo could declare a winner in case one warrior refused to surrender.

The field was unembellished in any way, shape or form. Nesmer stood at one end with his sword drawn and his shield up, and Fedradin stood at the other end with his sword drawn and his shield up, too. The two warriors stood about thirty yards apart.

"On your marks. Get set! And for the title of Greatest Warrior in Haxter, go!" shouted Uslo.

Both Nesmer and Fedradin charged at each other. They collided in the center of the field, swords clashing against each other. The sound of metal-on-metal resounded throughout the completely silent stadium. Fedradin sent a flurry of blows at Nesmer, which the elf parried with skill. Nesmer returned Fedradin's attack with his own sequence of blows, each one bouncing off Fedradin's sword. This pattern repeated itself many times, the swords colliding with massive amounts of force. The pattern was broken when Nesmer was swinging his sword at Fedradin, and Fedradin lunged out with a kick. Nesmer was caught in the middle of a swing, which he stopped short as he stumbled backwards. Fedradin advanced towards the elf, lunging with his sword. The elf, who had regained his balance, blocked the sword with his shield. Fedradin pulled his sword backwards as Nesmer launched another attack.

Fedradin blocked the first few swings with his shield, but as Nesmer began to launch his second attack, Fedradin swung his own sword. Nesmer was swinging his sword as well, so the swords collided in midair. Instead of letting the swords bounce off each other, both warriors pressed their swords together. The swords were interlocked, pushing against each other with a large amount of force. The warriors staying in this position for many minutes, until Fedradin planted his foot on Nesmer's chest and sent him flying. Nesmer's sword slipped off Fedradin's sword, just barely missing amputating Fedradin's leg by a few inches.

Fedradin advanced on the fallen elf, who was desperately trying to get to his feet. Fedradin swung overhead but was blocked by the elf's shield. Nesmer scrambled backwards, trying to avoid Fedradin's blade. Fedradin advanced on the elf, again swinging overhead. Once more Nesmer blocked the blade with his shield and scrambled backwards. Fedradin advanced and was about to swing his sword once more, when Nesmer kicked him in the stomach. Fedradin stumbled backwards, which gave Nesmer the chance he needed to get to his feet.

The elf did not only get to his feet, but he also advanced on Fedradin, swinging his sword. Fedradin parried the blow with ease and swung his sword back at Nesmer. The elf blocked the blow on his shield, and he slashed out at Fedradin with his sword. Fedradin blocked the sword with his own sword, and the two warriors began fighting intensely, their swords clashing back and forth faster than was visible to the spectators.

Fedradin parried one of Nesmer's swings, but the blow knocked the sword out of his hand. The weapon landed in the sand. Fedradin dove towards it, dodging Nesmer's attack. Fedradin grabbed up his sword, spinning to catch Nesmer's blow. His grip was loose, and once again he lost the sword. He backed up, raising a shield to stop Nesmer's sword. He fell back into the sand. Nesmer began to repeatedly smash his sword into Fedradin's shield. As Fedradin raised his shield once more to block the sword, it was sent spinning off his arm.

Nesmer pulled his sword back. "I yield!" shouted Fedradin.

A crazed smile passed Nesmer's lips. "Not today." Nesmer swung. Fedradin rolled to the side, and the blade struck the sand an inch to the side of Fedradin's head. Nesmer pulled his sword back once more, a crazed look in his eyes.

"No!" shouted Uslo, who slammed into the side of Nesmer. The elf went flying into the sand. Uslo stood up. "Elf! You are disqualified. Fedradin, you are the winner!"

A silence passed through the crowd like no other. Slowly, the audience registered what had happened and the humans broke out in cheers.

Chapter 47

Awards Ceremony

FEDRADIN

FEDRADIN STOOD ON THE highest of the three pedestals, to show that he placed first in the competition. Sapplezul stood on the second highest, since Nesmer had been disqualified. Bafflagen stood on the lowest pedestal. Uslo then started the ceremony.

"Greetings!" said Uslo, "We are here today to congratulate these three warriors, especially Prince Fedradin, on their success this past week at the Gii Games. All four hundred warriors fought valiantly, but the skill and determination of these three warriors was matched only by each other's. First, I would like to congratulate Bafflagen, representing the flayer race, on placing third place in the Gii Games!" The flayers in the audience cheered, as Uslo walked forward and placed a bronze medal around his neck. "Next, I would like to congratulate Sapplezul, representing the chultra race, on placing second in the Gii Games!" The chultra in the crowd cheered, as Uslo walked forward and placed a silver medal around his neck. "Finally, I would like to congratulate Prince Fedradin of Narven, representing the human race, for the level of skill and adroitness he had demonstrated over this past week. The winner of the Gii Games is Prince Fedradin!" The humans applauded madly, as Uslo walked forward. Instead of bestowing a medal upon Fedradin's shoulders, Uslo presented Fedradin with a golden trophy. Fedradin thrust the trophy in the air, and the humans cheered louder and louder. "But remember!" said Uslo, silencing the humans. "That is not all Fedradin wins..." Uslo presented a bag of money to Fedradin. "Fifty thousand fellyers!" said Uslo, as the humans continued to cheer. "And finally, the prize you have all been competing for most intensely, the sword, Baxcanador!" Uslo handed Fedradin the sword, still in its sheath. Fedradin slowly drew out the sword, savoring each piece as he pulled it out. The perfectly crafted pommel with the emerald on it, the hilt, the cross-guard. All of the pieces perfectly shaped and sized...all the way to the tip. Fedradin thrust the sword in the air, like he had with his trophy, the humans roaring their approval. Fedradin did regret the way he had won, but Nesmer *had* tried to kill him. "Once again, thank you to all the warriors who competed, all the spectators who came to the Games, and to anyone else who might have helped us construct this competition. Congratulations to the winners, Sapplezul and Bafflagen, and of course, Prince Fedradin. Good bye, everyone. See you next year."

Chapter 48

A New Force

NESMER

"YOU LOST TO THE human?" came a voice from the far end of the cave, which was shrouding in darkness.

"No, I tried to end him once and for all and they disqualified-" Nesmer desperately tried to explain. The elf stood at the opening of the cave, where some light managed to trickle in.

"You had already won?"

"We never truly would have won unless he was dead."

"But now *he* will win! He has the sword!"

"Master, he doesn't even know how to wield the sword."

"And you assume he won't figure it out?" shouted the voice. "The sword could bring the entire plan down! We've worked too long with the Minions and their Master to have it all end like this."

"The Minions don't seem too worried about the sword..." said Nesmer.

"That's because those arrogant Sages fancy themselves indestructible! I've seen Baxcanador at work, and it has enough power to destroy all of those self-aggrandizing bastards. All of them! With ease!"

"What shall we do?" asked Nesmer.

"I need to warn the Minions of the sword's potential, and when they ignore me-"

"If!" exclaimed Nesmer.

"When! When they cast me aside as a doomsayer, I will take matters into my own hand to rid ourselves of that 'Prince of Destiny.'"

"The Minions have already awakened Black Arrow from its slumber. What could be more powerful than Black Arrow?"

"If you think Black Arrow is powerful, wait to you see what I have hidden up my sleeve."

Part II
The Legendary Eight

Chapter 49
A Little Problem

FEDRADIN

FEDRADIN SET OUT FOR Narven the next morning. His Ridders had congratulated him many times, and he began to split the money up amongst them. He kept much of it for himself, but he gave out nearly thirty thousand fellyers. He split most of the thirty thousand fellyers between Shah, Draslupp and Kekk. He then gave large portions to Dethroid and Axto. Finally, he gave what was left over of the thirty thousand to Bev and Yexico.

When the carriage set out the next morning, all seemed fine. They rode along for around an hour or two, when they hit a bump in the road, and they heard their back axle snap. The carriage came to a stop on the side of the road, and Fedradin got out of the carriage to take a look at it. Dethroid came with him, but the rest of the Ridders stayed in the carriage. The horse driver walked over to inspect the damage, but when the horses were spooked by something, he went over to calm them down.

"How are we going to fix it?" asked Dethroid.

"I don't know...don't you know some mending spells?" asked Fedradin.

"Magic was never really meant for fixing things...so, no."

"We could lash the pieces together with something."

"I do know a binding spell. Do you want me to try it?"

Fedradin thought for a moment. "No. If you bind the pieces of the axles together, the carriage won't roll straight."

"What should we do?"

Fedradin thought for a moment, when it hit him. Literally. One moment he was thinking about how to fix his broken carriage, the next, he was hit in the head by something falling out of the trees. He looked down to see what it was, and it turned out that it was something even less appealing than an acorn.

"Breetex! What the hell are you doing here?" said Fedradin.

The dwarf looked up, rubbed his head and said, "Don't look at me. I wanted to hide out on a boat to Osup and go there. Aserax is the one who wanted to follow your carriage."

"Aserax's here too?" asked Fedradin.

"'Course she is." At that moment, Aserax tumbled out of the treetops.

"Hello, Prince!" she said happily.

"Why won't you leave me alone?" said Fedradin.

"Hey, it isn't my fault. You're the one who was dumb enough to harbor us in the first place," said Breetex. "Why don't you just harbor us again? Temporarily."

"No," said Fedradin. "Not again. I've already angered the elves enough."

"Please!" said Aserax. "At least just until we reach Narven. Then we'll be on our way."

"I don't think you should," said Dethroid, to whom Fedradin had explained Breetex's and Aserax's sitation once they had left their room.

"Wait," said Fedradin. "I have an idea." Ten minutes later the carriage was on its way down the road.

"So how did he fix it?" asked Bev.

"Let's just say he had a little help," said Dethroid. Then, to Fedradin. "The same thing would've worked with two logs."

Fedradin shrugged. "My way is more fun."

BREETEX

"Aserax?" Breetex said.

"Yes?" she replied.

"Are we really desperate enough for help that we're serving as an axle?" The dwarf and the elf were tied together at their ankles, facing opposite ways, their hands tied to the ends of the axle.

The two remained in that position, spinning around and around, all the way through the Mendelgar Forest, across the Ozreek Moutains, and into the Craggy Keep. When the carriage stopped, Dethroid undid the binds holding the two to the axle. Breetex and Aserax ran off east into the mountains.

As soon as all the Ridders stepped out of the carriage, a messenger came up to Fedradin.

"Urgent request for Prince Fedradin by Lord Thereeko," said the messenger.

"Probably just his congratulations," said Fedradin to mollify his Ridders, who were standing with worried expressions.

How wrong he was.

Chapter 50

A Summons

FEDRADIN

FEDRADIN WALKED WITH THE messenger to the castle. He let out a small sigh; it was hard to adjust from the towering fotress of Gii to the relatively dilapidated castle of Narven.

They walked through the building, passing bowing servants and Fedradin's solar, where he was first offered his enrollment in the Gii Games. They eventually reached the solar of Lord Thereeko. The messenger dropped back and stayed at the door, motioning for Fedradin to continue.

Fedradin walked in to the room, and he realized that he had never entered the room before. It wasn't a large room, but big enough for two or three people to be comfortably sat at once. At the near side of the room, a few chairs were spaced out around an unlit fireplace, with woolen rugs in between them. At the far side of the room, there was a huge cushioned chair, on which sat Thereeko. The chair faced a window, which faced Narven Lake. Thereeko was an obese man, lacking a neck as his chins rolled over to his chest. He had small, pudgy hands that grasped a golden cane.

"Welcome, Fedradin, my cousin," said Thereeko. "Congratulations on winning the Gii Games! For the honor you have brought to the human race and the recognition Narven will no doubt receive, I would like to present you with this." A servant walked into the room, carrying what looked like a large shell. The lord proclaimed the item as, "A kappa shell shield."

Fedradin gasped. He took the shield in his arms, caressing it with his hands. As he did this, Thereeko sent the servant away.

"I had my servants shape it identically to your old shield," said Thereeko.

"My Lord, I cannot thank you enough for this." Fedradin could not believe it. Kappa shells could deflect spells and were practically unable to be scratched. Also, the shield came from a kappa, were extremely rare and hard to slay. It truly was an exceptional gift.

"Nonsense, 'tis the least I can do," said Thereeko. A moment of silence passed as Fedradin examined his new shield, and Thereeko seemed to be deep in thought. Finally, "Cousin, I fear that this moment of happiness must come to pass. I cannot have you stay in my city anymore."

"What? Why?"

"You're simply too dangerous, what with that new magical sword and now the title of the Greatest Warrior in Haxter. I'm sorry, there's just nothing I can do."

"Why?" Fedradin clutched the hilt of his sword, Baxcanador.

"You know, I can't have you running around my city! People will be scared!" "People?"

"Yes."

"Does 'people' include you?"

"I mean, I don't really think that-"

"Thereeko! The only reason you're banishing me is because of your own paranoia!"

"Please, I'm not banishing you, I'm respectfully asking you to leave my city and never return."

"So I can refuse?"

"I would prefer if you did what I asked you to do."

"Cousin, I'm not leaving."

"I always valued our relationship, Fedradin. If you leave now without me forcing you to, perhaps we could leave our cousinship untarnished."

"No, coz. I am not going to leave my home just because you fear me."

"You don't think I see what you're doing?" roared Thereeko. "Naming yourself *Prince* just to spite me! Fine. If you will not leave by your own free will, I will force you to leave. By noon tomorrow, if you are still in this city, I will have you ejected by my guards."

"That's preposterous."

"Is it? Try me, cousin."

"You know, maybe I will overthrow you. It wouldn't be hard to slay a fat, paranoid bastard such as yourself with my new sword." Fedradin smiled and took a step forwards.

"Guards!" shouted Thereeko. "Take this man away from here!" Fedradin pretended to draw his sword from its sheath as the guards grabbed him by the shoulders. "Cousin, I hate to do this."

"No, you don't. You're thoroughly enjoying it," murmured Fedradin.

Thereeko ignored him. "If you have not left this city by noon tomorrow, I shall put a price on your head. I don't care if you're the Greatest Warrior in Haxter. I'll have you killed just the same."

"You don't have the guts," spat Fedradin.

"Try me, cousin. Just try me."

Chapter 51
And Try Him He Did

FEDRADIN

FEDRADIN HAD CANCELED CLASS for the day, giving the Ridders a day's rest before they resumed. He had visited Misk, at least he had tried. When he arrived in the hospital wing, Misk was nowhere to be found. He tried asking the Scholars, but they didn't seem to know anything. The only person who seemed to know anything was a boy named Quynn. The boy was from New Swenvip, and he told Fedradin that one day Misk had disappeared.

Odd.

Fedradin was sitting in *Bits and Pieces*, his swordbelt buckled to his hip, his shield strapped to his back, and his pouch (all the items inside refilled) slung over his shoulder. This was the position he was in when the church bells tolled for noon. He heard the church bells ring twelve times from inside the city, and he chuckled to himself.

"Thereeko was bluffing now, wasn't he?" Fedradin said to the sprites trapped in glass jars. Only a few moments passed before he was contradicted.

"The lord wasn't bluffing!" shouted a voice as the door slammed open.

Fedradin was used to this by now. "Draslupp, you're invisible." Draslupp materialized in front of Fedradin's face.

"Lord Thereeko just put fifty thousand fellyers on your head! People are coming this way! They're going to kill you!"

"Calm down. I'm sure this is just an elaborate scheme to try to get me to leave."

Draslupp took a deep breath. "You hear that?" Fedradin could hear the din of people shouting in the distance. "All those poor farmers are desperate enough for some money that they would kill you."

Fedradin stood up. "Well, what do you want me to do? I can't turn invisible like you."

"You could hide. No one knows you're here."

"They'll never think to find me where I work," said Fedradin.

"No need for sarcasm. Why don't we fight back?"

"I will not kill innocent civilians."

"Far from innocent! They want to kill you!"

"But they don't! They just need money. None of them actually wants to kill me."

"Nonetheless, your death is a goal of all of them."

The noise from the people grew louder. "I need to escape, Draslupp."

"How? Out the window?"

"Actually, yes!" Fedradin walked over to the window that overlooked the lake, about forty feet below. "I can reach the lake from the window."

"The fall will surely kill you!"

"Unless-" At that moment, the door to the shop burst open. Axto stood in the doorway, wielding his halberd. His eyes widened when he saw Fedradin. Without missing a beat, Draslupp plucked an arrow from his quiver and shot Axto in the stomach. "Draslupp! He could have been trying to help me!"

"After all he's done to you, you think he will help you right now?"

"It's a possibility!"

"It's also a possibility that all these people are trying to give you presents for winning the Gii Games."

"Could they-"

"Fedradin!"

Axto's body in the doorway attracted the attention of other people. A man had come to the door. "Hey!" he exclaimed when he saw Fedradin.

Draslupp, again, had an arrow aimed at the man in a heartbeat. Fedradin quickly knocked Draslupp's bow to the side as Draslupp released the bowstring. The arrow flew through the air, hitting a shelf and knocking it over. The merchandise hit the floor, the more brittle of the merchandise shattering on impact.

"Stop shooting people!" scolded Fedradin.

"What else should I do?"

Before Fedradin could answer Draslupp, Fedradin had to pull himself and the Domer out of the way of a flying tomahawk. The tomahawk crashed into the shelf behind Fedradin, knocking it over. The shelf that was hit by the tomahawk, knocked over the shelf behind it, and so on and so forth, the process resembling dominoes.

The two had taken shelter behind Fedradin's counter.

"I need you to help me jump out the window," said Fedradin.

"How? The fall will-"

"Yes I know. But-" The man who had thrown his tomahawk came running around the corner, and Draslupp quickly shot an arrow into the man's stomach. Fedradin did not have time to chide Draslupp. "Break the window. Then, as I'm falling, shoot an arrow into the lake water, close to me."

"Why?"

"Trust me. Now do it quickly! More will come."

Draslupp turned invisible and ran over to the window, smashing it with the end of his bow. When he had destroyed the window enough for Fedradin to jump through without cutting himself on the broken glass, Fedradin ran forward and dove out the window.

DRASLUPP

As soon as Fedradin jumped, Draslupp went to shoot the arrow, and upon releasing the bowstring, Draslupp was jostled by another farmer, looking for Fedradin, but because Draslup was invisible, as well as the bow and arrow, the farmer crashed into Draslupp. The arrow's flight was disrupted because of this, and it flew in a different path than Draslupp wanted it to. The arrow was going towards Fedradin.

FEDRADIN

Fedradin was soaring through the air, the wind whipping through his hair. He saw the lake fast approaching, and he saw that he was on a path to strike the lake a safe distance from the shore. All was going to plan.

Except.

Where was the arrow? If Draslupp's arrow didn't break up the lake's surface, he would perish from the collision. In the distance, he thought he heard Draslupp yell out, so he turned his head to look back up at his store. What he saw was an arrow, about five feet away, flying straight at his head. Instinctively, he ducked, and the arrow passed over him, striking the lake.

Fedradin looked back down at the lake to see that he was a few feet away from the lake. He closed his eye as he entered the water, going so far in that he hit the bottom of the lake, though not hard enough to hurt himself.

Fedradin swam to the top of the lake and gasped for air. He immediately dove back under the water, worried that someone was going to spot him from above.

Thus began Prince Fedradin's life as an exile.

Chapter 52
Reunion, Once Again

FEDRADIN

FEDRDAIN WAS WALKING WEST, cold, tired, hungry and wet. He was about to lie down and sleep on the rocky ground, when something caught his eye.

Smoke was rising, and it wasn't in the direction of Narven. Fedradin made his way towards the smoke, his sword drawn. He was hoping that whatever was making the smoke was friendly.

He walked for about ten minutes, and by the time he was close enough to see the flames creating the smoke, it was dark. Near the fire, he could make out silhouettes moving around.

Fedradin moved towards the fire, when he accidently kicked a rock. It tumbled down the mountain slope, hitting other rocks on its way down. The silhouettes froze, afraid of the noise.

Before they fled, Fedradin quickly called out, "I come in peace!"

"Fedradin?" yelled back a voice. A familiar voice.

"Breetex? Can I ever get away from you?"

"Apparently not!" he called back. "Come join us!"

Fedradin walked to the fire. When he arrived, he could see Breetex and Aserax clearly. He saw that there was a deer on a spit, roasting over the fire.

"Are you hungry?" asked Fedradin, with typical sarcasasm.

"What? Why do you...Oh. Aserax is a good hunter and she likes venison," said Breetex.

"I love venison," said Aserax, smiling.

"I know," said Breetex. "You brought home a hundred pounds of it!"

"Not a hundred pounds."

"How would you know? I carried it!"

"The antlers aren't meat and they're really heavy-"

"Believe me, I know!"

"Hey!" said Fedradin. Breetex and Aserax stopped bickering. "I wanted to know if you were going to eat the entire deer."

"Oh, sure you can have some," said Breetex.

"Hold on a moment there," said Aserax. "I believe I am the one who hunted it."

"Are you planning on eating the entire deer?"

"No, but I do think I have a right to have input on who eats it."

"Well, then, your Highness, may I eat the deer?" asked Breetex, bowing.

"I don't know, how much are you planning to eat?" The argument went on for a while, so Fedradin decided to start eating. By the time the three went to sleep, all three were full with delicious venison.

Chapter 53
The Lair of the Berseron

FEDRADIN

BREETEX, ASERAX AND FEDRADIN awoke the next morning, right at the crack of dawn. The fire had burned itself out, the embers still glowing faintly. They ate some more of the deer, before discussing what the next day had in store for them.

"I don't see a reason not to stick together," said Breetex, biting into his venison.

"I don't want to have this prince following me around," said Aserax. "He's a fugitive!"

"We're fugitives, too," said Breetex.

"You more than me, Breetex, you more than me."

"If I may weigh in," said Fedradin. "I could get into much trouble for being around you as well."

"I suppose..." said Aserax. "But I still don't understand why he can't just buy us berth on a ship to Osup."

"No one will take us, Aserax," said Breetex. "It would be worth a lot more for them to just turn us in to the elfish army."

"I'm sure smugglers would do it! Plus, Fedradin has a lot of money!" said Aserax.

"You're willing to trust smugglers with carting us to Osup? They would take our money and turn us in!"

"My money we're talking about," Fedradin chimed in. The dwarf and elf ignored him.

"What about a commercial ship?" asked Aserax.

"We'd be caught by someone trying to play hero. They would turn us in."

"What about-"

"If I may interrupt," said Fedradin. "I don't think getting to Osup or Stentor or Mazlek is a feasible task. I say we should all head out to the Mendelgar Forest and make a life there."

"So you're just giving up?" asked Aserax.

"No more than you are by trying escape to Osup."

The three argued for a little bit longer, but it became clear that Fedradin's idea was their best and only option. Within a few minutes they packed up their few belongings and started off in the direction of the Mendelgar Forest.

They walked all day, only stopping for lunch -which Aserax hunted— at noon. When night fell, they made camp in a clearing by the side of a cliff face. They lit a fire and ate the remainder of the two rabbits they Aserax killed for lunch earlier and were about to fall asleep when it started to rain. As night descended, the rain turned to snow.

The three decided to look for a more sheltered place, when Fedradin noticed a small hole in the side of the cliff face. He walked over to the hole and peered inside. He saw that it was almost a type of slide, about four feet in diameter, going down into the depths of the cliff. Breetex and Aserax walked over to him.

"Do you think it's safe?" asked Aserax.

"I can't see why not," said Fedradin.

"Famous last words," scoffed Breetex.

"Why do you think it unsafe?" asked Fedradin.

"It's clearly a lair of some sort," said Breetex.

"I don't recognize it as a lair of any monster I know," said Fedradin.

"What about monsters you don't know?" asked Aserax.

"I'm an expert on monsters. I've read a book cover-to-cover-"

"I've read a book on mushroom eating. Does that make me an expert?" said Aserax, who picked a mushroom from the ground.

"I sure as hell hope not. You just pulled up a poisonous one," said Fedradin.

"My point exactly!" said Aserax.

"Fine, but I still don't think it's a lair."

"What else could it be?" asked Breetex.

"An abandoned mine?" said Fedradin.

"In that shape? It's obviously a lair!" Before Fedradin could respond to Breetex, he was pushed into the hole by something, something that wasn't Breetex or Aserax. He slid down the tunnel, trying desperately to see what he was fighting. All he could make out was a vague silhouette.

The tunnel opened up into a chamber. The monster crawled on top of Fedradin, so he threw it off of him, sliding the monster across the floor of the chamber. Fedradin drew Baxcanador, and the sword immediately started giving off light. The sudden light made Fedradin almost drop the sword, since it was so unexpected.

He distantly heard Breetex's call, "It's a lair!"

The light from his sword allowed him to see the monster. It looked vaguely like a rat, but much larger, at least six times the size of a normal rat, about seven feet long. Its back had bone plates on it, to act as armor. Its tail had a large ball on the end that most likely acted as a club. Its teeth stuck out of its mouth like a normal rat, but they had a fresh coating of blood.

Fedradin swung his sword, but the monster eluded him, darting off into the shadows. He followed the beast's movement with his sword, using it like a lantern, but he wasn't able to find the monster. He kept searching, until finally he felt something collide with his back. He fell forwards, sliding across the stone, his sword coming out of his hands. He looked back, and the light cast from his sword showed him a blurred figure of the creature. It was having trouble finding him, for it was not accustomed to the light. Still, the monster was adjusting to the light rapidly. He knew he had to gain the upper hand on the beast before it could see better than him, and he knew just how to do it.

He scrambled away from the monster and back towards his sword. He picked up the glowing weapon with his dominant right hand, while placing his left hand over an eye, so he could not see out of it. He then walked to the monster, guided by his sword, and swung Baxcanador at the monster. The monster could not see well, but it could see well enough to avoid the sword. Baxcanador hit the stone ground below sending up a spark.

Fedradin again swung his sword at the monster, and it dodged it once more. To an outsider, it may have seemed like Fedradin was failing in doing the job of killing the monster. However, he was accomplishing his goal. The monster had to focus on the light of the sword to track it down and evade it. Fedradin repeated the process, so that the monster spent much time looking at the light. Even the spark that gave off a little light from when he struck his blade on the ground was intentional.

Fedradin got into a pattern with the monster: find, swing, miss, repeat. He repeated this many, many times, for about half an hour. When finally his arm began to ache from swinging the heavy sword so many times, he decided it was time to finish off the creature once and for all.

Without him doing anything, the light from his sword went out. He quickly switched his left hand from his left eye, to his right. He was immediately able to see extremely well in the dark, for his left eye was already accustomed to the dark. The monster, however, was frozen in shock from the sudden light to dark difference. Fedradin knew that the monster's eyes would adjust to the dark fast, so he knew he had to make his move.

Fedradin ran forward and swung his sword down on the monster. Startled by the sound of him running, the monster had moved away from him slightly, so Baxcanador collided with the armor on its back and not its head. The monster recoiled from the attack and ran away. Fedradin pursued it, as it ran around in circles in the chamber.

He finally was able to inflict some damage on the monster. The point of his sword's blade nicked the side of the monster, and it squealed in pain. It started running again, but before it got too far, Fedradin was able to slice off one of its ears.

Instead of running away this time, the monster turned to face Fedradin. Most likely its eyes had finally adjusted to the darkness. Fedradin pulled his left hand off his right eye, so he could see slightly better, because his right eye had adjusted to the dark. The monster leapt towards him, quickly, and before Fedradin had a chance to swing his sword, the monster tackled him to the ground. As it tried to bite into him with its teeth, Fedradin picked it up and threw it across the chamber. The monster crashed into the stone wall, and before it could regain its composure, Fedradin ran forward to kill it. As he swung his sword, the monster swung its club-tail. Baxcanador collided with the monster's neck, cutting its head clean off. Before he could do anything, even react to the situation, he felt something collide with the back of his head.

He awoke, at a time that he did not know. He could figure out that the night had passed, for small amounts of sunlight trickled in from the tunnel. He looked around the cave, and saw something.

Three silhouettes stood in the chamber, two smaller ones, which he assumed were Aserax and Breetex, and one larger one. The larger figure was examining the body of the monster. Fedradin had no idea who the larger figure could be, and whether or not he was endangering Breetex's and Aserax's life. He had a pounding headache, but that didn't stop him from performing his next action.

Fedradin sprung from his prone position at the large figure. He grabbed whatever it was by the shoulders and pulled it to the ground. He reached for his dagger on his foot, but before he could pull it out, he felt a knife against his throat.

Chapter 54

The Necromancer

"THERE IS A REASON prophecies exist, Master!"

"Prophecies are guidelines, Oxlo."

"No, they are not. There are some things that cannot be changed, some things that fate controls. Destiny is one of those things, and the Prince is the one destined to find the Demon Callers, no one else."

"But we know where the Demon Callers are."

"We know where they are and how to get them, yes, that much is true."

"But?"

"But, the question is whether or not we *can* get them. The Prince is destined to be the only person able to."

"You bring up valid points, Oxlo, but I believe four Sages, including one Full-Sage, will be able to find the Demon Callers."

"All I'm trying to tell you is that we're tempting fate by doing this."

"Oxlo, I have tempted fate plenty of times and I am fine. The whole point of fate is so that it can be tempted."

"If you say so, Master," said Oxlo, who bowed and backed away. The Minions stood in the royal chambers of the castle of Bal-gastar. The Master still had the appearance of Flyc.

"Tawassa, step forth and tell me about what you have learned about the whereabouts of the crystals."

Tawassa stepped forth and said. "Well, as you know, the earth crystal is in the hands of Krile Wandhand. I have located the water crystal, and it is in the hands of a woman, actually. Her name is Neomie, and she is the sister of that wizard we have been tracking."

"Interesting," said the Master. "How about the air crystal?"

"In truth, I have absolutely no idea where it is."

"Fine, I suppose. Don't bother expending any effort in trying to find the *most powerful crystal*."

"I have been trying. I have been trying so-"

"No, no. I believe you," said the Master, semi-sarcastically. "And how has the search for a replacement Sage of Fire been going?" He was not, in fact, referring to replacing Tawassa. He was referring to giving the fire crystal that had once belonged to Flyc to another person to create another Fire Sage.

"Actually, I have three candidates. One is-" Tawassa was interrupted by a flash of smoke, coming from behind him. When the smoke cleared, two figures appeared. One was a very tall man, standing about seven feet high. He wore a long, black robe that came down to his ankles and up to his forearms. The robe appeared to be well used, for at the edges it was frayed and torn. Just the bones remained on his arms and legs. Around the figure's stomach was a belt, and on the belt human skulls were chained. The figure carried a large scythe, one farmers used for cutting wheat. The blood stains on the blade showed that the tool had not been used for its original purpose. His head looked like a normal, bald, human head but badly scarred. One scar went straight through his lifeless, left eye. Behind him cowered the second figure, an elf.

"Necromancer, what brings you to my humble abode?" asked the Master, bowing. All three Minions were already bowing.

"I have come here to warn you about a new power this 'Prince of Destiny,' now wields. He holds Baxcanador, the mightiest of the Seven Blades. This new weapon could easily mean the end of what we mean to start!" said the Necromancer.

"I have one of the Seven Blades," said the Master. "Why should we be worried?"

"I too have one of the Seven Blades, yet I am still worried! The reason is that the last two blades were the most powerful, and those are two blades we do not possess."

"Why are the last two blades so powerful?" asked the Master.

"What most people are unaware of is that the cyclopsi forged the first five blades in the fires of Mount Dacoil, just an ordinary mountain. When they saw the evils that the first five blades had done, they moved to Mount Kzit, where the dragon, Silvamore, who ruled Haxter before the humans, lived until he fled after the Conquest of Dragons. However, Silvamore's magic was so great, that he left traces of it in the fires of Mount Kzit. When the cyclopsi made their last two blades, it was with the magic fires. They created these two blades in order to kill the villains who controlled their other blades. They were never given the chance, as they were slaughtered by the villians that the last two blades were intended to kill. Baxcanador was given to the Fiefdom of Gii and it remained there up until the recent Gii Games. The other blade was never found, and its location is a mystery up until today."

"So you came here to give us a history lesson?" asked the Master.

"I came here to warn you."

"That you did."

"And to propose that you consider Nesmer to be the new Sage of Fire."

"Nesmer? Is he that craven elf who is hiding behind you?"

"Yes."

"Can he...you know."

"Yes. He is able."

"Why do you think this elf should be the Fire Sage?"

"He would gladly hunt down the Prince, for he lost to the Prince in the finals of the Gii Games."

"So he's responsible for Baxcanador falling into Fedradin's hands?"

"No, Master. It is fate that the blade went to Fedradin. You can't tempt-" said Oxlo quickly.

"Shut, up, Oxlo," said the Master, waving a palm. Suddenly, Oxlo doubled over, as if an invisible fist had hit him in the stomach.

"I am responsible," said Nesmer, trying to ignore Oxlo. "And I wish to right my wrong."

"Tawassa?" said the Master.

"Yes, Master?" said Tawassa.

"Are any of your candidates more suited for this job than Nesmer here?"

"No, sir," said Tawassa. "I believe Nesmer is the perfect candidate."

"Well, then," said the Master. "I bestow upon you the fire crystal." The master placed the necklace that held the crystal around Nesmer's neck. "Go find the Prince of Destiny and bring me his head."

Chapter 55
The Wizard and the Prince

FEDRADIN

"FEDRADIN, NO!" SHOUTED ASERAX. "His name is Kerwan. He's our friend!"

"I'm not the one holding the knife," said Fedradin, slowly getting off Kerwan. Fedradin noticed the end of a wand protruding from Kerwan's pocket.

"But you are the one who slew the berseron?" asked Kerwan, placing his knife back in its sheath.

"If you mean that...dire rat, I think it was, then, yes," said Fedradin.

"That 'dire rat,'" said Breetex, "has been stealing treasure from dwarfish and elfish cities for ages. Look at the size of its hoard!"

Fedradin looked around the chamber until he spotted something he had not seen the night before. A pile of treasure, full of gold and silver and gems, was packed into the back left corner of the room.

"Wow. How did it steal that much?" asked Fedradin. "And why haven't I heard of this monster before?"

"Well," said Kerwan. "You haven't heard of it before, because it is thought of as a particularly farfetched rumor made up by the elves and dwarves. It is able to steal that much because it is able to control particularly weak-minded creatures of the forest. It can, well, could, control the rats in the kitchens, for instance, and they would steal one coin at a time from the elfish or dwarfish treasury. Eventually, it was able to accumulate this much treasure." Kerwan gestured to the hoard.

"And how do you know so much about this creature?" inquired Fedradin.

"My master, Biggs, explained to me the origins and tales of all the Greats."

"What are the Greats?" asked Aserax.

"The Greats," replied Fedradin. "are the only-"

"Only *known*," interrupted Kerwan.

"-naturally magical creatures to inhabit the Base Plane," said Fedradin ignoring Kerwan, even though the wizard was right. "There are six-"

"Were seven," said Kerwan.

"-Greats: the Great Lizard, the Great Lion, the Great Falcon, the Great Shark, the Great Bear, and the Great Ape. I have now learned there was a Great Rat, too. There is another creature that often is thought of as a Great and that is the chinside, which has no magical abilities, but it is still the most deadly animal in Haxter," said Fedradin.

"What created the Greats?" asked Breetex.

"A great mystery," said Kerwan and Fedradin at the same time. Fedradin looked over at Kerwan.

"Where is your master now?" asked Fedradin.

"My guess would be decomposing in Swenvip Swamp, covered loosely by a layer of dirt," said Kerwan.

"So he was killed?" said Fedradin.

"By Krile Wandhand of Desert Wind."

"What was the disagreement?"

"Krile wanted a magic crystal we were carrying around, for some religious purpose."

"Hmm," said Fedradin. "What brought you to this cave?"

"I heard your two friends over there yelling at the tunnel," Kerwan said as he gestured towards the tunnel's opening.

"You were making quite a racket fighting the berseron," said Aserax.

"We were worried about you when the noise stopped, so we tried to get you to respond to us by yelling," said Breetex.

"Anyways, when I showed up," said Kerwan. "I thought I would go down into the tunnel and have a look around. When I saw the dead berseron, and you lying on the ground, I figured that you had killed the berseron and then fallen asleep."

"Actually, it-" started Fedradin.

"What?" asked Kerwan.

"Nothing. Your assumption is completely accurate."

"So, here we are," said Kerwan.

"Here we are," said Breetex.

"Here we are," said Aserax.

"Here we are," said Fedradin. The four looked around awkwardly for a moment or two. "What to do now..."

Chapter 56
Roger

ROGER

THE PAST FOUR YEARS had been quite eventful for the urchin who lived in the rafters of the castle of Bal-gastar. After the event in the kitchen, life had been rough on him, for his was a guilt-ridden, paranoid existance. There was not quite as much outrage as one might expect for the murder of a woman in the kitchens, so Roger was not hunted, at least not for long. He eventually got over the fact that he was a murderer, for he committed his crime for survival, and what was an urchin's main goal? To survive. He soon started to steal from the kitchens once more.

He often found himself reflecting on the moment when he had shot a beam of light at the woman and killed her instantly. He had tried to figure out how he had accomplished the task, by trying to kill the rats that sometimes crawled across the floor of his small room by pointing his palm at the rats and straining hard. His attempts proved unsuccessful until one day, the rat he was trying to kill bit his finger. Roger let out a cry of pain and a blue beam of light flew out of his palm. The beam collided with the rat, and it let out a squeak of pain. The rat rolled onto its side, dead.

With newfound vigor, Roger kept trying to kill rats. Again, he was not able to kill the rats, until finally when he had his palm pointed at a rat, he noticed a nail sticking out of a wall. Out of his palm flew a purple beam, and the rat was hit with a volley of spikes. In ran around in a circle, squealing in pain, until finally it fell over and died. After this event, he realized that whatever spell he created was directly related to whatever thought he was thinking when he tried to create the spell. Based on this observation, Roger started experimenting by thinking of various things as he tried to kill the rats. After a week, he had figured out a white spell, which cut the rat in half, a brown spell, which shocked the rat, and a yellow spell, which bound the rats. Thus ended Roger's experiments with the rats.

The second thing to happen to Roger was the return of his old childhood friend, Sgire. Roger had been sitting on the rooftops of Bal-gastar, eating a pilfered apple. He was watching the people pass below as they went about their business, ignorant to the boy above their heads. All was normal with the day, when something out of the ordinary happened.

"Roger? Roger, are you up there?" called a voice. Roger looked into the crowd of people, trying to pick out who had called out to him. He found someone that looked familiar...awfully familiar.

"Sgire? Is that you?" he replied. The girl, well, almost woman, was holding out an apple to him.

"Yes!" she cried. "I got you this."

"Thanks, but no thanks," said Roger, showing her the apple in his hand. "Why don't you come up here and join me?"

Sgire nodded and started scaling the wall. Roger reached a hand over the wall, and she took it, Roger pulling her onto the top of the roof. When she sat down beside him, he saw her in a whole new light. The last time he had seen Sgire had been when he was twelve, and he was sixteen now. He felt a whole new attraction to her that he had never felt before. Instead of the brother-sister type of love, he felt something different for her. Everything about her he liked: the way her black hair tumbled over her shoulders, the way her brown eyes intelligently viewed the world, her red lips, and just about everything else. He also noticed that she carried a sword on the side of her frilly, but dirty, dress.

"What brings you back here?" asked Roger.

"Well," said Sgire, biting into the apple she was holding. "I didn't like my aunt's estate very much."

"You can't just leave because of that reason. Can you?"

"Oh, she didn't let me go. I ran away."

"And you came back here?"

"No. I actually enrolled in the army."

"How did you get in? I didn't know they let in girls."

"They don't. I cut my hair really short and exchanged my dress for some pants. They bought my outfit for a while until..."

"Until?"

"Until...until I started developing some feminine characteristics."

"What? Oh, oh. I understand now," said Roger.

"When they noticed they sent me back to my aunt's, but when I got there, I heard some awful news. Roger, did you know my mother is dead?"

"What? That's terrible! When did it happen?"

"About three months after I left. By then I had already run away and they were unable to tell me."

Roger's heart missed a beat. Could it be...? "What did she die from?"

"She died in a kitchen accident."

Oh no, thought Roger. *I killed her mother.*

Sgire went on to tell Roger that she had come back to Balgastar after her aunt allowed her to leave and grieve. However, Sgire had no intentions of returning to the estate.

"I'm going to run away from here and try and leave this all behind. You should come with me, Roger!" He told her he'd think about it and returned to his pitiful room.

As Roger dithered over whether or not to go with her, he made yet another discovery. He had found a new section of the rafters he was able to get to, and if he got to the right spot, he could see down into the royal chambers.

He sat there for a few hours, watching Flyc move about, when in entered three men he had never seen before. Two looked normal, while one was covered in scales and had an odd looking tail. The men began to argue, and Roger could hear snippets of what they were arguing about. This went on for a while, until a tall man and a small elf entered the room in a puff of smoke. When Roger saw the man who entered, a half skeleton abomination, he quickly crawled to his room, where he waited for his adrenaline rush to wear off.

The next day, he tracked down Sgire, who was packing a small bag in the center of the city.

"Sgire, I have to show you something-" started Roger, who was interrupted by a man reading off a parchment scroll in the center of the square in which Roger and Sgire stood.

"Lord Uslo of Gii wishes me to inform you of the winner of the Gii Games. Prince Fedradin Quickblade of Narven," said the man, as a few people snickered at the mention of Narven, "has triumphed over all at the tournament and earned the title of the Greatest Warrior in Haxter."

"Anyways, last night I found out I could look into the royal chambers. I was looking in, and a lot of strange things happened."

"So?"

"So, I want you to come to the spot I was talking about with me tonight."

"Why?"

"I want to see if you can figure this out."

Chapter 57
The Temple

FEDRADIN

FEDRADIN, KERWAN, ASERAX AND Breetex had decided to go look for Krile Wandhand and extract revenge on him for killing Kerwan's master. Fedradin had heard of Desert Wind, and he knew they had built their base in Widow's Desert. They would have to travel west.

The four had escaped the chamber -after filling their pockets with gold from the berseron's hoard— by inching their way up the tunnel, pressing against the sides with their hands and feet. When they finally escaped, they started walking towards the desert, staying off the Road.

The group walked all day, finally making camp when darkness fell. Breetex and Kerwan lit a fire as Fedradin and Aserax went hunting: Aserax to kill something and Fedradin to carry it back to camp. Aserax moved silently through the woods, but Fedradin stepped on branches a few times, or rustled leaves, scaring off potential prey.

"Can you please be quiet?" snapped Aserax when Fedradin's sword knocked into the side of a tree, scaring off a young deer.

"I'm sorry," said Fedradin, "I'm not used to hunting." The two kept walking through the woods, until they arrived at a place where the shrubbery was so thick that they couldn't see through. Fedradin stepped forwards and used his sword to cut through the vegetation, until he could see through the bushes. What he saw on the other side amazed him.

"You have to see this," he called out to Aserax, who came over to him.

"What?"

"Look!" In front of them was a temple, constructed completely out of mossy stone. The temple was in a loose cone shape, with a room at the top. On the sides of the temple, large blocks created a form of large steps, too big for humans. In the center of each side was a stone staircase leading to the top of the temple.

Before either one could say a word, something emerged from the top room of the temple. It coiled around the temple, turning to face Fedradin when it had circled the entire temple. It was a gigantic snake, which appeared to be made out of bronze. It had large fangs in its mouth, which instead of dripping venom, dripped sparks of electricity.

"Are you going to fight it?" asked Aserax.

"If it attacks me," said Fedradin, but his sword and shield were already raised. "You need to go get Breetex and Kerwan." Aserax darted off, silent as a field mouse.

Fedradin looked back at the bronze snake. It was staring at him, looking as if it were not going to do anything, when it spit a large ball of the electricity at him. Fedradin ducked down beneath his kappa shell shield, and the electric ball bounced off of it.

The serpent, unhappy with the results of its attack, hissed. Fedradin ran forward to the temple, up the stairs, until he reached the serpent. The snake snapped at him with its metal fangs, missing him by inches as he jumped off the side of the stairs.

He landed on one of the large blocks, which constituted the side of the temple. The snake came down the stairs after him, and when it reached him, Fedradin swung his sword, the blade coming down on the top of the snake's head.

Instead of slicing through the metal of the snake's head like he had expected, the blade bounced off its head, leaving a dent in the snake's head. It reared back, spitting a ball of electricity at Fedradin. He used his shield to reflect the electric ball again, and it collided with the serpent. The serpent jerked about and retreated from Fedradin.

"Fedradin!" shouted Kerwan. Fedradin turned to see that all three of his accomplices had arrived at the scene.

"Kerwan, get me a pail of water!" shouted Fedradin.

"Why?"

"Just do it!" Kerwan ran off to get a pail of water, while Fedradin turned to fight the serpent. The serpent lunged forward, and Fedradin hit its head away with his shield. Fedradin quickly followed up with a swing of his sword to the side of its head. The blade, once again, only left a dent.

"Fedradin, I got the water!" shouted Kerwan. Fedradin ran down the stairs of the temple to retrieve the water Kerwan was holding. The water was contained in a hollowed out squash half.

"Interesting bucket," said Fedradin as he grabbed it from Kerwan. He ran back towards the serpent, which was sliding down the temple in pursuit of Fedradin. He took the squash, and he threw the water at the serpent's head. When the water hit the serpent, the bronze snake had a spasm and it crashed to the ground. Fedradin saw sparks shoot out of the side of the serpent's head, and it lay still.

"Fascinating," said Kerwan, "you used water to destroy the mechanical magic that makes it work."

"Exactly."

"Is it just me, or does someone else need to find out what's inside the room at the top of the temple?" said Aserax.

"I'll go with you," said Breetex.

"We're all going up there. There could be anything in that room," said Fedradin.

All four members of the group started walking up the stairs to the top of the temple, sidestepping the body of the bronze snake. They arrived at the room and entered into it, looking around. Inside, there was a layer of dirt, which had an impression shaped like the bronze snake in a coil-like form.

"It must have been dormant for a long time," observed Kerwan.

"That's not what caught my eye," said Fedradin. "Look in the center of the coil!" In the center of a coil, were two objects. One was silver in color, and it was half buried in the dirt. The other was a scroll. Aserax pulled the silver object out of the dirt.

"It looks like a compass," she said. "But it's not working." Fedradin looked at it and saw that the needle was spinning out of control.

"Let me try," he said. Fedradin took the compass in his hand, and immediately the needle pointed in a direction, not north, but a direction nonetheless. "The bronze snake must have been guarding this."

"Why? It doesn't work," said Breetex.

"It works for me," said Fedradin, showing the straight needle.

"But its not pointing north!" said Breetex.

"I wonder why," murmured Aserax. "Are we going to follow the compass?"

"What does the scroll say?" asked Kerwan.

Fedradin unraveled the scroll and read: *"This compass is the guide to a treasure beyond any imagination. Behind eight guardians lies this treasure, which some call 'Finadek's Treasure.' Follow the compass if you dare, to discover the most fantastic treasure in all of Haxter."* Fedradin looked up. "It's signed 'TF.'"

"It could be a trap," said Breetex.

"I don't think so," said Kerwan. "It was guarded by a bronze snake. Why would 'TF' go through all that trouble just to protect a trap?"

"I agree with Kerwan," said Fedradin. "I would like to follow the compass to the fabled 'Finadek's Treasure', but if Kerwan would rather go to the desert..."

"My desire for treasure outweighs my vengefulness. If you follow the compass, I will travel with you," said Kerwan.

"I guess it's decided," said Fedradin. "We'll follow the compass."

Chapter 58
The Two Spies

SGIRE AND ROGER CREPT to the spot Roger had found the previous day. There they looked down into the royal chambers, where Flyc sat on his throne facing a man wearing peasent garbs. Three knights stood, holding spears, in between Flyc and the peasant.

"I swear, my lord, yesterday I locked up a flock of two hundred sheep. This morning I had but seven!" pleaded the peasant.

"What do you want me to say? It seems the wolves have taken a liking to your sheep."

"Not wolves, your Excellency, it was the Wolf Riders!"

"Wolf Riders! The men who ride wolves the size of horses?"

"Yes, your Honor."

"And what prove do you have of this?" said Flyc, chuckling.

"What else could have taken nearly two hundred sheep?"

"Wolves, thiefs, barbarians? Certainly not Wolf Riders."

"No! Only Wolf Riders could have done this!"

"What I am supposed to do about Wolf Riders?"

"Launch an attack! Others have suffered loses like mine, but haven't had the courage to bring it to your attention."

The smile left Flyc's face. "I'm losing patience. Leave my chambers at once."

"What about my sheep?"

"Honestly, I don't give a rat's ass about your damn sheep. I need you to leave."

"But—"

"Guards! Kill this man."

The peasant was barely able to open his mouth to scream before three spears pierced his stomach, the tips poking out his back.

"I'm done with hearings for today," said Flyc. "Send the rest of them away."

A few minutes later, when the body was cleaned up, the guards turned to Flyc, their armor shimmered, and they materialized into two men and a strange abomination.

"Master, I cannot stress this enough to you. We must not kill the Prince!" said Oxlo.

Erch sighed and said, "Oxlo, the decision has been made. We have a Fire Sage and a Uäile that are already trying to track him down. We can't call them back now.

"However, since you keep claiming that this man is the 'Prince of Destiny', there is a good chance that fate will have our assassins fail. In case of this situation, we will have to have a head start on tracking down the first Demon Caller.

"However, if this man truly is the Prince of Destiny, we will fail to accomplish this goal and he alone will succeed. In case of this situation, I have a task for you, Oxlo.

"With Frin's help, I would like you to create an army. I don't give a damn what you create as long as it can fight well. We will use this army to seize the Demon Callers if we lose them to the Prince.

"Finally, to complete my plan, I will create a...distraction amidst the LNR, which will be blamed on the humans, so the Prince will not be able to rally an army, in case he forsees what we are doing."

"And what are you going to do with the Demon Callers once we acquire them?" asked Frin.

"They are called Demon Callers, Frin, what do you expect me to do with them?"

ROGER

The men argued for a little while longer, but Roger was still turning over every word of Flyc's plan in his head. He had been able to hear the entire plan this time, for Flyc was speaking louder today. Roger was confused for Flyc referred to his race as 'the humans.' Anyways, Roger was more concerned about what Flyc was saying. What were the Demon Callers? What was the distraction he was going to create? And who was this prince they were trying to kill?

"Roger, we should go," whispered Sgire. The two backed out of the rafters and into the Roger's chamber. "What the hell was that?"

"I was hoping you could help me answer that question," said Roger.

"That can't be Emperor Flyc in there! Whatever that is, it wants to destroy...well, everything"

"That's why I need you to weigh in. We can't just sit back and let those men destroy Haxter."

"We need to find someone who can stop this evil plan, someone who is strong enough to kill all of those men."

"But who...?"

Sgire and Roger looked at each other. Simultaneously they said, "The Greatest Warrior of Haxter."

Chapter 59
The Cabin in the Woods

FEDRADIN

THE PARTY HAD WALKED in the direction of the compass, east, it turned out. They followed the needle for miles, until finally darkness started to fall. No one wanted to stop and make camp for the night, urged on by a strong sense of curiosity, so they continued. As the sky darkened, they found themselves in front of a cabin that was leaning on the side of a hill. Branches from the trees surrounding the cabin hung down over the clearing in which the hill and cabin existed. A deer on the side of the hill chewed on the sparse grass, as a slight drizzle began to come down.

Wait a moment, thought Fedradin. *I've been here before.*

Breetex walked forward, and the deer on the hill tried to run away, but its frail legs buckled underneath of it, and it collapsed to the ground, making, loud, threatening noises. Quickly, Breetex ran forward and slashed the deer's neck with his tomahawk. He beckoned for the others to follow, hissing, "Come on! This is where the needle points."

Aserax and Kerwan walked forward, but Fedradin was reluctant to follow, for he knew how this scene ended. When he did follow, he was shaking his head, trying to warn his counterparts of what was to come. Breetex, Kerwan and Aserax all made it onto the porch at the front of the cabin, when the door burst open. Three animals, which Fedradin could not make out, knocked Breetex, Kerwan and Aserax to the ground. Fedradin knew what happened next. Out of the door walked a figure, which appeared to be female. This was when Fedradin's dream always ended, so he had no idea what would happen next.

"Who goes there?" said the figure.

"We mean no harm!" shouted Fedradin.

"And yet you kill our friend the deer."

Our? "Is there someone else with you?" said Fedradin, trying to change the subject from the dead deer.

250

"Just me and my animals," replied the figure. "I merely wish to know what brings you to my front porch in the middle of the night."

"We are on a quest," announced Fedradin. "We are following a compass that we found guarded by a bronze snake in a strange temple."

"My animals have told me of this temple, but I always thought it to be hogwash. From what I've heard, the great beast that guards the temple is very strong. You must be a great warrior," said the figure. "Won't you come in? All of you. I've been quite lonely out here in the woods, and I wish to speak to humans."

The travelers entered into the dimly lit cabin, sitting down in one of the rooms. There were cushioned chairs facing a fire that on which they sat, as their host bustled to the kitchen to fetch some food for her guests. Fedradin could now see the woman in greater detail. She was a short woman, but still a good deal taller than Aserax and Breetex. She wore a grey, worn, hooded robe, which came down to her ankles, and on her feet were boots. The hood on the robe was over her head, which Fedradin had assumed was for the rain, but she had not taken it off since coming inside. The robe opened in the front to reveal the woman's tight black shirt. Fedradin saw black hair coming out the sides of the hood of the robe, and her cobalt eyes flicked back and forth as she moved about the kitchen. Her cheeks were slightly freckled, and her nose curved up just slightly. A ringmonkey, or lemur, from Mazlek, perched on her shoulder.

The animals that had tackled Breetex, Aserax and Kerwan were a flashdog, a catdragon, and a homunculus. The flashdog looked like a normal dog with yellow fur, but its ears were elongated. Fedradin also knew that the dog could teleport a few feet in any direction in a flash, hence its name. The catdragon looked like a miniature dragon, about the size of a large housecat. The homunculus looked identical to the one Fedradin had seen in Gii,

Those weren't the only animals in the small cabin. Fedradin saw a zaplizard, a small lizard that hummed with electricity; a naul, a winged monkey; and a brown zelt, a small bat with a shell that flew around the ceiling with the naul. Fedradin watched them for a few moments, until his strange hostess came back.

She was carrying a few platters of food, which she laid on a table in the center of the chairs. On one were fruits and vegetables cut up a placed around a white, creamy dip. Another had various slices of meat, while yet another had bread rolls. Fedradin also noticed her put a large dish full of scraps and a bowl full of water on the floor. The monsters came towards it and started eating. The lemur leapt down for the hostess's shoulder and grabbed a piece of mango.

"Thank you for this wonderful meal..." said Kerwan, his voice trailing off when he was unable to produce a name.

"Tiserae. My name is Tiserae." When Tiserae said this, Fedradin saw a fat creature that was in the kitchen lumber towards the food. It was green, roughly square in shape, with six arms, five eyes, and a huge mouth.

"No way!" exclaimed Fedradin. "How on earth did you manage to capture a zorne?"

"It was hard," said Tiserae. "but I have a talent for capturing and domesticating wild monsters."

"I can tell," said Fedradin.

"Yep, these aren't even my rarest pets," she said, gesturing around the room. "I have more that are in cages in another room. They just aren't as domestic as these ones are."

"I'd like to see them," said Fedradin.

"I'll show them to you after we finish eating," said Tiserae. "Though, first I want to hear about how you wound up at the temple."

The four went on to explain to her everything that happened, from the lair of the berseron, to the temple, to her cabin. By this time, the five sitting in the cabin had eaten all the food.

"I read about all these creatures, but I haven't seen have of them in the flesh."

"Read about them, like in *A Narv's Research*? I've dreamed of getting my hands on that for years."

"I would show it to you, but I left it back at Narven when I had to escape."

"Why did you have to escape?"

"Lord Thereeko exiled me, for he feared me."

"I was exiled, too. In a sense..."

"We're fugitives, too!" said Aserax, cheerily.

"Aserax!" exclaimed Breetex.

"Cut me a break," said Aserax. "She's a crazy, exiled lady that lives in the middle of the Mendelgar Woods. What's she going to do? Who's she going to tell?"

"I'm not crazy!" said Tiserae.

"Okay," said Aserax. "It's perfectly normal to live nowhere near anyone else and with a thousand monsters."

"It's not the life of my choice," said Tiserae, but she made no intentions of elaborating.

"Anyways," said Fedradin, desperately trying to change the subject. "You must be a good sorcerer, to have a homunculus and all."

"Yes. I do it in my shop."

"Your shop?" asked Kerwan. "And a room just for monsters? Where are all these rooms?"

"Right here in my cabin," Tiserae said cheerily. "It has four rooms, a kitchen, a sitting room, a monster kennel, and my shop. Out back I keep the larger monsters."

"Where do you sleep?"

"Not in here! I sleep in the trees like a bat."

"Of course," said Aserax. "You're definitely not crazy."

Chapter 60
Departure

KERWAN

THE GROUP OF TRAVELERS slept in the sitting room, though "sleeping" was a bit of an overstatement. With all the monsters wandering about the cabin, Kerwan could not sleep at all. Staring at the ceiling all night, Kerwan's eyes adjusted to the darkness well, so he looked around the room. He noticed something odd after a while: the rug by the fireplace had an indentation in it that looked exactly like Tiserae. Eventually, he drifted off, forgetting his observation.

When dawn finally broke, Kerwan used it as an excuse to get up and walk outside. He saw Tiserae, like promised, hanging upside down from a branch with her arms crossed. The lemur was draped over the branch, sleeping. Her hood was still on over her head, but there was a small gap in between the top of her head and the hood where Kerwan thought he could see something, so he walked over to Tiserae to pull back her hood. His hand was touching the fabric, when her eyes shot open.

Tiserae swung her legs that were wrapped around the branch, over the branch and over her body, so her body began to rotate, like she was doing a back flip. Her feet collided with the back of Kerwan's head, sending him flying forwards. He crashed to the ground, looking back, with his bronze knife suddenly in his hands. Tiserae faced him, two large, undulating blades sticking out of the sleeve of each arm from under her wrists. The lemur, woken suddenly, scrambled up Tiserae to her shoulder.

"Oh, it's just you, wizard," said Tiserae. "I thought that it was a...monster...or something."

"Sorry I woke you from your sleep."

"That's fine," said Tiserae, the blades retracting back into her sleeves.

"How do you do that?" asked Kerwan, observing the blades.

"With a device I invented in my shop," said Tiserae, pulling back the sleeve on her right arm. Kerwan saw a small contraption that was fastened on her forearm. Kerwan did not see many parts, but he did see a small ruby on it. The blade was underneath the device, pinned to Tiserae's forearm.

"How does it work?" asked Kerwan.

"I summoned some imps into the rubies on each device."

"Impressive."

"They're only second ring imps."

"Impressive nonetheless."

"All the others are asleep, I'm sure. I could show you my other inventions."

"I would love that." The two walked back to the cabin, going through the kitchen and into the shop. It was a large room with many tables cluttered with various objects. In the corner, there was a shooting range with a well-worn target. Tiserae then showed Kerwan a few inventions including: a contraption that shop ninja star-like objects at a high rate of speed. This was fastened to the top of the forearm with a trigger that was attached to the handle of the weapon. There was also a bow that split apart into two blades held together with the bowstring.

"The interesting thing about this bow," said Tiserae, "is that I wove fibers of nemean lion hair into the bowstring, so it cannot be broken by any blade. I also did that with my robe. Go ahead, shoot me with the bow. It will bounce off." Kerwan took her up on her challenge and he shot an arrow into her side, and as she said it would, the arrow bounced off.

Tiserae also showed him a knife that could shoot out of its handle, and still be attached by a retractable chain.

"Those are my best inventions," said Tiserae.

"They're fantastic. I can't believe you built all of them."

"It did take me a while," said Tiserae.

Kerwan took a breath, "How would you like to join us on our quest?" he blurted out.

"Your quest?"

"In the temple, we found a compass and scroll. It said that the compass would lead us to a treasure of epic proportions. Finadek's Treasure, if you've ever heard of that."

Tiserae looked around her cluttered room. "Why not? I'll have my homunculus feed the pets while I'm gone."

"Or you could bring a few with us..." said Kerwan.

"Really?"

"Sure!"

"Thank you, Kerwan. I have been so bored around here recently."

FEDRADIN

Fedradin awoke to Kerwan shaking him.

"Wake up," said Kerwan.

"What? Why?" asked Fedradin.

"Let's go. We need to keep going on our journey!"

"The needle pointed here. We need to stay here until we find out why it did."

"It pointed here so we could pick up Tiserae. The needle is pointing in a different direction now, look, see, it works for me!" Kerwan shoved the compass in Fedradin's face to prove his point. Sure enough, the needle was pointing in a slightly different direction.

Fedradin pushed the compass away from his face. "Why are you so eager?"

Kerwan looked around, "Look, I already invited Tiserae to come with us. She said yes, but if we don't leave soon, she might change her mind."

"You did what? We can't go about inviting people on this quest willy-nilly. Breetex, Aserax and I are all fugitives. We never know who might turn us in."

"What was the point of the compass bringing us here then changing directions? If we don't have her come with us, it might jeopardize whatever the mission is that the compass is leading us to."

"Let me see that," said Fedradin, grabbing the compass from Kerwan. He looked at the needle, but it he saw that it was pointing a slightly different way than when they had first received it. "Well I'll be damned."

"See?" said Kerwan.

"Why did it work for you and me, but not for Aserax?"

"Maybe it will now? But can I have your final decision on whether or not Tiserae can join us?"

"Sure, she can join us," said Fedradin, moving over to Aserax. He shook her awake.

"What do you want?" asked Aserax groggily.

256

"Can you try the compass again?" Aserax held the compass once more, and immediately the needle started to spin out of control. Fedradin took it from her, and the needle straightened out. Fedradin woke up Breetex next, allowing him to try the compass. Again, it started spinning. Finally, Fedradin took the compass to Tiserae, and when she held it, the needle spun, but not quite as fast as when Breetex or Aserax had held it.

As Fedradin tried to figure out the compass, Tiserae prepared breakfast and Breetex, Aserax and Kerwan packed their pitiful belongings. Tiserae decided against bringing monsters along with her, even though the decision had obviously been a painful one for her. She locked all of her monsters in the kennel, other than the homunculus, which had been put in charge of feeding the monsters. Fedradin followed her there, looking at the many creatures that were behind wooden bars. Tiserae then proceeded to the shop, were she picked up her detachable bow. She also threw a couple of her other inventions into a bag. She returned to the sitting room, where all of the others were sitting around eating the remainders of breakfast.

"Aserax, I want to give you something to prove I have a bit of sanity left after being cooped up in the woods all these years," said Tiserae.

"Why were you stuck in here for so long? And why can you leave now?" inquired Aserax.

"Unimportant," said Tiserae. "I want to present you with a bow I created. You can pull it apart by pressing the two buttons on the sides and pulling. You will get two separate blades, one at each end of the bow halves. They are connected with the bow string-"

"Which has nemean lion hair fibers in it!" exclaimed Kerwan.

"Thank you, Kerwan," said Tiserae. "Yes, the bowstring is almost unbreakable."

Aserax picked up the bow gently, examining it. She slowly pulled it apart, revealing two swords. She did a few practice swings with it.

"Wow. How did you make this?" asked Aserax incredulously.

"Much time and effort," replied Tiserae.

"And you're giving it to me?"

"If it will prove I'm not crazy," said Tiserae. "Then yes."

"I'll have to test it out later," said Aserax. "But I appreciate this. I guess you are, in fact, sane." With that, the group departed from the house, in the direction of the needle.

Chapter 61
Abominations

VASIRD

VASIRD DANGLED FROM THE noose, but he was not dying. He didn't even feel pain. Was he in fact dead? Was this heaven? Was it hell? The screams of terror as he tried to remove the bag from his head gave him a resounding 'no.'

Finally, Vasird was able to rip the bag off of his head with his clawed hands. He looked around the square as people started to run away in fear. Anyone who met his eyes was immediately turned into stone.

Vasird tried to claw through the rope holding him up, but before he could, the rope was cut, and he tumbled to the ground. The executioner, who had been standing on the platform, jumped down to ground, avoiding eye contact with Vasird. He swung his axe down onto Vasird's stomach. Yet, Vasird was not dead and he felt no pain. Other people came up to Vasird and chopped away at him with various weapons. Some inadvertently made eye contact with him and they turned to stone instantly. The men kept chopping and cutting until finally they had minced Vasird into many pieces. He had not yet died, even though only his head was in one piece. The men tried to break apart his head, but their swords and axes could not penetrate or leave any marks.

The lordling of Haneou walked forward, carefully avoiding eye contact, and wrapped a towel around Vasird's head. He then had someone carry the head down to the shores of the Vaad Sea, where they cast it into the seas from high on the cliffs. Vasird felt himself sink to the bottom of the ocean.

Thus ended the sad tale of Vasird. Or so they thought.

IRROTHURE

Irrothure had found himself in a cave. He saw a large imprint of the beast he turned into on the dust of the floor of the cave. He must have spent the night sleeping on the floor. He walked to the outside of the cave and looked around. The cave was on the side of a cliff overlooking the woods, which he assumed were still the

259

Mendelgar Woods. In the distance, the spires of the cathedral in Alta.

Good, he thought. *I'm not too far from home*. But did he want to be back at his log cabin, just so the monster inside of him could destroy it? Maybe his new ability was a sign that it was time to progress his life forwards. He could live in his cave, turning into the monster whenever it happened. He could question travelers who came close to him to try and find out what turned him into the monster he was now. If he ever did find out what caused it, he would crush it into the ground. He felt the transformation coming...

COID

Coid slashed the head off a goblin, which was trying to stand up, with his sword. The goblin's head tumbled down the slanted floor of the lair. In front of him, many goblins were bound together with chains forming three separate lines. Other, unchained goblins walked down the lines, holding their weapons menacingly, in case a chained goblin tried to escape.

"You are all my prisoners now," said Coid. "I have slain your leader with the greatest ease-"

"Lies!" shouted a chained goblin. "Our leader cannot be killed! Especially not by filth like you."

"Bring the spoken one forth," commanded Coid. Two unchained goblins walked forward, unchained the goblin and brought him to Coid, holding him by the arms. When they reached Coid, the goblins pushed the goblin to the floor. Coid looked down at the goblin, which was being held on the floor by blades. "You are quite right in saying I never killed your leader. Bring him forth!" Three goblins brought out a larger, fatter goblin, with an odd looking headdress. "Do you all recognize this goblin as your leader?" The goblins murmured their assent. "Good." With a stroke of his sword, Coid sliced off the head of the goblin. He grabbed it and picked it up, showing it to all the chained goblins. "Your leader is dead now! Each of you will now be asked to join me and my goblin army in the new goblin capital of Goblicoid. You will pledge your allegiance to us or suffer the worst consequences, starting with this goblin here."

Coid waved off the goblins pinning the goblin to the floor. They stepped back, and Coid pulled the goblin on the floor to its feet by the fat rolls on its neck.

"Do you pledge your allegiance to Goblicoid?" asked Coid.

"I rather die than join you," spat the goblin, in garbled Commonspeak.

"So be it," said Coid, then to the chained goblins. "Watch your comrade, goblins, as he is punished!" Coid stared into the eyes of the outspoken goblin, as two red beams flew out of Coid's eyes. The beams burned into the eyes of the goblin, burning them to ashes. The chained goblins gasped, some screaming in fright. The outspoken goblin shouted in pain, as Coid put a chain, connected to two different hooks, in the ceiling. He then stabbed the hook not in the ceiling through the outspoken goblin's right foot. The goblin screamed in pain. "You!" Coid pointed to a goblin with a whip. "Whip this goblin until he is dead!" The goblin with the whip started to whip the outspoken goblin harder and harder, until finally:

"I'll join! I pledge my allegiance to Goblicoid!" shouted the outspoken goblin.

"It's too late," said Coid. "You already made your decision." The goblin with the whip continued to whip the outspoken goblin until it was silent. "Who's next?" All the other goblins immediately pledged their allegiance to Goblicoid. "Excellent. Now, have these new members go to their treasury and take all the treasure back to Goblicoid. And unchain them, for heaven's sake!"

"No!" shouted a goblin. "I refuse to allow you to take the treasure!"

"Is that so?" said Coid, who ripped the hook out from the foot of the dead goblin and off the chain, and he threw it at the goblin which had refused, so that when it hit the stubborn goblin, it ripped the goblin in half. "Does anyone else have something to say?" The goblins proceeded to walk to their treasury and started carrying treasure back to Goblicoid, following a goblin that led them.

Coid oversaw the goblins carrying treasure, when one particular piece caught his eye. A sword was being carried by a small goblin. Coid grabbed the sword from the goblin. *Could it be?* thought Coid. He pulled the blade out of its sheath slightly and gasped. *Jurn.* It was one of the Seven Blades. Coid looked down at the cowering goblin, slashing its head from its shoulders. Coid turned the blade over and over, looking for a blemish that could tell him the sword was a fake. He could find no such blemish.

First his powers and now the sword. Nothing could stop him now.

Chapter 62
Lexinon

KERWAN

THE TRAVELERS HAD BEEN following the compass for two days when they found themselves in Lexinon, a small town inside the fiefdom of Gii.

"I sure hope this compass doesn't take us to Narven," said Fedradin, fearing the bounty on his head, as they entered into the fiefdom of Gii. The travelers walked farther into Gii, passing through a few small farms and inntowns here and there. Inntowns were towns that developed around inns off the Road that never really were marked on maps or given names, but could reach very large sizes. Finally they arrived at Lexinon.

"Do you think we should go in?" asked Breetex.

"I'm not going in. I'm an elfish princess! I'm sure everybody knows my face," said Aserax.

"Don't flatter yourself," replied Tiserae. "Though, I would not like to go into town either."

"Why?" asked Aserax.

"No reason."

"Even though I'm not particularly excited to go to a town close to where a bounty was placed on my head, we all need a change of clothes and a good meal," said Fedradin.

"I agree," said Kerwan.

"Why doesn't he go into town?" asked Breetex, pointing to Kerwan. "He could buy all the stuff we want."

"I don't have money," said Kerwan.

"I do!" said Fedradin. "I have twenty thousand fellyers worth of diamonds in my pouch."

"Isn't it heavy?" asked Tiserae.

"Yes! That is why we need to spend it. Are you opposed to going into Lexinon, Kerwan?"

"No, I guess it would be fine," said Kerwan. The travelers told Kerwan what to get, such as some clothes and good food. He then left for the city.

Lexinon wasn't very large, at least not compared to the cities in Swenvip. On the outskirts, there were small farms, giving way to the center of the city, which was just a market street in the center and housing developments on the side. Kerwan walked into the market street and began pursuing the various stands looking for what his partners had asked for, thinking about his bronze knife.

ASERAX

Meanwhile, Aserax tested out the new bow that Tiserae had given to her. She went out hunting with the bow, tracking a large deer. She finally caught up to it in a clearing, eating grass. Aserax pulled back the bowstring, aiming at the deer's head. The elf released the bowstring, the arrow flying perfectly straight, and it when straight through the deer's eye. Aserax dragged the deer back to the camp.

"What do you think of it?" asked Tiserae when Aserax returned.

"The arrow flies true," said Aserax. "This is a great bow. Thank you."

Kerwan arrived on the scene, loaded with clean clothes and baskets full of food.

"Come get it while it's hot!" The travelers proceeded to change clothes (except Tiserae) and cook the food that Kerwan brought. They ate hot food and drank ale flavored with stentspice late into the night, until they finally one by one, fell asleep.

Chapter 63

Narven

ROGER

SGIRE AND ROGER HAD set off in the direction of Narven as fast as possible. Neither one had fully realized how long the journey was to Narven, but even if both had known, neither would have cared. They both had no place to go, so running off to Narven to try to engage Haxter's most talented warrior had almost been just a good distraction.

It had taken them almost a month to cross through the Plains of Flyc, Swamp Swenvip, the Mendelgar Woods, and the Ozreek Mountains, but the two travelers finally arrived at Narven, then walked through the city to the walls of the Craggy Keep. Guards were stationed outside the portcullis.

"Halt," said the guard, raising a palm. "Name and business?"

"I'm Roger, and this here is my friend Sgire," said Roger.

"We seek entrance into the castle," added Sgire.

"Why do you wish to enter?" said the guard.

"We request to speak with Prince Fedradin," said Sgire.

"Prince Fedradin is not present in the castle currently."

"Do you know his whereabouts?" inquired Roger.

"Negative," said the guard.

"May we still enter the castle? We've been traveling for days now," said Sgire.

"You may not. There is plenty of space for you in Narven."

Defeated, Roger and Sgire retreated to Narven, where Roger took note of the city. It was an odd city, for pastures surrounded the outside of the main city. He saw a small building near the wall where he could hear the sounds of swords clashing together. Sgire and Roger walked up the path through the pastures, towards the city.

When they arrived in the "city" part of the city, they were not breath-taken, in fact, they were a bit disappointed. The main town of Narven was a collection dilapidated buildings clustered together around a market. Behind them, the Craggy Keep sat atop a hill, which overlooked Narven Lake. Roger saw a path that led up to a ledge on a mountain and over the city wall. On the ledge, there were a few various stores and shops.

"Where shall we stay for the night?" asked Sgire, looking around.

"I suspect an inn," said Roger.

"Do we have the money to pay for a room at an inn?" asked Sgire.

"I don't have money, of course," said Roger. "You have some, correct?"

"No, I'm as broke as you are. Maybe some innkeep will take pity on us?"

"And don't come back here, you lousy kids!" shouted the innkeep. He had actually picked both of them up by the collar of their shirts and thrown them out the door of his inn.

"That was the last inn in Narven," said Roger.

"I suppose we'll just have to sleep outside on the ground another night," said Sgire, disappointedly.

"Hey, I'm used to it," said Roger. "I've slept on stone floors for sixteen years." He had lived in his room as long as he could remember, with no recollection of who his parents were.

"You may be," said Sgire. "but I'm sick of sleeping on the ground! I miss my bed in Bal-gastar."

"Excuse me," said a man who walked up behind Sgire and tapped her on the shoulder. "Are you the two who were looking for Prince Fedradin earlier today?"

"Yes," said Roger. "Why do you ask?"

"I will give you lodgings. Just follow me back to my house," said the strange man.

Sgire, looked at the man with disgust. "My mother warned me about people like you. You're disgusting! I'm only sixteen."

"Oh, don't flatter yourself. Anyway, you have a sword and I am unarmed. Please, I can help you find Prince Fedradin," said the man.

"I think we should go with him," said Roger.

"He'll just lure us back into a corner alley and-"

"I don't really care, Sgire. I'm an urchin. I've been an urchin for sixteen years! I trust my instincts, and my instincts tell me to trust this man. I'm going to go back to his place and sleep in my very first bed. I don't care if you follow me." With that, Roger turned around and started told the man to start walking. The two left, the man slightly confused at what had just happened.

Sgire held her ground for a moment or two, but Roger and the man were about to pass out of her sight. With a sigh of exasperation, Sgire ran after them, into the darkness of the night.

Chapter 64
The Village

FEDRADIN

"GREAT," SAID FEDRADIN. HE checked his compass for the umpteenth time to see if they were following it correctly.

"What's wrong?" asked Tiserae.

"The compass is telling us to go into Narven," replied Fedradin. "The fief where I'm a wanted man."

"We have to follow the compass," said Kerwan, unhelpfully.

"I guess so," said Fedradin. "But we'll have to be careful." The travelers started walking through the Ozreek Mountains, hiding whenever a shepherd came down the path towards them. After a while, the path curved to the right, while the compass told them to go straight, and so they began their trek across the rocky slopes. Eventually, they found themselves in a small village, nestled into the side of the mountain.

About ten makeshift huts circled around one log building. Each hut was built out of small stones, with a wooden door. The roof was made out of thatched branches. Fedradin could make out a few people, mostly elder looking men bustling from building to building, going about their business with seriousness.

"Hello!" shouted Fedradin. One elder, who was on his way to the central log building, looked up frightened and darted quickly into a hut.

"It's okay," Fedradin heard another elder yell from inside the log building. "That's the Prince of Destiny." *What?* An elder walked out from log building. He had dark skin and a long, grey beard, which dangled down to his waist and constituted the only hair on the man's head. His head was bald, and he carried a scroll in his right hand and a wooden staff in his left. "Welcome to our village! Please make yourselves at home."

An hour later, Fedradin, Breetex, Aserax, Kerwan and Tiserae all sat around a circle in chairs, watching the elder who had greeted them brew some tea in a kettle.

"I'm guessing you all have some questions on our operation out here," the elder stated, "So, I'll give you some background knowledge. My name is Qint. I am the leader of this organization, called Thunderflash."

"Thunderflash? Like James of Dire?" inquired Fedradin.

"He was one of the more famous members," said Qint, as he poured boiling water into a teapot, where he added some tealeaves and allowed it to steep. "He also was one of our more ambitious members. He created many things, mostly monsters."

"Why did he create so many monsters?" asked Fedradin. "I've always wondered."

Qint sighed, "I guess since you're the Prince of Destiny, I should tell you, it took you long enough to get here-"

"Hold on. Why do you keep calling me 'the Prince of Destiny'?"

"Well, of course you're the Prince of Destiny! You're the one who received the prophecy!"

"I received no prophecy," insisted Fedradin.

"You were a baby when you received it. Maybe your father destroyed it. I should have asked him before..."

"Before what? His suicide?"

"Heavens no! You actually believe your father would kill himself?" Qint chuckled. "You don't know much about your father do you?"

"He loved Relwasa dearly!" exclaimed Fedradin. "It drove him to death when she was burned up in that inferno!"

Qint burst out laughing, "Someone has certainly kept you out of the loop of your own history!"

Fedradin flushed with anger. "Who would tell me? I practically raised myself! Both my parents are dead."

"Son, I have so much to teach you," said Qint as he poured out the steeped tea into china cups. "To begin your story we must go back as far as our own history. You see, when the humans came from across the Silver Sea to Haxter, there were six powerful kings each on one of the six boats, all sailing for the newly discovered land. Whether they were fleeing or expanding is still a mysery today. There was King Narven, King Swenvip, King Gii, King Viven, King Borave, and King Bal-gastar. Each founded his own kingdom, and the kingdoms soon began to war over territory. As I'm sure you know, King Bal-gastar triumphed over his opponents and founded the Empire. Bal-gastar's brother, Lord Creo, wanting his own kingdom, split off and founded the city-state of Creopolis. Despite many attempts to conquer the city, King Creo -for that was what he was now- fended off the attacks by sheltering between the Mendelgar and Bal-gastar rivers. Years passed, and when King Creo III wanted more land, Emperor Flyc I built the Flyc Cannal to hold back Creo's army. He then placed three castles on each river junction, naming them Whitewater, West Water and East Water. The people of Creopolis have had to pay heavy taxes ever since on goods shipped down the rivers. It was around this time period, almost two hundred and fifty years ago, when your father was born.

"Your father was merely a boy when the Base Plane was attacked, which came soon after the founding of the Empire. The demons poured through the portals that were appearing everywhere, and the three main races that were in Haxter - the dwarves, elves and humans - fought back. Unfortunately, we were losing the battle. Badly.

"Then something out of the ordinary occurred. Four crystals shot out of Mount Sage in a large eruption. There was an air crystal, a fire crystal, an earth crystal, and a water crystal. When one wore them, he gained the ability to control the crystal's corresponding element. Your father found, and picked up, the fire crystal, and he used it to fight wave after wave of the demons. All would have been well if the other crystal holders had fought the demons likewise. Unfortunately, the other three turned against their fellow humans because the crystals made them power hungry. Your father, Zantor, decided then that he had to do something. One by one, Zantor killed off the evil crystal holders, Sages, they were called, the name of course stemming from the name of the volcano in which the crystals had formed. Every time he would kill a Sage, he took their crystal and fused it to his own. When Zantor had collected all four of the crystals, he was able to control all the elements. With reinvigorated power, he charged back into the war with the demons and fought them off, making them retreat back into the Chthonic Plane from whence they had come."

270

"Wait a minute!" announced Kerwan. "Driving back hordes of monsters! That sounds like what Rotnaz did when he drove back the goblins!"

"Think about that name, Kerwan," said Qint smugly.

"Rotnaz...Rotnaz. Hey! That's just Zantor backwards!"

Qint nodded and continued. "Before the demons could regroup and come back with more troops, Zantor knew he had to find a way to close the portals to the Chthonic Plane, so he assembled a group, which he named Thunderflash, to create a device that would shut down the portals to the Chthonic Plane. Of course I wasn't alive quite yet, but from what I have heard, Thunderflash was able to create three devices, which they called Demon Callers, that together could close all portals to the Chthonic Plane, in every plane, or open a massive one. No matter how hard they tried to rid the devices of the ability to open portals, the gods forbade them from isolating the Chthonic Plane completely. Thunderflash accepted these conditions and closed the portals to the Chthonic Plane, and they have remained closed to this day.

"Zantor wanted to destroy the Demon Callers immediately, but afraid of the portals opening again, Thunderflash decided against it. Instead, they devised a series of defenses to avoid anyone stumbling upon the Demon Callers.

"As you know, Sages have the ability to live for extended amounts of time, so Zantor continued living for many more years. Around thirty years later, though Zantor was now forty or fifty, he had not seemed to age much. During this time, though the portals to the Chthonic Plane were closed, a demon escaped to the Base Plane by some other means. The demon, of course, was the prophet, Erch.

"Erch persuaded some of the weaker-minded creatures in Haxter to join him in the fight to seize the Demon Callers. Zantor, upon finding out of Erch's evil plans, quickly assembled an army to combat Erch and his army. Once again, Zantor overcame Erch. Nothing was heard of from the either prophet for many years, until finally, Zantor met your mother, Relwasa. The two quickly fell madly in love. This was around the time I was born.

"One day, soon after *you* were born, the castle of Narven was attacked by three Sages, believed to be Erch's Minions. During the fire, Relwasa was killed. Your father wanted to scour Haxter looking for the men responsible for the death of his wife, but Thunderflash decided that revenge would skew his decisions. They sent him to Southern Glaciers, telling him to return when his revenge died down. He refused vehemently, so we had to use force to banish him to the glaciers. We know he is alive, and we have offered to bring him out of the glaciers, for it has been nigh on twenty years he has been down there. He refuses to come back though. He still thinks that the anger he has towards Erch will skew any decisions he may make while up here.

"Since then, I have become a senior member of Thunderflash."

"So, my father isn't dead?" said Fedradin.

Qint chuckled. "I know. I have given you a lot to take in for one night. Maybe you should come back tomorrow for the rest of the story..."

"No," said Fedradin. "You must tell me of the prophecy."

Qint said, "Well, I guess so. Around your birth, Thunderflash intercepted a prophecy on its way to you. We copied it, keeping one for ourselves and passing the other along to you. The prophecy says, well, I can show you!" Qint ran out of the building in the direction of the log building.

"So, *Prince of Destiny*," mocked Aserax.

"Oh, shush. We're all aware that this man is insane," said Fedradin.

"Almost as insane as Tiserae," said Aserax, nudging Tiserae.

"Hey! I thought we agreed!" said Tiserae.

"I'm kidding," said Aserax.

Fedradin ignored them. "This man cannot possibly be right about my past, about Haxter's past! Demons? This is insanity."

The group debated for a few more minutes, until finally Qint returned with a scroll.

"Sorry that took me so long," said Qint. "We have many prophecies filed in that room." Qint rolled out the scroll across the table. The scroll read:

> To lead. To fight. What must be done to find what is destined to be found. If he dies, never will they be found.

272

But what is to be found, one must wonder? Oh, yes. Hidden away for the power is too great. The power? You wonder again. In the sea of death, despair and misery is where you will wander.

"What? Is this about the Demon Callers?" asked Fedradin.

"Precisely," said Qint.

"And I'm supposed to find them?"

"Correct again!" said Qint.

"Wait!" announced Kerwan, "The compass, it directed us here. The note was signed by 'TF,' obviously Thunderflash." Qint nodded. "It said that it would lead us to a treasure beyond imagination..."

"Go on!" said Qint gleefully.

"And now you're telling us that we need to find the Demon Callers..."

"Yes..."

"So, Finadek's Treasure, this treasure beyond belief is the Demon Callers?"

"Precisely! The compass will guide you to the Demon Callers, Haxter's most valuable treasure."

"Why? Why can't I just leave them where they are?" asked Fedradin.

Qint's face grew serious. "You see, the Demon Callers are not just behind defenses. They are also *hidden* all over Haxter. The other day, one of us was kidnapped. He hasn't returned since then, so it is safe to assume he was tortured to death or killed. We can deduce that he revealed some, or possibly all, of the secrets of our defenses and their locations. With an enemy who is informed about the Demon Callers' location, we cannot rest easily. I actually need you to track down the Demon Callers and move them to a safer and more fortifiable location, specifically Slevee, the Keshnul capital."

"I'm sorry, Qint," said Fedradin. "but your story seems slightly..."

"Insane!" interjected Aserax. "You sound insane!"

"I know. I'm asking you to reevaluate everything you know about yourself and about Haxter," said Qint. "But you have to trust me."

"Why?" asked Fedradin.

"I'll show you something tomorrow to try to earn your trust. Your decision could either save or doom Haxter."

Chapter 65
The Invisible Boy

SGIRE

THE STRANGE MAN LED Roger and Sgire back to his dwelling, which was a small, one story house crammed in between two other houses, both identical to it. The three entered into the house, ducking under the small doorway.

"Draslupp! Come out! We have company," shouted the strange man. At that moment, a boy appeared in front of the two sixteen year olds. Roger and Sgire jumped back in fright from the sudden appearance.

"The name's Draslupp," said the boy, who was probably around seventeen years old. Draslupp extended his hand. Tentatively, Roger shook it.

"My name is Roger, and this here is my friend Sgire," said Roger.

"Pleasure to make your acquaintance," said Draslupp, tipping an imaginary hat towards Sgire.

"And my name is Dethroid," said the strange man. "But enough formalities. You folks came here looking for Prince Fedradin?"

"That is true," said Sgire.

"And why do you seek the prince?" asked Dethroid.

"That doesn't concern you," said Sgire.

"Why not?" asked Draslupp.

"We need to tell the prince something," said Roger looking at the two men across from him. "Something secret."

"It would be helpful to know what you want to tell Fedradin, but I guess it is unnecessary as well. We believe that we have tracked down the prince," said Dethroid.

"We know he left into the mountains when he was exiled," said Draslupp.

"He was exiled?" asked Sgire.

"Yes, by Lord Thereeko," said Dethroid. "Anyway, I have a theory that he went to a small village out in the mountains that I discovered a few years ago."

"We were going to check at that village for him, and I guess if you two would like to come along with us that would be fine," said Draslupp.

"I guess we should," said Sgire. "It's very urgent."

"But I have one comment," said Roger. "Where are those beds we were promised?"

Chapter 66
The Air Crystal

FEDRADIN

FEDRADIN WALKED OUT OF the hut he had slept in overnight. Tiserae was already up, watching the sunrise over the mountains, sitting on a log by a small fire. Fedradin noticed her hood was still up. "Beautiful sunrise isn't it?" said Tiserae, without turning around to see Fedradin.

"What, you have eyes in the back of your head or something?" asked Fedradin, sitting down on the log next to her.

"I've developed something of the sort," she replied.

The two sat quietly for a few more minutes. "You do realize your hood is still up, right?"

Tiserae touched her hood. "Yes, I do."

"Is your hair a mess?"

Tiserae laughed. "Something like that." Fedradin looked over at her, and only then did he truly note her beauty. The way her black hair caught the first rays of sunlight amazed him. How her eyes searched the horizon with hope and determination stunned him. He was about to open his mouth to make a comment on it, but he stopped short, instead, just sitting on the log, watching the sunrise.

"Fedradin! You've awakened!" said Qint. Fedradin stood up and turned to face Qint.

"Hello, Qint," said Fedradin.

"Now, of course you remember yesterday, when I promised you something to earn your trust?"

"Obviously."

"And you do remember what I told you yesterday about the crystals used by the Sages to control the elements?"

"Yes..."

Qint procured a small, white crystal from his pocket. "Shortly after Narven was attacked and your mother killed, Mount Sage erupted. Like during the Demon War, the Goblin Wars, and the Uäile rise to power-"

"Uäile?" asked Fedradin.

"We will get to that topic eventually," said Qint. "But, anyways, four crystals came out of Mount Sage when you were just a baby. One member of Thunderflash found this crystal, the air crystal in the Mendelgar Woods. We have no idea where the other three crystals wound up."

"Why didn't the person who found the air crystal just take it?"

"Have you heard of the Oracle?"

"No, but I can assume-" Fedradin was interrupted.

"The Oracle is a person who has the ability to view all the prophecies that are sent out by the gods. The Oracle also has additional insights into destinies and future events," said Qint. "We brought this crystal to the Oracle when we found it, and she told us that it belonged to you; however, before I bestow this crystal on you, I must caution you."

Fedradin looked at Qint, his hand extended to grab the crystal, which was attached to a loop of string, like a necklace. "What?"

"If you choose to use this crystal, you will live longer than any of your acquaintances. You will be nearly immortal; however, if you choose *not* to use the crystal, you may fail to obtain the Demon Callers and doom Haxter to demon rule for eternity."

"Well, then it's obvious what I must do." Fedradin put the necklace with the crystal around his neck. He stood there for a few seconds, expecting something to happen.

"How do I use this thing?" asked Fedradin.

"You think I was going to just give you the crystal and send you on your way? Come with me. I'll show you the ropes."

Five minutes later, Fedradin, with his crystal, and Qint, leaning heavily on his staff, stood in a field, not too far away from the village. A large rock sat on the center of the field.

"Alright, Fedradin, I want you to lift that rock," said Qint, gesturing to the boulder.

"How?"

"Just look at that rock, and think about lifting it with your mind," said Qint. Fedradin stared at the boulder, imaging the rock lifting up into the air. "It may help to point at it with your palm," suggested Qint. Fedradin lifted his left palm, straining with his mind and body strength. He strained for a while, but it seemed hopeless. Fedradin was about to lower his hand, when the air around the boulder seemed to condense, turning into a hazy fog. "Good! Now, try to lift the air around the boulder. It may help to use your palm to help control the air." Fedradin raised his palm, and the air around the boulder moved upwards, pulling the boulder into the air with it. Fedradin cried out in alarm, and the boulder fell out of the air.

"Wow!" said Fedradin.

"That was good," said Qint. "Now I want you to try to control the boulder and make it loop up in the air."

Fedradin once again stared at the boulder and raised his palm. The air condensed around the boulder, and Fedradin lifted his palm. The boulder started floating upwards, so Fedradin swung his arm around. The boulder made a loop-de-loop in the air.

"Good," said Qint, as Fedradin lowered the boulder to the ground. "You're getting the hang of it."

Fedradin looked at Qint. "Now what?" he asked.

"Now you need to practice." Qint continued to give Fedradin various challenges, such as time trials and stacking. They stopped at noon, when both became hungry and Fedradin grew tired. They walked back to camp, where they found four unexpected visitors.

Chapter 67
Across The Sea

TRUMBELL

HE KNEW THE DARK got all the men who were out after night fell. There was no way to navigate the forest in the unfathomable blackness of the night, made even darker by the overhanging canopies of the thick forest. It was for that reason that Trumbell decided to stay on Dragonsback Ridge, where he could just make out his surroundings from the weak moonlight that squirmed its way through the clouds.

Trumbell had not moved since Joloak left, all the while realizing how stupid he had been. With only a spear to protect him, how was he to survive the night? Evil things lived in these woods like giants and mngwas and so many things that would enjoy him as a midnight snack.

The night gales began, and Trumbell began to shiver. If he were to survive the night, he'd have to move to a lower location. The colonist began to pick his way down the ridge in the direction -he hoped— of Sequo, the colony on Qassar.

Noise. He froze in his tracks, his spear at the ready. He waited a few seconds, tensed and ready for action, when a cricket chirp startled him into almost dropping his spear. Slowly, he began to move again, deciding to get into the treeline to wait out the darkness.

Noise again, but this time, he knew for sure it wasn't a cricket. It was a chattering noise, almost insect-like, accompanied by a clacking of some sort. He began to move towards it, despite every fiber of his being telling him to turn and run. The sounds grew louder as he got closer, the chattering and the clacking, and his heart pounded while his curiousity burned.

Firelight lit up the hillside and Trumbell dove to the ground to avoid being seen. He glanced up to see that he had been behind a bush the whole time. Trumbell turned his head to see long, ant-like shadows dancing around as the fire crackled. But ants couldn't have made as much a din as this. And they couldn't light fires either.

Painfully slowly and quietly, Trumbell pulled apart the bush in front of him to see what they were. He pushed his head forwards, and there they were in plain sight. Two, human-sized insects, both holding spears were huddled around a fire. They had long, ant-like torsos, and six legs sprouting from a muscular abdomen. Trumbell gasped.

Immediately, both creatures turned their heads towards him, spears raised high in the air. He didn't need the advice to run.

ASH

The Spice Sultan paced the room. His soldiers had been gone a long time. Too long. Too long for going in, slaughtering the no-good orcs, taking control of the city, and coming back. That was the plan. For the Spice Sultan, things went according to plan.

The door slammed open, Ash turned to see Fane enter the room, with a man by his side. Fane walked over to Ash's desk and placed a disgusting orcish head on the desk. It was green, and looked like the head of a pig crossed with the head of a bat, with a squashed up snout, beady eyes and large, protruding ears.

"I found our friend F'ntok. We disagreed on whose city it was."

"By the gods, what happened to your arm?" Ash pointed to the bandage wrapped around Fane's shoulder, which was stained red from blood.

"A flesh wound. Anyway, that leads me to introducing you to my new friend here, Hunnex."

"You did this to Fane?" accused Ash, whipping out his sword.

"No! A bloody orcish archer did. Calm your nerves!"

"A pleasure to make your acquaintance," said Hunnex, mockingly while faking a curtsey to Ash.

"This man here is the reason you have F'ntok's head and not the other way around. In fact, he bandaged me up after my injury."

Ash looked Hunnex up and down. "Is there anything I can reward you with for your bravery?"

Hunnex stared back at Ash, his gaze unwavering. "Just leave the Orcslayer Guild alone."

There was a trumpet. A human trumpet, no an orcish one.

"Orcs!" came the shouts from the wall.

Fane pulled out his sword, Hunnex nocked an arrow, all before Ash could react to the calls. The three men -with Ash chasing after— arrived at the wall, where a horde of orcs stood, spears and shields in hands. An orc stepped forward and yelled up at the wall, in the language of Orc. Once it finished, Ash turned to Fane.

"It says that the orc we killed wasn't F'ntok. It was F'ntok's brother, and now he wants revenge."

GRENT

"I *hope* that you will go through with this, King Dunlock. I've been through a lot getting here," said Grent, who was drying himself. He had gone to the bathhouse in Dunlock's keep immediately after entering, for to get past the slaves, he had crawled through the sewers, after getting smuggled through West Water in a trading cog.

Dunlock had him meet him in the menagerie, which was where Grent found him now. Throughout the room, there were strange and exotic creatures chained or caged, captured in the foreign lands of Mazlek, Osup, Stentor, the Jade Isle, and even a few from Qassar. There were animals, such as a hippo, crocodile, julamus, gabol, kangaroo, manatee, ostrich, parrots and macaws, chinchillas, bison, zebra, moose, elephant, tiger, lion, dire wolf, boar, bears, gorillas, peacocks, seals, penguins, and leapords. Glass tanks full of fish, quetzals, and snakes rounded out the color spectrum in the room.

Ignoring Grent's jape, Dunlock responded with, "What do you see in this room?"

"I see a king with a passion for animals."

"Is that what you see?"

"Yes. What else would I see?"

"Look harder."

"I still see only many dangerous animals."

"True. But what I see, I see the world."

"How so?"

Dunlock scooped up a chinchilla from a pen. It squirmed and swung its squirrel-like tail. He soothed it by petting its gray fur.

"A chinchilla. From the Silver Sentinels. I probably saved it from hunters when I captured it."

"Just so it can die here."

"Better here, where it can eat and sleep, then on some merchant's coat. Do you not agree?" Grent was silent. Dunlock released the chinchilla back into its pen. He turned and walked a few paces to the bison chained to the wall. He gave it a stroke and turned back to Grent. "A bison. From the Boiling Island. We captured it and brought it back here." Dunlock pointed. "A julamus from Mazlek, a seal from Osup, an ostrich from Stentor, a gorilla from the Jade Isle, a moose from Rach in the Shapiro Archipelago. There's more, from all over the known world."

"Somewhat like your slaves."

"Exactly like my slaves. Slaves I can no longer use. But these animals are also like you, like Creopolis."

"They are trapped."

"Precisely. The only problem is that now, they are chinchillas." He picked up the creature by its tail to show Grent. The rodent squeaked. "But they have the ability to be crocodiles." Dunlock threw the chinchilla into the gaping maw of the crocodile, which snapped it up greedily.

"So what are you trying to say?" Dunlock smiled, but said nothing. He put a finger to his ear, gesturing to listen. The distant roar of slaves could be heard.

"I will let them earn their freedom," said Dunlock. "With an attack on Haxter, the LNR, and specifically, Whitewater."

Chapter 68
Unexpected Visitors

FEDRADIN

FEDRADIN RECOGNIZED DETHROID AND Draslupp as two of the visitors, but there were also two children that he did not know. Many people had come out of their huts and were now gathered around the unexpected -and seemingly unwelcome— company, such as Kerwan, Breetex, Aserax, Tiserae and a few elders.

"There you are, Fedradin!" said Dethroid. "We were wondering where you had run off to."

"Dethroid, how did you know I would be here?" inquired Fedradin, suspiciously.

"Just a hunch," the wizard replied.

"Why have you sought me out?" asked Fedradin.

"We wish to tell you that Lord Thereeko has repealed the bounty on your head."

"That is all? Why did you bring along so many people?" demanded Fedradin.

"Draslupp was looking for something to pass the time without your classes," said Dethroid. "And these two young lads wish to inform you of a top secret item, which they have not even shared with me." Fedradin searched the again and again for another visitor who he hoped was hiding.

"Where is Shah?" asked Fedradin. His hunger to learn the answer overpowered the curiosity to hear the "top secret" item the two teenagers wanted to tell him.

"She would have come with us, but she has gone to Borave to set up another Ridder's business there," said Draslupp.

"What a shame! I would have had a Lear copy my monster book for her."

"Fedradin, before she left, she took the book off your desk," said Dethroid.

"Really? Well, at least it's being put to good use," said Fedradin, who took a deep breath. "Now, what did you to want to say?" he asked, gesturing towards the two kids.

"What? Oh, well, um," stammered Roger.

"We would really like to tell you in private," said Sgire, helping out Roger.

"You can say it right here, thank you very much," said Fedradin.

"Fine," said Sgire. "Roger and I were in the castle of Balgastar, looking into the royal chambers when something odd happened."

"Emperor Flyc was talking with these three strange men," said Roger, "I think I heard him say two names: Frin and Oxlo. Flyc was telling them of some terrible plan, I think involving ripping apart the LNR, finding some things he called Demon Callers, and killing a man he referred to as the Prince of Destiny with a Fire Sage and a Uäile."

"Frin and Oxlo?" said Kerwan, from out of nowhere. "Two of the three Minions?"

"I assume," said Qint.

"There was a third man there, too," said Sgire.

"Tawassa?" said Kerwan.

"Probably."

"Hold on!" said Fedradin. "Why does Flyc want to kill me? Is he too threatened by my new powers?"

"Whatever this thing is," said Qint. "It can't possibly be Flyc."

"And why not?" asked Dethroid.

"Because Flyc is the Fire Sage! Something must have happened to him," said Qint. "Probably involving the Minions. Maybe they hypnotized him and stole the Fire Crystal."

"I don't think so," said Sgire. "The men referred to him as Master."

"Maybe the hypnosis made him delusional, and they are just humoring him," suggested Breetex.

"Or," said Dethroid. "A more frightening possibility is that Erch has risen to power again."

"And how do you know of Erch?" said Qint. "Thunderflash made sure to try to cover up his existence."

"Apparently you didn't do a good enough job," said Aserax.

"How did you cover it up?" asked Kerwan. "I know much about the past of Haxter, but I never heard of the 'Demon War' until just recently."

"It's a long story..." began Qint.

"Who is Erch?" asked Draslupp.

"That doesn't concern you," said Qint.

"Yes it does! All of us are in this together now, including Roger and Sgire," demanded Draslupp.

"Fine!" said Qint, who repeated the story of Erch and Zantor. "After the attack on the castle of Narven, no one knows what became of him. It is quite likely he has been able to switch bodies with Flyc since then. And how we covered it up, you ask? We started a new religion, claiming him prophet. We changed the name of the prophet, to something as simple as Zantor's name backwards. Then, we started the Goblin Wars, allowing Zantor to triumph. Afterwards, we hid Zantor away for a time, allowing people to forget Zantor completely, claiming that he ascended into the heavens. We had the bible tell of only one of his victories, the one at the Goblin Wars. Finally, we used Thunderflash members to conduct the masses, so as to make sure the Demon Wars were never mentioned. Slowly, over a few generations, the Demon War disappeared from history as well as 'Rotnaz's' true identity. "

"But why?" asked Breetex, uncomprehendingly.

"Because we knew there was a strong possibility that Erch would come back to power, and we didn't want the populous to be frightened, or the Demisio-following creatures to attack!" Silence followed because Qint had yelled his sentence with frustration and candor.

After a moment, "Is anyone concerned that a Fire Sage and a...what was it Roger?" said Fedradin.

"A Uäile," said Roger.

"A Uäile, thank you, are trying to kill me?" said Fedradin.

"*He's* the Prince of Destiny!" said Roger to Sgire.

"You're an Air Sage, you'll be able to fight them off, especially with Baxcanador," said Qint.

"'Right, a Fire Sage I can probably deal with, but what is a Uäile?" asked Fedradin.

286

"A Uäile," started Qint. "Is a creature that is believed to have fallen from the skies on the Large Rock as a tiny being. The Rock, of course, became the Kaastone, which is worshipped in Kaa. The being on the rock split apart into four separate pieces, and each one crawled to a different corner of Haxter. They each found a place to hide as they grew into large, black, cocoon-shaped oozes. All was well until from their cocoons they formed into human-shaped creatures and started terrorizing Haxter. At around this time Mount Sage erupted again, throwing four more crystals into the air, two of which were claimed by Frin and Oxlo. The two made a deal with the Uäile and started fighting with the creatures against the humans and the Air and Rock Sage. Though Frin and Oxlo killed the Air and Rock Sage, the humans still overpowered the Uäile, killing all of them except one, which Frin and Oxlo helped hide away somewhere in the heart of the Mendelgar Woods, where it is too dangerous to travel for most. The last Uäile is still alive today, and the Minions probably enlisted her to help them find and kill you."

"What became of the other Rock and Air crystal?" asked Tiserae.

"The Minions' Master, who is believed to be Erch, took them away from the two young Sages, who he had taken control of. He could not use the crystals, for he already possessed a Rock and Air crystal," said Qint.

"Wait!" said Kerwan. "My Master told me no Sage has ever been anything besides human!"

"Once again, Thunderflash has been trying to keep Erch and the demon attacks secret. Who was your Master?" asked Qint.

"Biggs," said Kerwan proudly. "Biggs was my Master."

"Biggs? Did I hear you correctly? Biggs is a senior member of Thunderflash!" said Qint.

"*Was*, I'm afraid," said Kerwan. "He was killed by Krile Wandhand, who now has control of the Rock Crystal."

"'Tis a shame," said Qint. "Biggs was a good man."

"Nonetheless, a dead one," said Kerwan.

"I have a question," said Breetex, trying to change the subject away from Biggs. "The crystals that have been shot out from Mount Sage, do they exist forever?"

"Good question," said Qint. "For the most part, yes. However, there are a few ways the crystals can disappear. One, if the crystals are thrown back into the fires of Mount Sage, they are destroyed. Two, if a Sage collects four crystals, all different kinds, and the Sage is killed, the crystals disappear with him."

"Or her!" said Aserax.

"I guess that's a possibility," said Qint.

"Roger, you forgot the army portion of Flyc's plan!" said Sgire, now remembering.

"An army?" asked Fedradin, alarmed.

"I'm afraid so," said Roger. "They are going to create an army to take the Demon Callers if you get them first."

"What are we going to do?" asked Aserax. "If we get the Demon Callers first, the army will forcibly take them from us. And if they get them first, their army will stop us from taking them."

There was a moment of silence, while everyone was thinking. "I think I have an idea," said Fedradin, finally. "Qint, how is the first Demon Caller hidden?"

"The Demon Callers are extremely powerful..."

"You will speak in front of all of us, Qint!" demanded Fedradin.

"Fine! Each of the Legendary Eight guards a rock, which all together can open a tomb to the first Demon Caller. You need the silver compass to guide you to each monster and finally to a tomb, which opens if you have all the rocks of the Legendary Eight."

"And are each of the Legendary Eight spread out over Haxter?"

"I assume so..." replied Qint.

"Then," said Fedradin, "while we look for the Legendary Eight, we shall try to enlist the help of the races to fight the army Erch is creating and guard the Callers."

Chapter 69
The Distraction

FLYC

THERE WAS AN LNR meeting in the recently built LNR building near the middle of Haxter, in the Plains of Flyc, named after the first Emperor Flyc to rule over the humans, after Sir Balgastar. Emperor Flyc III was present, along with every other leader of the other eight races. They were sitting around a table in a room, which had large windows all around it. The leaders were discussing some issue, something about goblins and an indestructible head. Flyc wasn't paying attention to the conversation so much as he was looking at the window, waiting for something.

That something finally arrived when figures clad in red came smashing through the windows on all sides of the room. Alarmed, the leaders all looked around at the intruders, four in total. The figures drew swords.

"Guards!" shouted Hulten Sharpaxe. Quickly, a figure ran forward and slashed Hulten down with its sword. The rest of the leaders then took action, drawing various weapons. Duztil, the chultra, swung his sword at one of the figures, who ducked the blow. Haze, the half celestial, pulled out a knife and fended off one of the figures, who had launched himself at her. Sadly King Westel of the animal cultures was not able to get his axe up in time as another stabbed him through the eye with a knife. Now, all the leaders had armed themselves, but the guards had not yet arrived.

Flyc stood in the back of the room, watching the figures and the leaders fight. It was an intense battle, Prince Poltax of the elves and the Wrethig of the Flayers leading the fight. He saw the Wrethig about to slash one of Flyc's figures down, so Flyc walked up and hit the Wrethig in the back of the head with the handle of his knife. The Wrethig fell forwards, as the figure delivered the finishing blow. Flyc looked around, to find that the figure that he had helped to kill the Wrethig was now the last figure left. Flyc quickly plunged his dagger into the figure's chest, for the leaders were now staring at him, and to do otherwise would be suspicious.

"We killed them all," said Flyc. "I wonder where the guards were?"

Duztil walked forward and pulled the red mask off one of the dead figures. "They're human.

Chapter 70
The Search Begins

FEDRADIN

SURE ENOUGH, THE COMPASS'S needle had switched directions, pointing west. Draslupp and Dethroid had gone home to Narven, as well as Roger and Sgire to Bal-gastar. Fedradin, Kerwan, Aserax, Breetex, Tiserae and Qint had departed the village the next morning in the direction of the needle. The members of Thunderflash had supplied each person a horse -and Aserax and Breetex a pony.

Fedradin was saddling his horse, when he was grabbed. He turned, hand on his sheath, to come face to face with a woman. Her long, yellow fingernails cut into his skin, her skin was badly burned and her face was covered in rags.

"Beware!" she rasped, pungent breath in his face. "Beware! Your journey has begun! You will be betrayed by the men you hold most dear." Fedradin tried to break away as she fell into a coughing fit. Instead of releasing him, she grabbed even harder. "The merging yak! The invisible relative! The patched icicle! The grim gatekeeper! The bargaining plant! The magical orphan! Trust none of them. Each one will betray you!" Fedradin tried harder to free himself, but her grip only tightened. Finally, he saw an arrow sprout from the back of her neck, and she slumped over, dead. Fedradin freed himself from her deathly embrace.

He saw Qint holding a bow. "That woman has been sleeping for years. You have power, Fedradin, more than you know."

"Woman rise from the grave to give me warnings. Lucky me."

"There's no harm in warnings. I've never seen a man die because he was warned about something."

"It's false warnings I'm concerned about."

"And false warnings you'll get. But you should never disregard anything, no matter if it comes from the lips of the Oracle or the lips of a comatose woman."

Fedradin scoffed and finished saddling his horse. He was shaken by the warning; it had been the same one from his dream at Gii.

"How are we to enlist the help of other races?" asked Qint, once they were galloping along. "We shouldn't tell them of the Demon Callers."

"I don't see how we can avoid the subject," said Fedradin. "We are asking them to submit an army to defend the Demon Callers."

"What about the army Erch raised?" asked Kerwan.

"No one has proof that such an army exists," said Breetex. "There's no solid, factual basis."

"We can figure this out later," said Fedradin. "The closest races to us right now are the Keshnul, dwarves and elves, and we're still in the Ozreek Mountains! We have plenty of time."

The party entered into the Mendelgar Woods, riding their horses through Gii. In a few days, as they exited Gii's boundaries, the walking started getting rough for their horses, with so many roots and loose rocks, the Road in the forest untamed. The group slowed their horses down, but as the trees grew denser and denser, the low hanging branches started to hit them in the face, and they had to get off and walk the horses. Finally, darkness fell. At least they assumed, for it was hard to tell through the thick layers of leaves overtop their heads.

"Should we make camp?" asked Tiserae.

"I guess so," said Fedradin. "We can't see anything anyway." Fedradin pulled out an enchanted torch from his pouch and lit it to look at the compass. The needle was spinning around in circles, like it had with Aserax. "No!"

"What happened?" asked Kerwan, who came over and looked at the compass. "Let me have a go."

"Here," said Fedradin, handing over the compass. Kerwan held it, but the needle was still spinning in a circle.

"Did it break?" asked Kerwan.

"No," said Qint. "It's trying to tell us we are in the right place to find the first of the Legendary Eight."

Chapter 71
A Ruined Reputation

FLYC

FLYC BARELY AVOIDED GETTING killed by the leaders of the nine races. He escaped to Bal-gastar, and like fire, word about what happened at the LNR building spread. Flyc had quickly locked himself in the castle, doubling the guard around it. There he stayed as his civilians found out about what had happened and began protesting outside the castle, demanding for a new emperor. The guards meticulously made sure to keep the angry humans away from the castle.

DESMOND

Meanwhile, all the way in Liola, there was a meeting of the dwarves.

"We can't fight two wars at once!" insisted the newly appointed King Desmond, slamming his fist on the mahogany desk.

"The humans killed King Hulten! Do you not wish to reciprocate?" inquired King Desmond's war adviser, Yentrical Dixie.

"Hulten was my father, Dixie. Of course I want to attack the humans!"

"Why don't you?" said Dixie. "I see it as a logical course of action!"

"It is far from that," announced Desmond. "We simply do not have the resources to pull soldiers and supplies from the war with the elves to march on Bal-gastar!"

"What if we go to the flayers...or animal cultures for help? Flyc killed their leaders as well."

"Nonsense. We could never hope to gain the support of other races."

"And why is that?"

"We and the elves are threatening to tear apart the LNR with this war. No one would risk sending troops to support either side."

"How could you say that we might ruin the LNR? Flyc killed three leaders of the races!"

"How do you not see it, Dixie? There is no proof that Flyc killed those men, but any fool who opens his eyes can see us fighting the elves. I will not have us be the race that brought the end of the LNR."

Chapter 72
Ambush Soup

FEDRADIN

THEY HAD SPENT THE entire day wandering through the woods looking for whatever monster they were supposed to find first. Unfortunately, their searches had been to no avail, for as the sun began to set, they came back to camp empty handed. Kerwan had the honor of cooking this particular night, so he decided to create a stew. He had sent Breetex and Aserax out to find meat to add to the stew, Qint and Tiserae out to look for spices to flavor his concoction, and Fedradin to find some root vegetables as Kerwan made the fire and fetched the water needed for a stew.

Fedradin dug around the forest for a while, but he had found no vegetables. He moved farther and farther away from camp, but kept coming up empty handed. He thought about the warning he had been given. He had no theories for who any of the men were, except for the invisible relative. He had a sinking feeling it was Draslupp.

Eventually, he realized that he was going too far, so he decided to begin making his way back to camp. As he turned around to start doing so, something strange happened. A black ooze started to well up from the ground, spreading out through the clearing in which he stood, coating the grass thinly.

"What in the name of..." Fedradin's voice trailed off as the ooze started coming back together, forming an attractive, young, blond woman. The ooze seemed to transform into skin tight, black clothes, which barely covered her.

"Hello, so-called 'Prince of Destiny,'" she said, walking forward. A quiver and bow seemed to grow from the ooze and form on her back and in her hand.

Fedradin eyed the bow, slowly sliding the kappa shell shield off his back and onto his forearm. "Hello..." replied Fedradin as his other hand slid to the hilt of his sword.

"You probably do not know who I am," said the woman, slowly approaching Fedradin. He backed away at an angle, so the two began circling each other.

"I do not," said Fedradin. "But you seem to know who I am. Have we met before?"

"Not in person," said the woman, slowly drawing a black arrow from her black quiver. "Some refer to me as Black Arrow, one of the four Uäile to have landed here on the Large Rock, as you humans call it. Fedradin drew his sword out slightly farther. "I have been sent here to kill you," Black Arrow continued, "by Erch and his minions."

"You can try," said Fedradin, as he raised his palm. The air condensed around the legs of the Uäile and Fedradin darted away from her. Black Arrow tried to follow him, but the binds around her legs tripped her, and Black Arrow fell to the ground. Fedradin felt a drain on his energy, so he released the binds. Black Arrow tried to stand up, but before she could do so, Fedradin pulled out Baxcanador and slashed at the woman. Black Arrow rolled to the side, narrowly avoiding the blade. She leapt to her feet, as Fedradin swung again, so Black Arrow caught the sword on her bow, the bow blocking the sword like a shield. Fedradin's sword bounced off the bow, and before he could bring it around to swing again, Black Arrow fired an arrow. Fedradin used his shield to block the arrow, and the arrow bounced off harmlessly.

The two faced each other again, both breathing heavily. Fedradin launched into a fury of attacks with his blade, Black Arrow dodging or blocking each individual swing. Finally, Fedradin slipped up by not bringing his blade around fast enough, and Black Arrow slammed him in the side of the face with her bow. Fedradin fell backwards, unable to get his shield or sword up as Black Arrow swung her bow twice more, quickly. The blows sent Fedradin crashing back into the dirt.

Black Arrow pinned his arms on the ground with her feet. She pulled out an arrow, nocked it and pulled back the bowstring.

"I'm sorry, Prince of Destiny," said Black Arrow. She released the arrow, as Fedradin planted his feet in her stomach. He pushed out with his legs sending the Uäile flying as the arrow flew off the bowstring, burying into the ground an inch above his head. Fedradin sprung to his feet and moved towards Black Arrow, who had dropped her bow. As the Uäile reached for the bow, Fedradin quickly slashed with his sword, the blade connecting with Black Arrow's neck. Her head fell to the ground.

Fedradin backed away, pleased with his work, when he noticed that her head was smiling. She gave him a wink, and she and her body melted down into the black ooze. Fedradin ran back to camp as fast as he could, not bothering to look for any more root vegetables.

Chapter 73

Disappointment

THE MINIONS HAD BEEN cooped up in the royal chambers for days, so all they could do was wait for either Black Arrow or the Necromancer to come and give them news. Finally, one day, something shook them from out of their doldrums. Out of the chimney came a black ooze, sneaking its way down to the Minions.

"I believe this is our friend Black Arrow," said Erch, as the ooze formed into the young woman.

"Indeed you are right," said Black Arrow, as she fully formed. "Though, sadly I bring bad news."

"Go on ahead, nothing you can tell me will upset me," said Erch.

"The compass is gone," said Black Arrow.

"What?" shouted Erch. "I retract my previous statement."

"And I failed to kill the Prince."

"No!" shouted Erch again. "How could you fail?"

"The Prince is more powerful than I imagined."

"See? He will beat us! He will destroy us all!" said Oxlo.

"Shut up," muttered Frin.

Erch ignored the two, "At least Nesmer, the Fire Sage, still might be able to kill the Prince."

"I can try again!" said Black Arrow.

"Nonsense, you have proved yourself unworthy," said Erch. "Instead, I want you to focus on getting the silver compass back from that Prince."

"Fine," said Black Arrow. "As you wish." She melted back down into an ooze and climbed back up the chimney of the royal chambers.

"Frin, Oxlo, step forward," said Erch. The two walked towards Erch. "Is my army ready?"

"Almost. We are assembling it now," said Frin.

"Perfect. That Prince has no idea what I have in store for him."

Chapter 74
The First of Eight

FEDRADIN

"WHY DIDN'T SHE DIE when I chopped her head off?" asked Fedradin.

"That was the secret that kept the humans from overpowering the Uäile for ages," said Qint. The entire group was walking through the forest, all armed and looking for one of the Legendary Eight. "The key to killing a Uäile is to chop off a key part of its body, where the brain of the creature that makes it up is kept. One kept its brain in its left eye, another in its right ear, and the last in its left hand."

"Where do you think this one keeps its brain?" asked Fedradin.

"It could be anywhere that's not attached to its head," said Qint.

The group continued to walk for another hour or so, until they came across something odd. There was a clearing in the woods, but it wasn't a natural clearing, as Fedradin could tell by the trampled grass and bracken and the stumps of trees.

"This was made by an animal," said Tiserae, as she investigated the clearing. "You can see where it made its nest." Tiserae gestured to a padded down area of leaves and ferns.

"What could possibly be that large?" said Aserax.

"What are we tracking again?" said Fedradin, his tone showing that he knew the answer. At that precise moment, a large monster jumped out from the trees, landing in the middle of its clearing, sending up a cloud of leaves and bracken. The monster looked primarily like a large lion, for it was covered in lion-like fur, it had a head like a lion and even a mane. However, the monster was stockier than a lion, and stood lower to the ground. At the ends of its legs, near its eagle-like talons, the lion fur gave way to crocodile resembling scales. Instead of a lion's tail, the monster had a large scorpion-like stinger. On its head, above and between its eyes, there was a rhinoceros-like horn and on its back, two large bat-like wings protruded.

299

Qint eyes glowed red. "The Chingow," he murmured, and his eyes went back to normal. Qint stumbled backwards, dazed.

"Qint, what happened?" exclaimed Kerwan.

He smiled. "I must have neglected to tell you," the old man replied. "A spell was placed on me when I was appointed head of Thunderflash."

"Should we be concered?" asked a confused Kerwan.

"No, no. It's perfectly safe...I hope," he said, grimacing. It appeared he was in a significant amount of pain.

Fedradin had already run forward to face the Chingow. He swung his sword in an arcing movement at the monster. The Chingow leapt away, narrowly avoiding the blade. It faced Fedradin, then sent its scorpion tail flying at him. Fedradin used his shield, and the tail bounced harmlessly off the turtle shell. Fedradin advanced, thrusting his sword at the Chingow. The tip of his sword hit the scales of the bottom of the monster's leg and it bounced off, just like the monster's tail had against his shield. Alarmed by the blow to its leg, the Chingow hit Fedradin with the back of its scaled foot, sending him crashing back into the leaves. The monster bounded over to him, raising its clawed foot for the finishing blow.

Before it was able to finish Fedradin, Aserax's arrow collided with its shoulder. The Chingow roared out in pain, and looked for its attacker. Quickly, Fedradin got to his feet and slashed it across the chest with his sword. The Chingow backed away and took to the air, flapping its wings. Fedradin returned to his group of comrades, never taking his eyes off the monster.

"I can shoot it down," announced Kerwan. He pulled out his wand and began firing spells at the monster. First Kerwan fired a black beam, which the Chingow eluded by rolling to the side. Kerwan shot another spell, a purple one. The beam split up into many different spikes, as the Chingow dropped underneath the spell. The Chingow was low to the ground now, no longer above the tree level, though it was still flying. The Chingow started to circle the clearing, coming towards the group. Kerwan started firing black spells in rapid succession, trying to stop the monster from getting near them; however, the black spells always managed to miss the Chingow, crashing into trees and exploding. The wooden debris from the trees went flying everywhere, one flaming branch nearly embedding itself in Tiserae's head. Aserax joined in with Kerwan, shooting arrows at the oncoming monster. Still, it was to no avail, as the Chingow got closer and closer to the group, its horn thirsting for blood.

"Everyone, get down!" yelled Fedradin, flattening himself on the ground, pulling Breetex and Kerwan down with him, Kerwan firing one last spell. Qint and Tiserae were smart enough to do the same, but Aserax decided to shoot one more arrow. Fedradin saw this and pulled her down, but on her way to the ground, the Chingow grabbed the back of her tunic and carried her off, taking to the skies. Kerwan leapt to his feet, aiming his wand at the monster.

"Don't!" shouted Breetex, knocking the wand from Kerwan's hand. "You could hit Aserax!"

Fedradin raised his palm, about to attempt to condense the air around the Chingow's wings, but he realized that Aserax could get hurt.

"Someone has to go up there!" said Tiserae.

"Or someone has to bring it down," said Fedradin.

"Aserax will get hurt!" insisted Breetex. Fedradin smiled. He looked around for anyway to get up to the monster. Finally he spotted a large tree that was flexible but still strong.

"Help me with this," said Fedradin. He walked over to the tree and climbed it. He grabbed the top of the tree and jumped to the ground, so that the tree bent backwards, facing the Chingow. Fedradin's feet were a few feet from the ground, so his accomplices began pulling on him, until finally he reached the ground. They then held the top of the tree to the ground. "Wait here. I'll bait it."

Fedradin ran out into the clearing, waving his arms to draw the attention of the Chingow. The monster noticed him and snarled, diving towards to grab him up. Fedradin scrambled backwards, as the monster approached.

"Now!" he yelled, dropping to the ground. The tree swung out, slapping the Chingow across the face, but it didn't let go of Aserax. Instead, it carried forwards, and hit Fedradin as he tried to stand up.

As he collided with the side of the Chingow, he felt its talons grabbing for him, so he grabbed its hair and climbed to its back.

It took to the air, angry, as Fedradin pulled Aserax from the clutches of its talons. Quickly, before the monster could throw Fedradin or Aserax off its back, the Prince of Destiny grabbed Aserax and threw her off the Chingow's back, lowering her to the ground with a cushion of air he created underneath her.

The Chingow tried to shake Fedradin off, so he plunged his dagger into its side and held on for dear life. The Chingow spun around and around, Fedradin just staying on by holding onto his knife. The Chingow then started to buck back and forth, once again Fedradin only staying on due to his knife. The monster tried valiantly for a few more minutes, until it finally decided to come back down to the ground.

The Chingow landed and started running around the clearing, trying to knock Fedradin off. When it was unsuccessful, it started running into the woods. Remembering what he had learned with the drane in the Gii Games, Fedradin pulled out Baxcanador and stuck it into the right side of the Chingow, for he was too far away to slit its throat. He pulled out his dagger from the center of the Chingow's back and stuck it in the left side of the monster.

He tested the theory he had developed with the drane by pushing his sword farther into the Chingow's side. The large monster let out a cry of pain and jerked to the left. Fedradin pulled out the sword slightly and pushed his dagger into its left side harder. The Chingow jerked to the right. Using what he had now discovered, Fedradin maneuvered the Chingow back into the clearing. He made the beast run circles around the outside of the clearing.

"Quick!" he shouted to his comrades. "Cut down a tree in front of the monster!" As he rode around, they started to cut at the base of a large tree. Finally, the tree was about to fall over.

"Fedradin! We're ready!" shouted Breetex. Fedradin nodded, and kept the Chingow going towards the tree. When he got close to the tree, he signaled for someone to push to the tree trunk. Kerwan pushed the tree and it fell forwards, towards the Chingow. The trunk smashed into the head of the Chingow, Fedradin leaping off the side of the monster to avoid getting hit by the rest of the tree as it collapsed.

Fedradin looked back at the Chingow, and it was clear that it was dead, for its head was crushed like a grape.

"We killed it!" shouted Aserax in victory.

"Way to go, Fedradin!" cheered Tiserae.

"Thanks," said Fedradin. "But we need to find the rock that it is guarding."

"It's right here," announced Kerwan who was looking at the crushed remains of the Chingow's head. "It seems like it kept the rock in its head." The wizard picked up the rock and showed it to the group.

"I hope that the compass works now," said Fedradin.

"Why don't I go back and get the compass?" said Kerwan. "If it does-"

"When it does," interrupted Qint.

Kerwan ignored him. "I'll bring it back, along with all our stuff, so we can just leave from here."

"Sure," said Fedradin, catching his breath and smiling. "That'd be great."

Chapter 75
The Weak Link

KERWAN

KERWAN WALKED BACK TO the camp where they had stored the silver compass. They had deemed it a good idea to store the compass there when they had set out in the morning, but now Kerwan realized that if anyone wanted to, they could easily swipe the compass. Their camp wasn't far enough off the Road for that not to be a possibility.

He arrived at camp, slightly anxious about whether or not the compass would be there when he arrived. The camp looked just how they left it, with all their stuff piled by a tree, including extra food, clothes, and Tiserae's bag of inventions. Kerwan moved over to the pile and rooted through it until he found the compass. He picked it up and it worked perfectly, pointing in another direction.

Reinvigorated, he concentrated, trying to send the bronze knife to his hand. He had tried this before, but to no avail. The knife simply wouldn't budge. Maybe he had imagined it. Maybe he just didn't remember pulling the knife. But so many times. With Nirrue, and Fedradin. It couldn't just be he was blacking out.

He saw the horses and ponies tethered to a tree, and he realized that he had forgotten to take into account how hard bringing the horses back to the group would be. He would have to go fetch the group and bring them back to the campsite to get their horses. The whole trip had been utterly pointless. He was about to set off when something odd happened.

"Hello there," came a voice from the woods.

Kerwan turned to see a beautiful, blond woman step out from the trees. She wore a skintight, black outfit that hardly covered her at all. "Hello," said Kerwan, backing away slowly. "Do I know you?"

"No," said the woman, walking even closer to Kerwan. "I'm just a lost traveler walking through the woods."

"Not on the Road?" She said nothing. "Do you need something?" asked Kerwan.

"No, I just haven't had the chance to talk to a human in a while," she replied, now close enough to touch Kerwan. That she did, stroking the jerkin Kerwan was wearing.

"Again, you'd have a chance to do that if you'd gone on the Road."

She ignored him again. "It's been such a long time since I've been anywhere near another human..."

"I have my eyes on another woman, so if you wouldn't mind talking your hands off me..."

"Oh, I don't see any other woman around here," said the woman, pulling Kerwan closer. "She would never know."

"Really. I don't feel comfortable with this-" Kerwan was cut off as she kissed him. He tried to push away, but she pulled him closer. Finally, he was able to break free. "Please, this isn't right-"

The woman grabbed his head and pulled him closer. She started to caress him, running her hands up and down his shirt. Kerwan was about to pry her hands off of him, but he froze, stunned by her beauty. He reached out to pull her close to him, but suddenly, before he knew it, she had planted a foot in his stomach and sent him flying.

"I got all I need," she said, flashing him the compass.

"The compass!" shouted Kerwan.

"It's amazing how easily a woman can manipulate a man these days," she said, as Kerwan fumbled around for his wand. "Looking for something?" she asked playfully, waving Kerwan's wand around like a baton.

"Vixen," he seethed, pulling out his warhammer.

A black quiver full of black arrows materialized on her back, and a black bow materialized in her hand. She nocked an arrow on the bow and drew back the bowstring. "Like I said," she said. "I have no use for you." She released the bowsting and it flew through the air towards Kerwan.

The wizard braced for death, closing his eyes and putting his warhammer in the air in a pitiful attempt to block the arrow. He heard the twang of another bowstring, and after a second, he realized he wasn't dead.

Kerwan opened his eyes and looked around. Embedded in a tree to the left of him was an arrow, pinning a black arrow against the tree. He saw that Aserax stood to his right, holding a bow.

"Not today," said Aserax menacingly. The woman was startled for a moment, but she quickly recovered, nocking another arrow and shooting it in the direction of Aserax. The elf dove to the side, avoiding the arrow.

FEDRADIN

Fedradin had come to the campsite, for he had realized that Kerwan would need help with the horses seconds after Kerwan left. The rest of the group came with him. When he had arrived on the scene, Fedradin was startled to find Black Arrow kissing Kerwan. He quickly found an explanation to the situation, when he noticed her hand sneaking into his pocket, pulling out the compass and Kerwan's wand.

Black Arrow had shot an arrow at Kerwan, but Aserax was a good enough shot to be able to intersect the arrow with another arrow and knock it off its path. Black Arrow returned Aserax's attack by shooting an arrow back at her. Luckily the Uäile missed.

Fedradin quickly tried to think of where Black Arrow might be keeping her brain. She probably wouldn't keep he brain where her brethren had, so Fedradin ruled out ears, fingers and toes. Where would Black Arrow keep her brain...

Then it struck him. Black *Arrow*. Could it possibly be that easy?

"We need to break her arrows," announced Fedradin.

"Why?" asked Qint.

"I think that is where she's keeping her brain," Fedradin replied. With that, he leapt towards Black Arrow, swinging his sword back and forth. The Uäile turned to look at him, but he hit her in the stomach with his elbow, knocking her down. He ripped off her quiver, trying to pull the quiver away. Black Arrow hit Fedradin in the side of the head with her bow, knocking him sideways off of her, dropping the quiver.

Black Arrow jumped on him, pinning him to the ground as sh grabbed back her quiver. Black Arrow rolled off of Fedradin,

306

swinging the quiver back onto her back, before Fedradin was able to react at all.

"Weakling," scoffed the Uäile. Before she could do anything else, Black Arrow was tackled by Breetex.

Fedradin jumped up, yelling, "The quiver! Get the quiver!" Breetex wrestled the quiver away from Black Arrow, jumping to his feet. Black Arrow shot out her hand, grabbing Breetex's ankle. He tripped, but he hurled the quiver away as far as he could before he collapsed.

Kerwan ran to the quiver, and was about to swing his warhammer down to crush all the arrows, when Black Arrow managed to tackle him from behind. Kerwan quickly rolled on top of the Uäile and pinned her arms to the ground. Fedradin ran up to the quiver, along with Breetex, Tiserae and Qint. They began to snap the arrows one by one until finally, only one remained. Fedradin picked it up.

"I hope this works," he said. He snapped the arrow over his knee, and immediately, a screeching sound could be heard. It was inhuman, to say the least, and it was coming from Black Arrow. Fedradin turned to see the Uäile slowly but surely shriveling up. Eventually, there was nothing left of her.

"I can't believe it," said Qint. "First the Chingow, then the final Uäile. You truly are the Prince of Destiny."

Chapter 76
Into the Mountains

FEDRADIN

THE GROUP CONTINUED TO follow the needle, which took them on a northern route. Fedradin realized that they were close to the Dwarfish and Elfish Kingdoms, so, along with going off the Road, he asked if they should try to enlist the help of the two races. Breetex and Aserax protested, for they wanted to procrastinate that particular mission for as long as possible. The group respected their wishes and continued walking.

They made camp, the night passing quite uneventfully. In the morning, they set off again. The woods had thinned out enough for them to ride their horses, so they saddled up and started riding. They traveled much faster on horseback, the trees thinning out more and more. Eventually they reached the edge of the forest, and entered into the Liola Mountains. Fedradin also realized that they had entered into the borders of the Keshnul Kingdom. They started to climb a mountain path, spiraling higher and higher into the air. As the scenery never changed, they began to worry that they had gotten lost, when along came a planeblood shepherd, urging his sheep down the mountain path, towards the good grazing down below.

"Hello, sir," called Fedradin. The planeblood looked up from what he was doing. "Can you tell us where this path leads?"

The planeblood looked quite disgruntled. "Why, of course, this path leads to Slevee! But what business could yous human scum possibly have there?"

"Excuse me?" asked Fedradin, angry with the planeblood.

"That's right! Yous humans had Sir Hulten Sharpaxe killed! Along with the Wrethig and King Westal."

"King Hulten!" cried Breetex. "What could have happened?"

"They's been saying four red men came from thems windows of the new, fancy LNR buildin.' Emp'r'r Flyc help 'em an' ev'ry thing."

"Oh gods," murmured Fedradin. "On the bright side, we've just found the way to convince the races to join our fight."

The group had carefully skirted Sleeve, deciding to recruit the help of the Keshnul after they had found the second of the Legendary Eight. The needle had taken them almost to the coast of Haxter, but it told them they were in the right place before they reached the Great Costal Cliffs. They started searching for another Legendary monster the next morning. They climbed mountains and walked down ridge lines, until finally, they could see the cliff face of a mountain about a half a mile away. Qint's eyes glowed red, and he announced that they were about to face the Yethregon.

As he spoke, two rams began butting heads on the cliff face, the sound echoing all around the mountains. A large monster stepped out from a cave on the cliff face. It grabbed the goats by the fur on their backs and ate them whole, one by one. The monster looked like a large yeti, with white fur, stained and matted by dirt, sweat and blood. It had an hairless, ape-like face, hands and feet, with sharp, bloody teeth, and two ram-like horns that protruded from the top of its head.

Fedradin was viewing the next of the Legendary Eight: the Yethregon.

Chapter 77
The Yethregon

FEDRADIN

FEDRADIN CLUNG TO THE cliff face with one hand. And that hand was slipping. He scrambled for a foot hold, but all that he accomplished was to send some pebbles tumbling down to the ground hundreds of feet below. Fedradin's hand slipped, and he began to fall. His descent, however, was stopped abruptly as Tiserae grabbed his wrist.

"Didn't think I was going to let you fall, now, did you?" asked Tiserae as she helped him back onto the ledge on which they were battling the Yethregon.

Before Fedradin could answer, he pulled Tiserae to the ground as a large boulder shattered into pieces on the rocky spot on which they had just been standing. As anyone could tell, things were not going well.

The battle was taking place on a few different ledges. Fedradin and Tiserae stood at the bottom ledge, closest to the cliff face. Another ledge worked its way in, above the bottom ledge. There were two more ledges, above and closer to the mountain. Above those two ledges, the Yethregon stood, a stack of boulders piled next to it. Behind it, there was its cave. Qint and Kerwan stood on the third ledge from the top, and Breetex and Aserax stood on the second. Fedradin and Tiserae climbed up to the third ledge from the top, joining Qint and Kerwan. A boulder flew through the air towards the group of four, so they scattered, the boulder shattering nearby.

"We have to find a way to bring the monster down!" announced Kerwan.

"How?" asked Fedradin.

"We need to knock it off the cliff," said Kerwan.

"Once again I ask, how," said Fedradin. The group scattered as another boulder smashed into the ground.

"I have some rope," said Tiserae. "We could trip it."

"Great idea," said Kerwan. "Pass me the rope." Tiserae pulled a surprisingly long coil of rope from her pocket and threw

310

it to him. He caught it, unraveling it almost immediately. "Fedradin, tie an end of this rope around your chest."

"Why?"

"You go around one side of the Yethregon, I go around the other side. We jump off the ledge and pull it down with us."

"That's your great idea?" asked Fedradin skeptically.

"You have a better one?" Fedradin tied the rope around his chest.

Once he finished, "Let's do this."

Kerwan turned to Qint and Tiserae. "We need you two, Breetex and Aserax to distract the Yethregon while we pull it down," said Kerwan. Qint nodded. Kerwan and Fedradin started to climb up the side of the mountain, passing Breetex and Aserax and avoiding boulders, though there were few, for the rest of the group was distracting the Yethregon, and it was focusing all its boulders on them.

Finally, Fedradin and Kerwan reached the top ledge were the Yethregon stood. They split up, each taking shelter behind the ledge on which the Yethregon stood. Kerwan held up three fingers, two fingers, one finger. Both men climbed the ledge and ran forwards as fast as they could, the rope catching around the Yethregon's legs. They tried to get as far back as possible, pulling against the tension of the rope. Finally, they heard the Yethregon fall forwards, and they expected the tension on the rope to cease, because the Yethregon was supposed to fall over the rope and down the cliff; however, it increased, and the two men were pulled back towards the cliff face. The rope must have been caught on the Yethregon.

Fedradin, sliding down the ledges turned to face the oncoming cliff. The Yethregon, when it had fallen forwards, had caught the rope on its leg. It was now dragging the two men down the cliff, bouncing them ruthlessly on the rocks. But that was not what concerned Fedradin.

The Yethregon was showing no sign of slowing down, and if it didn't, it would pull Fedradin and Kerwan off the cliff.

The Prince pulled out his sword, but he was bouncing too vigorously to be able to chop the rope safely. In fact, he dropped his sword entirely because of the bouncing. The Yethregon grew closer and closer to the cliff, and Fedradin saw from the corner of his eye that Kerwan had cut his end of the rope. The rope started to pull towards Fedradin without anything to counter Fedradin's weight at the other end, but it wouldn't clear the leg of the Yethregon before the monster fell off the cliff.

Fedradin tore at the knot on his chest, but it wouldn't come undone fast enough. When all seemed hopeless, he was saved from a gory death on the sharp rocks below. Breetex jumped on the rope in front of Fedradin and with a swing of his tomahawk, he cut the rope. Fedradin immediately pulled Breetex to the side, and the two rolled off the rope, as the Yethregon plunged to its doom.

"I sure hope the rock wasn't in its head," said Breetex, as the Yethregon slammed into the rocks below, splattering everywhere.

"If it was, we aren't getting it now," said Fedradin

"Maybe it's in the cave," said Kerwan.

"Good idea," said Tiserae.

The group started to climb up the ledges, towards the cave. They eventually reached it, and they entered into the cave. Inside, the floor was strewn with hay. In the center of the hay, there was a bare area, where it appeared the Yethregon had slept the night before. In that spot, lay a red rock, similar to the one that was inside the Chingow's head.

"Two down," said Fedradin, picking up the rock. "Six to go."

Chapter 78

A Not-So-Welcome Back

SGIRE

SGIRE AND ROGER RETURNED to Bal-gastar, though not with the sense of satisfaction that they had expected. Sgire hadn't realized it, but she now felt the longing to join the Prince's adventure.

Sgire was slightly upset at first over the idea of going back to Bal-gastar, but Roger had argued that they had no other place to go. They might as well stay put and at least attempt to monitor Flyc, otherwise known as Erch; however, when they arrived in Bal-gastar things were much different from when they had left.

The castle was built at the top of a cliff, overlooking Lake Bal-gastar. The rest of the city stretched out in front of the castle, winding its way down in to William's Meadows, where the pastures were. There was one major cobblestone street that wound its way up the hill to the castle. It was usually visible from far away, but today it was crowded with people, all angry civilians who were protesting. Roger and Sgire tried to make their way up the path, but there was absolutely no way to pass through.

Sgire tapped on the shoulder of one of the protesters. "What's happening?"

A haggard man turned around. "Where've ya been? Livin' unda a rock?" The man chuckled, as Sgire struggled for a response. "Our great emp'r'r, Flyc, up in that castle just sent s'm a our men to attack the LNR buildin.' The o'er races are now threat'n'in' to boot us out the LNR."

"Thank you so much sir," said Sgire. The man turned around and went back to shouting his profanity at Flyc.

Roger and Sgire backed up from the crowds. Roger said, "We need to get up to the castle."

"How?" asked Sgire. "We'll never get through the crowds."

"I'll show you how an urchin does it," said Roger. He grabbed Sgire's hand and pulled her over to one of the houses on the left side of the cobblestone road. Roger put his foot into a foothold, created by the gaps between two clay bricks that helped constitute the house. He climbed to the top of the roof in this fashion, where he looked back down at Sgire expectantly. Sgire hesitated for a moment or two.

"What? Are you scared?" taunted Roger.

"No!" said Sgire indignantly. She started to climb the side of the house, making good progress, until she slightly missed a foothold and slipped. She let out a cry of terror and started to fall. Before she could, Roger shot out a hand and grabbed her wrist. He pulled her up to the top of the roof, and she rolled onto the roof, laughing. Roger started laughing too, for a second, but they both grew serious fast. "What next?"

"Watch and learn," said Roger. He ran to the end of the roof. He leaped off the roof and landed on the adjacent roof, slightly up the hill, he looked back gesturing for Sgire to follow. The girl shrugged, running forward and propelling herself off one roof and onto another. She landed safely on the roof, looking around. To her right was the cobblestone road, filled with angry civilians. To her left were smaller roads, weaving in between houses. There were civilians in those roads too, though there weren't quite as many. Roger started running again, and Sgire chased him, jumping from house to house.

Finally, they arrived at the final house. The house was the closest to the castle, and from their vantage point, the two could see the whole dramatic scene. Guards, armed to the teeth, were preventing the crowds from getting to the castle, though they were still trying. On the castle walls, row upon row of archers stood, arrows nocked on their bowstrings. The crowds were shouting, protesting and cursing. It was a horrific scene that went on for hours, Roger and Sgire scarcely moving, so mesmerized by what was happening. Finally, as the sun started to descend in the west, a voice could be heard, bellowing from the castle, though the speaker remained unseen:

"Attention to all rebels," came Flyc's voice. "There will be a strict curfew tonight. Anyone caught out of doors in the next ten minutes shall be publicly executed tomorrow."

"We ain't goin' anywhere, you traitorous bastard!" shouted someone.

"Yeah!" echoed someone else. "You think your big voice is goin' scare us off?"

More and more voices started shouting insults and threats at Flyc.

"Enough!" Flyc said, silencing the crowds. "I *hate* to do this, but guards, show them we mean business." Each guard lifted their weapon.

ROGER

"He wouldn't dare," whispered Roger. The guards swung their weapons at the closest person to them. Archers loosed the arrow on their bowstrings. The screaming started. Pain. Terror. People started fleeing from the guards, leaving the dead behind.

Sgire cried out in terror and clutched Roger. Roger cradled her head as he watched a guard mercilessly finish off an injured man who tried to get to his feet. Roger watched the blood start to trickle down the cobblestone path, passing the few brave souls that dared to stand their ground. He felt a coursing anger pulse through his veins; the only time he had felt this way was when that woman had...guilt struck him as suddenly as lightening. Sgire's mother...

He lifted Sgire's head, the area around her eyes red, for she had been crying. "We should go, Sgire," said Roger.

"But those people..." said Sgire, breaking into tears again.

"They will be avenged, Sgire," said Roger, giving her shoulders a squeeze. "I will avenge them."

Chapter 79
Sleeve

FEDRADIN

THE GROUP RODE BACK into Sleeve, with the two rocks they had taken from the Legendary Eight. On the way, Qint reminded Fedradin that they could be honest, for the ruler of Sleeve, Princess Haze, knew about their plans and would help them out regardless.

They arrived in Sleeve at nightfall, so they decided to make camp outside the Keshnul capital and request audience with Haze in the morning. Before they went to sleep, Qint tapped Fedradin on the shoulder.

"I'm going to show you something new," said Qint.

"What is it?" asked Fedradin.

"It has to do with Baxcanador," replied Qint.

"My sword? What could it do?"

"You know that your sword is profoundly magical, right?"

"Yes, of course."

"Do you know how to access that magic?"

"Well...actually, I guess I don't."

"Alright then, I'll show you." The two walked away from the campsite. Qint took Baxcanador in his hands. "I never possessed one of these blades, but the Oracle told us that you would be carrying this when you arrived, so she taught me how to." Qint slashed back and forth with the sword, bringing it back to a level position. "The sword actually can respond to your thoughts and desires. If it senses a goal in your mind, it will do everything in its power to help you."

"Yes, I know that. I used that ability when I fought the Great Rat."

Qint looked up. "You have slain the Great Rat?"

"Yes."

Qint shrugged. "Interesting. How did you use the sword?"

"I made it glow."

Qint chuckled. "If that's your idea of using Baxcanador to its full extent, you've got another thing coming."

"Why?" asked Fedradin.

"I'll show you." Qint closed his eyes, and appeared to strain. After a moment or two, the elder disappeared into thin air.

"Holy..." exclaimed Fedradin. However, Qint almost immediately reappeared.

"The stronger your desire, the more easily it will help you," said Qint, passing the blade to Fedradin. "But for now, I want you to try and ignite the blade."

"How?"

"Want it. Desire it. *Need* it. Try to aim your thoughts towards how much you want your sword to catch fire."

Fedradin looked down at the blade, which looked quite ordinary from where he was looking at it. "Here goes nothing." Fedradin closed his eyes and thought. Thought about his want for the fire, thought about his desire for the fire, thought about his need for the fire. Slowly, the blade began to glow, like a dying ember.

"Picture the fire," said Qint. "Imagine a raging inferno."

Fedradin suddenly had a picture of the castle of Narven burning. He saw the fire consuming every last turret of the castle, leaving the charred remains of the rock in its wake. He saw his mother perishing in that fire, though possibly at the hands of one of the evil three men: Frin, Tawassa, and Oxlo. He was filled with a sensational rage, coursing through his entire body, from his forehead to his feet. He yelled out in anger, and Baxcanador ignited, shooting a thirty foot high flame into the air. Fedradin was startled, and he almost dropped the blade, the fire height diminishing greatly.

All was quiet for a few seconds, until Qint murmured, "You have some serious problems."

"Princess Haze will see you now," said announced a beautiful celestial girl. She led the group past several heavy oaken doors and into the royal chambers where Haze stood in a brilliant white gown.

"Hello, humans," said Haze. Her head was turned and she was looking out a large window at the Liola Mountains beyond. "What do you seek?"

"We seek help from your powerful race," said Fedradin, stepping forward. "As you know, there is reason to believe Erch has infiltrated the Human Empire."

"I am aware," said Haze, without turning around. "and that is why I forgive your race for the atrocity at the LNR many days ago."

"And we are grateful for that," said Fedradin bowing.

"Is this about the Demon Callers?" asked Haze, cutting the Prince off before he add any other apologies.

"In a manner of speaking, yes. We believe that Erch has created an army to seize the Demon Callers from us, if we ever track all three down."

"And what should I do with this information?"

"We may be in need of your troops to help us fight the army if the situation ever arises."

"If such an event occurs, my Keshnulian forces will be armed and ready to come to your assistance," agreed Haze.

"Thank you, Princess Haze," said Fedradin. "That is all we ask of you."

Chapter 80
Liola

BREETEX

ADMITTEDLY, BREETEX HAD NOT been thrilled about going to Liola, the dwarfish capital, but he knew that what had to be done had to be done; nonetheless, he had refused to enter the city. He would stay with Aserax safely outside the capital. He had offered to follow the needle of the compass, which now pointed in a new direction, west, but they had all decided that it was a bad idea for him and Aserax to go alone.

After a day of riding, the group, minus Breetex and Aserax, entered into the dwarfish capital.

KERWAN

Kerwan felt out of proportion in Liola, for it was sized for four or five feet tall dwarves. Whenever a dwarf passed by, Kerwan felt like a giant. The group, Qint, Kerwan, Fedradin, and Tiserae, were making their way to the castle in the center of the city, when they were arrested by the dwarfish guards.

"We just want to see your king!" said Tiserae.

"You know, that would be one hell of a lot easier if you damn humans hadn't killed him!" yelled one of the guards.

Another said, "Ignore him. We'll take you to see the king, but we'll have to escort you."

The dwarf guards led the group to castle, where one ran ahead to alert the king of the visitors. The dwarf came back, informing the other guards that the king would see them.

The group was led to the royal chambers of the castle of Liola, where the guards allowed them to enter, standing at the doors with their axes raised.

"Humans?" said the dwarf that stood at the end of the room. He was slightly taller than the other dwarves, possibly standing four and a half feet tall. He had a dirty blond beard, and two intelligent blue eyes. "You sure have some courage coming here after what happened at the LNR building."

"Please, King..." said Fedradin, his voice trailing off as he failed to come up with a name.

"Desmond."

"Well then, King Desmond, we wish to gain your assistance in the task of-"

"Throw them out," said Desmond, before Fedradin could finish his sentence. "Get them out now."

The guards walked out from the oaken door. "Wait!" yelled Fedradin, the guards hesitating. "We believe that Emperor Flyc is putting together an army."

A guard grabbed each member of the group and was about to pull them out of the chamber. "Wait," said Desmond. "Leave them." The guards unhanded them and moved back to the door. "Go on about your army."

"We believe that Flyc is creating an army," said Fedradin. "We don't know what for, but he already killed off Sir Hulten Sharpaxe. There is clearly no limit to his actions."

"And you wish my forces to..."

"To be prepared to rise up against Flyc's army," finished Fedradin.

Desmond thought for a moment. "I'm sorry. First of all, I already discussed this with one of my yentricals. We are in a heated war with the elves right now, as I'm sure you know, and we cannot afford to pull troops out of that battle to fight an enemy that might not yet exist. I'm sorry, but please show yourselves out of my kingdom."

Chapter 81
Three

FEDRADIN

FEDRADIN DECIDED NOT EVEN to bother going anywhere near the borders of the elfish kingdom. Prince Poltax was bound to find out about Fedradin's entrance into the kingdom, and that Prince wanted Fedradin's head on a stick. And within the elfish boundaries would be the perfect place to get it.

Fedradin also avoided the elfish kingdom for unselfish reasons. Breetex and Aserax dreaded going into the boundaries where they could both be captured, so he respected their wishes. He also knew that it would be futile trying to enlist the help of the elves, so he skirted the empire.

Instead, they continued to follow the compass in a general westerly fashion. They passed by the Floating Quoll Mountains and entered into the Cientile Plains. This was when the compass started spinning, telling them they were in the right place. They made camp for the night, waiting until morning to pursue the third of the Legendary Eight.

The next morning, Fedradin arose bright and early. He stuck his sword in his sheath and slung his kappa shell shield over his back. He adjusted his pouch until it was at the right place. He then sat on the ground, watching the sunrise, waiting for the rest of the group to get up.

He heard someone walk over, and he looked over to find Kerwan sitting on the ground in close proximity to him.

"'Mornin,'" said Kerwan.

"Good day for hunting monsters," said Fedradin.

"Never been a better day," chuckled Kerwan, looking down at the ground and pausing. "Look, I've got this secret, and I've got to tell someone."

"And what is that?" asked Fedradin, casting a sideways glance at Kerwan.

"I think I'm falling in love with Tiserae."

Fedradin's heart skipped a beat. He fumbled for a response for a moment or two, before saying. "You sure seem faithful."

"That Uäile came at me! It wasn't my fault!"

"I'm joking," said Fedradin, who looked away from Kerwan. The rest of the morning was passed in awkward silence as they waited for the others to arise.

They began the search for the third of the Legendary Eight once they had eaten breakfast. They mounted their horses and began to ride around the Cientile Plains, searching for a Legendary Eight. Finally, they came across a flat area of the plains, where there were a few large holes in the ground.

Qint's eyes turned red, and in a monotonic voice, "The Mulluk." At that moment, a monster shot out of one of the holes in the ground. It looked like a gigantic mole, with large, clawed hands. It let out a roar, then flipped around and dove back into its hole. As it disappeared, Fedradin caught a glimpse of a dolphin tail-like piece to the bottom of the Mulluk.

Fedradin looked around, trying to find where the monster had gone. Suddenly, he heard a roar from behind him. Fedradin turned, but he wasn't fast enough, as the Mulluk send him flying with the back of its hand. Fedradin crashed to the ground, next to a hole in the ground, rolling to his feet as soon as possible. He looked at the hole where the Mulluk had last been, but the monster was gone. Suddenly, he felt the Mulluk hit him once again and he flew through the air, back towards the group.

"Get away from the hole!" yelled Fedradin, and the group scattered as the Mulluk launched out of the hole. It flailed about, trying to find a target, but ultimately failed. It quickly dove back into the ground.

"We need to get it out of the ground," said Kerwan.

"Kerwan, you're too close!" said Breetex. As he uttered those words, the Mulluk appeared in the hole next to Kerwan, and grabbed the wizard by the back of his shirt.

"Kerwan!" shouted Fedradin. He ran over to the hole, but the wizard was nowhere to be seen. "I'm going after him," announced Fedradin.

"No, that's a stupid idea," said Tiserae.

"That Mulluk could be ripping Kerwan apart right now. Is that what you want?"

"No, but..."

"No, but what?"

"At least tie a rope around yourself." In a few minutes, Tiserae had tied a rope around Fedradin's chest.

"Two short pulls means get me out," said Fedradin. He walked over the hole and started repelling down the side. He repelled farther and farther, until finally he reached a flat bottom, where he could see an intricate cave system that the Mulluk had been using to get to the various holes so fast. In the center of the cave system, amidst pillars of dirt, Fedradin could see Kerwan from the light streaming in from the holes. But he couldn't see the Mulluk.

"Kerwan!" shouted Fedradin. He could already feel tension in the rope and he knew that he couldn't walk much farther.

Kerwan looked up. "Fedradin!"

Fedradin gestured for Kerwan to walk over. "Quickly! Before the Mulluk finds us!"

Kerwan got up unsteadily, "I'm not sure that's a possibility anymore." Kerwan pointed behind Fedradin, who turned around. There was much more of the cave system behind him, but that was not what caught his eye. The Mulluk was in front of him, frothing at the mouth. It grabbed Fedradin and started to pull him across the cave.

BREETEX

Breetex was holding the rope, listening to a muffled version of the conversation between Kerwan and Fedradin. Suddenly, the rope became taut. Breetex had to pull back on the rope just to keep himself from falling into the hole.

Aserax ran over to him, and grabbed the little bit of slack that was behind him. She started pulling with all her might, saying, "Two short pulls means bring him up. What does one long, steady pull mean?"

KERWAN

Kerwan saw that the life was slowly being squeezed out of Fedradin. With the rope around his chest tightening, due to a gigantic mole monster pulling on one end, and what he assumed was a dwarf, an elf and two humans pulling on the other. Kerwan knew he had to act before the rope broke all of Fedradin's ribs. The wizard pulled out his wand, pointed it at the rope, a safe distance from Fedradin, and he fired a white spell. The beam flew through the air and severed the rope, sending the monster tumbling backwards.

TISERAE

Tiserae and Qint had now started to help pull on the rope, but it was a losing battle. Slowly but surely, they were inching closer and closer to the edge of the hole. Breetex was about to go over the edge, when suddenly the rope went slack and they went flying backwards, piling up on top of each other.

FEDRADIN

Fedradin desperately tried to free himself from the grasp of the Mulluk, but with the rope tightening around his chest, he couldn't move much. When he felt his ribs about to snap, the rope went slack and the Mulluk flew backwards. The gigantic mole loosened its grip on Fedradin, so much so that Fedradin was able to worm his way out of its grasp. While the Mulluk fell, Fedradin launched himself into the air, jumping off its chest. The monster smashed into the ground, and it was temporarily dazed. Fedradin saw a perfect opportunity to finish it off. He drew Baxcanador and held it with both hands above his head. The Prince landed atop the Mulluk's head, brining his sword down into its eye.

The Mulluk let out a squeak of pain, but it quickly died. Fedradin drew his sword, which was covered in blood, so he went to wipe it on the fur of the Mulluk. However, before he had the chance to do so, the blood disappeared on the blade. Strange.

"Fedradin, that was amazing!" said Kerwan, running over to him.

"Thanks, but this lair freaks me out. Let's find the rock and get out of here."

"You mean this rock?" asked Kerwan smugly, procuring a red rock, identical to the other two.

"Precisely! Let's get out of here."

Chapter 82
A Wizard's Kind of Vengeance

FEDRADIN

"WE ARE RIGHT NEXT to Widow's Desert, Fedradin. Give me one good reason why I can't!" shouted Kerwan.

"You'll die," replied Fedradin, nonchalantly.

"I don't need you to tell me what to do, you arrogant Prince!" shouted Kerwan. "I can make that decision for myself!"

"Yes, but it's a stupid decision."

Kerwan shook his head. "Of course you don't understand. It wasn't your master who was killed."

Fedradin pushed Kerwan to the ground roughly. "You think I don't understand the need for revenge! My mother was killed by one of the Minions, my own cousin tried to have me killed! But I haven't run off in search of them. No! I've kept a level head. Kerwan, you think you're an expert on vengeance, but you've got plenty to learn."

Kerwan got to his feet, his face red with anger. "So your mother is dead? And your cousin doesn't like you? I pity you so much." Kerwan bowed to Fedradin in a mocking fashion. "I was sold. Sold to pay the ransom of my father. Just like my sister before me, and my brother before her. I don't even know my siblings' names! And the worst part is, I don't know if I was sold for enough money to pay for my mother! I have no idea what happened to my family! I will never know what happened to them! But I do know what happened to Biggs, and I can do something about it. I am going to find Krile Wandhand and fight that evil man, regardless of whether or not I live." Kerwan turned on his heels, saddled his horse and started to ride in the direction of Widow's Desert.

Fedradin watched him leave, practically ignoring Tiserae as she explained how she had put the rocks from the Legendary Eight and the compass in a bag.

KERWAN

Kerwan was prone in the sand, on the edge of a crater. In the crater lay the camp of Desert Wind. It was a pitiful sight to see, small wooden shacks together in a dense cluster. To the side of the shacks was a large sandstone temple, similar to the one where the bronze snake had been. He saw some members of the gang walking around in their hooded robes. Some were leading camels laden with various goods.

Kerwan was trying to find Krile Wandhand. He needed to isolate the wizard, now a Sage, and kill him. Kerwan realized, now that he looked out across the desert, that he had possibly bitten off more than he could chew. Maybe Fedradin had been right. Maybe this was a stupid idea. Maybe he should have stayed with the group...

He heard footsteps in the sand behind him. Quickly he spun around, his wand colliding with the face of...Fedradin?

"What the hell are you doing here?" asked Kerwan.

"The compass told us to come this way, so I decided that we might as well follow you."

"We?" asked Kerwan. The wizard turned back and saw Tiserae, Qint, Breetex and Aserax on the horizon.

"We all came out to help you kill this man," said Fedradin.

"Thanks, but I'm not sure if this is a plausible feat," said Kerwan. "I have no idea where he could be, and I don't want to have to fight the whole village."

Fedradin thought for a moment or two. "I have an idea."

FEDRADIN

A few minutes later, Aserax had joined the Prince and the wizard. She had nocked an arrow on her bow, drawn the bowstring back, and had it pointed at a member of Desert Wind, who had drifted away from camp to urinate. He was standing behind a house, for privacy's sake. Aserax released the bowstring, and the arrow flew through the air, hitting the man in the head. He collapsed to the ground without a sound.

"One down," said Aserax, drawing another arrow. The three waited atop the edge of the crater for another few minutes, until another member of Desert Wind came to look for the man. Aserax quickly loosed am arrow in the direction of the second man, the arrow striking him in the neck. He, like the other man, collapsed to the ground, dead.

"Cover us, Aserax," said Fedradin, as he and Kerwan started sliding down the sandy slope, towards the two bodies, and they successfully reached the bodies without raising any alarm. Fedradin began to take the robe off one of the members, kicking the body under the house. He motioned for Kerwan to do the same. Before long, the two were dressed in the Desert Wind robes, hoods drawn up all the way. They walked into the camp, and began to scout.

Members walked by, but never talked about the location of Krile. Finally, Fedradin gave up and tapped the shoulder of one of the men bustling about.

"Excuse me, do you know where Krile Wandhand might be?" asked Fedradin.

The man looked at him suspiciously. "And what is it to you?" he replied.

"We wish to, uh..." stumbled Fedradin.

"We wish to discuss a top secret item with him," said Kerwan, coming to Fedradin's aid.

"Um, alright," the man said slowly, eyeing Fedradin and Kerwan. "He's in the temple, of course."

"The temple!" said Fedradin. "Of course!"

"Yes. Why we should have thought of that!" said Kerwan. Quickly the two turned and walked to the temple, the man watching them as the left. Finally, he shrugged and went back to his business.

As Kerwan approached the temple, he noticed that it was different from the one with the bronze snake. It had the same room at the top, but it also had an entrance at the side. Kerwan turned to Fedradin.

"Should we just enter?" he asked.

"We're here to kill the man," said Fedradin, "Does it matter if we break some etiquette?"

Kerwan agreed and the two walked into the temple. Inside, there was one massive room, almost completely empty, except for a man meditating in the center. Kerwan recognized that man. It was Krile Wandhand.

Without looking up, Krile said, "I knew you would come for me, wizard."

"You killed my master. Did you expect something less?"

"I expected something sooner."

Kerwan grew angry. "For your information, I have been on a quest of highest importance."

"Good heavens, you must have gotten very lost."

"Don't flatter yourself, Krile," said Kerwan, trying to control his anger. "We haven't been tracking you at all."

"Really? You say that, yet here you are."

Kerwan clenched his fists. "Don't let him anger you, Kerwan," said Fedradin.

"Oh! You brought some back-up. How nice."

"I will best you one-on-one, Krile. He's just a precaution."

Krile opened his eyes and stood up, pulling back his hood. Kerwan saw the classic Desert Wind tattoo on Krile's forehead, but that was not what caught his attention. Under Krile's eyes was a red birthmark shaped like a horseshoe. Exactly like the one under Kerwan's eye.

"Brother," whispered Kerwan.

Krile smiled. "It's about time you were able to put two and two together, brother."

"You're alive! How can that be?"

"I was sold to some brigands by mother to pay for father, and I was able to escape. I came to this cult, worked by way up to the top, and now, I'm the Rock Holder."

"How did you know I was your brother?"

"I saw the red birthmark when I first met you. Why do you think I let you live?"

Kerwan opened his mouth but no words came out. Finally, he shook his head. "I do not care if we are of the same kin, Krile. I shall have to kill you for the death of my master."

"So be it, brother. But I must warn you, I will not spare your life again." Kerwan drew his wand and warhammer, while Krile drew his own wand and a knife. Fedradin stepped back, letting the two brothers fight. He knew that he was going to step in if Kerwan began to lose.

Kerwan shot a white spell at Krile, which he dodged. Krile returned the spell with a brown one. Kerwan ducked and the spell flew over his head. This went on for a while, Krile and Kerwan shooting spells back and forth. One came quite close to Fedradin's head, but he was able to duck it.

Soon, the commotion from the spells attracted the attention from the members of Desert Wind. They came to the doors of the temple, looking in, but before they could act, Krile yelled at them to stay out of the fight.

Finally the spell battle came to an end, when the spikes from a purple spell clipped Krile in the shoulder, knocking him down. Kerwan ran forward, swinging his warhammer down at the ground. Before the hammer could reach Krile, though, the man disappeared and reappeared behind him. Krile raised a palm and the ground beneath Kerwan shot upwards, sending Kerwan flying. The ground went back to normal, and Kerwan smacked to the ground. Krile walked over to Kerwan, pointing his wand at Kerwan's head.

"Good bye, brother," said Krile. "It was a short pleasure."

Fedradin knew he had to act. He raised his palm, and the air condensed around Krile. Fedradin moved his palm to the side, throwing Krile into the side of the temple. The members of Desert Wind around the temple gasped, not sure what to do. Quickly, Fedradin ran forward, pinning Krile to the ground, holding the blade of Baxcanador against his neck.

The members of Desert Wind around the outside of the temple started to move forwards.

"Stop!" yelled Fedradin. "You move another inch and I slash this man's neck." The cult members froze in place. Kerwan stood up and walked over to Krile. He looked into Fedradin's eyes, and Fedradin nodded.

"Good bye, brother," mimicked Kerwan. "It was a short pleasure." In one quick movement, Kerwan swung his warhammer into Krile's skull. Quickly, Fedradin pulled the earth crystal from the neck of Krile.

"Fedradin! Look!" shouted Kerwan, as the Desert Wind members walked towards them. Fedradin glanced up, sword at the ready.

"Get your weapons out, Kerwan," said Fedradin in a level tone. "There's no where to run."

The cult members formed a circle around Kerwan and Fedradin and slowly closed in, but none attacked. Fedradin, itching to fight, had to restrain himself as the cult grew closer. Suddenly and simultaneously, the members took a knee and kowtowed.

Fedradin did not sheath his sword, but instead whispered to Kerwan, "What's happening?"

One of the members rose to his feet, and a startled Fedradin nearly relieved the man of his head. "You killed our master and took his Rock, and with it, his place as our leader. Your wish is our command."

"I wish I wasn't the leader of a cult," said Fedradin.

"Then you shan't be any longer. Pick one of us to take your place and be on your way."

Fedradin turned to Kerwan, who shrugged. "You seem fit for the position," said Fedradin, gesturing to the man in front of him.

"Thank you," said the man, kowtowing once more, "My name is Tyration. And as a gift of gratitude, I will let you keep the Rock Crystal."

Another man rose to his feet, and pulled out a knife. "Not so fast. I invoke the Rashimi Clause." Tyration spun to face the man.

"As you wish, Sauner," said Tyration bowing. He as well pulled out a knife. Fedradin and Kerwan were pulled back to the edge of the circle. The two rolled back their sleeves.

"What's going on?" murmured Kerwan.

"Any member of Desert Wind has the right to challenge the Rock Holder, when he receives the crystal, with the Rashimi Clause," said a cult member. "This way, the Rock Holder stays the strongest of us all. A Rashimi is a fight to the death."

Tyration and Sauner slid their knifes across their forearms, drawing blood, but never losing eye contact with each other. The pulled their knives back, still bloody, and faced each other.

"Rashimi," hissed Sauner.

"Rashimi," echoed Tyration.

Sauner launched himself at Tyration, knife slashing out. Tyration parried the blow, but was knocked to the ground by Sauner's momentum. Tyration rolled over, kicking out and catching Sauner in the knees. He stumbled back, and Tyration leapt to his feet, swinging his own knife. Sauner was able to block it, before he toppled over. Tyration stepped to the side to avoid Sauner's feet as he kicked out. Sauner climbed to his feet, but before he could lash out, Tyration attacked him with a flurry of blows.

Sauner was able to block the blows, but he was always one beat behind. Finally, Tyration slipped his knife past Sauner's defenses and stuck the blade in his shoulder. Sauner dropped his knife and reeled backwards. Tyration jumped forward, slashing Sauner across the cheek. The man fell backwards, fear in his eyes.

And for good reason.

Tyration brought the knife down on Sauner's chest, and killed him instantly. "Rashimi," announced Tyration, holding up his bloody knife. "It is done."

Chapter 83
Motivation

ROGER

ROGER AND SGIRE WERE sitting in a tavern. Neither had ordered a drink, much like almost all of the customers. There was an uncomfortable silence as people sat at the tables, trying to digest what had just happened.

Roger was slightly restless. He didn't want to be cooped up in a bar, scared of the guards patrolling outside. There was a window in the side of the bar, which looked out onto the cobblestone street. From there, Roger could see the guards, but he was noticing that they were coming fewer and farther between. He looked out over the tables of people, the atmosphere of defeat, hopelessness, and despair filling the room like smoke. Roger looked over at Sgire, and that what was the worst of all. She was sitting there, clutching a silver amulet, running in between her fingers. She had once told Roger that her mother had given her that amulet as a child. That was all that was left of Sgire's mother.

Roger couldn't bring back Sgire's mother, but he could help the people in the room. He climbed onto the table, heads turning towards him.

"So that's it?" he said, not loudly, but his words filled the silent room. "We're just going to give up?" There was no answer to his question, until finally a man said:

"Shut up, kid. There's nothing more we can do."

"There's not? That man, that traitorous man, cooped up in that castle right now is looking down at us. He's probably laughing. He's amused by the fact that he has won. At the sight of some blood, we run away. From him. From his guards." Roger paused. "But we shouldn't have run away. Those men, those good women, even a few *children* as I recall, were cut down by his soldiers and we ran. We fled leaving our loved ones behind. Our husbands, wives, brothers, children, parents. We left them to die!"

"My husband was killed by those soldiers," said a woman, looking down at her shoes.

"See? I stayed behind slightly longer than most, and I saw something. Something horrifying. A man. As innocent as any one of you was knocked to the ground by a sword. But he hadn't died. He lifted his head proudly, to see all of you leaving him. And that was the last sight he saw! The last sight he'll ever see, for a guard killed him with a quick blow to the head. He could've lived. The man good be here with us right now, but we left him." Roger turned to the woman who had spoken up earlier. "Ma'am, that man could have been your husband. And you left him." The woman broke into tears.

"What ya sayin' kid?" said someone else.

"I'm saying it's not too late! We can fight back. We can find the man who destroyed our reputation, who tried to bring about the end of Haxter. And we can kill him! The innocent men and women who died today should not have died in vain. Will not die in vain! We will avenge them! We will march to that bloody castle, and we will prevail! Do not let this woman's husband have died in vain. Do not let the eight year old child that was murdered today die in vain. Do not let Sir Hulten Sharpaxe or King Westel or anyone else who was slain by Flyc die in vain! We will fight. And we will win!" People started cheering.

"How are we gonna fight 'em? We ain't got thirty people in here," someone said.

"We'll rally an army. Everyone go to a different tavern or house or theater and convince them to fight. We'll need as many people as possible to bring an end to this bloody bastard."

Chapter 84
Halfway There

FEDRADIN

QINT HAD SHOWN FEDRADIN how to use the earth crystal. It was much like the air crystal, except that one could use it to control the element of earth. Fedradin had taken the earth crystal off the necklace that Krile had and he had attached it to the air crystal. The two crystals fused together to form one that allowed Fedradin to use both elements.

When Fedradin had told Qint about Desert Wind letting them go, Qint voiced his surprise. He told Fedradin that Desert Wind was one of four mysterious tribes that collected a certain type of crystal. Besides Desert Wind, which of course collected the earth crystals, there was Tidal Wave, which collected the water crystals, Spark Light, which collected the fire crystals, and Tempest Gale, which collected the air crystals. Qint wondered why they had given up an earth crystal to outsiders.

"Maybe they were just happy to be free of Krile," said Fedradin.

"That seems to be the only possible solution," replied Qint.

KERWAN

The group was out to find the fourth member of the Legendary Eight. The compass had told them that they were in the right place, smack in the middle of Widow's Desert. They had left their horses tethered to a tree in an oasis they had found, which irritated Aserax, for she hated walking. Still, she trudged through the sand one foot after another, waiting for something to happen. That something finally did, when Qint's eyes turned red.

"The Cunderswud," said Qint.

"The Cunderswud?" said Kerwan. "I've heard of the Cunderswud." Kerwan had seemed a lot happier now that he had killed the man who had killed his master. Aserax did not know that Krile Wandhand had actually turned out to be Kerwan's brother. Neither did anyone else in the group besides Fedradin. "They say that if you see the bottom of its foot, it is a bad omen and you will never retur-" Kerwan was cut off as the Cunderswud exploded out of the sand. It looked like a large, purple-scaled lizard, with eight legs, four on each side. It had a long tail with a razor sharp spike on the end that swished back and forth dangerously. The monster roared and small fangs were visible in its mouth.

Fedradin had been knocked over by the gigantic lizard, and he was now trying to regain his footing. The Cunderswud walked over to him putting one of its feet in the air.

"Oh no," murmured Kerwan.

Quickly, Fedradin waved his palm and some of the sand on the desert flew up into the eyes of the Cunderswud. This distracted the monster long enough for Fedradin to get away. The Cunderswud advanced, swinging its spiked foot at Fedradin. Fedradin pulled out his kappa shell shield and was able to deflect the foot, but the force of the blow sent him flying. Fedradin crashed to the sand far away from the Cunderswud. Kerwan fired three black spells at the Cunderswud, but the gigantic lizard braced itself and the spell exploded harmlessly on its hard scales. The Cunderswud then dove into the sand, leaving a hole that quickly filled itself in.

"Where did it go?" asked Kerwan. His question was soon answered as the Cunderswud erupted from the sand, nearly swallowing Kerwan with its open maw. Kerwan ran in terror, the Cunderswud's snorts sounding almost like laughter.

By now Fedradin had returned, wielding Baxcanador proudly in his right hand. The Cunderswud turned to Fedradin and dove in the sand.

"Fedradin! Watch out! It's going to come out of the sand under you!" shouted Aserax.

Fedradin nodded. "I've got this." The Cunderswud emerged from the ground, swallowing Fedradin whole.

"Fedradin!" cried Tiserae. It seemed as if that was the end of Fedradin, as the Cunderswud set its sight on the rest of the group. They scattered, trying to escape from the monster before it killed any more of them. That was when something amazing happened. The Cunderswud started to twitch. It started started whimpering in pain. Its stomach started to inflate, much like a balloon. It got larger and larger, until finally, the monster popped, exploding outwards, sending scales flying, like shrapnel. Aserax fell to the ground, as to minimize the area where the scales could hit her. Finally, when all the scales had stopped flying, she looked up to see Fedradin face-down in the sand, covered in a liquid of some sort.

"Fedradin, are you okay?" cried Aserax, running forward. She lifted up his head, his eyes flickering open. He spat out some sand and said:

"Remind me never to do that again." With those words he passed out in Aserax's hands.

Chapter 85
Plitsky

PLITSKY

PRINCE PLITSKY HATED PRINCE Poltax with all his might. Prince Plitsky was the next of kin for the throne, but after Poltax had become engaged to Plitsky's twin sister, Aserax, Poltax had moved up above Plitsky in the race for the throne, because Aserax was five minutes older than he. Plitsky had grudgingly accepted this, for it was the way it worked. However, when Aserax had run off with her dwarfish lover, Plitsky had expected King Juern, his father, to officially bequeath the throne to Plitsky. However, this was never done, though nor was this done for Poltax. Still, when the Gii Games came around, Juern had decided not to go, and sent Poltax in his place. This filled Plitsky with anger, for it was essentially a foreshadowing that Juern would bequeath the throne to Poltax.

Plitsky had come up with many plots to kill Poltax, and he was about to carry one out, when one day something changed his mind. He had awoke to a strange, blue light. After a cursory glance, he found the source of it: a blue orb floating above his head. Plitsky grabbed the orb and brought it down. He looked at it, but I looked like an ordinary orb. He got out of bed to dispose of it, but when he did, he received a sharp pain in the hand with which he held the orb. Plitsky dropped the orb on the floor, and it exploded in a white mist, leaving a scroll behind. Plitsky picked up the scroll and read it.

You will become king if you do whatever is necessary.

Plitsky's wife rolled out of bed. Her name was Gnue, and she happened to be the sister of Poltax. She despised her brother. "What is it, Plitsky?"

"I know what I have to do."

Chapter 86
A Vision

FEDRADIN

KERWAN HAD BEEN ABLE to find the rock from the Cunderswud in the bottom of one of its feet that were spread out across the desert. The rest of the group brought the limp, unconscious body of Fedradin back to the oasis where they had left their things before searching for the Cunderswud.

When he finally awoke, the various gunk and goo he collected while inside the Cunderswud had crusted over due to the intense heat of the sun. He quickly stripped down and bathed in the pool of water in the oasis, cleaning himself of the filth that covered his skin. What had he been thinking? He willingly let a gigantic monster *eat* him? And for what? If he asked Qint, he was sure he would get an answer along the lines of, "It's for the sake of the world, and if you fail Haxter is doomed."

Fedradin got dressed and rejoined the group, who were preparing to leave. Kerwan was looking down at the compass, the rest of the group looking down at it as well.

"I think it's pointing to the Biztil Rainforest," said Kerwan. There were murmurs of agreement. Fedradin walked over, mildly irritated by Kerwan taking over the group. *Kerwan* wasn't the Prince of Destiny.

"So we're headed to the rainforest now, are we?" asked Fedradin, keeping his voice friendly. At least, he tried.

"That's where the compass is pointing," said Kerwan.

"'Right, then. Let's get going." They were about to mount their horses when a voice came from behind them.

"Not so fast," the voice said. Fedradin turned, slowly. Behind him stood a humanoid monster, about seven feet high. It had grey skin and a bald grey head that looked melted slightly. It was barefoot, and wielded two maces in either hand. And it was angry. Fedradin recognized it as a deathwielder, an undead monster. "I have been sent to finish you off, once and for all!" said the deathwielder. Fedradin hopped down from his horse, pulling out his sword slowly.

The deathwielder angered by Fedradin's lack of intimidation, charged forwards, swinging its maces. Fedradin pulled out his shield and blocked the swing, the mace bouncing off and colliding with deathwielder's chest. The monster stumbled back, and Fedradin advanced, swinging his sword, the blade slicing across the monster's chest. The deathwielder collapsed to the ground, clutching its wound, as Fedradin stepped forwards to deliver the finishing blow. He raised his sword high in the air, but before he was able to bring it down, the deathwielder swung its mace, catching Fedradin in the shoulder and sending the Prince flying.

Fedradin crashed to the ground, his sword flying out of his grip. The deathwielder advanced, preparing to swing its mace. "Don't worry," said the monster. "It won't hurt for long." The deathwielder brought back its mace, but as it started to swing, a flash of white light lit up the oasis. A white beam flew towards the deathwielder cutting its head clean off. The monster fell to the ground, headless and dead.

"Are you alright?" asked Kerwan, the one who had shot the white spell.

Fedradin felt anger surge through his body. "Get out of my face, Kerwan," spat Fedradin.

"Excuse me? I just saved your life!"

"I don't need your help! In fact, I don't need any of *this*. I was perfectly happy with my Ridders, in my castle. I never wanted to be *Prince of Destiny*. How is it fair that someone else decided I need to save Haxter?" There was complete silence as everyone stared at Fedradin. "I'm leaving. Kerwan can be Prince of Destiny for all I care."

Fedradin grabbed his sword and jumped on his horse. "Fedradin! Wait! We need you!" said Tiserae.

Fedradin looked down at her. "I frankly don't care. Everywhere I turn, someone has been sent by their master to kill me! I went my whole godsdamn life without a single assassination attempt, and I sure as hell don't need any undead beasts rising from the ground to kill me! Good-bye. Good luck with the Demon Callers." With that, he turned the horse and galloped away, leaving the shell-shocked group to figure out what to do next.

Night had fallen. Fedradin sat in the sand of Widow's Desert, staring up at the stars overhead. What had he done? Was Qint right about him dooming Haxter by refusing to go along with their idiotic quest? Maybe he should go back to the group...But then again, Draslupp had told him Thereeko had un-banished Fedradin from Narven. Should he go back to his home with his Ridders? As he looked out over the endless desert Fedradin battled with these thoughts, until something upset the balance.

An image appeared in front of him. It was white, shimmering, looked human, and began to speak.

"Fedradin? Son? Is that you?" said the image.

"Father?" whispered Fedradin, feeling like he had lost his mind.

"Son! What are you doing in this desert?"

"I could ask the same of you."

"I am not in the desert. I am in the Glaciers and for very good reasons, too. But why have you abandoned your group? They need you."

"I'm sure they can handle it on their own."

"Of course they cannot! Only you received a prophecy, Fedradin. Not them. You!"

"But-"

"Please, son, if not for them, do it for me. The same men that killed your mother are after the Demon Callers. You must stop them at once!"

"Why can't you, father?"

"I can't leave the Glaciers, you know that. I still harbor anger for Erch; I mustn't go anywhere near anyone else."

"That makes no sense!" argued Fedradin.

"It will in time, son. But until then, you must stop these evil men from getting the Demon Callers! If they do, they will kill so many more. Please son, do it for me! Do it for your mother, if not for yourself."

"But father-"

"Please Fedradin, I can't maintain this conversation much longer. But before I go I must hear you say it. Will you find the Demon Callers?"

Fedradin thought a moment. He saw his father's agonized face, when suddenly it flickered. The picture of his father began to get fainter and foggier. A sudden picture popped into his head. It was the rainbow over the canyon he had seen on his way to Gii. That was the kind of beauty that would disappear if Erch ever came to power.

"'Right!" he blurted out to as the picture of his father faded. "I'll do it."

Chapter 87
A Failed Attempt

PLITSKY

PRINCE PLITSKY HAD SET out to kill King Juern, his own father. He knew how bad of an elf that made him, but the thought of the throne falling into Poltax's hands was too much for him to handle. Before Juern could bequeath the throne to Poltax, thus making it nearly impossible for Plitsky to assume the throne, Plitsky needed to kill Juern. After the king died, without an official bequeathment of the throne, Plitsky would assume the throne, for he was in fact the next, living, male heir.

Plitsky had set out in the morning, holding an ivory dagger carved out of the black rhinoceroses of the plains, in order to find the king and kill him.

GASODO

Meanwhile, in the courtyard of the castle of Axler, an elf by the name of Gasodo was sitting with his back turned to the opening of the castle. He was thinking about his daughter, Gnue when something terrible happened.

PLITSKY

Prince Plitsky stabbed the elf he thought was his own father once, then twice, then thrice, all in the back. The man died instantly falling backwards, revealing his face to Plitsky and the fact that he was not, in fact, King Juern. This was Gnue's father, Gasodo, who he had just cold-bloodedly murdered. Plitsky was inundated with panic, and quickly, he darted away, before anyone else came by and saw the crime scene.

Chapter 88

A Night in the Jungle

FEDRADIN

FEDRADIN WAS WAVING A flaming stick at a gambol, trying to keep it at bay. He wore tattered robes and was starving. How did he wind up like that? To answer that question, one must back up many hours. Fedradin had returned to his group, and from the oasis, they went to Ezent, the capital of the Chultra Kingdom.

"Please, King Duztil, Emperor Flyc could already have assembled his army! He could be marching this way right now!"

"How can we trust humans? How will we ever be able to trust you again?"

"I'm not asking you to trust us-the humans, I mean. I just ask that if Flyc assembles an army, you will have your troops help fight him. The Keshnul army has already decided to do this."

Duztil thought for a moment or two. "I will accept your offer. If Emperor Flyc raises an army my forces will help destroy it." Fedradin turned to the rest of the group excitedly. "If! You prove that you're worthy. Survive one night in the jungle with no weapons and I will pledge my allegiance to you."

From there, Fedradin was stripped of all his weapons and led into the jungle, blindfolded, by two chultra. Fedradin was glad that he couldn't see as he was led away from Ezent, for the city was built entirely in the large rainforest trees. Wooden bridges through the tree tops led to the various houses built around the tree trunks. The bridges weren't exactly the sturdiest and Fedradin never really felt comfortable on them.

Finally, the chultra spun him around five times then removed the blindfold. Then, they backed into the rainforest, each going a separate way. The sun began to rapidly set, so Fedradin lit a fire in the clearing in which he had been deposited.

The sun went down behind the trees and darkness descended over the rainforest. That was when things started to get hairy. Quite literally.

Fedradin knew that many of the creatures in the rainforest were nocturnal, and scared of fire, so Fedradin lit a stick to act as a temporary torch by smashing two rocks together and making sparks. He sat on the ground, waiting for something to come and attack him, when he saw the eyes. He could see yellow animal eyes pierce the heavy darkness of the rainforest, more pairs than he could count. The Prince of Destiny jumped to his feet, waving his torch madly.

"Get!" he yelled loudly. "Be away with your filth, you ugly curs!"

A few of the eyes disappeared into the darkness, but certainly not all of them. Fedradin continued to wave his flaming stick, until one of the monsters attached to one of the pairs of eyes stepped forth from the trees. It looked like a cross of a lion and an ape. It stood on all fours, but instead of paws it had ape hands. It had a mane, but instead of a lion's face it had an ape's. It had dark blue fur and skin, which was stained with blood and dirt. It opened its mouth to roar and displayed row upon row of sharp teeth. Fedradin recognized it as a gambol.

"I said back!" screamed Fedradin desperately, thrusting his torch in the monster's face. The gambol jumped back as the flames bit into its skin, but it didn't run away. In fact, it seemed to only grow angrier. The gambol jumped forwards, Fedradin swinging his torch and moving to the side. The gambol missed Fedradin, but turned to jump again. It did jump, but Fedradin was once again able to use his torch and evasive maneuver to avoid becoming the gambol's dinner.

This process went on for a long time, the gambol leaping, Fedradin dodging and swinging his torch, until finally another gambol stepped out from the trees. Then another. Then another. Then another. Fedradin quickly saw that he could not fight five angry gambols, so he decided to run. He sprinted away from the gambols and into the forest.

He heard the monsters led out a howl, to signal to their other gambol friends that prey was on the loose. Fedradin tried to ignore their calls and focus on the path ahead of him. His flickering torch was hardly enough light for him to navigate the obstacle-ridden jungle floor. He had to avoid roots, thorny plants, trees, rock faces and whatever else might have been trying to trip him up and leave him as good as dead for the gambols.

Fedradin came to a screeching halt. In front of him was the swiftly moving Oxler River. He saw no way over it, nor around it. He looked back over his shoulder and saw the gambols closing in on him. He needed to act, and he needed to act now.

Fedradin spotted a log floating slowly down the river. The gambols were feet away. He took a running headstart and leapt for it, flying through the air, a paw passing inches from his back. Fedradin landed on the log and let out a sigh of relief as he drifted away from the gambols.

He lay back on his log, watching as the trees zoomed by. He was calm, relaxed and confident, until he heard the sounds of a waterfall. He sat straight up, and looked forwards, to see where the river ended and the falling began. His log was moving at a good clip towards the edge of the falls. Fedradin stood up on his log and began looking for a way out.

He could swim for it, but he'd never make it. He could try to survive the fall, but he'd drown. He could...grab that branch! Fedradin launched himself at a low hanging branch, stemming from a tree leaning dangerously far over the waterfall. He grabbed the branch, right as his log went tumbling over the edge. He dangled there, feet soaked from the spray of water, when he heard the branch crack.

As the branch continued to moan and groan, Fedradin climbed hand over hand along it towards the trunk of the tree. When the branch finally snapped off the tree, Fedradin's left hand was still clinging to it, his right hand grasping another one. The limb splashed into the river and soared off the edge of the waterfall. Fedradin swung himself, releasing the tree. He landed on the bank of the river and was able to grab a root with both his hands before his legs, in the water, were taken by the current.

The only thing between him and his death was a root. His whole body was pointed towards the falls, his knuckles white from grasping the root, his muscles screaming in pain. As his hands began to slip, he summoned an immense amount of strength and was able to thrust his left leg forwards, landing his knee in the muddy bank. After, it was easy for him to pull his right leg from the water.

Soaked, muddy, sweaty, tired, and bloody -though whose blood it belonged to was a mystery- Fedradin pulled himself up the bank and collapsed in a heap, and fell into a fitful sleep, waking when a chultra stirred him with its foot.

Chapter 89
Rebellion

ROGER

ROGER WAS AMAZED BY how many people had come out, risking their lives for the small chance of bringing down Flyc. The blood-stained cobblestone streets were now almost as full with people as they had been earlier in the day. The guards that Flyc had claimed would be monitoring the streets were nowhere to be seen, so it was quite easy for Roger to rally his army.

People had armed themselves with various things, such as bits of wood from chairs or tables, torches, pitchforks, knives, broken glass, and some went unarmed, relying on their fists. Roger's army marched towards the castle, all yelling and protesting. Next to Roger was Sgire, who had taken out her sword. Roger had merely a knife in his hand. And of course his magic.

Finally, they arrived at the top of the cobblestone path to find something that they had not expected. Soldiers were everywhere, hundreds of them lined up in front of the castle, swords at the ready. On top of the castle, hundreds of archers stood in a line, bows drawn back, arrows pointing at Roger's army. Flyc stepped out from the castle, drawing a chorus of insults, curses and profanity from the army. Some threw their weapons at him.

"So you have come back, despite my threat," announced Flyc, his voice projected by an unseen device. "That was unwise of you, and that is why I was able to predict that you would do exactly this." Flyc paced for a few moments. "I will once again offer you the choice of fleeing. If you do not, I will have to be forced to kill each and every one of you." He stared at the crowd, but not a single soul moved.

"We will kill you Flyc!" shouted Sgire.

"Is that so? Guards, leave not one of these rebels alive." There was hesitation in the ranks of the army. "Fire at will!"

The archers hesitantly released their bowstrings, the arrows raining down on the rebels. Many of the arrows buried themselves in the buildings surrounding Roger's army, most likely on purpose, but a few found their marks in the rebels. The archers fired more arrows that rained down on the rebels, surprisingly few actually reaching their marks. It seemed some of the archers, shaken from the previous event when they had shot civilians, had intentionally missed. Even if the arrows were inaccurate, the rebels still took shelter from them, so Flyc commanded the soldiers on the ground to attack the rebels.

The soldiers charged the rebels, causing a cease fire from the archers, afraid of hitting their allies. The soldiers all had swords and maces and spears, but the rebels had a better reason to fight, fiercely fighting back with their assorted weapons. Roger had never seen such intense combat, rebels beating soldiers to death with pieces of wood, soldiers decapitating rebels with their swords. Roger also fought, using his magic powers to electrocute the soldiers one by one. Blood started to pour down the cobblestone street as more and more people fell, equally as many soldiers as rebels.

LIDER

It was awful. He had fought against goblins, but nothing could prepare him for what he was watching now.

Sergeant Lider was gazing upon human soldiers slicing through rebels with their blood stained, no, drenched, blades. The rebels were fighting back, but they were slowly loosing the fight, their makeshift weapons no match for Flyc's army. Lider saw a child throw a stone at a soldier, which bounced harmlessly off the soldier's helmet. The soldier turned, annoyed with the thrower of the rock. Lider had expected, upon knowing that it was merely a child, that the soldier would turn and keep fighting the armed adults; however, the soldier took his sword, pulled it back, the eyes of the child wide with fright. *He wouldn't,* thought Lider, but the soldier showed no intentions of stopping. The sword was now in the ideal location to stab the child.

"No!" shouted Lider, who slashed with his sword, killing the man with a single stroke. "Get out of here, kid." The child didn't need to be told twice.

Lider winced. He had just become a traitor.

ROGER

Roger knew that he would lose. There were simply too many, well-trained, well equipped, soldiers for the few poorly trained, poorly equipped, civilians to kill. Roger was killing many soldiers, but he was starting to get surrounded, and his energy was beginning to drain. He saw Sgire in the corner of his eye, her blade flashing back and forth, felling many soldiers, but she too was getting overwhelmed. Roger was about to yield to the soldiers, and hope for mercy when something spectacular happened.

A soldier, clad in black armor, killed two soldiers from behind. Quickly he slashed the heads off two soldiers who looked his way, and stabbed a third in the chest. The last soldier who remained in front of Roger ran in fright, Roger killing him with a brown spell before he could get too far.

"Thank you, kind sir! May I have the privilege of knowing your name?"

"Lider. My name is Lider," said Lider.

"I would tell you mine, but there is no time for formalities. We have soldiers to kill!" Roger and Lider began making their way to Sgire, killing any and every soldier in their path. When they were finally able to get to Sgire, she was swamped with soldiers, barely blocking all the blows that were sent her way.

"Roger!" she cried. "Help!" Roger and Lider quickly killed the soldiers around Sgire.

"Roger, your hands..." started Sgire.

"No time to explain," said Roger.

"Look!" shouted Lider, pointing up the blood drenched cobblestone path. The few soldiers left were retreating up the path, running from the rebels. Roger turned to his rebels and encouraged them on.

"Attack! Let us make these bastards pay for their crimes!" shouted Roger, to fewer rebels than he wanted. The rebels charged up the path, chasing the soldiers. It would be a grueling fight, but Roger was confident he would win.

Chapter 90
Golbicoid and an Asteroid

COID

COID WAS PROUD OF his city, located to the west of Borave, in the plains of Flyc. It was built like a goblin den, so it was entirely underground. There was an opening chamber, where goblins guarded a gate that led into the rest of Golbicoid. There were then paths that split up and led to sleeping chambers of the goblins, the jail, the church, the communal space, the royal chambers, the treasury and the barracks. Coid was most proud of the treasury, where he had collected all the treasure of all the goblin tribes he had conquered.

After conquering countless goblin tribes, Coid had moved on to conquering the hobgoblin and bugbear tribes, the goblins' fiercer cousins. He wanted them in his ranks, for he was planning on raising an army with the goblins. This army would be forever in the service of whatever force gave Coid his powers after he freed his fellow slaves in Histam. Until then, he occupied his time with conquering hobgoblin, bugbear and goblin tribes.

UÄILE

It fell from the sky, just like the Large Rock had, but this rock was much smaller. It was the Small Rock, if you will. The rock crashed to the ground, somewhere in the midst of the Mendelgar Forest. All was quiet for many minutes, the birds stopped chirping, the wind stopped blowing, as the rock lay in the forest, giving off smoke. From off the rock slithered a microscopic organism. As soon as it cleared the rock, the organism began to multiply, building on top of itself until it formed the shape of a beautiful blond woman, similar to that of Black Arrow.

The Uäile sniffed the air, tasting it with a forked tongue. A sword as black as death appeared in her flawless hands. She spoke, in a language that could be understood by all, be it the humans, chultra, or chipmunks. "It seems my daughters have failed."

Chapter 91

The Gravorg

FEDRADIN

THE CHULTRA HAD FLOWN on a roc over the jungle, searching for Fedradin. It had quickly found him, napping on the edge of Phantom Falls, which he learned it was called. He had taken a ride back on the roc to Ezent, where he took a short nap, in preparation to find the next of the Legendary Eight.

Pharaoh Duztil had assured Fedradin that the chultra would happily fight side by side with Fedradin if ever a time came up in which that was necessary. Fedradin thanked Duztil and went on his way, following the needle.

The needle actually took him and his group back into the jungle, when it told them they were in the right spot. They began to search for the next Legendary Eight, wondering where it could be, when finally they came across a cave.

Qint's eyes glowed red, "The Gravorg," he said in a monotonic voice. Fedradin walked towards the cave, but Kerwan stopped him.

"The Gravorg, much like the Cunderswud, actually has a strong mythological background. Rumor has it that the Gravorg can switch the flow of gravity, smashing you on the top of the cave."

"So what the hell am I supposed to do with that information?" asked Fedradin, grumpily, from his lack of sleep.

"I think we should tie a rope around you, or something that will be short enough that you won't hit the cave roof."

"'Right, that sounds fine. I take it Tiserae has rope?" As he spoke, Tiserae pulled out a coil of rope from her robe, which still had its hood up.

Moments later, Fedradin had a coil of rope tied around his chest, and the rest leading off to the group. They walked to the cave so they could see Fedradin, and grabbed the rope. Fedradin walked into the cave, expected the worst from the fifth Legendary Eight. He imagined a gigantic bear or demon, but what he saw shattered all those expectations.

The monster was about the size of a ferret. It was white, with black stripes, much like a skunk. It looked like a rodent, with black beady eyes, a long tail, and furless hands. The Gravorg was coiled around a jewel, about five inches in diameter. Next to the jewel was the rock that the Gravorg was guarding. Scattered around the cave were bones, from the looks of it human. It truly was an eerie situation.

The Gravorg looked up at Fedradin, and immediately everything in the cave, besides the Gravorg, the jewel and the rock, floated up into the air. This happened quickly, and the rope around Fedradin's chest stopped him from smashing into the rock ceiling of the cave.

Seeing that Fedradin had not perished on the stone ceiling of the cave, the Gravorg changed the flow of gravity to back to normal, and Fedradin fell towards the bottom of the cave. He realized that he should have thought out the plan better, but as he started to fear splattering on the stone below, he figured out a way to save himself. Fedradin waved his palm at the ground, and all the dirt that had floated up with him fell down to the ground faster than he, creating a cushiony landing space for him.

The Gravorg grew angry by Fedradin's survival, so it quickly started switching the gravity. Up, down, up, down. Fedradin grew too discombobulated to keep track. As the Gravorg seemed to take a break from switching gravity, Fedradin heard Kerwan call out.

"The jewel! You have to destroy the jewel!"

"Why?"

"That is one of the five jewels that Bal-gastar had made for his five wives. Each one holds an immense amount of power, for they were designed to keep his wives ageless forever. However-" Before Kerwan could finish his history lesson, the gravity switched again. Kerwan was close enough to the cave the he too floated up, but it wasn't strong enough for him to smash into the ceiling.

As Fedradin floated in the air, he saw a bone next to him. He grabbed it with his left hand, and as the gravity switched he threw it at the Gravorg. This action, however, stopped him from bringing the dirt down to provide him a soft spot for landing. Still, as he saw his death approaching, the gravity switched, as

352

the Gravorg stopped the bone from coming into contact with the jewel.

"Kerwan! You need to shoot the jewel with one of your spells!" shouted Fedradin, as the Gravorg turned the gravity to back to normal. Fedradin waved his palm and the dirt fell to the ground, helping him land. Kerwan landed on the dirt, too, and he shot a black spell at the Gravorg. At that moment, Fedradin pulled out Baxcanador.

Then, two things happened at once. One, the spell exploded near the Gravorg. Two, the Gravorg reversed gravity. The spell sent the Gravorg, the jewel and the rock flying. The reversal of gravity became lessened as the distance between the Gravorg and the jewel increased. Fedradin floated in the center of the cave, as his sword had left his hand and started to move upwards. Before he realized what had happened, the sword cut the rope his was attached to, leaving him freely floating.

"Fedradin! If the Gravorg gets to the jewel, it will send you flying into the top of the cave!" shouted Kerwan, unhelpfully. Fedradin tried to move towards the Gravorg, which was squirming in the air, with a swimming motion, but it didn't work. He remained motionless, thrashing about like an imbecile.

He saw that the Gravorg had figured out how to move through the air, slowly, by wagging its tail furiously. He didn't have a tail, so obviously that wasn't an option, so Fedradin had no idea how to move. He finally figured it out, when saw a bone float near its head. He reached out and grabbed it, throwing it in the opposite direction of the jewel.

His plan worked and he started floating forwards, towards the jewel. He grabbed another bone near him and repeated the process. He also used the spyglass from his pouch, his dagger and a shoe. Finally, he reached the jewel, just before the Gravorg.

Fedradin threw the jewel in the direction of Kerwan, and the effect of the zero-gravity gradually faded as the distance from the Gravorg to the jewel increased. Fedradin's feet touched the ground, and things began to rain down around him, like the bones and dirt and the Gravorg...And his sword! Fedradin dove to the side, just as Baxcanador plummeted from the sky, burying itself in the dirt. Fedradin walked over to get his sword, in order to finish off the Gravorg, but before he could, the ferret-like animal bit his forearm. He tried to shake it off, but it wouldn't budge. He had to use one of the bones to bludgeon the monster off of him. It started to run towards its jewel, but before it could get too far, Fedradin took Baxcanador and chopped it into two separate pieces.

As Fedradin started to look for his knife, his shoe and the rock, Kerwan slipped the jewel into his pocket, unseen by anyone except Tiserae.

Chapter 92
Despair

PLITSKY

PRINCE PLITSKY HAD COMMITTED an unimaginable crime. Not only had he killed his father, but he had killed his wife's father, too. Plitsky returned home that afternoon, to find his wife, Gnue, in hysteria.

"Why?" she sobbed. "Why was he killed?"

"What is it, Gnue?" asked Plitsky.

"My father! He was stabbed in the back while sitting in the courtyard!"

"He was?"

"Yes...and your father was killed too, my dear Plitsky," said Gnue.

"No!" said Plitsky, feigning surprise.

"Yes! Who could have imagined it, both our fathers in one day," cried Gnue. Gnue cried for another few minutes, before drying her tears on her sleeve. "I must leave."

"What? Why? How long will you be out?"

"I don't know, Plitsky, but I need some time alone right now." Plitsky watched her walk out the door. He stared after her for a couple moments, then realized that something odd was happening. He walked after, jogging to catch up. Gnue was nowhere to be seen, so he asked around Axler. He was given the direction in which Gnue had last been seen going. He ran along until he arrived at a bridge, over a river that fed into Axler Lake.

Gnue stood on the handrails of the bridge, pacing back and forth, her eyes red.

"Gnue! What are you doing?" shouted Plitsky.

"I cannot bear to live in a world without my father!" she exclaimed.

"No, Gnue! What about our three daughters? What shall become of them?"

"They are all perfectly fine young elves now," said Gnue. "They have no need for me anymore."

"You are their mother! They will always have need of you!"

"I don't *care*, Plitsky! If I don't get a father, they don't get a mother!"

"Gnue, I beg of you, think twice before you do this."

"I've thought twice! I've thought thrice! I thought a million times! I'm going to jump, Plitsky, and there is nothing you can do to stop me!"

"No!" Plitsky ran forward, trying to reach the bridge before Gnue jumped into the swiftly moving river. He was unsuccessful, as his beautiful wife cast herself off the bridge. Plitsky grabbed the air where his wife had last stood, and he whispered to himself, "This is my fault."

Chapter 93
Across The Sea

JOLOAK

JOLOAK DID NOT SLEEP all night. As soon as the sun peeked its head over Dragonsback Ridge, Joloak was out of the gate, machete in hand, ready to search for his partner. Fender stayed back in Sequo. He was able to recognize a hopeless cause when he saw it.

Joloak was combing the ridge, looking for any trace of Trumbell, when he saw footsteps in a patch of mud. He walked over, examined them to find paw prints instead of human ones. Discouraged, Joloak stood up, to find a haggard looking man staring him in the face. He leapt back, before he realized who it was.

"Trumbell! You're alive!"

Trumbell stared back at Joloak, for a long time. "They're back."

"What -?"

"They. Are. Back."

FENDER

"They're back," murmured Trumbell.

"I need more information than that," said a vexed Fender, who had been trying to get Trumbell to elaborate for nigh on an hour.

"They're back."

"Godsdammit!" shouted Joloak. "We need more!"

Trumbell looked at Joloak with an expression of terror. "They're back."

"That's fantastic. Who are we speaking of?" said Fender.

"They're back. They're back. They're back!"

Joloak stepped forward and slapped Trumbell as hard as he could across the face. The man toppled backwards, knocking the chair over as well. Trumbell crashed to the ground, sliding across the stone floor. Joloak walked over to him.

Trumbell looked up and said, "They're back."

"Who?" screamed Joloak, kicking Trumbell in the ribs.

"They're back!" choked out Trumbell. Joloak prepared for another attack. "The Formiant. They're back."

TRUMBELL

"I've never run faster in my life," said Trumbell. "The creatures, they gained on me no matter how fast I ran!"

"What happened?" asked Joloak.

"They caught me," said Trumbell. "Brought me back to their camp. There were so many Formiant." He shuddered. Joloak and Fender waited for him to continue. "They branded me. Treated me as a prisoner, wrapped me in some spider web. But in the night, I was rescued. I don't know by who, or even more frightening, what, but I ran. And when I heard the fights begin, I didn't stop, didn't go back. I kept running. No idea where I was going. Didn't care really, as long as it was away from the horrible bugs."

"Formiant," said Fender cautiously. "Haven't been seen for sixty years, more. Our fathers helped drive them over the Ridge. They were never seen again."

"Until last night!" exclaimed Trumbell. "I saw 'em with my own two eyes! They're back, and they're comin.' We need to alert the mainland."

"The mainland? Haxter? The *Empire?*" said Fender incredulously. "We haven't received word from them in months! They've forgotten about us! They think we're crazy!"

"That may be, but I'm leaving tomorrow for Haxter. They need to know about the Formaint!"

"I'm sorry, Trumbell, but I forbid you from leaving. We need every man here to protect us if the Formaint attack!"

"If I bring back hundreds of men to help us, it will be worth it!"

"The Empire will laugh at you! They will not give us men!"

"Challenge accepted." Trumbell walked for the door.

"Stop!" yelled Fender. Trumbell turned, dirk in hand, the knife up against Fender's throat.

"You don't control me." Trumbell pulled the knife off Fender's neck, turned and walked for the door.

Fender turned to Joloak. "He's stupid."

"He may be stupid," said Joloak, "But he's not careless."

FANE

Fane flung Ash to the side as the orcish archers fired at the wall. Fane blocked the arrows that came near the Spice Sultan with his shield, then yelled, "Ash, get your ass back in the fotress!" The fat king didn't need to be told twice. He waddled back into the fotress as fast as he stubby legs could carry him. Hunnex was fighting along side Fane's archers, felling orc after orc as they charged the gates.

"Use the oil and rocks if these creatures bring out ladders!" yelled Fane. "Any foot soldier on the wall, come with me to make a welcoming committee for the orcs!" Fane ran down the steps, twenty other men behind him. When the arrived at the bottom, the wooden door to the fotress was being beaten with some sort of orcish ram. "Do not let this line break when the orcs come through!"

As soon as Fane finished his words, the door shattered open, and orcs spilled into the hallway. Fane's men were able to slaughter about fifteen suprised orcs as they came through the door immediately, but the sheer number of orcs rushing into the castle overwhelmed the soldiers and they retreated, losing ground as the relentless orcs attacked.

Luckily, the orcs didn't wear armor, so Fane was able to slash open their stomachs and gut them as he was attacked, but his other men didn't find the same success. As he saw one of his soldiers lose a head to one of the creatures, he shouted to one of his men, "Get reinforcements! Make sure you bring Hunnex!" The man turned and ran as Fane beheaded another creature. The bodies piled up as Fane stabbed and slashed, but still he was forced to retreat, his men dying around him all the while.

An orc toppled backwards as an arrow was sent through its heart. Another twang and a second orc was impaled. Fane turned to see Hunnex nocking yet another arrow. "I would advise ducking," was all the man said, as he sent an arrow into the orc charging Fane, as Fane dropped to the ground. "That's two lives you owe me."

"How did it look from the wall?" said Fane, knocking the blade from an orc's hand before slicing it in half.

"The orcs seemed endless," said Hunnex, as he loosed another one of his deadly, accurate projectiles.

"That's what I want to hear," said Fane sarcastically, killing an orc.

"Until the rest of the Orcslayer Guild arrived," replied Hunnex. The man reached into his quiver, but found nothing there. "Damn!" he cried.

"I have an extra sword," offered Fane, who chopped his way through a few orcs. There was a cry and another one of Fane's men fell.

"I've never used a sword before," said Hunnex.

"Better late then never," said Fane, tossing a weapon from his second sheath to Hunnex. "Use the pointed bit."

HUNNEX

He didn't know if his stance was right. He didn't know if his grip was right. But he was blocking the orcish blades and managing to kill the orcs if they got close, so he figured it was good enough. That was until an orc knocked Fane's blade out of Hunnex's hands, the weapon clattering to the floor. The orc approached Hunnex, a look of glee on its ugly face.

Hunnex scrambled backwards, looking for something to protect himself. The orc followed, grinning from ear to ear. Suddenly, Fane appeared out of nowhere, slicing the head off the orc. He turned to Hunnex, smiled and said, "Now we're even."

"Not quite," said Hunnex, but Fane had continued to fight, slashing the orcs back as they came.

The humans continued to get pushed back, until the Orcslayers came bursting in the door, slaughtering the orcs from behind. The humans began pushing their way towards each other, killing every orc in their path, until none remained.

Exhausted, the few soldiers who were left standing, a panting Fane, and a bloodied Hunnex, met the Orcslayers. Hunnex stepped forwards, embracing a woman from the Orcslayers, who did likewise.

"I thought you were dead," said the woman.

"I would be if you hadn't shown up."

Fane stepped forwards, "I don't believe we've met."

The woman moved past Hunnex and extended a hand. "Fevra," she said. "And I have to ask, what could you have done to anger the orcs so?"

ASH

Ash, Fane, Hunnex and Fevra sat around Ash's table.

"Wine?" asked Ash, as servants brought out bottles.

"I'll have some," said Fane. Hunnex also accepted Ash's offer, wheras Fevra waved off the drink.

"So Fane tells me I owe you Orcslayers for both Stent and Welnn," said Ash.

"Indeed you do," said Fevra, her long red hair pulled back in a long braid. To Ash, she was strikingly attractive, with her freckles and nice figure.

"If I've been battling orcs my entire life, how have I never even heard of your guild?"

"Two thoughts," said Fevra, "one, it doesn't look like you've been battling orcs you're whole life, it looks like you've been feasting your whole life on your precious stentspice that *he's* been fighting to protect." Fevra pointed at Fane. Ash fought to keep rage from surfacing on his face.

Fane leaned over and whispered in his ear, "Remember she saved your life." Ash faked a smile.

"Second," continued Fevra, "we've kept our guild secret, because how do you think the orcs would like it if they found out about a certain Orc*slayer* guild?"

"Point taken," said Ash, taking a gulp of wine, "But why have you taken so long coming to my aid?"

"I don't know how much you know about orcs, probably little, but orcs are a tribal race, and it seems as of late, the tribes have come to together, and chosen some sort of king. I believe he sent you a letter the other day?"

"F'ntok!" said Fane.

"Precisely," said Fevra. "With unity these orcs pose an actual threat to Stentor and possibly even the mainland, Haxter."

"But we killed them all today!" said Ash.

"*You*, did nothing but cower in your room," said Hunnex. Ash forced a smirk, as he clenched his fists.

"That?" said Fevra, "was the welcoming party. F'ntok wasn't a part of it."

"What do you mean?" said Fane.

"I mean, that there are more orcs in Stentor that we ever knew. When they aren't killing each other, they breed like flies. Ash, Fane, we're all going to die if we don't get help. There aren't enough humans in Stentor to combat the creatures."

Ash stood up. "I'll take our fastest ship to Uiklo on the morrow."

Fevra stood up as well. "I hope it's a very fast. For everyone's sake."

DUNLOCK

The main rivers of Haxter: the Oxler, the Mendelgar, the Silver, the Bal-gastar, the Haxter, and other connecting rivers had all been cleared of rocks and dug deeper by the LNR so ships could sail up and down them. It was one of the few good things the LNR had done.

So the actual sailing wouldn't be a problem. The problem was Truz. Controlled by the chultra, it was one of the gates to the Haxter riverway and was fiercly guarded by the freakish cat warriors.

Grent had gone back to Creopolis to rally his troops, while Dunlock raised a fleet and crewed it with his slaves. So many slaves volunteered, that Dunlock was able to crew all his dromonds, galleys, cogs, xebecs, frigates, carracks, balingers, koches, triremes, and some whalers he had captured off of the Osupenese shore.

` That armada was the one he now had to get through Truz. He had long since given up on stealth. Maybe if he had stolen a few longships from Osup he could be able to slip them through the gates of Truz under the cover of nightfall, on a moonless night. But a few longships would not be able to take down Whitewater.

His dromonds might.

It was the gloaming as he brought his fleet towards Truz. The large gate that barred the Oxler River from the Trade Sea could be seen leagues off, catching the moonlight on its rusted metal. The tower that held the gate dwarfed the rest of the town, a golden dome on top making its mark on the night sky. A few more buildings rose up around the gate and stretched back down the river, but none could even come close to the massive size of the gate.

"What's the plan?" asked Kolan, who came up from belowdecks of the flagship, *Redemption*. A few knights followed behind him, Sir Fern, Sir Unk, and Sir Beck. Sir Fern's bond was of reasonable length, noted Dunlock. A good ten or twelve rings were linked together and dangled from his swordbelt. Sir Beck and Sir Unk had a measely one ring. "These are some coinswords I picked up before we left. There's more on some of the other dromonds."

"You there," said Dunlock, pointing a finger at Fern. "What's your name?"

"Sir Fern Tradeborn, the Trade Knight, son of Frem, if it please your Grace."

"A bastard," said Dunlock. "But an acknowledged one, by your surname."

"Yes, your Grace."

"How much do you know of Truz, Trade Knight?"

Fern smiled. "How much do you want to know?"

FERN

"Few people know this," Fern said, "but Truz is left mostly abandoned at night." Fern was captaining a small skiff, with muffled oars, as he rowed with his other coinswords towards the gates of Truz. "The chultra have taken to sleeping in trees, to protect themselves from the beasts of the rainforest." Another pull of the oars. "The sleeping arangements are back a ways, in the rainforest." Pull. "The only ones here are the sentinels in the Golden Dome, which is largely run by coinswords, like us." Pull.

"Why does this matter?" spat Beck as he pulled. "I'm just doing this for a few fellyers. Maybe a link or two." Pull.

"To get those fellyers, you'll have to listen to me." Pull. "If we can get in, we can slay those guards and open the gate before they wake up the rest of the chultra." Pull.

"Won't they have spotted us already?" asked Unk. Pull.

"I've been in that Dome. When they're not drinking, they're playing cards. When they're not playing cards, they're drinking.

When they're not doing either, they're dead." Pull. Soon, they arrived at gate. They had not been spotted. "This wall has taken a beating," said Fern to his crew, laying a hand on the wall that supported the gate. "From arrows to boulders to spells, it has given it nice handholds."

Fern began his climb, finding nicks and arrow slits to wedge his feet in as he made his way upwards. All would have been well, accept for Beck's clumsy footing. The coinsword put his weight on a chunk of stone wedged in the wall, which broke off underneath him. He went tumbling down the wall, knocking taking another coinsword with him, screaming all the way.

Damn! thought Fern, as he heard the muster of men in the Dome. He froze, pressing himself tight to the wall, as the guards poured out on the barbican. Fern looked down in horror to see one of his men leaning backwards, fingers in an arrow slit, to catch a glimpse of the guards. A shout and soon the man was feathered with an arrow, falling down to the ocean below. A guard came over the wall and peered down to see the rest of the men pressed as flat as they could.

"Damn!" yelled Fern, this time aloud, as the guard went running back to the rest, and he heard cries of, "Someone wake the chultra!"

Two chultra, who had both removed their shells to give them mobility, leapt over the edge of the barbican. Ropes had been tied around them, Fern could see, as they repelled towards him.

One targeted him, and the chultra swung at him. He released his toes from an arrowhead he had been using as a foothold and slid underneath the chultra. Angered when it missed, the chultra tugged on the rope and swung once more, lower. With his fingers barely gripping the arrowhead, Fern quickly had to decide his next move.

He leapt backwards off the wall as the chultra passed, grabbing its back legs as it passed. The chlutra, in an attempt to rid itself of Fern, rotated its hips so that Fern was sent smashing into the stone wall. Dazed, he nearly dropped off the chultra -his left hand releasing from the chultra's leg, but managed to retain his grip. As the chultra swung again, preparing to smash Fern, he knew he couldn't hang on for another bout with the wall.

A thought struck him -luckily before the wall did the same-and he remembered a chultra friend of his suffering after his shell was removed, in the place where the shell used to cover. Fern loosed his right hand and sent his fist into the chultra's back.

"*Pza!*" it cried, and as it recoiled, Fern just barely skimmed the wall. He fumbled for his sword, pulled it out, but he scraped against the wall once more and it tumbled from his hand.

His grip on the chultra's leg slipped. He slid a few inches down its leg, but regained his purchase as he reached its ankle. The chultra shook its leg, but a blow to its back stilled it.

Fern reached for his knife and found it -right as the chultra sent him smashing into the wall. His grip faltered, and he fell - only to be saved by the rope of the second chultra that had descended lower to fight his other men. On instinct, he slashed the rope below him with his dagger.

He remembered the first chultra tugging once to descend. Fern tugged twice. He began to lift, clutching the rope. The first chultra attacked once more, but Fern fought him off with the knife, sending the chultra reeling with a slashed arm and cheek.

Fern arrived at the top of the barbican, jumping forward to give himself the element of surprise. He landed on a soldier out front, supposedly the sentry, but Fern could smell the stentspice on his breath. He slashed his throat. Fern pulled the man's sword from his sheath and got to his feet, sword at the ready.

The soldiers were shocked to see him standing there. None had a weapon out, unless one could consider a wineskin a weapon. Fern attacked and felled the man who had pulled him up, twisting to catch the blow of another soldier. The swords pulled back and kissed once more, lighting the night sky with sparks. The battle raged, until Fern went to parry and his cheap steel broke under the pressure of his adversary's blade.

His abandoned knife was behind him, he held splinters in his hand, his backup was likely dead, and by now other guards had nocked an arrow to their bowstrings and had Fern in their aim. He threw down his weapon and yielded.

"What a nice bond," said the soldier to whom he had yielded. "I'll now be *Sir* Wendel Domeswatch." Fern closed his eyes as the soldier grabbed his bond and prepared to pull it off.

"I would have gone with Sir Wendel Dunghead," came a voice from the top of the wall. Sir Unk flew at Sir Wendel, cleaving off his head. Unk flung Fern a sword, which he caught with ease. The bowmen loosed their arrows, and Unk was taken in the arm. Luckily for him, not his swordarm.

Fern and Unk cut through the bowmen as they tried to reload, leaving a pile of corpses in their wake. A few men yielded, but with no place to keep prisoners, Fern and Unk were forced to kill them.

More men appeared at the top of the wall, until there was Sir Fern, Sir Unk, Sir Walt, Timund, Big Tum, Bonesholt, Kifford, Gabryl, Linton, Slenk, and Waprid. "We have to get the gate open," announced Fern. "Big Tum, Kifford, and Waprid, I need you to help me turn the wheel. The rest of you..." The shrieks of the chultra could be heard in the distance, a wave of brown visible as the chultra charged towards them. "Hold them off with the bows." Fern came over to Unk, who was trying to pick up a bow. "You can't fight," said Fern, pointing to the red flower blossoming through Unk's boiled leather. He had pulled the arrow out himself.

"I cut his bloody head off. He's paying for this wound in hell, I'll tell you that. It's hard w' no head."

"Unk, you will die if you fight."

"You'll all die if I don't."

Fern left Unk to struggle with holding the bow with his left hand to help get the gate open. He entered the Dome Room, where empty bottles of wine lay scattered, Grape Islands, Vineyard, Vale, Jade Isle. These men drank well. Barrels of stentspice were cracked open and spilled, games of Hex lay about unfinished, and cards for Drago were strewn about. In the middle of the room, a large wooden wheel stood, its purpose to open the gate.

The guards had flung chairs and tables at it when they had heard Beck's screams. The debris was so that the wheel could not be turned unless it was cleared. Fern's men were standing around. *No one ever said coinswords were smart.*

"Clear the debris!" he screamed, and the men began to work. Soon it was done, but Fern realized something bad. The spindle of the wheel had been cracked in the chaos. It would snap off soon and then the gate wouldn't open. "Spin the wheel!" ordered Fern. "Don't break the middle of it or we can't open the gate." Fern had chosen the biggest men for the job, but it was still a long process. They twisted very slowly, but it opened still, until Fern heard when he was dreading. A loud snap. The wheel came to a stop and wouldn't budge.

"To the battle!" cried Fern. "And hope the gate is open enough."

DUNLOCK

Excitement grew onboard *Redemption* when the gate began to swing inwards and open. Dunlock had seen the battle atop the barbican, but could not determine the winner from so far away. Suddenly, the gate came to a screeching halt, too narrow to let any of his dromonds pass through.

Impatient, he called for his catapult-ships -one of his own creations. Three cogs with mounted catapults pulled forwards, and flung huge boulders at the gates. One hit the Dome and made a clanging sound that rang through the city, another hit the wall the soldiers had just climbed, and the third knocked the gate open slightly more.

"We're going to have to ram it open," said Kolan. Dunlock passed the command to a few koches, crewed mostly by slaves. The koches were used by the Osupenesse for when they sailed around the Icicle to trade with the Grefture. They were made to break ice easily. And how different were ice and metal gates?

The captains took the orders, despite the sureness of their ship's destruction. A few slaves jumped ship when they heard, but could not swim and sank below the tranquil waters to a watery grave.

The ships went full speed, oars beating the water furiously. The koches crashed into the gates, slowly opening them ram after ram. Suddenly, as a destroyed koch crashed once more, the gates flung open suddenly with a wooden snap that could be heard far away.

"Forward!" shouted Dunlock as his ships rushed forwards towards the now open gate. The koches he had sent were now sunk, and the other ships picked up as many surviving crew members as they could capture. Many still drowned.

Dunlock passed the gate and sailed down the river, surprised at what he found.

FERN

The chultra were all around them, swarming from their nests to attack. His men fell one by one to either the chultra darts or machetes. Unk managed to stay alive though, slaying chultra after chultra with his very bloody sword.

After the Dome was struck by a boulder, and the wall shaken by another, all who remained were Fern, Unk, Big Tum, Bonesholt, Kifford, and Slenk. Fern's borrowed steel felt so heavy as he struggled to lift it, and the chultra seemd to have an endless suppy of soldiers.

Ships began smashing the gate, and Fern heard a crack. *The wheel gave way*. The gate swung open and ships rushed in. Fern took the opportunity and dove off the barbican, landing on the deck of *Redemption*. He heard a crack, but knew it wasn't the boat. It was the bone in his leg.

DUNLOCK

The amount of chultra was astonishing. They leapt onto boats and attacked his men with their long knifes and poisoned darts. He pulled out his sword, but none were bold enough to attack the flagship. His other ships however...they showed no restraint. A few ships had been burned by torch-bearing chultra.

There was no telling how many men he lost on the Oxler River that day. As his ships pulled away from Truz, the chultra pursued on foot as far as they dared. His archers took out most of them.

Only Fern, Unk, Big Tum, and Bonesholt made it back. The rest had died either in battle, falling off the wall, or drowning when they dried to jump back onto the boats. Kifford had been impaled on a mast.

But he had made it through. At the cost of a few men and a few ships, he was on his way to take Whitewater and win back all he had lost. *Redemption* sailed through the waterway, with its mission painted on its hull.

Chapter 94
Voyage to Vau

FEDRADIN

FROM THE GRAVORG'S CAVE, they decided to ignore the needle, which pointed southwest, and go and try to enlist the help of the flayers. They traveled to Uiklo -the trading post between the flayers, svaadi, chultra, Stents, Corsairs, Jade Islanders, and Westlanders— and they chartered a boat. It was a small yacht, with two sails and a cabin below the main deck. They also hired a skipper to help them sail to Vau, the island where the flayers lived. Fedradin noticed the strange boats from Stent moored to the docks, as the dark-skinned Stentoriks unloading barrels of stentspice with the oversight of the supercargo.

The group left the port of Uiklo behind. They set off the next morning, sailing through the waves. Tiserae was staring off the side of the boat. Fedradin came up to her and joined her at the starboard side of the boat.

"Hello," said Fedradin.

"Hello," said Tiserae.

There was a moment of awkward silence, as both parties had not said another word. "Are you feeling seasick?" asked Fedradin. "I'm feeling seasick."

"Actually, I am, a little bit."

"The waves are pretty big today."

"I guess."

Fedradin looked over at Tiserae, who appeared very disinterested. "You ever wonder what's on the other side of the ocean?"

"Probably some other landmass."

"I've been thinking, what if that landmass is the other side of Qassar?"

"What?"

"What if you traveled across the ocean so far one way that you reached the unexplored part of Qassar?"

"No way. Not possible."

"Why not?"

"You'd fall off the world, you wouldn't go around it."

Fedradin shrugged, staring into the ocean, waves gently undulating. "Your inventions are really neat."

"Thanks, I've spent a lot of time working on them."

"I know. You said you summoned some spirits to help you?"

Tiserae turned to Fedradin. "Like you know a thing about summoning," she said in a joking tone.

"Try me!"

"Okay, what are the three main types of spirits?"

"Easy: imps, djinns and genies."

"How many rings of the spirit world are there?" asked Tiserae.

"Twelve, next."

"What's the ring with the most power?"

"The twelfth, obviously."

"What's the fourth and rarest type of spirit!"

"Um, well, that would be, um..."

"Ha! It's an efreet!"

"I knew that! I must have been around too many of the other kind of spirits." Tiserae laughed at his joke, even though it was only a particularly bad pun. Fedradin looked into her eyes. Her eyes were looking into his. "You look beautiful in the moonlight, even with that ridiculous hood." Fedradin moved his hand to pull her hood down. Tiserae turned to the side and brushed his hand away. Fedradin moved his hand to her shoulder, turning her so that she faced him again.

"Sorry, I just don't like anyone seeing my hair. It's all messed up."

"That's okay. The rest of your beauty makes up for it." Fedradin leaned in and kissed her, and after a few seconds she kissed him back.

KERWAN

Kerwan was standing behind one of the masts, watching Fedradin and Tiserae as they kissed. He was full of rage, mostly directed at Fedradin. He had told the Prince that he was in love with Tiserae, but Fedradin still went ahead and kissed her!

Kerwan reached into his pocket and pulled out the jewel, holding it so that it caught the moonlight and gleamed. It was certainly a sight to see. The jewel that had been of a bronze-ish color before now looked red, just as red as Kerwan felt angry.

Kerwan slipped the jewel back into his pocket, looking back at Tiserae and Fedradin. He would have need of the jewel in time. All in good time.

FEDRADIN

Later that night, Qint took Fedradin out onto the deck of the boat.

"What did you bring me out here for?" asked Fedradin.

"I suspect that you may have a confrontation with the Fire Sage soon, so I need to show you something before then. To use the fire crystal to its full potential, you will need to create fire out of nothing. Right now, you have only had to control the elements that are around you. Now, I want you to learn to create those elements and control the elements you create. Understand?"

"I'm following you."

"Great. Because air is all around us right now, it would be impractical for you to try to create more of it. Instead, I want you to try to create a handful of sand, and throw it in my face."

"How?"

"Like you use your crystal normally. Just think!"

Fedradin pointed his palm at Qint. He strained, thinking about creating sand. He wanted to create sand. He needed to create sand. Slowly, grains of sand began to form in the air, collecting together to assemble a small handful of sand.

"Think about Widow's Desert, Fedradin! Think about all that sand!" The grains started to form faster and faster. Finally, the collection of sand was big enough to be considered a handful. Fedradin pushed his palm towards Qint. The sand flew into the elderly man's eyes and mouth. Qint, brushing the sand from his eyes and spitting out a glob of it from his mouth said, "I think you've figured it out."

Chapter 95
The Battle of Bal-gastar

ROGER

THE SOLDIERS WERE IN a defensive position around the door, shields down in front of them, swords pointed out. A few archers had run down from the wall and joined the soldiers, picking up close combat weapons on the way. Now Roger, Sgire, Lider and the remaining rebels, maybe fifty of them left, faced possibly seventy five or a hundred soldiers guarding the entrance to Bal-gastar.

FLYC

Flyc looked down at the battle from the window in his royal chambers, Oxlo, Frin, Tawassa standing behind him. A soldier burst into the room.

"The rebels are gaining ground on us, your Excellency!"

A smiled crossed Flyc's face. Without looking he pointed his palm at the man standing behind him, and a ball of fire erupted from his palm. The soldier caught fire and started screaming in pain. He fell to the ground, the smell of burning flesh filling the room. Flyc waved his palm again, using his air powers to circulate the air to ameliorate the smell.

"What are you happy about, Master, they are getting closer to us!" said Frin.

"If I wanted these rebels dead, they would be dead Frin. I obviously want them alive."

ROGER

Roger sent a beam of black light into a clump of soldier from his hand. The beam exploded, killing a few soldiers on impact, but the shockwave sending many others crashing to the ground. The rebels advanced, beating to death any soldiers who had fallen out of line.

"Roger, how are you doing that?" asked Sgire, as the soldiers regrouped.

"There's no time for that, Sgire, we're fighting now!" The rebels charged forwards, throwing themselves at the soldiers' shields, beating the strips of metal with their various weapons. A few pushed through and broke the soldiers' first line, but they were quickly killed by the spears and swords of the soldiers. Roger fired two more black spells at the soldiers, killing many, and sending even more flying into the grasps of the rebels, where they were quickly killed.

Roger raised his palm to fire more black spells into the crowds of the soldiers, when he was tackled from behind. Roger and his mysterious assailant rolled down the cobblestone path. Finally, Roger was able to break free of his attacker, throwing whoever it was away from him. He finally was able to see his attacker. Surprisingly, it was Sgire.

"What are you doing?" shouted Roger.

"They never figured out what my mother died of, Roger. I saw you kill all those soldiers without a weapon. Roger, I think you killed my mother."

"Fine! Okay? Yes, I killed your mother!"

"Roger! How could you?"

"I was starving, okay? I needed food and your mother tried to stop me!"

Sgire, started breathing, heavier and heavier, until she started crying. Roger had no time to console her, for the soldiers were advancing, the rebels retreating. Roger ran to try and help them, but it was no use. The rebels started to run away from the soldiers. Lider was the only one that had stayed to fight, so Roger ran up to join him. He knew that he couldn't use a black spell, for it might kill Lider. Roger began to fight the soldiers with only his knife, but it was in vain. Slowly, he and Lider became swamped with soldiers. After a while, they knew that they would perish if they kept fighting, so they lay down their weapons and put their hands in the air. A soldier raised his sword to finish off the two, when something amazing happened.

"Stop!" came the booming voice of Flyc. "Arrest those two men."

Reluctantly, the soldier who had wanted to kill Roger and Lider stepped backwards as two others grabbed them by the arms and walked them into the castle of Bal-gastar.

They were thrown into the Flyc's royal chambers, skirting a badly burned corpse, which struck fear into Roger's heart.

Flyc was standing by a window, which overlooked the entrance to the castle. The soldiers were regrouping, returning to their original, defensive position. "So, boy, you have decided to lead a, well, very unsuccessful rebellion against me. And you, soldier, have decided to betray me for these rebels."

"Your Excellency, what you're doing to these people is wrong! They are innocent civilians and you are killing them off like flies!"

"Silence, soldier. I will deal with you later. You first, boy. What have you been doing with your hands?"

"Oh, this?" said Roger, shooting a white spell at Flyc. Flyc waved his palm and the air in front of the spell grew denser. The beam collided with the dense portion of the air and disappeared into nothingness. Roger let out a shout of astonishment.

"You do not want to anger me, boy. Now I must know, how can you use magic without a wand?"

"I have no idea, your *Excellency*."

"Fine, if you refuse to tell me, then I will have you killed." Roger was grabbed by two soldiers by his shoulders. At that moment, when all seemed lost, Roger heard the doors to the castle give in to the mob. The soldiers unhanded Roger, distracted by the door. Roger, before either one could react, stabbed them both in the neck with his knife. They fell to the ground dead, and Flyc only laughed.

"What's to laugh about, emperor?" said Roger. "You hear that sound? That is the sound of my army climbing the stairs to come and kill you."

"That's how appears doesn't it?"

"What do you mean?"

The army of rebels emerged from the stairs that led to the royal chambers.

"There's Flyc!" yelled one rebel. "Let's kill that dictator!" yelled another. Flyc smirked as the rebels rushed forward. In an instant, he changed from a small man into a demon.

He was now eight feet tall and bright red. He had three horns growing out of his head, two on the sides and one above and

374

between his two red eyes. He had muscular arms that ended in claws, and a tail with a razor sharp blade on the end.

"I am Erch!" the demon promulgated. "You will bow down before me!" Purple fire rose from under his feet, enveloping him in a raging inferno. The fire went out, and Erch was gone.

Chapter 96
Smire

FEDRADIN

THE BOAT DOCKED IN Elatador, where the flayer supercargo was shocked to see humans. In fact, he refused to allow the boat to dock. Fedradin slipped the supercargo a diamond -for which he exchanged some of his fellyers— in order to dock. The actual docking process was very laborious, for at seeing how much money one could get out of Fedradin by a mere refusal, the skipper was not in the best of moods. When finally the boat had docked, Fedradin and his group set out on newly purchased horses for Smire, the capital of the flayers, where the new Wrethig was presiding. Fedradin knew that he was paying double for everything he was buying, but since the humans had killed the Wrethig, it seemed reasonable.

The trip across Vau was uneventful, until they stopped for lunch. They were sitting on the plains, eating the two rabbits and one squirrel that Aserax had hunted. It was like a normal lunch, with not much chatter, mostly everyone thinking about the journey ahead of them. They still had to hunt down and kill three more of the Legendary Eight, and that had proved to not be an easy thing to do.

They were about to saddle their horses and start to continue on their way to Smire, when ahead of them came a few flayers, each on foot. There were three of them, though only one had the slit in its throat that allowed it to speak Common. When they passed near the group, they stopped, one flayer spitting.

"What do you want?" said Fedradin.

"We mad," said the flayer said through the slit in its throat. "You kill Wrethig. We mad."

"Yes, I know," said Fedradin, "and we're sorry that our Emperor did that to your leader. Now, if you will let us pass we need to be on our way."

"You spineless worms. You trying run away from us."

"That is not true, we just need to get to Smire."

"Why, you kill new Wrethig too?"

"No."

"Why you go?"

"We want his help," said Fedradin.

"He help you? Hilarious humans. He support deranged crocodile before he support you. Actually, you humans just like deranged crocodile." The flayers began laughing, in a weird inhuman way.

Fedradin put his hand on the handle of his sword. Breetex grabbed Fedradin's arm. "No Fedradin! Killing them would be disastrous!" Fedradin, with much effort, pulled his hand off his sword's hilt.

After a few more minutes, during which Fedradin had to listen to the one flayer make fun of the human race, the flayers left, laughing to themselves as they went. Fedradin stared at them as they walked away in anger, but he finally tore his gaze away and saddled his horse. The group started riding north, going in the direction of Smire.

The rest of the trip to Smire was uneventful. They arrived at the flayer capital, to find that the entrance to the city was a hole. They walked over to the hole, where they were quickly arrested by two flayers and brought to the castle of Smire immediately, before any of them were able to utter a word.

The city of Smire was incredible. It was all underground, yet it had the eerie feeling like it was a normal city. The ceiling was high and painted blue, like the sky, and unseen magical devices cast light on the city made entirely out of marble. The flayers that had arrested the group brought them to a building at the end of the city, a one story building the width of the entire city, which was fairly wide. They entered the building, getting dragged by the flayer guards to a room. Inside, there was a flayer who Fedradin safely assumed was the Wrethig. The flayer had a crown made out of gold atop its head, and a staff with a large sapphire at the top. Fedradin also noticed that this flayer had the slit in its throat that allowed it to speak Common. The Wrethig sat on a throne, which was on a platform, which overlooked a rectangular hole, which was filled with a grayish-pink liquid.

The guards pushed the group to the ground, pointing their blades into their backs. One guard, who did not have a slit in his throat, started speaking in a mixture of clicks, grunts and hand motions. The Wrethig nodded, clicking and grunting something back.

"Why have you come, humans?" asked the Wrethig, in fairly good Common.

"We request your assistance."

"And you think that we will help you humans with anything? Get out of my city."

"Wait!" shouted Fedradin, as the guards began to drag him backwards. "You know that the actions of Flyc don't speak for the rest of the human race. That being said, what if a dwarf asks your assistance? Or an elf?"

The Wrethig thought for a moment. "I guess I would listen." The guards stopped pulling them away. Fedradin nudged Breetex.

"Oh, right! We have reason to believe that Emperor Flyc is assembling an army, and if that army ever marches, we would like your troops' support to fight that army."

The Wrethig thought for a moment, but said nothing. "Please! The chultra and the Keshnul have already said that they would help us!" said Aserax. The Wrethig continued to think, finally saying:

"I must consult my advisors. Wait here." The Wrethig clicked something to the guards and made a hand gesture, and the guards left the room. Qint got up and walked over to Fedradin, pulling him aside.

"Fedradin, there is obviously no chance that the Wrethig will support you. The humans killed his father!"

"Well thanks for killing *my* hope," said Fedradin. "What's your point?"

"My point is that you are going to need a vial of the brains from the elderpool."

"Elderpool? What's that?"

"You see that pool in front of us?"

"Yes."

"That has the brains from all the past Wrethigs."

"Including the one that was killed by Erch?"

"Yes. Now, the flayers use this to pass down secrets from Wrethig to Wrethig, and also to talk to the deceased Wrethigs."

"I follow."

"To get to the third Demon Caller, you will need to make a potion out of rare and hard-to-come-by ingredients and in that potion you will need a vial of the brains from the elderpool." Potion with rare ingredients? Sounded familiar.

"So I need to take some of it? Wouldn't that be an unspeakable crime to the flayers?"

"Yes," said Qint, slipping Fedradin a glass vial from his pocket, "but there is no chance in hell that the flayers join our cause. I suggest, so that you don't have to come back here, that you take it now."

"But-"

"Do it, Fedradin!" Fedradin reluctantly took the vial from Qint, and walked over to the elderpool. He dipped the vial into the brains, until it filled up to the top with the disgusting looking mush. He put the stopper back into the top of the vial.

"I'm sorry, but my advisers advise that-" The Wrethig stopped short as he saw Fedradin slip the vial of brains into his pouch. "What are you doing!" The Wrethig let out a loud series of grunts.

"Run!" shouted Fedradin, as the guards rushed into the chamber. Fedradin pulled out Baxcanador and swung it at the nearest guard. The flayer parried the blow with a black, undulating, obsidian blade and a wicked point. Baxcanador bounced off the flayer's sword, and the flayer swung at Fedradin, who blocked it with his kappa shell shield. Fedradin put his shield down and thrust his blade at the flayer, who ducked the blade. Fedradin swung at the crouched flayer, and it only avoided the blade by rolling to the side. It leapt to its feet, dodging another one of Fedradin's swings.

After a fury of blows from Fedradin, the flayer found an opportunity to swing at Fedradin, which he parried with Baxcanador. Before Fedradin could return the attack, the flayer swung an overhead blow at Fedradin, who caught it easily on the edge of Baxcanador. Again, Fedradin was not able to attack before the flayer sent its blade hammering into Fedradin's. This process repeated itself many times, until the flayer's blade collided with Fedradin's wrist guard. The vibrations caused Baxcanador to drop out of Fedradin's grip, leaving him open to the finishing blow from the flayer. It kicked Fedradin to the ground, raising its obsidian sword for the finishing blow.

Fedradin thought desperately for ways to avoid his oncoming death. His shield was underneath him, so it would be impractical to pull it out and use it. He could think of no more options, until he saw the obsidian blade catch the sunlight. *Obsidian. Obsidian is a stone. Stone is earth. Could this work?* Fedradin raised a palm, pointing it at the sword. As the flayer thrust the sword towards Fedradin, the sword began to curl up into a ball. The flayer, in confusion, looked at its sword, and in that moment of hesitation, Fedradin jumped to his feet, kicking the flayer to the ground. Quickly, Fedradin grabbed Baxcanador, stabbing it into the head of the flayer.

He looked up, to see the rest of the flayers dead, each with an arrow in its head. Fedradin looked to Aserax and she shrugged.

"I couldn't get a clear shot," she said.

Fedradin shot her an angry glance. "We have to run. If the messengers the Wrethig will surely send reach Elatador before us, they will sink our ship and we will never leave this godsforsaken island." The group turned and ran for the door to the building, running into the streets of Smire. Fedradin stole a glance behind them to see three flayers run out of the castle in pursuit. Still, since none had the slit in their throats, they were incapable of yelling for help, for their clinks and grunts could not be heard for away.

Fedradin weaved in between merchants and civilians, pushing his way through to get to the opening of Smire before the other flayers. Fedradin looked behind him to see that the flayers were having just as much trouble making their way through the crowded streets as he.

Fedradin collided with a flayer who carrying chickens, for he was looking behind him. The flayer crashed to the ground, her chickens falling to the ground around her. Fedradin, who had not fallen, jumped over the flayer, who was trying to round up her now freed poultry.

Finally, he made it to the gates of Smire, along with the rest of his group. They ran past the guards, mounted their horses and rode south as fast as they could. Fedradin looked behind him to see the flayers that had been pursuing them, stop at the gates, arguing with the guards there. Fedradin smiled to himself. This would be easy.

Chapter 97
Challenge

POLTAX

PRINCE POLTAX ANGRILY JUMPED to his feet.

"My sister and my father?" he shouted. "Who is responsible for this?"

"I don't have any proof, but it had to have been Plitsky, my own nephew," said an elf by the name of Vuinmore.

"Why would he kill his own wife?"

"He didn't. She drowned herself in the river after he killed Gasodo and Juern."

"Why would he do that?"

"He obviously wants the throne bad enough." Even though Vuinmore didn't say it out loud, he had ulterior motives.

"What should I do about it?" asked Poltax.

"You need to challenge him to a duel, show him who's really fit to be king."

PLITSKY

Prince Plitsky was pacing in the courtyard when Prince Poltax arrived.

"You!" Poltax shouted. "You killed my father, and now my sister is dead, too!"

"I did not!"

"Give it a rest, Plitsky. No one believes your story. It's obvious that you did this to give yourself an advantage for the throne."

"Now, Poltax, I cannot believe you would accuse me of such treachery!"

"Like my accusations are invalid! I challenge you to a duel, Plitsky. Tomorrow, here in the courtyard. The winner of the duel inherits the throne."

"But the throne belongs to me now!"

"Does it? I have a letter from Juern that bequeaths me the throne."

"You have no such letter, Poltax."

"Are you willing to bet your integrity that I don't? If you try to inherit the throne, yet I am the rightful heir, you will be destroyed."

"Why haven't you shown the letter to get the throne already?"

"I want you out of the picture before I become king."

Plitsky scowled at Poltax, biting his lip. "Fine," he said finally. "Tomorrow night, and I shall prevail." Plitsky reached forward a hand, and Poltax shook it briskly, walking away as soon as the deal was made.

BRUNUS

The next night, Brunus, a friend of Plitsky, was walking through the castle. Poltax and Plitsky were about to duel for the throne, and he was to make the event official. As Brunus walked down the corridors towards the courtyard, however, he noticed voices coming inside of a room. He stopped to listen, and he recognized Poltax's voice.

"Are you sure this is necessary?" asked Poltax.

"Yes, the poison will kill Plitsky instantly if you draw blood."

"Plitsky is your nephew, so why do you want me to win anyway?"

"I would *hate* to see the throne fall into the wrong hands."

"Technically speaking, Plitsky's hands are the right hands."

"Please, you will obviously make the better king. Plus, you have that letter from Juern, don't you?"

"You know that letter is complete hogwash! It just made it up to get Plitsky to agree to this duel." On those words, Brunus rushed off to find Plitsky.

VUINMORE

Vuinmore smirked as Poltax left the room. How gullible that elf was. Vuinmore shook his head. He waited until he was sure that Poltax was truly gone, and not coming back, before he poured red wine into a golden chalice. He looked around once more, reached his hand into his pocket and pulled out a glass bottle with a wrinkled and yellowing label that read: "Cyanide." Underneath the label, there was a depiction of a skull and crossbones.

Vuinmore unscrewed the cap of the bottle, dropping precisely five drops of the liquid into the wine. Quickly, Vuinmore scribbled out a note on a piece of paper with a quill and ink, which read:

> *Congratulations on your victory, Poltax! Please enjoy some of my favorite wine as a present for your success.*
>
> *Yours truly*
> *Vuinmore*

The elf turned away from the desk on which he had put the wine and note and walked towards the courtyard, where he would watch the throne fall into his hands, without him having to move a muscle.

PLITSKY

"Plitsky! Plitsky!" shouted Brunus running up to him. "Poltax has no letter from the king! The throne is rightfully yours!"

Plitsky turned to face his friend. "The whole castle must have heard of the duel by now. If I back out now, I will not gain the respect of my civilians. I shall have to duel this elf anyways."

"I also heard Poltax conspiring with someone in his room. They are poisoning Poltax's sword so that if it draws blood you die!"

Plitsky looked at Brunus. "I appreciate the information, friend, but if I accuse Poltax of cheating, and he is not, that too shall ruin me."

"Then, all I can do is wish you good luck." Brunus and Plitsky embraced; afterwards, both went their separate ways.

Chapter 98
The Skeleton Pirates

FEDRADIN

FEDRADIN WAS WRONG, VERY wrong. As he approached Elatador, he checked behind him one more time to see if he was being tailed. He had expected nothing to be behind him except the rest of his group, but he saw something odd in the distance. Three bird-like shapes in the sky told him that they were in fact being tailed, and their followers were rapidly catching up. Fedradin could make out the buildings of Elatador, and he could also make out the details of the birds that the three flayers were riding.

Fedradin recognized them as Smalhanien Birds, or gigantic eagles native to the island of Vau. There was only one colony of these birds, on the cliffs of Vau, which hunted down and ate deer whole. They were similar to rocs, but they were much faster and smaller. And they were gaining on Fedradin.

He and the rest of the group reached Elatador and continued riding through the town, for the Smalhanien Birds were now trying to find a way to dart down and grab any one of the many horses that the members of the group were riding. The streets were too crowded and the buildings too close together for the Birds to get a good angle, so instead, each one began screeching. Fedradin, if he had not been holding onto his speeding horses for dear life, would have covered his ears, but that was not an option in this case. He had to put up with the horrible noise, which permeated his brain. He saw the supercargo standing on the docks look up at the Birds and then at Fedradin and his group.

Fedradin reached the docks, dismounting from his horse, and setting his eyes on his boat, dead ahead. The supercargo put up and hand, signaling Fedradin to stop. Fedradin also raised a hand in a similar fashion, but instead of sending a stop signal, Fedradin sent a strong gust of air straight into the supercargo's chest, who flew backwards off the docks, colliding with Fedradin's boat, and falling into the water. Fedradin ran to his boat and jumped off the docks towards it, landing on the deck of the boat. He got up and reached over the side to help the rest of his group get on. He was pulling them in one by one, when he saw the three Smalhanien Birds start to nosedive at the ship. Fedradin instinctively cut the rope that held the boat to the docks, and the boat began to drift away from the docks.

"Fedradin, wait!" shouted Tiserae, who was still on the docks. She flung herself at the boat. Tiserae flew through the air, colliding with the side of the boat, Fedradin grabbing her by the forearm.

"Aserax! I need arrows in the sky, pronto!" he yelled, the elf nodding and shooting a volley of arrows in the direction of the Smalhanien Birds, forcing them to pull up out of their nosedives to avoid the arrows.

Fedradin pulled Tiserae into the boat, his attention now focused on her. "After all that and your hood is still down," said Fedradin. He moved to pull it back, but she grabbed his hand.

"Please don't," she said. "You have your secrets and I have mine."

Before Fedradin could respond, Breetex came running to their side. "Bad news," he said. "We left the captain at Vau."

"Does anyone here know anything about ships?" asked Fedradin.

"I do!" said Kerwan, quickly.

"Great!" said Fedradin. "What do we need to do to get the hell out of here?" The boat had drifted far enough away from the docks now that Fedradin wasn't concerned that they could be hurt by the mob of flayers now gathering on the docks. Still, they needed to start sailing the boat to get back to the mainland.

Kerwan, trying to answer Fedradin's simply, almost rhetorical question, looked like he had been struck by lightning. "Well, the first thing you might want to do is, um..."

"Give it a rest, Kerwan," said Tiserae. "You don't know a thing about boats. Luckily, I do." Tiserae took the helm of the boat. She began to call out commands to the group. Fedradin didn't understand half of what she said, but he could infer from context and complete the tasks she allotted him: raise the sail, duck as the boom came around, whatever she asked him to do he would, for it was effective as the boat began cruising along the ocean at a fast pace. "Where to boss?" asked Tiserae, once the boat had taken up a decent pace.

"I was thinking we go across the channel to Gaati."

"The svaadi port?"

"Yes. Plus, that's in the direction that the compass points."

"Copy that," said Tiserae, turning the boat south, giving Fedradin and the rest of the group a few more commands.

"Fedradin, I think you might want to see this," said Aserax.

"What?"

"The Birds, look they're flying away!" Fedradin looked up to see the Birds, sure enough flying away from their boat, the flayers on their backs.

"What do you know? They are!"

Gaati was in sight, but no one had any interest in entering a new kingdom during nighttime. They had laid anchor for the night, deciding on waiting until morning to go into the Svaadi Kingdom.

Fedradin was pacing the deck, the way lit clearly by the bright moonlight. He was too nervous to stop and go to bed, because of his low success rate with getting races to join his cause. Fedradin hoped the svaadi would accept his offer, for if not, he only had two more chances, with the animal cultures and the Grefture. Also, the animal cultures would almost certainly deny his request, their leader being one of the leaders who were killed by Erch, appearing as Flyc.

He finally tired himself out enough that he believed he was ready to sleep. He started to make his way to the cabin underneath the deck, when he saw a ship, not one hundred paces from his own ship.

Fedradin yelled out for help, while drawing Baxcanador. He continued to yell as the boat got closer and closer, until Fedradin could see all the details of the boat. It was solidly black, with three black masts, each with their own black sail. On the deck of the boat, Fedradin could see a crew bustle back and forth, but it was no ordinary crew. Each figure walking back and forth was only made out of bones. Fedradin could also see the shapes of the three Smalhanien Birds sleeping in the crow's nest, and the three flayers standing at the bow, looking forward at Fedradin's boat.

"We're under attack!" shouted Fedradin, his cries growing louder and more desperate. Finally, he awakened someone, who came running to the deck.

"What is it?" asked Breetex.

"Look!" said Fedradin, pointing to the boat that was rapidly approaching.

"Are those skeletons?"

"I'm afraid so."

As the pirate boat started to draw up alongside Fedradin's, two more people came running out of the cabin.

"No way! It's the fabled Skeleton Pirates!" said Kerwan. "You know, they are skeletons only because when a they hijacked a royal Princess's-"

"Shut up, Kerwan. We don't have time for a history lesson," said Aserax. Kerwan glared at Aserax. The pirate ship was now alongside their boat, and the skeletons had started swinging on ropes over to their boat, as Tiserae and Qint ran up from out of the cabin.

"Remember!" shouted Fedradin, as the pirates started boarding the boat. "You need to bludgeon the skeletons and shatter their bones to kill them."

"Actually-" began Kerwan who was interrupted by a skeleton pirate attack.

A skeleton landed on the deck in front of Fedradin. The Prince raised his hand, sending a strong gust of air that broke it apart. Its bones flew everywhere, some landing in Fedradin's boat, some in the pirates' boat, and some in the ocean. Two more skeleton pirates dropped down in front of Fedradin, both carrying clubs. Fedradin raised his palm to knock the skeletons backwards with his air powers, but one of the skeletons swung its club at him, knocking him to the ground, before he was able to fight back. Fedradin pulled out Baxcanador as the skeleton raised its club to finish off Fedradin. Fedradin swung Baxcanador so that the flat of the blade hit the side of the skeleton with enough force to shatter the skeleton. The other skeleton walked over to him, about to swing its club, but Fedradin raised his palm and blasted the skeleton away.

Fedradin looked around to see that the skeletons had retreated, going back to their boats to regroup. On their boat,

Fedradin saw each skeleton grab a rope that hung down from the boom, after being instructed to do so by the flayers.

"Aserax!" shouted Fedradin. "I need you to take out the skeleton on the far left!"

"What?"

"Shoot an arrow at the skeleton on the left so I can use his rope!" said Fedradin. The Prince ran forwards, jumping off the side of his boat, flying through the air towards the skeleton on the left. Fedradin saw Aserax's arrow fly past him and towards the skeleton. The arrow came near the skeleton, passing in between its ribs. Fedradin, his plan falling apart at the seams, grabbed the rope, swinging around it and kicking the skeleton off the rope. The skeleton broke apart, bones falling into the sea.

Fedradin stepped foot on the pirate ship, looking for the flayers, who were now sending the skeletons swinging onto Fedradin's boat. Fedradin ran over to the flayers, swinging his sword and decapitating one of them immediately. The other two turned to face him, and Fedradin swung his sword again, meeting blades with one of them, who had drawn a steel sword. The other retreated backwards, afraid to get in the way of his friend.

Fedradin and the flayer began fencing, Fedradin lunging, the flayer parrying, the flayer lunging, Fedradin parrying. Finally, Fedradin decided to try the trick he had used on the other flayer back at Smire. He pointed his palm at the flayer's sword, trying to get the iron in it to shrivel up. He was unsuccessful, he assumed, because the steel wasn't natural; it was iron ore that had been smelted. Fedradin and the flayer started fighting again, and out of the corner of his eye, Fedradin saw the other flayer running towards the Smalhanien Birds. He knew that the he couldn't let it reach the mainland to spread the news, so Fedradin picked up the pace in beating the flayer with which he was currently fighting.

He was able to push the flayer far enough away so he could raise his palm and shoot a strong blast of air at the flayer. The flayer flew backwards, flying off the side of the ship. Fedradin turned to see the last flayer as it climbed the ladder to the Smalhanien Birds. Fedradin looked at his sword, shrugged, and hurled it at the flayer. It soared through the air, flipping handle over handle, but it was slightly off target, too far to the right, and Fedradin saw that it would not hit the flayer.

That was, until it curved. The sword seemed to switch directions in midair, from missing the flayer by a few feet, it went to hitting the flayer in the back of the head. The flayer dropped off the ladder, smacking into the deck below. Fedradin made a move to go retrieve his sword from the remains of the flayer, when Baxcanador came flying back to him. Fedradin lifted a hand, and the handle of his sword flew right into his grasp. But now was not the time to be awestruck by his sword.

He looked to see skeletons, maybe fifteen of them, lining the edge of his boat, as his group attempted to make a stand. Quickly, Fedradin grabbed one of the ropes that hung down from the boom of the pirate ship, now empty, save the Smalhanien Birds. Fedradin backed up, ran forwards and jumped. Flying through the air on the rope, he lifted a palm, changing the rope's swing so that he came at the skeletons from the side. He started blasting air at the skeletons, sending almost all of them flying. The rope lost its momentum, so Fedradin dropped to the deck, facing the last four skeletons that were not shattered. Fedradin ran forward, smacking the side of a skeleton in front of him. It shattered as another skeleton came up behind him. Fedradin, sensing the skeleton out of the corner of his eye, swung his sword behind him, hitting the skeleton with the side of his blade as another came up in front of him. Fedradin raised the palm of the hand with which he was not holding the sword, and he blasted the skeleton into pieces. The last skeleton ran towards Fedradin, just as he finished with his air blast. Fedradin dropped his sword, grabbed an unattached arm bone, and smashed it down on top of the head of the last skeleton. The skeleton crumbled, breaking into pieces from the top down.

"Fedradin that was amazing!" said Tiserae. Kerwan scowled.

"Where did you learn to do that?" asked Aserax.

Fedradin opened his mouth, but no words came out. He had an answer, but he never liked sharing it because it made him sound insane. He decided just to tell his usual lie. "I couldn't tell you," he said. "I guess I just picked it up on the streets."

"So you're telling us that you defeated one of the mysteries of Haxter with skills you picked up on the streets?" asked Tiserae.

"Ahem," said Kerwan. "He did not defeat the Skeleton Pirates. Look!" Kerwan pointed to the pieces of the skeletons that were now moving towards the pirate ship. "There is only one way to defeat the Skeleton Pirates, and that way is...You know what? Never mind."

"Oh, come on, Kerwan! Tell us!" said Tiserae.

"No, you missed your opportunity. I was going to tell you, but Aserax cut me off."

"That was because we were under attack!" Tiserae exclaimed. "Tell us now that we're safe! We're all listening."

Kerwan shook his head. "Nope, I'm sorry, you missed your chance." He started to walk away, expecting people to beg for his story. When none did, he ran back to the group. "Fine! I'll tell you! The Skeleton Pirates were created when a ship full of pirates attacked one of Sir Bal-gastar's daughter's boat. They stole all the valuable cargo aboard and fled. Distressed, she ran to her father, telling him what had happened. Angered, Bal-gastar sent an armada out looking for the pirates. When he found them, he had them publically executed, before deciding that death was not punishment enough. With the help of one of the two Necromancer brothers, he had the pirates reincarnated as skeletons, to work for the rest of eternity as slaves in Bal-gastar. He made sure that they would always reassemble automatically if shattered, different from normal skeletons. The pirates worked for a long period of time, until Bal-gastar perished. The next emperor was being chosen, which was made much harder because of the fact that Bal-gastar had only girls. Eventually, Flyc was chosen, Bal-gastar's son-in-law. However, during this process the pirates, now skeletons, escaped from Bal-gastar and began roaming the seas, looting ships, cursed to live forever as skeletons."

"But you said they could be destroyed," said Fedradin.

"They can," said Kerwan. "And this is how. You are all aware that the two Necromancers were the only wizards strong enough to bring back the dead, correct? Good. Now, the Necromancers, when they brought back someone from the dead, that person would take the form of one of three beings: a zombie, a skeleton, or a ghost. Obviously, Bal-gastar decided that he wanted the pirates to be skeletons. But I digress. Whenever an undead was created, half their soul would go into their revitalized body, and the other half would go into a container of the

Necromancer's choosing, usually a crystal orb. If the undead being lost either half of its soul, either by being killed or by their orb being smashed, their soul would go back to the undead realms of the Hell Plane from whence they came. Now, of course these certain skeletons cannot be destroyed by bodily damage, so the only way they can be killed is by destroying their orbs. I believe that that is what the Skeleton Pirates are searching for, their orbs, so they can end their tortured existence."

"Thank you for the lesson, Kerwan," said Aserax, sarcastically.

"Oh, I have plenty more from where that came from. What mystery of Haxter would you like to hear about next: the Five Jewels of Bal-gastar? The Seven Blades? The Chaos Spawn? The Quoll Mountains? The Lost King? Ooh! How about the Heart?"

"Shut up, Kerwan," said Aserax. "I'm going to sleep. If you have so much energy, why don't you take first watch tonight."

Kerwan sighed. "Actually, I have always been in the pursuit of knowledge. I would be happy to listen to Kerwan all night," said Tiserae.

Fedradin, who had been looking forward to his bed, said, despite his exhaustion, "I'll stay up, too. The rest of you can go to bed if you wish." Kerwan shot Fedradin a dirty look. Breetex turned to walk down to the cabin, but Qint lingered a little while longer.

"As exciting as it would be to listen to you lecture me about things I already know, I need my sleep, for I am not as young as you. Good night, see you in the morning." Qint hobbled down the stairs to the cabin, leaning heavily on his cane.

"Now where should I begin?" said Kerwan. "How about the Quoll Mountains? As you probably know, the world began as shadows..." Fedradin quickly stopped paying attention.

Chapter 99
Duel

PLITSKY

PRINCE PLITSKY FACED PRINCE Poltax in the courtyard. A few other elves had come out to watch the duel, and they stood around the side of the courtyard, which was mostly clear, except for a stone bench in the center. Brunus stood on the bench.

"I want a nice, *clean* fight," he said, directing his swords at Poltax. "The winner of this duel will become the king of the elves, and the winner shall be the elf who either kills his opponent or forces his opponent to surrender. Are we clear on the rules?" Brunus turned to face both elfish Princes, who both nodded. "Then let the duel commence!"

Brunus stepped back and let the elves fight. The Princes charged each other. Prince Poltax ran slightly faster, so he had to jump over the bench to reach Plitsky. As Poltax flew through the air, Plitsky swung his sword, Poltax parrying the blade as he landed. Plitsky, determined not to let a good opportunity get away, swung again, knocking Poltax off balance as Poltax dodged the blade. Quickly, Plitsky pushed Poltax, Poltax tripping over the bench and falling onto the ground. Plitsky leapt over the bench, swinging his sword down at Poltax, who was prone on the ground. Poltax rolled to the side, desperately avoiding Plitsky's blade. Plitsky missed Poltax, his sword bouncing off the ground, and he raised his sword again, as Poltax delivered at kick to Plitsky's chest, sending him flying. Plitsky cleared the bench and hit the ground behind it, rolling to his feet instantly.

Poltax skirted the bench and ran at Plitsky, swinging his blade. Plitsky ducked the blow and thrust his sword at Poltax, who sidestepped the blade. Poltax swung at Plitsky, Plitsky dodged the blade, Plitsky swung at Poltax, Poltax ducked the blade. This pattern repeated itself many times, until Poltax feinted a blow. Plitsky dodged a blade that did not come, so he was unprepared for Poltax throwing his body at Plitsky. Poltax tackled Plitsky to the ground. He pulled out his sword and stabbed it at Plitsky's head. Plitsky moved his head right to avoid the blade, the sword millimeters from his head. Poltax stabbed downwards again, and Plitsky was once more able to dodge the blade. As Poltax raised his blade to finish off Plitsky, Plitsky jammed his fist into Poltax's stomach. Poltax had the wind knocked out of him, and that was enough for Plitsky to throw Poltax off of him. Poltax landed on the ground a little ways away and Plitsky ran over, jumping on top of Poltax.

Poltax had already drawn his sword, so when Plitsky landed on top of Poltax, swinging his sword, Poltax was able to parry the blow. Instead of drawing back for another attack, Plitsky pushed his sword down harder, Poltax pushing up to avoid being decapitated by his own blade. The two lay on top of each other like this for awhile, before Poltax used his foot to push Plitsky off of him. Poltax rolled on top of Plitsky, swinging his blade. Like before, only with the sides reversed, Plitsky used his sword to push back up, trying to not let either sword reach his neck; however, Poltax started pushing Plitsky's sword back towards Plitsky's neck, Plitsky losing the competition of strength. To avoid losing his head, Plitsky lifted one of his arms in attempt to slide Poltax's blade off of Plitsky's. The attempt was successful, and Poltax's blade slid down Plitsky's blade. However, on its way, Poltax's blade nicked Plitsky's skin.

Poltax's eyes lit up, and he hesitated for a moment. Plitsky wasn't dead.

Plitsky, taking advantage of Poltax's hesitation, swung his sword, the blade connecting firmly with Poltax's chest. Poltax fell backwards, clutching his chest as he started bleeding ferociously. Plitsky advanced, sticking his sword in Poltax's chest.

"Surrender, Poltax," said Plitsky.

"I will never! I would rather die than surrender to filth like you." Poltax spit at Plitsky.

"Your wishes shall be respected." Plitsky grabbed Poltax's sword from the dying elf's grip. He sliced Poltax's arm open, and instantly, Poltax closed his eyes and his breathing stopped.

"Congratulations, Plitsky!" announced Brunus, from atop the stone bench. "You have defeated Poltax, so you will be awarded the throne." The elves standing around started applauding their new king, before they left to go spread the word. Brunus walked over to Plitsky. "So you're immune to the poison?" said Brunus.

"I hope so," said Plitsky, looking down at his cut.

Vuinmore walked over to Plitsky thinking, *How has the poison not worked yet?* He was carrying a golden chalice filled with red wine. "Congratulations, nephew! I would like to give you some of my most precious wine as a present."

Brunus leaned in and whispered into Plitsky's ear, "Don't trust him! That was the man I heard conspiring with Poltax! Surely the wine is poisoned!"

Plitsky waved him off, like it was an unimportant matter, but it was just for show, to alleviate any suspicions Vuinmore might have regarding whether or not Plitsky knew about what Vuinmore had done. "We can talk about that later, Brunus. Now, Vuimore, uncle, I would love to have some of that wine, but only if you have some first."

"No, no, I insist! To the victor go the spoils!"

"I couldn't possibly! You said it yourself, this is some of your precious wine!" said Plitsky.

"No, I had some earlier. This is all yours!"

"Oh, dear uncle, if you don't drink any, neither shall I. It's called manners!"

Vuinmore was watching the throne slip out of his grasp. Maybe just the smallest sip... "Fine, I shall drink!" Plitsky looked at him in surprise. Vuimore tilted the chalice back slowly, and as soon as he felt the smallest drop of wine slide down his throat, he quickly tilted it forwards, choking down the poisonous liquid. He opened his mouth to say, "Now you drink!" when Plitsky grabbed the chalice and poured a large portion of wine down Vuinmore's throat. On instinct, he swallowed to avoid choking. Vuinmore collapsed to the ground, trying to get his body to throw up the poisonous contents.

"Is everything alright, uncle? Is there something wrong with the wine?"

"Drink it! The wine tastes-" Before Vuinmore could finish his sentence, he grabbed at his heart, ripping his shirt in the process. The elf collapsed to the ground. Plitsky grabbed Poltax's sword, and he stabbed it into the back of Vuinmore.

"His precious wine. Does he take me for a fool?"

Chapter 100
Mudmaw

FEDRADIN

THEY DOCKED IN GAATI in the morning. Fedradin was exhausted as he helped dock the boat, for he had stayed up most of the night listening to Kerwan lecture him and Tiserae about the various mysteries of Haxter.

"...and that is how the Fog Islands got their name," said Kerwan. He and Tiserae had picked up where they had left off in the morning.

"Yes, because they were very foggy," said Aserax, bored out of her mind.

"Well, yes, because of the will-o-wisps that breed there twice a year."

When they went into Gaati, they paid a svaad a few fellyers to take the boat back to Uiklo, because they had left their captain on Vau. Fedradin felt bad about leaving the captain, but he should have stayed on the boat. Still, Fedradin wondered what had happened to the man.

There were a cluster of rocks outside Elatador that had once been home to a nest of Smalhanien Birds. Now, it was home to a warning sign, which was a man hanging by his neck, a sign tied to the rope which read, "Beware all ye humans who enter." The man, of course, was the captain.

FEDRADIN

They followed the compass into the swamp, which happened to be in the direction of their next destination, Chaa, the svaadi capital. They waded through the swamps, Fedradin careful to keep the group away from monsters like will-o-wisps and red mists that tried to lure the travelers into the depths, where they would be eaten by the various creatures that skulked in the swamps. Kerwan might know much about the history of Haxter, but Fedradin knew even more about monsters. As they grew hungry and decided to stop for lunch, Fedradin checked the compass, which was now telling them that they were in the right spot to find the sixth member of the Legendary Eight.

They started searching the swamp, Fedradin in the lead, looking for a monster of some sort. They knew they found it when they came to a pool of swampy water in which floated a gigantic crocodile. "The Mudmaw," said Qint, his eyes turning red.

Fedradin looked at the Mudmaw, and the Mudmaw looked at him. Fedradin was about to try something with his power of the elements, when the crocodile opened its mouth and out shot a brown tongue. It grabbed Fedradin's leg and started pulling him closer, dragging him into the pool of swampy water. Quickly, Fedradin lashed out with its sword, cutting the tongue. He scrambled backwards, away from the Mudmaw, as its tongue retracted, returning to the crocodile's mouth. Fedradin returned to his group.

"Fedradin, look!" said Aserax. Fedradin turned to look at the Mudmaw. It now shot a group of four tongues, each that looked identical to its first tongue. It grabbed Aserax, Breetex and Kerwan, as Fedradin jumped over one of them. As the three were dragged towards the pool of water, each tried to cut the tongues. Breetex pulled out his tomahawk and chopped the tongue that was pulling him, and he was able to get free. Aserax shot an arrow into the tongue of the Mudmaw, the arrow cutting the Mudmaw's tongue. Kerwan's bronze knife, unseen by anyone, appeared in his hand, and he was also able to cut the tongue. All three of them ran away from the Mudmaw and back to the group.

"How are we going to defeat it?" asked Tiserae.

"I think I have an idea," said Fedradin, stepping forward. The Mudmaw shot out a tongue and grabbed Fedradin by the ankle. It began dragging Fedradin through the swampy water, and he pulled out Baxcanador but did not chop the tongue. He waited until he was close to the Mudmaw, and he raised his sword to stab it through the eye. The Mudmaw saw this, however, and flung him through air, Fedradin landing on the side of the swampy water opposite his group. He turned to face the Mudmaw, and he realized something. *Mud*maw. The tongues were made out of mud, and he could control them with his earth crystal.

The Mudmaw shot out its tongue again, and Fedradin raised his palm. The tongue froze in midair, the Mudmaw helpless to pull it back. Fedradin quickly stuck Baxcanador to the tongue. He then waved his palm, and the tongue snapped back, Baxcanador impaling the Mudmaw's eye. The monster let out a cry of pain, but the sword had punctured its brain. The gigantic crocodile rolled over into the pool of swampy water, dead.

Fedradin raised his hand, and Baxcanador flew into it, its handle going into his palm, for that was what he desired.

"Fedradin! You did it!" said Tiserae, running over to him. Kerwan frowned. As Tiserae affectionately congratulated Fedradin, Kerwan waded into the pool of swampy water to find the rock the Mudmaw was surely guarding.

Chapter 101
Urchin Emperor

ROGER

ROGER WAS UNCOMFORTABLE AT first, but he now enjoyed the feel of sitting on the throne. He had appointed Lider as general of the newly founded army, the soldier who had turned against his own army to help Roger's cause.

It was a weird feeling. Not three weeks ago, Roger had been an urchin on the very streets he now ruled over as Emperor of the humans. He had been voted into the position almost unanimously with a few votes being cast towards Sgire or Lider. Still, the position wasn't as advantageous as before, because it had a ruined reputation.

Roger and Sgire had not talked much since after the battle, and so when Roger saw Sgire outside on the terrace, he decided to walk over and have a discussion with her. He joined her at the rail, which overlooked Lake Bal-gastar.

"I never meant to kill her, Sgire," said Roger.

"I don't care, Roger, you did and that's all that matters," replied Sgire.

"No, it's not! I was starving and I needed food. And hey! You should take some of the blame, too, because it was you who got me used to a regular food supply."

"You're not seriously trying to blame me for your homicidal deeds, are you?" Roger remained silent. "Roger, my mother was all that was left of my family! My father was killed during an orc attack on his barracks. My sisters were killed as they were crushed by falling stone during the earthquake in Borave! My brother was on the expedition to create Sequo on Qassar when his boat sank in the Fog Islands! Now I'm alone, Roger, and it's all because of you."

Roger looked over at Sgire, who was tearing up. He waited a moment before saying, "I think back to that moment every day. It haunts me, knowing that I killed an innocent woman. I think to how it could have gone differently: maybe I could have eaten faster and gotten out before she came. Maybe I could have restrained my anger. There are millions of different things that could have gone differently that would have resulted in your mother being alive today. But you can't change the past. Obviously I would if I could, but I can't. Your mother is dead, and unfortunately, it was at my hands; however, you know what would never have happened if your mother was still alive? You would be at school right now, learning how to walk with a book on your head. Erch would be in control of the human Empire, destroying the respect of the human race even further. That man, Fedradin, would not know about Erch's plan, and he could be dead! And Erch would then easily obtain the Demon Callers! I know I killed your mother, and I couldn't feel more regret towards you or your family, but what's done is done." Sgire looked up at him, wiping a tear from her eyes.

"I guess I never looked at it that way..."

"Plus, now you get to be the empress of Bal-gastar," said Roger smiling, running a hand down Sgire's arm, holding her hand delicately.

"Oh, stop," she said, forcing a laugh, but not trying to extricate her hand from Roger's grasp.

"Come on," said Roger, pulling her close.

"Roger, you killed my mother." Immediately, he dropped her hand and stepped back. Sgire barely prevented herself from smiling. He was so easy to manipulate. And anyway, she had held in her heart no anger towards the murderer of her mother, for it was because of her mother's killer that she was able to escape school. Still, she was shocked to find that the identity of the murderer was Roger, but she wasn't angry.

"I know. It was an accident. I'm terribly sorry. I should not have-" Roger said quickly.

Sgire laughed, grabbed Roger by the shoulders and kissed him. "All is forgiven."

Chapter 102
Chaa

BREETEX

IT WAS BREETEX'S TURN to carry the bag full of six of the Legendary Eight stones and the silver compass. It was a heavy load for the four foot high dwarf, who felt much like a pack mule.

He, along with Fedradin, Kerwan, Aserax, Tiserae and Qint, were all headed in the direction of Chaa, the svaadi capital. After defeating the Mudmaw, they walked all day through the swamp, making camp when it grew too dark to continue on. In the morning, they set off again, arriving in Chaa early on in the day.

The svaadi were surprised to see humans (and of course a dwarf and an elf), but no guards arrested them as they traveled to the castle of Chaa. Fedradin requested council with the svaadi king, Greysvaad Moaand. Unable to speak Common, the svaad that guarded the royal chambers went inside to speak with the Greysvaad. After a few minutes, the guard came out, making a beckoning motion with his hand.

Breetex entered the room, along with the rest of the group. They came in to find Moaand sitting on his throne, awaiting the travelers.

"Humans! Why have you come to Chaa?"

"We seek your assistance," said Fedradin.

"To kill more leaders of LNR?"

"Of course not! Those were the actions of our traitorous emperor and they do not reflect on the actions of the rest of human race."

"Hmm. Okay. So, you don't steal vial of elderpool, that your emperor, too?"

"What?" asked Fedradin, pretending to be confused.

"Flayer tell me everything. You steal from elderpool!"

"We did no such thing!"

"You call me liar?"

"Of course not!"

"So did you steal vial?"

Fedradin looked over at his allies. Greysvaad Moaand knew they had stolen from the elderpool. There was no use arguing. Maybe honesty would win over Moaand. "Yes, fine, we stole from the flayers."

"So you admit it?"

"Yes. Now could we have help with-"

"No!" roared Moaand. "Get out of city!" Fedradin and his group froze. "Now!"

Guards started to pour into the room, so they darted from the royal chambers, running out the door as fast as they could. Fedradin turned to Qint.

"Thanks for the advice, Qint."

"I'm telling you, Fedradin, you will need that vial later on in your journeys."

"'Right, you better be telling the truth. Taking that vial cost me the support of the svaadi."

"Like the svaadi would have supported you anyways."

"I guess you're right." The group continued running until they cleared the the city.

"That was unsuccessful," said Breetex.

"No kidding," said Fedradin. "Thanks for the update."

Chapter 103
King Plitsky

PLITSKY

KING PLITSKY. HE LIKED the sound of that. Plitsky was sitting upon his newly-won throne, preparing to go to his next meeting with the council of elves. They would inform him of the latest issues facing the elves and ask him for a verdict.

He was on his way to the meeting when he passed by Brunus, who was also on his way to the meeting of the council, for he was part of the council.

"Hello, Brunus," greeted Plitsky.

"Hello, Plitsky," responded Brunus. They continued to walk in the direction of the council meeting room while they continued their conversation.

"I wonder what's on the agenda for today," said Plitsky.

"I hear it's going to be mostly tactics about the dwarfish war, and of course, discussions about what we need to do about the humans." At this point in time, the two had arrived at the meeting room, where the rest of the council had already arrived. Inside, Plitsky saw that the elves had a human gagged and tied to a chair.

"What is going on here?" said Plitsky.

"We caught this human in the streets trying to tell everyone that Flyc is actually a demon named Erch," said one of the council members.

"Erch? That sounds familiar," said Plitsky.

"It's the prophet of the Demisio religion," said Brunus. The human shouted his agreement through his gag.

"That seems like complete and utter crap," said the council member who had first spoken.

"Yes, it does seem a bit far-fetched, I agree with you completely, Merip," said Plitsky. "However, if that man were to lie and try to restore the respect of the human race, why would he tell such a ridiculous lie?"

"Because we would think exactly that! They knew we would believe them if they told a crazy lie."

"Listen, Emperor Flyc was a main proponent of the LNR. Why would he work so hard to build it, when he had ulterior motives to destroy it later?"

"Motives change, Plitsky!"

"Not without reasons, Merip!"

"There could be some things we don't know about!"

"Like what?"

"We don't know what we don't know!"

"Don't you have some theories?"

"He was mad at the other races, perhaps?"

"The humans won the Gii Games! Why would he be mad with the other races?"

"Once again, there could be reasons we don't know about!"

"Fine, Merip, I may not be able to change your mind about this, but this is ultimately my decision. Untie this man now!" Merip stared at Plitsky with anger as he cut the bonds with a small knife. The man collapsed to the ground, gasping for air.

"Thank you, King Plitsky!" said the man. "My name is Waprid and I am from Bal-gastar."

"Where the evil Emperor Flyc presides?" shouted Merip.

"Where the evil Prophet Erch *used* to preside! Where Emperor Roger now rules!"

"Emperor Roger? Who is this man?" asked Plitsky.

"He is the new emperor of the humans who led us to victory against Erch," said Waprid.

"Alright. Why does that concern me?" asked Plitsky

"We have reason to suspect that Erch has an army," said Waprid.

"Do you now? What proof do you have?" asked Merip.

"Roger and Sgire overheard Erch talking about it," said Waprid.

"And you were there when those two heard this information?" verified Merip.

"Well, not exactly..."

"So, no?" Waprid said nothing.

"Hold on a minute, Merip. I believe this man. Erch did not have a loyal army while posing as Flyc."

"But what about the power and influence he had as Emperor Flyc?"

"What influence? He betrayed the LNR! No one would support any of his actions. And for power, angry citizens generally don't do their best work."

"No! This is debate is insane! You are trying to tell me that Emperor Flyc is not a traitor, instead he is a demon straight from a religion that the dumbest of all monsters worship?"

"Strangely, it holds a factual basis, as long as you put even the slightest amount of trust into Waprid here. Still, I as king of the elves believe this story, so I have the final say. Waprid, you were saying something about an army?"

"Yes, as I previously stated, Roger and Sgire, two of the leaders of the rebellion, overheard Erch talking about his plan to create an army. What we would like to know, is whether or not we have your support if and when Erch raises such an army."

Merip interjected abruptly, "You absolutely do not!"

"Merip, are you king of the elves?" asked Plitsky. Plitsky turned to Waprid, "You have my race's full support if and when Erch raises an army."

"Thank you, King Plitsky," said Waprid bowing. The human quickly bustled out of the room, scared off by the livid stare from Merip.

Another council member stood up. "So the war with the dwarves."

"The war with the dwarves," said Brunus. The elves began discussing, but, much to Merip's chagrin, Plitsky made all the decisions.

Chapter 104
The Plains of Flyc

FEDRADIN

FEDRADIN WAS STARTING TO lose hope. He had been rejected by the svaadi, flayers and dwarves, three of the five races he had asked to join his cause. He was now on his way to the animal culture kingdom, where he would surely be rejected, for theirs was one of the leaders killed in the attack.

They were riding newly bought horses through the Plains of Flyc, trudging along, when something happened. In the distance, they saw a horse with a small rider on top of it. It came galloping across the plains towards them, and it soon came close enough to Fedradin that he could see who was riding it.

It was the elf Nesmer, the one who Fedradin had beaten to take the title of the Greatest Warrior in Haxter. The elf closed in on the group, but something must have spooked his horse, because it reared back and threw Nesmer off of it, running away.

Tiserae laughed. Nesmer leapt to his feet, dusting himself off and pointing his sword at her.

"Try me, woman, I dare you!"

"Nesmer, what are you doing here?" asked Fedradin.

"I have come to claim the sword from you."

"Claim? I believe I did beat you at the Gii Games."

"Maybe claim is not the right word, but nonetheless I am going to take it from you. It belongs to my master. And besides, this time, Uslo won't be there to save you."

"And who is your master?"

"Only the great and powerful Necromancer!"

"There are two," interjected Kerwan. "Which one is he?"

"He is the greater and more powerful one!"

"'Right, Nesmer. You've had your fun. Now would you please leave?"

"No! I must take Baxcanador from you!"

"I guess you can try." Fedradin pulled out the contested sword, and for dramatic effect, had it ignite. He jumped down from his horse, waving his flaming sword.

"You have fire?" said Nesmer in a tone as one use when addressing a toddler. "So do I." Nesmer pointed his palm upwards, and a ball of fire rose out of his hand, floating a few inches above his palm. The elf then threw the fireball at Fedradin, whose sword had extinguished. Fedradin dove to the side, avoiding the fireball, which exploded on the grass behind him, igniting the grass. Fedradin charged at Nesmer, swinging Baxcanador. The elf dropped to the ground, avoiding the blow. Nesmer, on the ground, blasted fire out of his palm at Fedradin's legs. Fedradin jumped over the fire, pointing his palm at the ground. He, knowing that the fire needed air to burn, created a vacuum around the fire with his air powers, extinguishing the fire instantly. Fedradin landed unevenly.

Nesmer jumped to his feet, swinging his own sword at the unbalanced Fedradin. Fedradin, regaining his composure, parried the blow, and swung his sword back. Nesmer dodged the blade by side-stepping, as he shot off a few fireballs at Fedradin. Fedradin pulled out his kappa shell shield, and the balls of fire bounced off. As Fedradin was behind his shield, Nesmer lunged forward, jumping over Fedradin's shield and kicking him in the face. Fedradin tumbled backwards into the grass, his shield to the side. Nesmer jumped on top of him and raised his sword to stab Fedradin. Quickly, Fedradin hit Nesmer in the side of the head with his shield, knocking the elf off of him. Fedradin jumped at the elf swinging his sword, but Nesmer raised his own sword horizontally as to parry the blow. Fedradin, however, did not let the blade bounce off Nesmer's blade. Instead he pressed down, trying to push Nesmer's blade into Nesmer's neck. The elf, as Fedradin became more and more successful, planted his feet into Fedradin's stomach and sent the Prince flying through the air.

Fedradin crashed to the ground, rolling into a crouched position with his sword at the ready. At that moment Nesmer came running forward, flinging three fireballs at Fedradin. Without time to use his shield, Fedradin decided to deflect the balls with his sword, his plan working perfectly. Nesmer bounded into the air, his sword over his head. Fedradin raised his palm, blasting Nesmer out of the air with a strong gust of wind. Nesmer plummeted out of the sky, crashing to the ground. Nesmer got up, but he was dazed. Fedradin took advantage of that opportunity to create a head sized boulder in midair, which he flung at Nesmer. The boulder collided with the elf's stomach, Nesmer flying backwards. Fedradin ran to Nesmer, who was now almost unconscious, and slashed the elf's neck with his sword.

Fedradin ripped the crystal, which was also on a necklace, from Nesmer's neck. He placed the new crystal with his others, the fire crystal fusing with the other two. Only then did he look around. Fire was everywhere, the group desperately jumping on it to try to put it out. Fedradin ran over to help put out the fire, and after a few more minutes, they were successful.

"Did you know that Yaalk was originally a svaadi city?" asked Kerwan.

"Really?" asked Tiserae, actually interested in what the wizard had to say.

"Yes! The svaadi arrived before the animal cultures, and because of that, they claimed a larger portion of Haxter. Unhappy with their small kingdom, the animal culture army attacked the Svaadi Empire, seizing more land and driving the svaadi back to the swamps."

"Fascinating, Kerwan," said Aserax sarcastically.

Kerwan replied, "I just thought you might want a little background knowledge on the city we are about to visit." Fedradin rolled his eyes and continued walking.

They were now in the animal culture capital of Yaalk. It was similar to Chaa in its layout, but all the civilians were gigantic animals. Many were alarmed to see humans, and some even ran away in fear. Still, they were not arrested by any guards that came by. Finally, they reached the gates to the castle of Yaalk. There stood two scorpion folk guards.

"Halt! What brings you humans to Yaalk?" yelled one of the scorpion folk.

"We wish to talk to your new king," said Fedradin.

"And you know why the king is new? Because you killed the old one!" shouted the other.

"Not really me personally..."

"Silence! Let us throw them in the dungeons and let them rot for eternity!"

"Why, yes, that is what we shall do!" announced the other scorpion folk. The two scorpion folk then proceeded to get behind the group, and with their swords and stingers, herded the humans into the castle, probably in the direction of the dungeons.

As Fedradin walked through the halls already plotting his escape, a yakio emerged from a room in front of him. And Fedradin knew that yakio...

"Fedradin?" said the yakio incredulously.

"Yuntile Stronghoof?"

"Actually, it's *King* Yuntile Stronghoof now."

"How did you win the throne?"

"First, I want to know why you are being arrested by my guards. What have you done?"

"The only reason we are under arrest now is because we are humans."

"Not true! We arrested the dwarf and elf too," said one of the guards.

"Go away! Both of you!" said Yuntile, sending the guards away. "Now Fedradin and friends, why don't you come into my chambers and have a proper chat?"

The group followed the yakio king through the passageways of the castle, finally entering into his royal chambers. Yuntile gestured towards the chairs facing a large bay window overlooking the Plains of Flyc, and they had a seat, while he chatted about his adventures in throne-getting.

"...and so I say that there is no way to find a suitable king unless there is at least a little bloodshed, so as my eight other cousins and I were seated around the table, maybe my arm slipped a few times and some poison wound up in the wine."

"King Yuntile, you wouldn't do that!" exclaimed Fedradin.

"No, no, no, no, no, no, of *course* not!" Even though he said this, Yuntile gave Fedradin a wink. "So, what brings you into Yaalk?"

"We actually wanted to ask your help in something," said Fedradin.

"What is it?"

"We believe that Emperor Flyc is creating an-"

"Hold on," said Yuntile. "Did you say Emperor *Flyc*?"

"Yes. He is the human emperor, isn't he?"

"May I ask you something, Fedradin?"

"Anything."

"How long have you been traveling?"

"A long time. Maybe a month at most."

"So you haven't heard any of the recent events?"

"No, I guess we haven't. The most recent thing we have heard is about the attack at the LNR building."

"Buclin! Fetch the town crier!" A beaverio who had been standing by the door waddled out of the room, and a few minutes later brought back a disgruntled squirrelio. "It is okay, crier. I only wish for you to report the news to my friends."

"Well, there was an announcement made by the flayers that they were attacked by a band of humans who stole brains from their elderpool." Fedradin's hand clenched around the glass vial in his pouch. "But it has been disregarded as slander." Fedradin's hand relaxed. "The elfish king has been assassinated by an unknown assailant and the new king is King Plitsky, as decided by a duel between him and Prince Poltax."

"What? Juern's dead?" said Aserax.

"And Poltax!" said the crier.

"My father and my ex-fiancé dead? And my brother king?" she muttered uncoherently to herself.

The crier looked around hopelessly, unsure what to do, but Fedradin made a gesture for him to continue. "And of course the biggest news, which is spreading around Haxter like wildfire, is what happened at Bal-gastar. According to many various human scouts that rushed to the various capitals, a rebellion, led by a little boy of sixteen named Roger, was successfully able to take down Emperor Flyc. When they were preparing to kill the emperor, he turned into Erch, the demon prophet from the Demisio religion. They claim, and maintain to this day, that the demon vanished from the site in a ball of purple fire. The boy Roger is now Emperor. We have sent members to verify this information, and the most we can say is that Flyc is not at Bal-gastar any longer."

"Thank you crier, you may go," said Yuntile. The squirrelio darted from the castle like a normal squirrel would. "Now, Fedradin, what do you think of that information?"

410

Fedradin looked over to see Aserax attempting to digest the piece about the elves. "I believe it."

"You believe that Flyc is a demon named Erch?"

"Yes."

"You do?"

"Yes. We have actually...had...suspicions that Erch was posing as Flyc," said Fedradin, stuttering to try to find the right words.

"You did?"

"Surprisingly, yes."

"Okay then. What did you want to ask me?"

"We wanted to know that we have reason to believe Emperor- I mean Erch is raising an army, and if that army marches on Haxter, we want to make sure you will join the fight with your army."

"Of course! If an evil demon attacks Haxter, I assure you, my troops will be on the front line!" His tone was slightly sarcastic, but Fedradin decided it was good enough.

"Thank you so much, sir!" Fedradin shook Yuntile's hand vigorously.

The group walked out the door of the solar. Yuntile stared after them for a while, then shook his head. If only he knew shortly in the future he would have to honor his word.

Chapter 105

Assembly

ERCH

"NO!" ROARED ERCH, NO longer appearing as Flyc. Behind him stood Oxlo, Fin and Tawassa. Erch was cradling the dead Mudmaw, the stone it was guarding nowhere to be seen.

"They beat us to another one, Master," said Oxlo, then murmuring. "Just like I told you they would." The Minions had fashioned a silver compass of their own, the Heart helping them to accomplish that task.

"What was that, Oxlo?" Erch's heightened senses allowing him to hear him.

"Nothing."

"That's what I thought."

"What are we going to do, Master?" asked Frin.

"We are going back to Dire Island, that's what we're doing." A flash of purple fire light up the swamp as the four teleported into their fortress on Dire Island. As soon as Erch was oriented, he began walking towards the cave on the side of their fortress where the Heart was. He entered into the cave and walked over to the Heart, the big, blue pulsing mass of what appeared to be flesh.

"Frin! You just used this to create the army, correct?"

"Yes."

"And the army is where now?"

"In the valley, awaiting further instruction."

"Good. Oxlo!"

"Yes, Master."

"Find me information on Nesmer's location, now!" Oxlo scurried out of the cave, returning five minutes later with a long face. "What?"

"Nesmer is dead," said Oxlo gravely.

"What? No!" Erch slammed his fist into his palm.

"I'm afraid so, Master. But what I did find out from our spy was that there was this meeting at a village in the mountains. I have the names of everyone involved."

Erch thought for a moment. "Give me a moment. I have a plan."

UÄILE

The Uäile was at Reedil, a happy elfish city. She was hiding in the trees, looking at the children playing. That wasn't right. Children shouldn't be happy. Why weren't her daughters in charge?

A sword as black as death materialized in her right hand. She stepped forth from the trees, walking towards the city slowly. When she arrived there, an elf walked up to her.

"Are you lost?" Without replying to the elf, she slashed him across the stomach with her sword. The elf dropped to the ground, crying out in pain. Without looking down, she took her foot and ground it into the elf's neck until he grew silent. A few nearby elves heard the commotion and ran over, the Uäile slashing them to the ground with her sword. One that she had not killed took a swing at her with its sword, but the Uäile's middle turned to black smoke, the sword passing through harmlessly. The elf looked at her, eyes wide with alarm.

"Who are you?" he whispered.

"I am Black Heart."

A few minutes later, all that was left of Reetil was a few burning buildings, not a single elf still alive. It was at that moment that Black Heart felt a pulling sensation towards a point. It was so strong that she knew that was where she had to go, even with the need to take over Haxter still festering in her heart.

COID

Coid was marching his army of goblins, bugbears and hobgoblins to Histam to emancipate the other slaves, when he was hit with the sensation. It was so sudden and so powerful that he disbanded his army, and turned to go to the source. He had a strong feeling that he was about to find out who had given him his powers.

AXTO

Axto's wound had finally healed from Draslupp's arrows. He was glad that the Domer had moved out of Narven. Axto was sitting

413

in his small house in Narven, practicing with his halberd. He, of course, had no family or baby to take care of, contrary to what he had told Fedradin.

In fact, he was angry with Fedradin. That Prince was responsible for him getting cooped up in a hospital for days on end, costing him a job that he had wanted. Obviously, Draslupp had shot him, but it was ultimately Fedradin's fault. The Prince was also responsible for the death of his brother, Junike. He would get revenge on Fedradin. Somehow. That was when he felt the pull. He knew where he had to go.

TYRATION

Tyration received all the respect he could possibly get. Any Rock Holder who had won a Rashimi battle was never questioned again. He had taken a crystal from Desert Wind's sacred vaults. It was an unprecedented action, an unpopular one, too, but he didn't care. He was the Rock Holder. The one and only.

All was well, until one day, a figure, half skeleton, half human came walking into the camp. The figure had demanded to see the body of Krile, and when he was refused, the figure killed off members of Desert Wind until his wish was granted. Tyration had quickly dug up the body of Krile from its grave, and gave it over to the figure. The figure had taken the body of Krile into a room, and a few minutes passed before Krile walked out of it, alive and well.

The old leader of Desert Wind quickly reassumed his title, killing Tyration after he invoked the Rashimi Clause. Krile was only in power for a few days, before he left suddenly, claiming that he needed to go somewhere, leaving the earth crystal behind.

HIJIMIN

The flayer, by the name of Hijimin, crawled out of the ocean, onto the beach, spitting out sea water. After getting knocked off the Skeleton Pirates' boat, he had hid in the water until Fedradin's boat was out of sight. When it was, he started to climb up the side of the Skeleton Pirates' boat, when he felt something. It was like his brain was sending him a message. He needed to go to a certain place, now! There was no time to get on the boat or get the Smalhanien Birds. He dove off the side of the boat and started fruriously swimming, never slowing or looking back.

ERCH

Erch watched each and every one of these people come to him by scrying. He smiled to himself. The Prince of Destiny would be in for a shock.

Chapter 106
From One Domer to Another

DRASLUPP

DRASLUPP HAD DECIDED TO leave the city of Narven after the event in the village in the mountains. Dethroid had vanished upon the return to Narven, and without him or Fedradin, no one was around to protect Draslupp. There was still much hatred against the Domers; not much time had passed since the Domer Dark Ages. Now, being the only Domer in Narven, he was constantly being knocked to the ground, robbed, vandalized, cursed at, spit at, and he had to take it, for if he used his invisibility, he would most likely be exiled, like Fedradin. With all this hatred in the city of Narven, Draslupp decided it was time for a change of scenery. He packed his bags and headed out to Smafa, a little town on the edge of the fiefdom of Narven. Maybe the people there would be nicer, though probably not.

He arrived at Smafa. It was a small town, with a small castle on a hill which overlooked a village, where a few people were out and about. A Rotnazian Church was on the outside of Smafa, where a few people were gathered, including a Rotnazian Lear. Draslupp started to walk over to the church, when he was tapped on the shoulder. Draslupp turned around to find a man standing there.

"Hey, kid," said the man. "You look hungry. Would you like some venison?"

Wow. People are nice around here, thought Draslupp. "Thank you! I've been traveling all day. Some food would be great." Draslupp took the meat out of the man's hands, wolfing it down with eagerness. When he looked up, the man was still standing there watching him. It was then that Draslupp noticed that the man had different-colored eyes. "What?"

"Were you up in the village the other day?"

"The village...What village?"

"You know, the one in the mountains."

Draslupp looked at the man with a suspicious glance. "No, I wasn't." Draslupp knew that what happened at the village was very confidential.

"Oh, come on, I was there, too!"

"Really, I don't remember you being there. And I have a good memory."

"I was there!"

"Then what were we talking about?"

"Um, well, of course, um, about Fedradin!"

Draslupp rolled his eyes. Obviously this man was lying. "Alright. What do you want?"

"I was, um, unclear about what we were going to do about the, uh, Demon Callers."

"I don't know who you are or how you know about the," Draslupp lowered his voice, "Demon Callers," he returned to his normal voice, "But I know that I am not telling you anything."

The man scoffed. "I would rethink that, Domer." The man pulled out a sword and pressed it to Draslupp's neck. Draslupp smiled and disappeared. The man, slightly frightened, swung his sword, the blade passing over Draslupp's head, for the Domer had ducked. Draslupp tackled the man, still invisible, bringing both of them to the ground. Draslupp pulled out a knife, but he needed to keep the knife visible. The man saw the knife, and was able to grab onto Draslupp's arm, though invisible, and he threw the Domer off of him. Draslupp crashed to the ground, turning visible.

"You'll pay for that, Domer!" hissed the man, slashing at Draslupp. Draslupp rolled to the side, the sword sending up a spark as it collided with the rocky pathway. Draslupp tried to get to his feet, but the man kicked him to the ground, pinning the arm that held the dagger with his foot. The man raised his sword over his head. "Good bye, Domer." The man stabbed his sword down, Draslupp bracing for impact. But it never came.

Out of nowhere, another man appeared, flying through the air. He collided with the first man, slashing his neck with a knife. The second man reached a hand to Draslupp. Draslupp got to his feet with the man's help. The two stared at each other for a few seconds until the strange, familiar-looking man broke the ice.

"Hello. I am Velk," said Velk.

"Velk, I know that name," said Draslupp, thinking.

"Yes, you and I competed in the Gii Games."

"I remember that! You tried to save Fedradin's life."

"That I did. And by the way, not only did I try, but I also succeeded."

"Well, I am grateful for that and saving my life right now!"

"My pleasure. A Domer is always ready to help another Domer."

"You're a Domer?"

"Of course I am, didn't you see me appear out of nowhere?"

"No, I was actually busy trying to *save my own life*."

"You didn't do a very good job of that, now did you?" Draslupp scowled, but Velk chuckled. "You were very brave using your invisibility at the Gii Games."

"Why didn't you?"

"So much hatred these days. Anyways, I'm a good enough fighter on my own, without the invisibility."

"You didn't prove that at the Gii Games."

Velk laughed. "You're funny! You say that, yet my fighting skills just saved your sorry life."

Draslupp shrugged. "Fair point," he said.

Velk looked at Draslupp, slightly nodding. "Draslupp, you've probably been wondering where all the Domers are." Draslupp nodded. "After the Dark Ages, we formed a cult. Where no one judges us or hates us. It's just us Domers and no one else, maybe about twenty of us."

"And where is this magical place?" asked Draslupp.

"If I told you, I'd have to kill you." Draslupp laughed, but Velk's face remained straight. "I'm serious. Put on this blindfold."

Chapter 107
Leivtante

BREETEX

THE JOURNEY FROM YAALK to Leivtante had been a rough one. Three long days through the hot Cientile Plains, the thick Oxler Forest, and into the towering Sumier Mountains. At the end of the third day, they could see Leivante, the Grefturen capital, perched on the top of a mountain. Night was falling then, so they decided to make camp on the rocky soil before heading into Leivtante.

"It sure is cold up here," said Aserax, rubbing her bare arms.

"We are pretty close to the Glaciers," said Kerwan.

"I'm going to kill some furry animal to use its hide as a blanket," said Aserax.

"Bring me back something," said Kerwan.

"I would love some blanket, too, please," said Qint.

"I'll go with her," said Breetex. "Make sure you don't get into trouble." Five minutes later, Breetex and Aserax was dangling upside down, a rope around their ankles, the end of which was attached to a thick tree branch. An ettin, its heads muttering to each other, had a pot of water boiling over a fire. Breetex looked to Aserax and said, "I did a terrible job."

FEDRADIN

"They sure have been gone a while," said Kerwan, painfully pointing out what everyone was thinking.

"Thank you captain obvious," said Fedradin.

"What do you think is taking them so long?" asked Tiserae.

"They could be having trouble finding game," said Qint.

"No, I saw two wolves and a bear on the way up here alone," said Kerwan. "Plus, Aserax is an expert tracker and hunter."

"Maybe we should go after them," said Fedradin.

"Let's give them a few more minutes," said Tiserae. A few more minutes passed.

"I'm going after them," said Fedradin.

"I'm going with you," said Tiserae.

"And me, too," said Kerwan, springing to his feet. The three looked to Qint, who waved passive-aggressively.

"I'll pass," he said. "I'm old. I need my rest." Fedradin shrugged and ran off in the direction of Breetex and Aserax, Kerwan and Tiserae following him. They started looking for the dwarf and the elf, when Tiserae noticed something.

"Look up there!" she announced. Kerwan and Fedradin came running over. Tiserae was pointing in the sky, where there were faint wisps of smoke.

"What do you think that is?" asked Kerwan.

"Last time I found those two the smoke guided me to them," said Fedradin, who started jogging towards the smoke. Tiserae and Kerwan exchanged a glance, and shrugged, before running after Fedradin. They found him, along with a two-headed troll, a boiling pot of water, and Breetex and Aserax dangling from a tree. Aserax saw the three and her eyes lit up. Fedradin made a shushing motion with his finger, as he drew Baxcanador with his other hand.

The ettin was picking its nose with its club as it sat on a rock, waiting for the water to boil. Fedradin crept out of the woods, slowly enough to avoid attracting the ettin's attention. He raised his palm, and the rock upon which the ettin sat lifted into the air. Alarmed, the monster's heads looked back and forth at each other, yelling something in their strange, a mix of Goblin, Troll, and Giant. Fedradin moved his hand to the right, and the boulder came out from under the ettin. The monster crashed to the ground, grabbing its club which had fallen out of its hands. Fedradin ran forward, swinging his sword. The ettin blocked the blow with its club, the sword shattering the club. The ettin, enraged, threw the splintered remains of its club at Fedradin, who raised a palm, using his air powers to stop the wood in midair. The remains of the club fell to the ground as Fedradin ran forward, jumped in the air and lunged with his sword, the blade slicing the ettin's shoulder. The monster roared in pain as Fedradin drew back his sword.

The ettin grabbed at Fedradin with its hands, Fedradin ducking to avoid getting clawed by its long, yellow fingernails. Quickly, he pushed the ettin back with his hands, before slamming into its chest with his feet, sending the monster flying.

Fedradin ran forward, pinning the monster to the ground before it was able to get back up. He raised a palm, pointed it at the ettin's heads and tried to send a burst of fire from his palms. However, he was not able to accomplish it. He tried once more, this time picturing the faint memories he had of the castle burning in Narven. Fire erupted from his hands, scorching the life out of the screaming ettin. After a few more minutes, Fedradin released the fire stream, because the fire was taking much energy from him. Tiserae and Kerwan emerged from the trees.

"Fedradin, that was amazing!" said Tiserae.

"It's what I do," Fedradin said dramatically, cutting Breetex and Aserax down with a swing of Baxcanador. The two fell on top of each other, all tangled up.

"I think that was only okay," said Kerwan. "I mean it was only a stupid ettin."

"Smart enough to capture Aserax and Breetex," said Fedradin, who turned and walked back to camp. Tiserae, Kerwan, Aserax and Breetex followed after him.

The next morning, after a long (and cold) night, the group headed into Leivtante, the Grefturen capital. They rode up the mountain path to the city on their horses. When they entered into the city, they came across a magnificent sight. The city was built into the side of the mountain; shops, houses and more were flat against the mountain. A path, the same path that led them to the city, looped around the mountain and allowed the civilians to get about. On top of the mountain was the castle, where the new king of the Grefturen race presided. As they walked up to the castle, the various faun, centaurs, and satyrs were shocked to see humans. Finally, they reached the doors to the castle, where two centaurs were barring the doors.

"Halt, humans," announced one. Fedradin and the others stopped in their tracks. "What do you wish?"

"We wish to see the king," said Fedradin.

"King Thrasp is not seeing anyone today. Especially not humans," said the other.

"Thrasp? I competed with Thrasp in the Gii Games!" said Fedradin.

"You know the king?" asked the first centaur, confused.

"Yes, we grew very close during the Games." Of course they had not.

"If he knows King Thrasp, we should let him in." After a few more minutes of bickering, Fedradin and the rest were let into the royal chambers. Thrasp, a centaur, was standing in a corner, sleeping. He was clutching a gold sword between his human arms, murmuring in his sleep.

"King," said one of the centaur guards, tapping on Thrasp's shoulder. "King!" Thrasp awoke with a start.

"What is it?" he demanded of the centaur guard.

"This man, your friend, is here to see you."

"Human friend? I have no human friends."

"Except me, Your Highness," said Fedradin, bowing before the king.

"Fedradin? From the Gii Games?"

"Yes, that is my name."

"You are not my friend."

"Should I have him thrown out, sir?" asked one of the centaur guards.

"No. I am now intrigued. Why are you here, humans?" asked Thrasp.

"I have come to request your assistance," said Fedradin.

"Assistance in what?"

"As you know, Emperor Roger claims that Emperor Flyc was actually the Demisio prophet, Erch."

Thrasp scoffed. "Yes, I am aware. I wonder where that urchin gets his imagination from."

"I don't know, sir," said Fedradin. "But I don't think he imagined it. I think he is telling the truth."

"Do you, now?"

"Yes, and I also believe that Erch has assembled an army that he plans to march soon."

"Really? Fedradin, may I ask, what have you been smoking?"

Fedradin laughed. "I know it sounds a bit ludicrous."

"A bit?"

"All I want to know is that if such army does march on Haxter, we can rely on your Grefturen forces to help us combat the fiend."

Thrasp looked at Fedradin with an air of befuddlement. After a few moments, he said, "Sure, if an evil demon tries to attack Haxter, I will gladly help you fight him."

Fedradin shrugged. "That's all I'm asking."

Chapter 108
Conspiracy

PLITSKY

KING PLITSKY WOKE UP with a terrible headache. He got out of bed, very dizzy. Everything was very fuzzy and unclear. He was probably just sick. Still, Plitsky knew that today he had to do something. Something important.

ROKA

The gong sounded from inside Axler. *What is father doing now?* wondered Roka, one of Plitsky's daughters with exasperation. She was picking apples with her sisters, Rola and Roga, in the orchards by their private estate. Together, the three sisters went into Axler to see what King Plitsky was up to.

The king of the elves was standing on a platform, seeming to be standing unsteadily.

"Greetings, elves," said Plitsky, slurring his words together. "I have called you here today to assign a new Count of Smore."

"But there already is a Count of Smore!" exclaimed Merip, from the crowds. "What is wrong with him?"

Plitsky ignored Merip. "I will give the position to whichever of my daughters loves me the most."

"We all love you equally, father!" said Roka.

"But especially me!" said Rola, winking at the other two.

"No way!" whispered Roga. "I want to be Countess." She turned to her father. "I love you the most father!"

"Tell me how much you love me!" said Plitsky.

"What are you going to do about the devastation of Reedil?" interrupted Merip.

"Silence! Now, girls, how much do you love me?"

"I love you more than a cool breeze on a warm summer's afternoon!" shouted Rola.

"I love you more than the heat from a fire on a cold winter's night!" shouted Roga. The two looked to Roka, who shook her head.

"And how much do you love me, Roka?" asked Plitsky.

Roka said, "Father, I have no words to describe to you how much I love you. You should just know that I do."

Enraged Plitsky scowled down at his daughter, "Tell it to me like your sisters, Rola!"

"I am Roka, father, and I refuse."

"Then off to the dungeons with you! Guards, I don't want to see her face until I am dead!" Roka was seized and dragged off to the dungeons. What had happened to her father?

BRUNUS

Brunus could not believe the scene that had just unfolded. Plitsky, the most loving and caring father in the world, had just sent his own daughter to jail. For no reason! Plitsky had then given the role of Countess of Smore, which was already being filled well by Fevin IV, to Roga, after she competed with her sister for who loved Plitsky the most.

Brunus was walking to the meeting room, where the council had planned to meet in secret, without Plitsky. Brunus entered, and the meeting was already in session.

"We should kill him! He's crazy!" shouted Merip.

"That's anarchy!" shouted a council member by the name of Unal. "We can vote him out of the throne."

"That would take too long to accomplish! We need this elf out of the picture now, before he does something like Emperor Flyc did! Look at the humans! Do we want to end up like them, telling pitiful lies in attempts for redemption?"

"May I remind you that the humans saved us during the Goblin Wars? Without the humans or Rotnaz, we wouldn't be here right now!"

"You're bringing religion into this?"

"Why not?"

"This is a strictly political matter! Religion has no place here!"

"And why the hell not?"

"Order!" yelled Brunus, silencing the two elves. "I don't know why you're discussing the political implications of Rotnaz, but why do you want to kill Plitsky?"

"Because he's insane!" said Merip.

"I agree that he is being unreasonable at the current moment," said Brunus.

"Yes, he is! He won't listen to any of us! He's becoming a dictator!" shouted Merip.

"Yes, but we don't need to kill him!" said Unal.

"Yes we do!" shouted a member of the council.

"Silence!" shouted Brunus. "I agree with Merip." There were murmurs of surprise and shock.

"But I thought he was your friend!" said Unal.

"He is my friend, but he needs to die!" said Brunus. "I believe that poison, from when he battled Poltax, is affecting his decisions for the worse. With him alive he will cost us the war with the dwarves, and worse. We need to kill him and we need to kill him now. He will not step down peacefully." Brunus unsheathed his unused knife, the metal blade gleaming in the light. "It's unfortunate, but we need to end this once and for all."

Chapter 109
Galeb Duhr

FEDRADIN

"**OVER THE RIVER AND** through the woods, to kill a monster we go," Aserax was happily singing a parody of a popular children's' song as she rode her pony down the rocky path on the mountain. They were on the ridge line of a row of mountains, riding along in the direction of the compass. The sun was overhead, but it wasn't warm. Far from that. They were passing into the colder regions of Haxter, nearing the Oxler Tundra and the Glaciers in the south. Finally, Fedradin decided it was time to stop for lunch. They dismounted their horses. Fedradin, as Aserax unpacked the food for lunch, sat on the ground, resting his back on a rock.

"And what in the name of hell do you think you're doing?" came a voice. It wasn't familiar. Fedradin looked around, searching for the speaker. "Get off me!" Fedradin was thrown forwards, startled, and he reached for his sword. He got to his feet, Baxcanador up and at the ready, as he searched for his attacker. But he could not find one. Was it a Domer that had attacked him?

Fedradin, alarmed to say the least, sat back down on the same rock. "What? You didn't learn your lesson the first time? Get the hell off me!" Once again, Fedradin flew forwards, crashing to the ground. By now, the rest of the group was watching this.

"Fedradin," said Tiserae. "It seems like...maybe...the *rock* was throwing you forward?" Fedradin turned to the rock and stared at it. The more he looked, the more he could see a human resemblance in the rock...Fedradin decided to experiment. He raised a palm, pointed it at the rock, and with his earth powers, attempted to lift the rock into the air. But it did not budge. He tried again, this time with air powers. The rock shot into the air, its...eyes...opening as it flew. Its arms and legs started flailing about, and it began to yell.

427

"Put me down, you addle-brained fool!" shouted the rock, which now, no doubt, had a humanoid shape. Fedradin, amazed at this creature, did not, so it made an obscene gesture with its hand. Upon seeing this, Fedradin released his hold on the monster, and it tumbled out of the air. The rock monster hit the ground, hard, falling fast due to its weight.

"What, what are you?" asked Fedradin. He had never seen a monster quite like it.

"I am-" the rock monster was cut off by Kerwan.

"It's Galeb Duhr!" announced Kerwan. "one of the four elemental creatures that were created along with the four Elemental Planes. The other three are Immoth, Magsla, and Varab Por, the water, fire and air creatures."

Galeb Duhr had dusted himself off. "I believe only we are allowed to call ourselves 'creatures.'" Galeb Duhr made quotation marks in the air. "What brings you into my mountains?"

"*Your* mountains?" asked Breetex.

"Correct. I make 'em. I own 'em." Galeb Duhr gestured around the mountains. "In fact all the mountains around you were made by me. Back when Haxter was mere shadows, I helped form these magnificent peaks you see today. Except the volcanoes. Me and Magsla worked on those together. Or the Quoll Mountains. Varab Por helped me with those."

"Kerwan was telling me about those mountains," said Tiserae. "But he didn't mention that the god-like creature called Galeb Duhr who created them was a three and a half foot tall monster made out of rock."

"Ah, I wish I still had my powers. But you dwarves and elves and humans and flayers and svaadi and chultra and...well you get the picture, are all tapping into the flow of magic I need to create mountains. There is simply not enough magic available at one time for me to use."

There was a moment of silence, until Fedradin broke it. "'Right. It was nice meeting a crucial piece of Haxter's history, but we're kind of in a race between an evil demon prophet for powerful pieces of magic that could bring an end to the world as we know it. Good bye." Fedradin turned to mount his horse, when Galeb Duhr cried out.

"Wait! What evil demon prophet? Do you mean Erch?"

428

"Yes. How did you know?"

"How many demon prophets are out there?"

Oh great, thought Fedradin. *Now the immortal, god-like, rock monster is being sarcastic.*

"It's just that Thunderflash erased that from history," said Qint. "Fedradin must have forgotten that you are old enough to have experienced the Demon War."

"More than experienced it!" said Galeb Duhr. "I fought in it! Those damn demons were burning everything in sight! They were wreaking havoc on the forests and mountains that I had worked my brains out to implement!"

"'Right, so you have a grudge against Erch. So do a lot of people," said Fedradin, turning away.

"Not true!" shouted Galeb Duhr. "Everyone who was alive back then has already died!"

"*Most* of them have," murmured Fedradin, thinking of his father.

Galeb Duhr ignored Fedradin. "Please let me go with you! I won't weigh you down at all!"

"What are you, two-three tons?" asked Kerwan jokingly.

"It was figurative, you idiot!"

"I'm sorry, Galeb Duhr. We don't need anyone else," said Fedradin.

"Fine, but before you leave can you do me one favor?" Fedradin turned to Galeb Duhr.

"And what would said favor be?"

"There are miners around here, human miners that are destroying these beautiful mountains, looking for only some small crystals that took me no time to create. Can you teach those miners a lesson?"

Tiserae, Aserax and Breetex looked at Fedradin beseechingly. Qint and Kerwan couldn't care less. "And you can't do this...why?"

"If I could drop an avalanche on those bastard's heads, I would. But I don't have enough power. And I don't have any weapons to kill them hand-to-hand. The short answer: no. I need your help."

Fedradin thought about it for another second. "Fine," said Fedradin. "We'll kill those miners." Fedradin went to mount his horse, but Galeb Duhr stopped him.

"You don't want to alert the miners by marching in on horses," said Galeb Duhr. "Just leave your things here, for the miners are only on the other side of the mountain." Fedradin shrugged. He was doing Galeb Duhr a favor, so the creature wouldn't do anything bad. No one's morals were that bad.

In a few short minutes, the group: Tiserae, Fedradin, Aserax, Breetex, and Qint, were looking over the edge of a cliff face, to see that below two men were picking away at the side of the same cliff face with pickaxes.

"This should be easy," said Aserax, drawing back an arrow. She was about to release the bowstring, when Fedradin grabbed her arm. "What?" she snapped.

"Those are just innocent people down there," said Fedradin. "They're just doing their job. We can't murder them."

"But what about Galeb Duhr's request?"

"Maybe we can talk to them. Ask them to go mine someplace else." Fedradin found a way down to the place where the two miners stood. He came up behind them and tapped one on the back. The miner turned around, alarmed by Fedradin. There were no other humans for miles around.

"What the-?" said the miner. "What are you doing here?" The other miner turned around.

"What is it?" The second miner's eyes widened as he saw Fedradin.

"Hello to you both," said Fedradin. "I am Prince Fedradin of Narven. I request that you move to a different place to mine." The first miner suggested a place for Fedradin to put a certain body part. Fedradin angered, but he controlled his impulse to chop the miner's head off. "There is a creature on this mountain and you are disturbing him. He has peacefully asked that you move."

"Buddy," said the first miner. "You seem like a smart guy. There could be thousands of fellyers worth of gems and metals in this mountain. If you think we're going to move just because an anonymous creature complained about us, think again." The miner raised his pickaxe to hit the side of the cliff.

"Please, this creature is very powerful-" started Fedradin.

"Enough!" shouted the first miner, turning around. "We came here to mine in peace, and you are destroying that goal!" With that the first miner swung his pickaxe at Fedradin, instead of the cliff face. Fedradin easily sidestepped the blow, the pickaxe slamming into the ground beside Fedradin.

"Nice try. May I suggest stepping into it next time?" said Fedradin, playfully. Out of the corner of his eye, he noticed the second miner fall dead, an arrow sticking out of the top of his head. The first miner had not noticed this however, and swung again. Fedradin raised his palm, and the pickaxe stopped in mid-air, caught by Fedradin's air powers. The miner's eyes widened with fear. Fedradin smiled. "Enjoy the taste of your own pickaxe," said Fedradin, waving his palm. The pickaxe slammed into the miner's cheek, knocking him to the ground. Fedradin saw one of the miner's teeth go flying out of his mouth. Fedradin walked away, letting the pickaxe drop onto the already unconscious body of the miner.

The group went back to where they had originally found Galeb Duhr, some still amazed at Fedradin's Sage powers. When they returned, it was quite different. The various bags they had kept clothes, food and other such supplies in were ripped open, things everywhere. Perched on the branch of a large oak tree was Galeb Duhr, holding a bag out of the cliff with a gleeful smile on his face.

"Well, we took care of those two miners you asked us to subdue," said Fedradin, angrily. "What have you been up to?"

"I have your bag!" said Galeb Duhr, his smile growing. "I have your compass and your six rocks and I have your bag!"

"What is he talking about?" asked Fedradin.

"I told you! I put all of the valuable stuff in one bag!" said Tiserae.

"And that was a good idea?"

"It seemed like one at the time!"

"'Right, so now we have to figure out to make sure Galeb Duhr doesn't drop the bag."

"So what if he does?" said Breetex. "Erch will never find the rocks in that ravine."

"He wouldn't need to," said Qint. "If Galeb Duhr breaks enough of those rocks, the tomb will burst open, allowing anyone to get at the Demon Caller."

"So why don't we break the rocks and go to the tomb now?" asked Aserax.

"I would love for you to give me directions to where the first Demon Caller is hidden," said Qint. "But Erch might know where the tomb is and he could be waiting there now."

"Focus," commanded Fedradin. "We need to save the bag!"

"Just let Galeb Duhr join us! There's no harm in it!" said Tiserae.

"I guess you're right...Hey! Galeb Duhr, would you like to join us?" asked Fedradin.

The creature looked up with a cry of glee. "Would I ever!" He jumped down from the branch and ran over to group, throwing the bag to them. In a few more minutes they were saddled up, Galeb Duhr riding with Kerwan, who had the strongest horse to carry the creature. Kerwan was happy to have someone as old as Galeb Duhr around to talk to about history.

A few minutes into the ride, Tiserae pulled up next to Fedradin and said, "By the way, it was a decoy bag."

Chapter 110
Sam's Colony

FEDRADIN

AS THEY ENTERED INTO the Oxler Tundra, they had to send Aserax out for fur, for the temperature was rapidly decreasing as the moved farther south. By the time they decided to crash for the night, they had reached Sam's Colony, the farthest south human settlement in Haxter.

Sam's Colony was a small, rundown operation. A few, dilapidated, wooden shacks stood together on the tundra. As a gale came roaring across the seemingly endless tundra, the shacks shook, but stayed upright. The piles of debris told Kerwan that the buildings had not always been so successful. The pile of debris was also aflame, with three figures huddled around it. Each figure was wearing a parka, hoods up.

"That fire looks nice," said Breetex, through clenched teeth. "I am not used to cold weather." It was true. Breetex was from up north, in Alta, which was much hotter than Sam's Colony. The group walked over to the fire, Breetex running over, getting as close as he could before catching on fire himself. The sudden appearance startled one of the figures, the closest one to Breetex.

"What in the name of-? What the hell? Are you a dwarf?" stammered the figure. A smile came to Fedradin's face. A dwarf was not the weirdest creature they had accompanying them.

Another figure looked over. "Hey! Whats we got on us hands tonight? That a dwarf?"

The third figure stood up. "Yeah, it is! That be a dwarf! We know what ta do wid'em dwarves down here at the Colony!" The third figure pulled out a knife, which appeared to be whittled out of bone. The other two also stood up, pulling out similar weapons. The smile vanished from Fedradin's face. Breetex backed away, his hand going towards his tomahawk, as the three figures approached.

"Hold up a second!" shouted Fedradin, jumping in between Breetex and the three figures, his hand on Baxcanador. He felt the temperature dropping every second, as the sun set in the west and it grew darker.

"What is this?" said the first figure. "We got visitors? We ain't had no visitors in years!"

"Yeah, you *had* visitors," said Fedradin. "Let's leave. We don't stay in a town that tries to kill our friends."

"No!" exclaimed the first figure, as the group turned away to leave. "Please stay! I'm Grepil, and these are my friends Minus and Ominate." Grepil gestured to the second and third men. "The only reason we was mean to your dwarf friend was that we hasn't seen anything like him around here in years, and wes thought something bad be going on."

Fedradin eyed the three suspiciously. Minus finally said, "C'mon we was about to cook up some stew. Would yous be wantin' any?"

Fedradin looked to his counterparts and shrugged. What could be the harm in staying for free food? "'Right. We could stay for just a while longer."

The figures' faces lightened up. "Great!" said Ominate. "I'll put the stew on."

Ten minutes later, the sun had set. The stew, made out of seal and whale meat, and a little seasoning, had been dished out to everyone in ceramic bowls. The stew was devoured with gusto, the hot liquid spreading warmth throughout previously cold bodies. Aserax had gone out to bring back more fur, killing three wolves. The fur temporarily helped with the cold, but it just wasn't enough to block out the freezing gusts of wind that tore down through the tundra.

"We hardly ever see any other souls," said Minus.

"Yeah! The threes of us be more'n half the town," said Grepil.

"Yeah, and the other two be on a fishin' trip down'n the Glaciers," added Ominate.

"Well, we're here now," said Fedradin.

"Yeah. Now wes got a few humans, a dwarf, an elf, and a...whats the hell is that?"

Fedradin turned to Galeb Duhr. "He's Galeb Duhr."

"Glaby-what now?" said Minus.

"Never mind," said Fedradin. "Is there someplace where we can sleep for the night? Preferably someplace warm?"

"Oh, sure. You can use those three cabins over there. Except for you, sweet thing, you can use my cabin, if you catch my drift," said Grepil, looking at Tiserae and winking.

"Yes, I caught your drift," said Tiserae, coldly. "I'll sleep in the cabins you've offered us already." Tiserae turned on her heel, walking towards the cabins. Fedradin watched her leave. He turned back to Grepil, winked and shrugged.

"You gave it a try." With that Fedradin followed Tiserae, the rest of the group following in his wake.

Chapter 111
A Meeting

AXTO

HE STOOD IN AN obviously man-made clearing, stumps everywhere, with the slight scent of smoke, in the middle of the Mendelgar Forests, near its heart, where it seemed that no human had ever passed through and survived. Maybe Axto was the first. Well, that was if he survived.

The man in front of him was tall, very tall, and bright red. Not rose red, but lobster shell red. A tail, equipped with a razor sharp blade, whipped back and forth cutting the brush behind him in half. He was admiring a set of claws, each one nearly four or five inches long, nibbling at them with the multitude of fangs in his mouth. Above the mouth, three horns protruded from his head.

This was their master.

This was Erch.

"Greetings! I have summoned you all here today for a very important reason." Behind Erch stood two men and an odd looking creature. Axto knew these to be the Minions. In front of Erch stood Axto, of course; a man that had appeared to have horns; a beautiful woman, wearing an odd, black one piece outfit that fit her tightly; a flayer; and a man in a robe, its hood lowered to reveal the man had a bald head, with a red tattoo on his forehead. Axto had heard the names: Coid, Black Heart, Hijimin and Krile mentioned. "I need your help, all of you." Erch paced back and forth. "And this is what I need your help for."

Erch went on to explain to Axto and the rest what he wanted them to do, and a smile came to Axto's face. This would be fun. After the Prince of Destiny had destroyed Axto's life by killing his brother and costing him a job, he would enjoy extracting revenge on him. Slow and painful revenge.

BLACK HEART

Black Heart also harbored anger towards the Prince of Destiny. This man was responsible for the death of one of her four

436

daughters. It was because of the Prince of Destiny that this planet did not belong to the Uäile race. She would make sure that this man paid for his crimes. She would make sure he paid with his life.

COID

Coid had no anger towards the Prince of Destiny, but he had a gut feeling that Erch was the one responsible for his powers, so he would do anything and everything to help Erch. He was ready to fight the Prince of Destiny. The man wouldn't stand a chance.

HIJIMIN

Hijimin, a gifted sculptor, wanted to destroy the Prince of Destiny. This was the man who took the brains of the elders from the flayers' sacred pool, and for what? There was no purpose for that, just to spite the flayers. If Hijimin found the Prince of Destiny, he would kill him.

KRILE

Krile Wandhand had known about the plan for a while and had been brought back from the dead just for this purpose. To find the Prince of Destiny, the man who had sent him to his grave in the first place. He had paid the Necromancer in advance to resurrect him, so he had not fought his hardest when Kerwan finally attacked Krile.

Chapter 112
Information

TYRATION

MUCH LIKE KRILE, TYRATION had been raised from the grave by the mysterious man. Members of Desert Wind had paid the man to do so, and the next day Tyration was walking around, alive and well. But he didn't spend much time walking around aimlessly. As soon as he was resurrected, he set off in pursuit of Krile, who had left a few hours before. Krile had left someone else in charge of the cult, but it was that person's idea to have Tyration brought back to life. That person, Portar, was also the member in control of the earth crystal.

Tyration followed Krile all the way through the Cientile Plains and into the Mendelgar Forest, where Krile walked into a clearing. Tyration crawled to the edge of the clearing, peering in through the shrubbery. As he lay there, he heard a man, if one could call whatever it was a man, talking to five figures, while three stood behind him. The man talked about a plan which involved seizing the "Demon Callers," which would allow the man to...rule the world? Was this man insane? It seemed so to Tyration. But all the figures around him were transfixed as he spoke. Were they insane, too? That was a possibility. Tyration thought for a few more moments, until he decided that even though there was a strong possibility that all these people were simply crazy, he had to tell someone. And he knew just whom to tell.

ROGER

Roger had sent eight recruits to capitals of the various races, with the explanation for what had happened with Emperor Flyc. He knew that telling all the leaders of the Nine Races that Emperor Flyc was actually a demonic prophet was a bit far-fetched, but nevertheless, it was the truth. He was also trying to help rally the army to fight Erch that Fedradin was attempting to rally. His operation was met with fairly good results: the chultra said they would help, the Keshnul said they would help, the Grefture said they would help, the animal cultures said they would help, and the elves said they would help. The svaadi slammed the door in the face of the messenger, and the dwarfish said they would not help fight an evil demon prophet. The flayers sent the head of the messenger back. There was not a clear answer to whether or not they would help, but Roger was able to jump to a conclusion.

Roger had also sent messengers to the fiefdoms of the Empire, explaining how there was a new Emperor in Bal-gastar. The kings of Borave, Viven, and Gii paid their respects to the new Emperor by bringing him a gift. They were all shocked to see that a boy was sitting atop the throne, but none questioned his authority. After all, he was the one who had brought down Flyc. The kings of Swenvip and Narven did not come to pay their respects. Instead, both kings sent a notice that they were seceding from the Empire, forming their own, separate kingdoms. Now, Roger was dithering over whether or not send out an army, composed of the Empire's soldiers, Boravian soldiers, Vivien soldiers, and Giin soldiers to crush the rebellion.

As he sat in his throne thinking about this, a man being escorted by guards came through the door. The man was bald, with a big red tattoo on his forehead. He wore a robe that came down to his ankles.

"Guards? Who is this man?" asked Roger.

"This here, sir, is Tyration," said one of the guards. "He claims he has important news regarding the...Demon Callers?" Tyration confirmed what the guard said with a nod of his head.

Roger looked down at Tyration, then back at his guards. "Alright, give us a moment." The guards backed out of the room. "Speak, Tyration," said Roger.

"Yes, Your Highness," said Tyration. "I was following a certain man, by the name of Krile Wandhand, into the woods. He came to this clearing, where there were about eight other figures. One of them was referred to as Erch. They started talking about how they were going take the Demon Callers."

"Where was this meeting you say?" asked Roger.

"It was in the eastern part of the Mendelgar Forest."

"Thank you for the information. You can leave now." Tyration nodded and backed out of the room. Roger rubbed his head. Yet another thing to think about. He knew that Erch planned to kill Fedradin already. That wasn't new. But the fact that Erch had waited so long to do this was...odd to say the least.

Roger shook his head. He needed to talk about this with someone. And Sgire was his first and only option.

Chapter 113
The Far South

BREETEX

BREETEX'S EYE FLUTTERED OPEN. He was a light sleeper, he always had been. The noise that had awoken him came from the creaking floorboards of his wooden cabin. He slowly turned his head to see that Minus was creeping towards the sleeping bodies of him, Aserax, and Tiserae. Minus pulled out an object, which Breetex guessed was a knife, but it was too dark in the cabin to ascertain. Minus bent down next to Tiserae (whose hood was still up) and pulled her purse silently towards him. Breetex knew that the six rocks from the Legendary Eight plus the silver compass were in that bag.

As Minus started to slink away, Breetex slowly reached for his tomahawk. *I have one shot*, he thought, as he grabbed the tomahawk. He carefully aimed the tomahawk at Minus and threw it as hard as he could. The tomahawk flew through the air, slicing the bag right below Minus's hand. Minus froze for a second, alarmed, as the bag fell to the ground, spilling its contents everywhere.

Breetex ran forward, his larger, battleaxe in hand. He swung, and Minus ducked to avoid decapitation. The man jabbed out with his knife, but Breetex grabbed his forearm, breaking the bone by kneeing it. Minus cried out in pain, clutching at his broken arm, but Breetex wasn't finished. With a flying kick, he sent Minus crashing into the wall of the cabin, the man falling to the floor, unconscious.

"What happened Breetex?" asked Aserax.

"Minus just came in here and tried to steal the bag!" said Breetex, gesturing to the bag filled with the items they needed to get to the first Demon Caller.

Tiserae looked up, from her prone position and said, "That isn't the bag," before turning over and going back to sleep.

Breetex looked at her, one eyebrow raised. "How many decoys do you have? And where is the real bag?"

Tiserae's reply was muffled because she was speaking into a blanket. "To answer your first question: many. To answer your second: did you really think that I wouldn't let the Prince of Destiny guard what he is destined to find?"

"If that's the case, then we should check on the other cabin," said Aserax.

"I'm sure they're fine," said Tiserae.

"In any case, I'm going to check on them," said Breetex, picking up his tomahawk. As started towards the door, it slammed open, catching him in the shoulder and sending him tumbling across the room.

"Is everyone okay in here?" asked Fedradin, faint sunlight streaming in through the door.

"Yes, we're fine," said Tiserae, still determined to fall back to sleep.

"Speak for yourself," said Breetex, rubbing his shoulder.

"Oh, I'm sorry," said Fedradin, but his tone was not very apologetic. Breetex shot him a dirty look. "We should get out of here," said Fedradin. "These men are bad news." Grudgingly, Tiserae packed up her blankets into a pocket in her coat, as Breetex and Aserax shoved their blankets in bags.

Aserax noticed Tiserae cramming an impossible amount of stuff into her pocket, so she spoke up. "What is going on with your pocket?"

Tiserae looked down at her pocket. "Oh, I invented this. I summoned a spirit, which transports anything I put in my pocket to a storage cellar near my house. If I want anything from my pocket, I simply think about it, and the spirit sends it back up."

"Fascinating," said Aserax, half serious, half sarcastic. Finally, they were all packed, so they exited the cabin, leaving the unconscious body of Minus lying on the floor. Fedradin, Kerwan, Qint and Galeb Duhr were already all packed up, and were gathered around the embers of the burned debris, eating cold, leftover stew.

"There they are!" said Fedradin.

"Sorry we're late," said Tiserae.

"No rush, or anything," said Fedradin. "Just trying to *save the world*." Tiserae could tell he was joking.

Tiserae joked back by mimicking him, "'*Right*. What's next on the agenda?"

Fedradin smiled a little, saying. "Same old, same old. Trying to kill some legendary monsters." This banter went on for a while, until Kerwan forced them to focus. After a few more minutes of preparation they were off. They were off to slay the seventh of the Legendary Eight.

QINT

As they walked out of camp to find the seventh of the Legendary Eight, Qint felt guilt well up inside him. He should tell them about what would happen when they slayed the seventh. He knew he should tell them, but whenever he tried, a searing pain ripped through his brain, only ceasing when he decided he wasn't going to say anything. It must be the spell that turned his eyes red and announced the name of the Legendary Eight monster. The same spell he needed to warn them about. He couldn't tell them directly, but maybe if he wrote in the dirt with a stick...

His brain was seized by an invisible force, and it felt as if his brain were being dissected by a trembling man with a flaming scalpel. He submitted to the force. He wouldn't warn anyone.

The pain stopped. Qint looked at Fedradin, the Prince's determined face examining the silver compass. If only the poor boy knew what was in store.

FEDRADIN

Fedradin and the others followed the compass through the Oxler Tundra until it told them they were in the right area, by spinning wildly. It wasn't long before Fedradin found the seventh of the Legendary Eight, for on the tundra, one could see for miles. They saw a figure of a monster on the horizon and they rode towards it. When they got close enough, Qint's eyes turned red.

"The Bebegan," he murmured. The monster looked similar to a dire polar bear, except that it had a whirlwind of ice chunks circling around it. Fedradin pulled out Baxcanador and began to fight.

The Bebegan swiped at him with its claws. Fedradin dove to the side, the claw ripping a chunk out of the frozen soil. He swung Baxcanador at the Bebegan's leg in an attempt to cut it off, but the monster retracted its leg before Fedradin got the chance. The Prince of Destiny jumped to his feet, facing the Bebegan, which was crouched down, growling.

As Fedradin prepared his next move, an arrow flew through the air towards the Bebegan, bouncing harmlessly off an ice chunk that was revolving around the monster. Kerwan tried a black spell on the Bebegan, by that too was intercepted by an ice chunk. However, Kerwan's spell exploded unlike Aserax's arrow, which sent the Bebegan tumbling across the ground.

Fedradin ran forward, along with Breetex and Tiserae. Fedradin got to the fallen Bebegan first, but he was hit by a flying chunk of ice. He fell to the ground, rubbing his jaw, where the ice had hit him. Breetex got through the field of ice without injury and swung his battle-axe at the monster. It hit the Bebegan in the side, the axe sticking into its side. The monster roared in pain, swinging its clawed paw at Breetex. The claws ripped through the dwarf's shirt, narrowly missing his chest; however, the claws did not go all the way through Breetex's shirt. The Bebegan, seeing that Breetex was not dead, swung its paw into the air, sending the dwarf flying. Breetex crashed to the ground far away from the monster. Tiserae, who also was able to make it through the field of ice, attacked the Bebegan while it was occupied with Breetex. The knives that were hidden in her sleeves came out, ready for action. She rushed forwards, stabbing the Bebegan in the chest. The monster roared, and as it did so, Tiserae stabbed again. And again. And again. She was pulling back to finish off the monster with a stab to the neck, when a chunk of ice collided with the back of her head. Tiserae fell forwards (but her hood did not come off), landing face first in the light layer of snow that covered the tundra. Fedradin saw that the Bebegan was raising its claws to finish off Tiserae.

"No!" Fedradin cried out in anguish. "Tiserae!" He raised a palm, desperate to do anything to save her. With his air powers, he ripped the Bebegan's arm off completely, throwing it to the side. But he wasn't finished. As the Bebegan ululated in pain, Fedradin raised his palm, and the monster floated into the air. It required a tremendous amount of energy and attention, but the adrenaline helped him with it. "Kill it Kerwan! Kill it!" He could already feel his strength draining.

The wizard started firing white spells at the Bebegan. Mostly, the spells did not reach the Bebegan, for they sliced the ice chunks in half, instead of hitting the Bebegan. A few did hit the monster though, cutting off various body parts. Finally, one spell reached the monster's neck, decapitating it immediately. Fedradin dropped the corpse of the monster, and fell to the ground, exhausted.

"Where's the rock?" was the last thing he was able to mutter before he passed out. Kerwan ran over to Fedradin, holding gorp similar to what Biggs had used to revive Utka. He started to feed bits of it to Fedradin, as the rest searched for the rock. Galeb Duhr was actually the one who found the rock, which (like the Chingow) was in its head. To be fair, the Galeb-Duhr was not actually interesting in finding the rock, he just wanted to crush the monster's head.

QINT

Qint was watching everything, Fedradin coming to, the joys over finding the rock. He saw Kerwan grab the silver compass, looking down at the needle.

"It says we're in the right location to find the next of the Legendary Eight," said Kerwan, baffled.

Qint could feel the transformation coming. He hated to admit it, but he was more frightened by his approaching death than the fact that the group might not get the last of the Legendary Eight rocks. To make up for this, he decided to shout a warning to the group.

"Look out, I'm-" Searing pain, worse than he had ever felt seized his brain slicing it into a thousand pieces. He collapsed to the ground clutching his head. Everyone looked his way, and he knew he needed to finish the sentence. Even though the pain grew even more, if that was possible, he choked out the remainder of the sentence. "I'm the last monster."

Chapter 114
The Dirty Deed

BRUNUS

BRUNUS HAD PUT ON the white, hooded robe Merip had supplied. He pulled the hood up so that it cast a shadow over his face, in an attempt to not be recognized during their dirty deed. He looked at the provided blades, all lined up across a table. Brunus was not sure whether or not to pick one up and use it to kill Plitsky. Inside his head, he was caught up in a swirling battle. On one side, he felt that he had to protect his friend, to stand up against Merip and the other members of the council. On the other, he knew the something was wrong with Plitsky; his judgements and decisions had been wildly poor and unpopular. The battle raged as Brunus stood there, but after a few minutes he knew what he needed to do. Brunus picked up a knife, hating himself for what he knew had to be done.

A few minutes later, the council (minus Unal) all dressed in white robes stood behind a pillar, waiting for Plitsky. They all had their blades out, ready to finish off their biased king once and for all.

As Brunus saw Plitsky emerge from his office, holding a scroll, he felt a pang of guilt. He needed to do something. He was about to shout out to Plitsky, to warn the king, when a piece of him strangled the cry. Deep down, he knew that the council had to kill Plitsky. The king was becoming a dictator.

"There he is!" announced Merip, running forward knife in hand. Plitsky looked up, alarmed. When he saw Merip's knife, his eyes widened, and he stuck out the scroll he was holding as a shield. Merip's knife embedded itself in the scroll, and as Merip made to retrieve the knife, Plitsky flung the scroll backwards, the scroll and knife clattering to the floor far away. Merip, angered, threw a punch at Plitsky's head, but the king was able to dodge the blow and follow up with a kick to Merip's groin. Merip collapsed to the floor in pain, as two other council members charged Plitsky.

One stabbed at the king earlier than the other. Plitsky was able to sidestep the first knife, knocking it free of the elf's hand; however, as he turned to avoid the second blade, the second blade entered his forearm. Plitsky cried out in pain as he fell to the ground, the blade retracting from his flesh. The elf who had stabbed him raised his knife for a finishing blow, but Plitsky, fighting through the pain, swiped the legs out from under the elf. The elf fell to the floor, Plitsky finishing him off by snapping his neck.

Brunus watched what was happening from in front of the pillar. Plitsky had been able to hold off the first three elves, but now the rest of the council had made its way over. Plitsky had picked up a knife, and Brunus, despite what he had decided earlier, hoped that the king would be able to fight the council off.

Plitsky was backing away from the angry council, until he hit a wall. When he hit the wall, he quickly lashed out with his knife at the closest elf. The blade struck an unprepared elf in the knee, and he dropped to the ground, screaming. He lashed out again, but his target was prepared this time and was able to deflect the blade. He stabbed again, but instead of just being deflected, he was disarmed.

Plitsky, defeated, put his hands over his head. "Okay, fellas, I don't want any trouble. What do you want? I can give you money, power, women?"

"We don't want any of that. We want your head on a stick," said Merip.

"Why don't we find a compromise? Instead of my head on a stick, you can have-" Plitsky was cut short by a stab to his gut. He doubled over, clutching at the wound.

"Did you enjoy that?" said Merip, though he wasn't the assailant. "There's plenty more where that came from."

"Please..." said Plitsky, weakly. Merip smirked.

"Get him." Knives from every direction began plunging into Plitsky. He rolled into a ball, he arms over his head and his knees pressed against his chest. Still, the knives found their way through, cutting into his chest, sides, stomach, back, not to mention that hundreds of cuts he must have received on his arms and legs. Throughout this time, Brunus (who was still standing apart from the group), could hear little to no sobbing or wailing coming from Plitsky. The king must have decided not to cry as he died, so only during certain stabs did a murmur of anguish find its way through his tightly closed lips. He was a brave king. It was a shame he had been poisoned by his own uncle.

After a few minutes, Merip called off the council and they ran in all different directions. Brunus, after they had scattered, walked over to Plitsky, who was bleeding out on the floor.

"Brunus..." murmured Plitsky.

"I'm sorry my friend," said Brunus. He pulled out his knife.

"You too, Brunus?"

"I'm sorry," Brunus whispered. With that, he slit Plitsky's throat. He had done it. He had killed his best friend.

Chapter 115
The Final Monster

FEDRADIN

FEDRADIN WATCHED WITH HORROR as Qint, the man who had taught him to use the crystal, morphed into something...something strange. First, his eyes glowed red, like Fedradin had seen them do before. Qint's arms seemed to expand, the skin seeming to stretch to contain the muscles within. Finally, the skin gave way, revealing massive rocky arms. Qint began to grow, the same thing that had happened to his arms happening to his legs. As he stood now about ten feet in the air, his torso and head grew so it was proportional to the large legs and arms. Then, slowly, his torso and had began to transform into the rock that constituted the rest of his body. Fedradin was now facing what looked like an enlarged Galeb-Duhr.

"You seek the last rock?" roared the beast that used to be Qint. Fedradin stood paralyzed, unable to answer. However, he was able to nod slightly. "Then you must take it over our dead bodies!"

Our? Fedradin heard what sounded like an eagle screeching first. Then, he saw a monster fly in from the horizon, beating its wings against the wind. It looked similar to a dragon, but it was smaller and frailer. But it still wasn't small *or* frail, just dragons were much more so. It had a long lizard-like tail which had an arrowhead shaped spike on the end. Also, instead of the gnashing teeth of a dragon, it had a beak of an eagle. It screeched as it grew closer to the group.

"We are the last of the Legendary Eight!" proclaimed the Qint-beast. "I am *Gesamador* and she is *Gesamadora*."

Tiserae said, mostly to herself, but it could be heard by everyone, "That translates to Thunder and Lightning in the lost language of the cyclopsi..."

"I don't care what it translates to," said Fedradin. "All I know is we need to kill those monsters. We destroyed all seven other of the Legendary Eight. We cannot let this last one stop us!" With that Fedradin sent a ball of fire flying at Gesamador, the rock monster. The fireball slammed into the chest of Gesamador, knocking him back a few steps, but not killing him or even shattering him.

"Puny human!" he roared. With that, Gesamador flung a boulder (which appeared out of thin air) at Fedradin. Caught in a moment of indecision over whether to use his air powers or his earth powers, it seemed like he would get hit by the boulder. Right as he ditched the idea to use his Sage powers and decided to jump away, the boulder shattered in midair. Fedradin was baffled by what had happened, until he heard Galeb Duhr say:

"I may not be able to control avalanches, but I sure as hell can destroy a boulder." Fedradin had an idea.

"Galeb Duhr! Try to shatter Gesamador!" shouted Fedradin. Galeb Duhr looked intently at Gesamador, but only a few pebbles fell off the stony nose of the monster.

"Is that Galeb Duhr? Hah!" laughed Gesamador, almost triumphantly. "Gesamadora!" The dragon-like creature swooped in from the sky, grabbing Galeb Duhr between her talons. She flew into the air, screeching in delight as she went.

"That's high enough!" shouted Gesamador to Gesamadora. Gesamadora released Galeb Duhr, the rocky monster plummeting towards the ground. Fedradin did not know what would happen to Galeb Duhr when it hit the ground, but judging by the screams of terror from Galeb Duhr, it wouldn't be pretty.

Fedradin, in an attempt to save his newfound friend, thrust out his palms, catching Galeb Duhr with a cushion of air he created himself. Galeb Duhr crashed into the cushion of air, Fedradin letting him down lightly. Galeb Duhr nodded to Fedradin, in thanks, before jumping back into the battle.

At the same time, the rest of the group joined in to the battle, for they had been paralyzed before. Aserax fired three arrows at Gesamadora, but the monster was able to avoid two of the three. The third stuck into her wing, but caused no major damage. Kerwan pulled out his wand and fired two white spells and a black spell at Gesamador. The white spells bounced harmlessly off of him, not cutting through, and the black spell exploded, only knocking the monster back a few feet. Kerwan began shooting spells at Gesamadora, but upon seeing him shooting spells, the monster swooped down and snatched him up. Breetex, before

Kerwan got too far off the ground, grabbed Kerwan's legs, in an attempt to keep the wizard on the ground, and was taken up into the air also. Tiserae, Fedradin noticed out of the corner of his eye, pulled something out of her magical pocket. To him, it looked like a bunch of grapes, but they seemed to be made out of glass and with a glowing core. Fedradin looked at her curiously, but she winked.

"Don't worry, you'll find out what they do," said Tiserae.

"Excuse me! Breetex is still up there with Kerwan! Do something! I can't shoot arrows; I might hit them!" shouted Aserax.

"'Right," said Fedradin, processing the situation. "Galeb Duhr, Tiserae, work on taking down Gesamador. I'll help Aserax with Gesamadora." They split, Galeb Duhr and Tiserae rushing to fight Gesamador as Aserax and Fedradin prepared to take down Gesamadora.

Aserax looked up at Gesamadora circling overhead. Kerwan was attempting to get a good angle to shoot a spell, as Breetex clung on to his legs for dear life. "What are you going to do?" asked Aserax.

Fedradin thought for a moment. "How afraid are you of heights?"

TISERAE

Tiserae and Galeb Duhr were facing Gesamador. They had come up with a plan, and they had reached a point where they were ready to execute it. Gesmador threw a boulder at the two, which he created out of thin air. Tiserae stepped to the side as Galeb Duhr shattered it with his ability to control the element of earth, like a Sage.

"Now!" shouted Tiserae. Galeb Duhr charged forward as she threw one of the glass balls in her hand. The ball flew through the air, colliding with Gesamador's chest. As it shattered against the rocky chest of Gesamador, there was an explosion that knocked Gesamador back. As he stumbled backwards, Galeb Duhr jumped into the air, kicking the monster in the chest. Gesamador fell backwards this time, landing on his back with a deafening thud. Tiserae ran to the fallen Gesamador, which was attempting to pick itself up, but was still on the ground. Tiserae ran onto the monster, running all the way up to its head. When she reached its head, she jumped into the air, throwing another one of her glass balls down at Gesamador's head. The ball exploded on impact, sending her flying outwards. Tiserae crashed to the snowy ground of the tundra, looking behind her. Her cloak had saved her from being burned by the explosion, so she only ached slightly from where she had landed. Galeb Duhr ran over to her, giving her a hand up.

Gesamador was not dead. She saw it get up, but its face had a large crack down the middle. He laughed as he stood up, saying:

"Nothing can defeat me! You all shall perish!" Upon saying this, a boulder, larger than any other he had created before, formed in front of him. He grabbed the boulder, before hurling it at Tiserae and Galeb Duhr.

"Break it, Galeb Duhr!" shouted Tiserae, as the boulder grew closer.

"Don't you see that I'm trying? I don't have enough power to break one this large." Tiserae, to avoid the boulder, moved to the side. She thought she was in the clear.

She wasn't.

The boulder curved to follow her step. Tiserae took a step back. The boulder followed her. She tried once more, and again the boulder followed her. At this point she lost her nerve, and she ran.

FEDRADIN

Fedradin had condensed the air under Aserax's feet, and he was now raising the condensed air higher up, towards Gesamadora. His plan was to get her high enough into the air that she could get a better shot at the monster that was circling overhead.

Gesamadora was flying in a loop, and she had just turned towards Aserax. The monster let out a screech, flapping her wings faster to reach and attack Aserax as quickly as possible. Aserax calmly drew an arrow, aiming it at Gesamadora, pointing it at her eye. As Gesamadora grew closer, she was about to release the arrow, when she was hit by something and was knocked off the condensed portion of air. The something being Breetex.

Fedradin had seen it clearly from where he was standing: Gesamadora had flicked the leg that was holding Kerwan (and through Kerwan, Breetex) at Aserax. Gesamadora had held onto Kerwan, but Breetex had not been able to hold onto Kerwan because of the incredible amount of force. Breetex had flown through the air, slamming into Aserax.

Aserax had lost her hold of the bowstring, and the arrow flew off into the distance, narrowly missing taking Breetex's ear with it, since the arrow had been so close to his head.

Fedradin saw both the elf and the dwarf start to fall out of the sky. He looked to Gesamadora to see that she was swooping low, and he realized what she was trying to do. Gesamadora was going to catch the two on the way down with her talons. But Fedradin knew how to stop this. He raised both his palms catching both Aserax and Breetex in a cushion of air. As Gesamadora swooped directly underneath Aserax and Breetex, Fedradin let them fall so that they landed on top of a slightly confused Gesamadora. Immediately, the two were able to understand what Fedradin wanted them to do.

Breetex ran over to the side of Gesamadora where Kerwan was hanging. Breetex reached out a hand, which Kerwan grabbed, and with his other he used his tomahawk to cause Gesamadora pain until she unclenched her talons. After around five or six tomahawk strikes (which barely punctured her scaly legs) Gesamadora released Kerwan, the wizard being pulled up by Breetex. Now that the three stood atop the monster, it was time for them to bring her down.

Fedradin, confident with his work with Gesamadora, turned to face Gesamador, who had his back towards Fedradin. Instead of facing Fedradin, he was facing Tiserae and Galeb Duhr. Fedradin seized the opportunity by leaping onto the back of Gesamador. He put his right arm around the monster's throat, attempting to pull him down backwards. But he was not able to do so, distracted by what he saw what was going on in front of Gesamador. Tiserae was running from a boulder, which was following her across the tundra. Fedradin shot out his left palm to try and stop the boulder, but it was too far away. He watched in horror as the Galeb Duhr valiantly dove in front of the boulder. The boulder sent Galeb Duhr flying, but it also shattered as it hit him. Tiserae was safe, but Galeb Duhr was sprawled unconscious on the tundra.

Gesamador let out a chuckle. Rage filled Fedradin's veins, and Fedradin pulled harder on his neck. Fedradin started pushing out on his upper back with his legs, while simultaneously pulling on his neck. Finally, the monster fell to the ground, Fedradin leaping back to avoid getting crushed. He had just used a simple takedown maneuver that could be used on humans -though on humans it would be with two hands, one around the neck and one on the back— on a gigantic monster.

Fedradin looked down at Gesamador as he tried to pick himself up once more. Fedradin needed to figure out a way to finish him off, and as he thought, a voice, no, a whisper, sounded in the depths of his brain:

Baxcanador.

He drew his sword, raising it high above his head. This was the end of Gesamador. He was about to bring the sword down, when he glimpsed something out of the corner of his eye.

Figures falling. Three of them.

KERWAN

Kerwan would normally cut the head off the monster with a white spell. But then again normally he wouldn't be riding on the monster's back. The Gesmadora was still searching for the three figures, who, not five minutes ago were all comfortably in her control. The scales, Kerwan assumed, were not very sensitive to pressure, so Gesamadora could not feel them on her back.

"I say we should cut off one of her wings," said Breetex. He was quietly discussing with Aserax and Kerwan over what they should do to harm Gesamadora and get to the ground safely.

"No," said Kerwan. "We don't know how stable this thing is and she might crash us straight into the ground without two wings."

"How about we hang off the front of her head?" proposed Aserax. "We might have enough weight to pull ourselves down to the ground."

"Too dangerous," said Kerwan. "And plus, we wouldn't have nearly enough weight."

"Alright, genius," said Breetex. "You come up with a better idea."

"That I have," said Kerwan. "Aserax, take apart your bow. Breetex grab you battle axe." Kerwan pulled out his warhammer, as Aserax pulled her bow apart at the center to reveal two blades and Breetex took the battle axe off his back. "You remember how Fedradin steered the Chingow? He caused pain to one side of it, and it went the other way to avoid the pain. He did that with right and left, but why wouldn't it work with up and down?" Breetex and Aserax shrugged. It was a good idea, and they were not too proud to back down from their own ideas if it would save their lives.

Thus began Kerwan chipping away at Gesamadora's scales with a warhammer, Aserax stabbing into the scales with her bow-blades, and Breetex cutting deeper than both of them with his battle axe. They heard Gesamadora screech in pain as she began to feel the attacks through her scales. Kerwan then expected Gesamadora to fly towards the ground. Sadly she didn't.

Instead, the monster twisted violently, sending Kerwan, Breetex and Aserax tumbling off the side. Kerwan saw the tundra rapidly approaching.

Should have gone with the wing idea. That would have been better, thought Kerwan as he fell towards the tundra. *That would have been a lot better.*

FEDRADIN

Fedradin quickly created a cushion of air underneath Kerwan, Breetex and Aserax. They fell into the air cushion, each one without injury. He started to lower them to the ground, as he looked for Gesamadora. She was circling overhead, but it looked like she had taken a lot of damage. Her eyes were a little foggy and her wing strokes were half-hearted. Kerwan, Breetex and Aserax were closer to the ground, but still far enough away that a fall would be fatal, when Fedradin was struck in the back by something.

Fedradin flew forwards, the air cushion disappearing as he lost his concentration. Baxcanador was knocked from his hand, for he had been focusing most of his energy on the air cushion, not on grasping his sword.

455

Judging by the rock fragments around him, Fedradin guessed that he had been hit by a boulder from Gesamador. He knew that the monster would be right behind him, but he had to do something before he could turn to fight the monster.

Fedradin created a cushion of air right underneath Kerwan, Aserax and Breetex, directly before they hit the ground. He only held it for a fraction of a second, just enough for the three to slow down to non-fatal speeds. He released the cushion of air, immediately lunging forward for Baxcanador. His finger tips were barely touching on the pommel of the sword, when he felt himself get pinned by a large foot. A large, stony foot. He tried to grab the sword, but it was mere inches out of his grasp.

"It is a shame I must destroy such a worthy opponent," said Gesamador. Fedradin twisted his head to look into the monster's demonic red eyes. Fedradin pointed his palm, of the hand that wasn't touching Baxcanador, at the monster's chest. He was about to blow the monster back with a tremendous air blast when the monster clucked disapprovingly.

"I wouldn't advise that," said the monster. "You push me away, and that boulder drops on your head." Fedradin noticed the boulder floating over his head for the first time. Fedradin thought about his options. He could blow Gesamador backwards and try to destroy the boulder before it hit him. He could destroy the boulder and most likely get crushed by Gesamador. He could take a hand off Baxcanador to destroy the boulder *as* he blew back the monster. He would have to go with the last option. He prepared to do so, when he heard Kerwan's voice.

"Smile, you boulder bastard!" shouted Kerwan. Fedradin turned to see the wizard shoot a black spell at Gesamador. The explosion that knocked Gesamador to the ground dazed Fedradin for a moment, so he did not do something about the boulder falling towards his head. He realized this once the boulder shattered into thousands of small fragments, which rained down around him. Fedradin looked for his savior as he stood up (and picked up Baxcanador), to find Galeb Duhr standing proudly, Tiserae standing next to him.

Galeb Duhr smiled and said, "I'm back." Fedradin nodded his thanks to the odd, smaller version of Gesamador, before turning to the life-sized Gesamador, who was trying to get up. Fedradin ran forward, leaping into the air and stabbing with Baxcanador. The blade, somehow, passed through the stone of Gesamador's chest, hurting the monster as it went. Gesamador yelled out in pain, as Fedradin retracted the sword, ready to stab again. Before he had the chance, though, Gesamadora swooped down, grabbing Fedradin in between her talons. But before she could get too far, Fedradin flung Baxcanador to the rest of the group.

"Use the sword! Kill the monster!" his cries faded as he was carried off.

GALEB DUHR

Galeb Duhr was the one who caught Baxcanador, though he was very cautious around it after what he had seen it do to Gesamador. Galeb Duhr ran forward, to stab Gesamador, but the sword bounced off the stone. He was about to swing again when he was stopped by Tiserae.

"Give the sword to Kerwan," she said.

"Why...?"

"Just do it! I'll explain later." Kerwan took the sword, not knowing why the task of slaying Gesamador had fallen to him. Kerwan charged Gesamador, which was still recoiling from Fedradin's assault, and stabbed the sword into the monster, which passed through Gesamador like a hot knife through butter. Kerwan stabbed the sword into the monster again and again, until finally Gesamador fell backwards, dead. Kerwan, as he looked at Gesamador's corpse, dropped the sword on the ground.

"That sword..." murmured Kerwan. "Let's just say I'll stick to my warhammer from now on."

FEDRADIN

Fedradin was glad to see Gesamador finally fall. It was now time for him to focus on his own problems. He looked up at Gesamadora, who seemed to be trying to carry him as far away as possible. In fact, the Oxler Forest was creeping towards him in the distance. Fedradin put out his palm, condensing the air in front of Gesamadora into a solid wall. The monster smashed beak-first into the wall, dropping Fedradin out of shock. Fedradin let himself fall to the ground, providing his own air cushion right as he hit the ground.

He saw that Gesamadora was dazed from hitting the invisible wall, and when she was able to regain her composure, she would come after Fedradin, so he ran towards the rest of the group as fast as he could.

He reached them right as Gesamadora came zooming back across the tundra hungry for the flesh of whoever had hurt her and killed her partner. Fedradin looked back to the rest of the group.

"What should we do?" asked Aserax.

"Watch this," said Fedradin. He turned to face Gesamadora, flying back from across the tundra. He picked up Baxcanador and hurled it at the monster. The sword traveled through the air towards Gesamadora. As it neared her, it made a sudden movement, driving its tip straight through Gesamadora's eye. The monster howled before falling out of the sky, crashing to the ground with an explosion of frozen soil, snow, and ice. Fedradin put out his hand and the sword retracted from Gesamadora's eye and landed in Fedradin's grip. There was awestruck silence for a while, until Breetex finally broke it.

"Look!" shouted Breetex. The corpse of Gesamador was turning back into Qint. The corpse of Gesmadora was turning back into a woman, but no one was much interested in her. Fedradin ran over to Qint, to find the man was still breathing, but he had holes in his chest from where Baxcanador had stabbed him.

"Qint!" cried Fedradin. "Can you hear me?"

"Fedradin?" murmured the old man. "You truly are the Prince of Destiny. Take this rock and go save the Demon Callers." A rock, identical to the rest of the rocks protected by the Legendary Eight appeared over Qint, floating in midair. Fedradin gingerly took the rock from Qint.

"We can't just leave you here, Qint, you're going to die," said Fedradin.

"That is *my* destiny," said Qint. "I guided you here, taught you the things you had to learn to defeat Erch, which is *your* destiny. Now go, time is of the essence! If Erch has fastened a silver compass of some sort he will know where the tomb is! You must get there before him. You must protect the Demon Callers. Leave me, Fedradin, please. Go and save the world!"

Fedradin reached down and squeezed Qint's hands. "I will not fail you. You will not have died in vain! Good bye, Qint, and may your soul be guided into heaven." Fedradin turned and walked away, repeating, "You will not have died in vain." The rest of the group said their good byes to Qint, before turning and leaving his side, too.

QINT

Qint knew that death would soon save him from his pain. As he watched the Prince of Destiny walk away from him, he thought to himself: *That boy's going to save the world. It's a shame I will not be alive to see it.*

Part III
Finadek's Treasure

Chapter 116
Discussions

ROGER

SGIRE AND ROGER STOOD on a balcony that overlooked the city of Bal-gastar. Soon after the rebellion, people had gone back to work, living out their normal lives, even though they were being ruled by a sixteen-year-old boy. A sixteen-year-old boy who had saved them from a cruel dictator, he liked to remind them.

"I think this is just Erch preparing to kill Fedradin," said Roger. "Nothing Fedradin isn't ready for."

"I can't imagine Erch would wait this long, Roger," argued Sgire. "I'm not playing devil's advocate just to sharpen my mind. I truly believe that you're wrong."

"How? There's no proof!"

"Quite on the contrary!" said Sgire. "There is a landslide of proof in my favor."

"Like what?"

"Like the fact that Tyration said there were eight figures standing around Erch."

"What does that prove?"

"Remember, we overheard that Erch was going to use a Fire Sage and a Uäile to kill Fedradin. That's only two! What accounts for the other six?"

"The Minions of course!"

"There are only three Minions."

"There could be more we don't know about."

"There's a chance. There's also a chance that this is something more serious than just the assassination of Fedradin."

"More serious?"

"Yes! Remember how Qint said that there was a tomb which would be opened by the rocks from the Legendary Eight?"

"I recall."

"What if this group is going to ambush Fedradin and his group at the tomb?"

"How would they know where-"

"They might! Can we take that chance?" exclaimed Sgire.

"Hold up, Sgire. Do *you* remember how Erch discussed creating an army?"

"Of course."

"If he wanted to take the Demon Caller from Fedradin, he would use his army!"

"And expose his army to all of Haxter? I'm sure Erch knows that you sent messengers to all four corners of the Haxter to warn the races about his army."

"Oh, please. Even I don't believe that helped at all. The other races have no respect for us humans."

"But many said they would help us, correct?" inquired Sgire.

"That may just be because Fedradin forced them into saying they would help fight. Maybe, when Erch does march his army across Haxter, none of them will have the guts to help fight."

"Erch would never be so reckless! He's been planning this for hundreds of years; he's not going to risk everything by sending an army to do something a group of eight could do."

"You're right. He has been waiting a while to do this. That's why he would be even more reckless."

"What?"

"He's sick of waiting, Sgire. He's sick of planning and plotting. He wants to act! He wants to kill!"

"Alright, then why did he wait so long to do something after deciding to kill Fedradin, if he's so reckless? Fedradin has to be almost done getting the rocks from the Legendary Eight..." Her voice trailed off as she and Roger both thought of a possibility that they hadn't before.

"What if he's dead?" Roger's voice was hardly above a whisper.

"Maybe Erch has killed Fedradin already. Maybe they now have the silver compass and are either going straight to the tomb or to find the last of the Legendary Eight," said Sgire.

"Summon Tyration!" yelled Roger to a guard who was standing close by. Roger turned to Sgire. "Hopefully he can guide us back to the meeting place. Hopefully we are not too late. Hopefully we can still save the world."

Chapter 117
The New Ruler

BRUNUS

OBVIOUSLY, ASERAX WAS THE rightful heir to the throne. But Brunus had been warned: if he brought up finding Aserax and giving her the throne one more time, he would be thrown out of the council. Plitsky had not bequeathed the throne to anyone, so the council was in the process of finding a suitable heir. Obviously, their first choice should have been one of Plitsky's daughters: Rola, Roga, or Roka. Roka had been let out of jail, for in Plitsky's words, "I don't want to see her face until I am dead." He was dead, so Roka's sentence was up. Roga had been denied the job of Countess of Smore by Fevin IV, the presiding count, because Plitsky was dead, and Fevin believed she was making up stories. She tried to get support from the council to fire Fevin, but they did not give her a second glance. All three women were at the meeting though, each one trying to assume the throne -even Roka.

"No! The throne has never been directly handed down to a female heir! We can't break tradition!" demanded Merip.

"That's because there has always been a male heir to fufill the position. Now that there is none to do so, we must give it up to one of Plitsky's daughters!" said Brunus. Merip was arguing to not let the throne fall into the hands of Plitsky's daughters, and to give it to a senior council member. He was supported by almost every council member, except Unal and Brunus.

"How could we do that without a precedent or law?" cried Merip. "That would be unthinkable!"

"Precedents need to be set, you do realize!" said Brunus. "And besides, there is no precedent *or* law in your favor either."

"*Au contraire*, my dear friend, King Lopin died without bequeathment, and the throne was passed to a senior council member."

"That was to King Juern, his only *son*."

"But nonetheless it sets a precedent in my favor, does it not?"

Brunus argued fruitlessly with Merip for another few minutes. After a while Brunus even demanded to see the elvish constitution to make sure that the word "male" was placed in front of the word "heir." Unfortunately for his side it was. Brunus tried one last argument.

"We were willing to give Aserax the throne after King Juern died. Why are we not willing to give the throne to one of these fine young elves right now? It is the same relationship."

Merip was silent for a moment. "We warned you, Brunus."

"What?"

"You brought up Aserax again! You're no longer welcomed by this council."

"You have to be joking."

"I wish I were. Guards!"

"You weasel! I know exactly what you did!" shouted Brunus in a moment of sudden realization.

"Do you now? If only you were on the council to voice your opinions. Guards!" Brunus was about to shout out what Merip had done, he felt himself being dragged out of the room, his mouth covered by a guard's hand. They threw him into the hallway outside the council room, slamming the heavy oaken doors behind them.

Brunus screamed at the doors, even though he knew they were soundproof. "Merip wanted Plitsky out of the throne as soon as possible, and he didn't want us to take the time to vote Plitsky out of the position! That is why he wanted to kill Plitsky! All he wanted all along was the throne for himself, and now with all the heirs out of the way he is going to reach that goal! Don't give him the throne!" A few minutes later, the council meeting was adjorned. The council members walked out of the room, avoiding eye contact with Brunus.

Brunus thought to himself, *Wow, I cannot believe how cleverly he did this. He made friends with almost every council member. He never stated that his goal was to assume the throne, so many of these foolish ambitious elves believed they had a chance to become king if they agreed with him.* Finally, the elf Brunus was waiting for emerged. It was Unal.

"Unal! Wait!" shouted Brunus, running to catch up with Unal.

"What do you want, Brunus?"

"I want to know what happened in there."

"Obviously Merip won the debate. They then held an election and Merip was voted into the position of king."

"I knew it! You want to know what I figured out?"

"I know what you figured out. I was the first one to see it! He's been calculating this whole time, positioning himself for this moment."

"But why did we agree with him to kill Plitsky and not simply vote him out of the position?"

"Because he was right! It would take a while to make it official. The entire council would have to vote against Plitsky *and* we would need at least half of the general council to agree with us *plus* a three quarters popular vote. Plitsky was making bad decisions and we couldn't allow him to continue doing so as we tried to remove him. Plus, Plitsky wouldn't listen to anyone else. He was deciding things all for himself. *And* Merip found a way for this all to behoove him. By killing Plitsky, he helped ensure the throne, for if Plitsky were alive right now, he would have defended his daughters with gusto, making sure that one of them got the throne."

"So what should we do?" asked Brunus.

"I guess we'll have to just let Merip become king. It can't be too bad."

"No, that is unacceptable! Merip is a decent council member, but as king, I think he will be too opinionated to be any different from Plitsky. He will lead us down a dark path."

"Well, do you have a plan?"

"If, per say, Aserax were to come back, do you think that Merip would give up the throne?"

"He sure as hell would not!"

"Allow me to rephrase that: do you think Merip would be forced to give up the throne to Aserax?"

Unal weighed the situation in his head. "I suppose if Merip were a truly terrible king that could be a remote possibility."

Brunus thought for a moment. "I'll take it."

"Excuse me?"

"I'll take the chance." Brunus turned on his heels.

"Where are you going?" called Unal after him.

"To find Aserax and bring her home. We desperately need her help."

Chapter 118
Pursuit

TYRATION

TYRATION HAD BEEN DISAPPOINTED in Emperor Roger's reaction to his information. The Emperor had seemed to completely disregard Tyration, and he had thought about going back to Desert Wind defeated, but instead he had decided to hang around Bal-gastar for a while, something in the back of his head telling him to stay in the city a little while longer. It turned out that it was a good thing he had listened to that something in his head, for not long after he had been dismissed from Roger's royal chambers he was fetched by a guard. The guard led him to back to the castle, where Roger, and a girl of similar age, were waiting for him.

"Tyration! I have discussed the information you have given me with my...affiliate," said Roger. The girl next to him gave him a quizzical glance.

"What have you decided to do?" asked Tyration.

"We first need to ask to a few more questions. Did the man who was refered to as Erch talk about a certain 'Prince of Destiny?'"

"Not from what I heard, no, but they had been talking before I arrived."

"Alright, then. Do you know think you could guide us back to where the meeting was held?"

"Sure. I followed the Mendelgar River back to the Bal-gastar and then back up to here. The river was very close to the meeting place."

"Sounds great. My...affiliate and I, Sgire, and I were wondering if you would be willing to lead us back to the clearing."

"Of course I would. I would do anything for the Emperor," said Tyration. "But I have to ask: why?"

Roger was about to answer, but Sgire answered for him, "You know how the possessor of the 'Demon Callers' has the ability to conquer all of Haxter?"

467

"Yes, the man called Erch made that fairly clear."

"Well, we want to stop him from doing just that."

ROGER

Luckily the group Tyration had spoken of had not left the clearing. Roger, Sgire and Tyration were all prone in the bramble and bracken as they watched the figures with fascination. Tyration had his sword; Roger had his natural powers and a crossbow, extra bolts strapped to his back; and Sgire had the sword which she had procured from the training facility she had been in while posing as a boy. Right now, the three were listening in on a conversation between the figures.

"There's something different about the way the compass is reading today," said one of the figures, a normal looking man wearing a black robe.

Compass? thought Sgire. *As in the silver one?*

"Sure is," said another figure, this one obviously Erch, looking down at the compass. "What do you think that means?"

"I think we just found out where the tomb is," said the first figure. "Come on, Hijimin, Krile, Black Heart, Coid, and Axto. Let us go find the first Demon Caller!" The men (and one woman) that the first figure had just called upon seemed to have been waiting for this particular moment for a long time, for they were immediately ready to leave. They each mounted a horse, which seemed to not have been there when Sgire was first observing the clearing.

They were about to ride off in some direction, when Erch stopped them. "Wait!" called the demon. "Where are you going, in case..."

"We are going east, and if I were to have a guess as to where, I would say we are about to travel to Mystike, you know, that island off the coast. It seems like a place that Zantor might have hidden the tomb," said the first figure.

"Alright, Oxlo, I'll see you once we're one Demon Caller richer." With that, Oxlo and all the people he had rode out of the clearing, traveling due east, leaving only Erch and two other figures standing in the clearing. However, the three figures did not stand around for very long. Soon after Oxlo and his brigand had disappeared into the woods, Erch, like he had done in Balgastar disappeared in a purple ball of fire.

Sgire looked to Roger. "I know where we have to go next."

Chapter 119
That Night

KERWAN

"I WONDER HOW RUMORS about Gesamador and Gesamadora were started,"said Tiserae. "If Qint and that other woman only transformed into the monsters when all the other Legendary Eight were dead, how did anyone even know about them?"

"I know!" said Kerwan, evoking a groan from Aserax. Kerwan ignored her. "Qint and that other woman were not actually Gesamador or Gesamadora. The two monsters were actually spirits that could invade a body and transform it into their physical form. The spirits were not just waiting to protect their rock, they were also terrorizing villages by taking over others' hosts and using them to transform into their physical forms." The group was walking through Swenvip Swamp, following the needle, which was pointing towards a fishing town by the name of Tier.

They arrived at the town, and found that the needle was not satisfied yet. They were not close enough to where the tomb was that the needle was spinning. Instead, they found that the needle was pointing out to sea, possibly in the direction of the strange island of Mystike. Night was falling, so Fedradin decided he would figure something out in the morning, maybe charter a ship that would take them out to into the ocean, to follow the compass farther. They went to a small inn near the docks, where they rented a few rooms for the night.

FEDRADIN

That night, Fedradin fell asleep on a bed-bug infested mattress, thinking about the task ahead of him the next day. Would he simply be able to walk up to the tomb and take the first Demon Caller? That would be too easy. He also thought about the warnings he had received. He had a sinking feeling that the magical orphan was Kerwan. Eventually, Fedradin fell into a spastic and disrupted sleep, worried by the surprise waiting for him.

ASERAX

That night, Aserax fell asleep doubting her choice of running away with Breetex. Her father had been assassinated while she was gone! But she couldn't have stopped it. Could she have? No, she couldn't have and she loved Breetex. With this argument raging in her head, she was barely able to get any sleep at all.

BREETEX

That night, Breetex fell asleep fearing the next day. He knew that there was no way that Gesamador and Gesamadora were the last defenses to the first Demon Caller. Something else was going to pose as an obstacle, and he hated being unprepared. He was also wondering what was making Aserax so restless as she tossed and turned in their bed next to him. Still, even with these concerns on his mind, Breetex was able to get some sleep, aware of how much it would help his fighting skills if (or more likey, when) they needed to fight their way through an obstacle.

KERWAN

That night, Kerwan fell asleep with anger festering in his heart. Fedradin had seduced Tiserae, even after Kerwan explained his emotions to him. No matter how hard Kerwan seemed to try, he could never impress her; the woman was more attracted to Fedradin's abilities as a fighter than Kerwan's brains. Kerwan put his hand in his pocket, feeling the jewel. This helped sooth his anger, and he smiled to himself. He would prevail. He would be Tiserae's lover at the end of all this.

GALEB DUHR

That night, Galeb Duhr fell asleep happy as could be. He was ready to go and get the first Demon Caller. He had created most of Haxter, and he wanted to help save it. He harbored absolutely no fear, for he was practically immortal. Even after getting hit by a boulder he had gotten up unscathed. As he imagined winning medals and ribbons for his part in saving the world, Galeb Duhr drifted off into gentle sleep.

TISERAE

That night, Tiserae fell asleep fearing something that none of the others did. She checked for the umpteenth time that her hood was still on her head. This had been a mistake. She should have stayed in her cabin and listened to what her father had told her...*No*, she yelled at herself. *There is a reason their compass guided them to me. I must help them fight, even if it goes against the will of my father. I just hope that I can do so without them finding out my secret.* With her hands on her hood, Tiserae found sleep.

ROGER

That night, Roger fell asleep outside of New Gii. In the morning, he, Tyration and Sgire decided that they would take the risk of going to Mystike. There was no guarantee the "tomb" that was spoken of would be on the island, but it was where the Minions had predicted the tomb would be, so that was where they were headed. Roger was slightly fearful of the next day and the fight that would surely ensue, but what he was mostly frightened about was the girl sleeping next to him. Had she really forgiven him? How could she have? He had killed her mother! Of course he feared losing his life the next day, but he feared losing Sgire even more. With these thoughts in his head, Roger fell into a fitful sleep.

SGIRE

That night, Sgire fell asleep worried only about the task ahead of her, Roger and Tyration. She had to essentially take Fedradin's place as Prince of Destiny and save the Demon Callers, but she wasn't sure she was able. Sure she had gone to a military school, but had hardly covered the basics before her true gender was found out. But she had Roger beside her. His mere presence helped her feel safe. Sure he had killed her mother, but because of that she had escaped from her awful schooling at the women's school and was able to help warn Fedradin about a despicable plot. And anyway, she knew Roger was still torn over the thought of what he had done. He regretted it every day of his life, and she could feel it. In fact, from the way Roger was tossing and turning in the bed they shared, she could tell he was thinking about what he had done. In an attempt to make him feel better, she moved closer to him, wrapping her arms around his chest. With the reassuring feeling of him so close to her, she feel into a deep sleep.

TYRATION

That night, Tyration fell asleep thinking about the day ahead. He had warned Roger and all, and that was great, but now he was scared to think of actually fighting the men he had seen in the woods. They were formidable to say the very least. He wanted to help save Haxter, but he wanted to continue to live even more than that. He had already died once. Once was enough. Tyration drifted off into sleep, thinking of ways to back out of the fight he was fairly sure he wouldn't live through.

BRUNUS

That night, Brunus fell asleep with the urgency of finding Aserax pressing on the back of his mind. The elf that had just assumed the throne was a power crazy council member, and after years of being ignored had probably built up quite a bit of rage. Brunus couldn't even begin to imagine what horrors would befall the Elfish Kingdom with Merip as king. Brunus fell asleep, completely ignorant of the battle that was about to take place that could decided the fate of Haxter, worried only about the elfish throne.

UNAL

That night, Unal fell asleep, hoping that Brunus's searches would find Aserax. Like Brunus, he believed Merip would become a bad king, but there was nothing he could do about it. Right? He could have gone with Brunus to look for Aserax, but he was needed in the council. His opinions would be listened to. Right?

POLTAX

That night, Poltax did not fall asleep. He was being carried out to a graveyard by two other elves, who thought he was dead, in a sack. His claustrophobia had kicked in long ago. He was barely able to handle his fear because of the glee he felt due to the fact that the entire elfish race thought he was dead. But he wasn't. Somehow the poison hadn't killed him. Poltax was thrown on the ground roughly, and despite himself, he let out a gasp, an audible noise. The gravediggers must have heard it, because they sliced open Poltax's sack -relieving his claustrophobia— and as they did so, he sprung outwards, grabbing a shovel and killing both of them. Poltax was free. He would get the throne. He would get the throne soon.

MERIP

That night, Merip fell asleep with the title of King of the Elves, the title he had been dreaming of ever since he was elected to the council. Merip had been ignored by countless kings, his opinions deemed inferior. Even though he always criticized those kings for ignoring him, he planned to do the same to his council. Sure, he would become a hypocrite, but who wasn't these days?

DESMOND

That night, Desmond fell asleep with the weight of the war on his shoulders. He knew the elves were in turmoil, and he should strike now. But he couldn't bring himself to do it. He wanted to find peace with the elves. He didn't want it to be on him when the LNR fell apart.

YUNTILE

That night, Yuntile fell asleep comfortable in his king bed. Sure, he had used murder and deceit to get there, but it was worth it. He was almost glad for all the turmoil Flyc had caused the races. Almost.

THRASP

That night, Thrasp fell asleep wondering how in a few short weeks he had gone from warrior to king. He had made some enemies upon his coronation, especially Prince Rann, a satyr who had been the heir to the throne. Thrasp tried to put it out of his mind. He was safe...right?

ZOCATRAR

That night, Zocatrar fell asleep ashamed. All his fellow finalists were becoming kings. Yuntile, Thrasp...what was he? Nothing. Just a "thank you" from Desmond. The boy knew nothing about being a king! He was hardly an adult at all. Zocatrar, clutching his hand on his axe, managed to fall asleep.

WRETHIG

That night, the Wrethig of the flayers fell asleep thinking of the knowledge lost from the elderpool when that human had stolen from him. The Wrethig vowed revenge. He would rally the slaadi, and he would crush the life out of every human in Haxter, Osup, Stentor, Qassar and the rest of the known world.

MOAAND

That night, Greyslaad Moaand fell asleep, worried that he had allied himself with the wrong side. Should he have supported the flayers? He didn't have much of a choice. He owed them a favor. A huge favor.

HAZE

That night, Haze fell asleep concerned about the instability of the LNR. Elves and dwarves fighting, flayers and slaadi in an alliance, evil demons marching on Haxter...How could it all end well? Haze fell asleep contempling a solution.

DUZTIL

That night, Duztil fell asleep worried about the War of Gems. He was concerned that soon he would be dragged into it, if the elves called in their favor. No one knew about the favor. What would that do to the LNR...

IRROTHURE

That night, Irrothure fell asleep in his cave far away from the cabin he used to call home, bones scattered around him. He had taken to eating deer, which were plentiful around the forest and tasted pretty good. It wasn't a glorious lifestyle, but what else could he do? He couldn't go into a town and risk transforming into the monster that now seemed to dominate half his life. He would be hunted down like a mad dog! *No, no*, he said to chide himself. *You will not completely turn into that monster. Why the effect of that would be bad would be because innocent people would die at your hands, not the fact that others would hunt you down! You will continue to be human, despite what the monster is trying to do to you! You will have morals, standards to live up to. You're human, not a monster.* Irrothure fell asleep, proud of himself for remaining who he had been before his transformation. *You will not become a monster. You will not turn evil.*

VASIRD

That night, Vasird fell asleep with a fish in his mouth. It was so boring on the ocean floor. To pass the indefinite time that he had to spend in the ocean, he made a game, trying to see how long he could keep a fish in his mouth before it got scared and swam away. His record was currently a week, and he was trying to break it. *Oh gods,* he thought, *let this misery be over! Kill me! Kill me now!*

TRUMBELL

That night, Trumbell fell asleep thinking about the sail ahead of him. His big journey through the Fog Islands and to Narven, to warn the mainlanders of the Formaint. He tried to distract himself as his thoughts constantly were dragged back to how many ships sunk in the Fog Islands, but the thought of drowning where no one could hear him scream kept surfacing, unlike the man in his vision. What had his decision cost him? He had nearly killed Fender. When he returned to Sequo -if he returned to Sequo— what would become of him?

JOLOAK

That night, Joloak fell asleep full of fear. He had supported Trumbell; he had found the crazy man. And what had Trumbell done in return? Nearly killed Fender and completely destroyed Joloak's reputation as he stuck his neck out for him. Formiant? Old wives tales! They were all butchered in the Formiant Wars so long ago. But he had brought this upon himself. Even when Trumbell stormed out, Joloak took his side, Joloak drifted to sleep angry with Trumbell, but even angrier with himself.

FENDER

That night, Fender fell asleep wondering if Trumbell could be right. Could Formiant lurk behind Dragonsback Ridge? Could those creatures storm Sequo, and from there the gates of Balgastar? It was the colonists job to protect the Empire's realm from threats from Qassar, and if Fender mistrusted his companions, how was the job to get done?

ASH

That night, the Spice Sultan fell asleep angry with Hunnex and Fevra and Fane, but especially himself. If only he had stood on the wall with a sword held high, he wouldn't have to make up for his cowardice by sailing the pirate-ridden Trade Seas in search of reinforcements for the war against the orcs. Why did Fane send him back inside the palace? *It isn't Fane's fault. It's yours.* He often had to remind himself. But the Spice Sultan begging for help on the western shores of Haxter? Who would respect him? No one even knew who he was as it was in Haxter. And to show up and request men die for him? Finally, he was able to put himself to sleep with the thought that he was the best man for the job. At least the Spice Sultan himself would be asking for troops, not the Spice Sultan's merchant. He fell asleep hoping he wasn't prone to seasickness.

FANE

That night, Fane fell asleep with the thought that he shouldn't have sent Ash inside. The poor, fat man wanted nothing less than to sail to Uiklo. He'd get beaten, stolen from, killed! And it was all Fane's fault. The Spice Sultan had been happy to stand around, fighting no one, but no, Fane had to protect him. But what if Ash had died? Fane would take the Spice Seat no doubt. And that's what he wanted, right? It's why he kept so close to Ash? Fane fell asleep anxious for Ash, and curious of his own motives.

HUNNEX

That night, Hunnex fell asleep in the palace of Stent wondering who he should side with. The obvious choice would be the Orcslayers, but if what Fevra said about them was true, then he didn't want to fight to the death against an infinite orcish horde. He liked life, and it seemed the people of Stentor knew how to preserve it. Fevra was crazy, he knew that, but so was Ash. The question was, who was the sanest?

FEVRA

That night, Fevra fell asleep disgusted with the fat sultan. Nepotism, no doubt, was how he got the throne. But the Spice Seat wasn't supposed to be inherited. Or maybe he won a spice-eating contest. She knew someone needed to go to the mainland, and that someone was not going to be her. It was pleasing to see how perfectly her guilt trip worked. Ash jumped at the change to right his wrongs faster than he must have done at a freshly baked pie. Fevra smiled. There was no way the man came back alive.

DUNLOCK

That night, Dunlock fell asleep as his boat sailed down the river. Was it a mistake? Should he have ignored Grent? Maybe he could have sold his slaves back to where they were from. No, he needed Haxter. Without it, the slave trade would fail and that would mean blood on his hands. He wouldn't be the Corsairian King who let the LNR ruin the kingdom. He would be the king who conquered the mainland and taught the Haxterians that they were more that just pirates!

GRENT

That night, Grent fell asleep with an army armored and ready for Dunlock. He had heard about the attack on Truz, and he assumed that his allies were on their way. He smiled. Finally, Creopolis would not be under the control of Haxter or the LNR. They would rise up and take the land as they should have long ago. Grent would be remembered forever. He just hoped it was for winning the war.

KOLAN

That night, Kolan fell asleep worrying about Fern's leg. He was helping the knight as best he could, but he needed magic to fix the leg in time. And he had no coinwands. Maybe he should hire some. Other Scholars were treating the other injured at the Battle of Truz, but many more men were dying than living. And those who were living wished they were dead. Kolan's best treatment was amputation, which wasn't a popular choice. With those thoughts to mind, he fell asleep.

FERN

That night, Fern couldn't sleep with the horrific pain in his leg. He hoped it would set in time for the battle at Whitewater. He wanted to fight, that was how he made his living. As the boat rocked, he winced. It was going to be a long night.

UNK

That night, Unk was in pain, much like Fern. His arrow wound was getting worse, possibly infected. He legs were both broken after jumped onto a carrack, and his Scholar just continued to leech him and offer amputations. Unk had little time left to live. He could feel it.

SHAH

That night, Shah fell asleep in the city of Borave, wondering what had become of Fedradin. She had his book, the book that had been a part of him, sitting on a table not far from where she slept. She still felt guilty for taking his book, he had loved it so much, but he was banished. What good would it do him? Shah felt an immediate impulse to do something, but it was soon smothered by common sense. What could she possibly do? Plus, as a disturbing thought came to her. What if he was dead? With that horrific thought in her head, Shah fell asleep.

DRASLUPP

That night, Draslupp fell asleep in a compound in the Ozreek Mountains. Many other Domers slept near him, some visible, some not. He had thought that coming to this compound would be good for him, but it turned out that he might have been better off staying at Smafa. He was different from all the Domers. They were drawn up, shy, afraid of the outside world, just because of their condition and the hatred surrounding it. Draslupp didn't know if he should leave or not. He really didn't have any place to go. Smafa? Smafa might be better- *Forget it! Smafa would be no different from any place you could go. People hate Domers, that's the sad truth. I'll have to make do up here, with these Domers.* Draslupp was able to put himself to sleep with this thought in his head, but in the back of his head, he knew that he wouldn't be able to stand it up here. He would have to do something eventually. The question was: what?

VELK

That night, Velk fell asleep painfully aware that Draslupp was not comfortable in the Domer settlement. The boy was going to bring around some kind of change. And Velk didn't like that. No, he didn't like that at all. Things were good the way they were and did not need to be change. Change was bad. And Draslupp meant change. Velk put the thoughts together. Draslupp was bad.

SAPPLEZUL

That night, Sapplezul fell asleep thinking about Shah. Had everything really been her fault? Was he just scapegoating her for all the misery in his life? Probably. He should apologize, but he couldn't leave the Chultra Kingdom. They were preparing for war and didn't want anyone coming in or out. They were preparing for war against the dwarves.

THEREEKO

That night, Lord Thereeko fell asleep with his thoughts on one thing, and one thing only, Fedradin. His thoughts had been centered around his cousin ever since the lord had been forced to use force to make Fedradin leave. Everyone in Narven had despised him for that. If only they knew. If only they knew he was doing them a favor. If they knew his motives behind what he had done, which were *not* fear and jealously, they would be erecting statues of him. He had bought them all a little more time. But that time was going to expire soon. That was why he had seceded from the Human Empire. Not because his pride was too high to bow down to a sixteen year old boy! Emperor Roger had the potential to be a great Emperor. The reason he had seceded was for more time. More time for his people to live. More time for him to live. Lord Thereeko of Narven fell into a nightmare racked sleep, his worst thoughts being turned into the disturbing and twisted images that played out in front of his eyes.

USLO

That night, Lord Uslo fell asleep thinking about Fedradin. Fedradin had passed Uslo's test, the Gii Games. Uslo was a member of Thunderflash, and the Games had been put together just to test Fedradin's abilities. But was it worth it? Uslo had received loads of criticism about the Games, so much so that Gii had become the laughing stock of Haxter. And Uslo didn't like that. He was a lord first, and a Thunderflash member second.

F'NTOK

That night, F'ntok, the orcish king, fell asleep with a stomach full of delicious stentspice washed down with human blood. His whole army would have their fill, once they ravaged Haxter and took what was rightfully theirs. Before the elves, dwarves, humans or even the dragons, the orcs had run Haxter how they wanted. Until the damn celestials came and chased them to the far reaches of the world, where they were forced to slowly die in the desert. F'ntok would have histories written about him when he sailed across the Trade Seas to Haxter and took back his land. And not a single creature would escape his wrath.

THE NECROMANCER

That night, the Necromancer fell asleep with his thoughts focused on what had been his goal for the past...many...years. That goal was the reason he was supporting Erch's hairbrained scheme. The Necromancer couldn't care less about taking over Haxter. He just wanted the jewels. There were five. He had four. The desire to possess the final jewel grew everyday. As he looked down at his wrist, all he could see was the missing spot on a band where he kept his jewels, not the rest of the filled spots. And the worst part was, he knew where the final one was, and he was *so* close to obtaining it. He just needed to play his cards right, meticulously manipulate every situation, and he would have all the jewels. Now what would he do with all the jewels? The Necromancer smiled. He would do many, many things.

FRIN

That night, Frin fell asleep worried about his army. Would it pass his master's test? The Master was very particular, and after Frin used all the resources he did creating the army, Erch would be even more so. *They can fight. They can fight well.* His army was fantastic. He shouldn't worry about Erch. But worry he did.

ERCH

That night, Erch fell asleep smiling about the surefire success of his plan. The Prince of Destiny would be destroyed by the ambush, and afterwards, Erch would have all the time he needed to collect the Demon Callers and take down Zantor. Zantor had defeated him twice, but the Sage was getting old. Erch would persevere. Finally, Zantor would crack. Finally, Erch would rule Haxter.

Chapter 120
Shadow Versus Destiny

FEDRADIN

THEY HAD NOT HIRED a skipper this time. Instead, they had let Tiserae captain the ship they chartered from the supercargo of Tier. The rest of the group acted as the crew, pulling ropes, ducking under some swinging log Tiserae called the 'boom.' And it was surprisingly effective. Fedradin knew little about boats. Narven, his birthplace, was not on the sea, so he had never bothered to learn about them. He had always suspected more or less that eventually he would become the lord of Narven, where one needed absolutely no knowledge about ships. He never expected that the fate of Haxter would fall into his very own hands, and that he would have to sail across a channel to an island that may be where the first Demon Caller was. Tiserae had been following the needle, sailing as fast as she could towards whatever it was pointing to. Soon enough, Fedradin found his prediction had been correct, as the island of Mystike came into view, the compass pointing directly at it.

Finally, they arrived at the island. There was no dock, obviously, so Tiserae sped the boat up fast enough that it slid up the beach when it landed. She then jumped out of the boat and tied a rope around a large rock that she had Fedradin create with his earth powers.

"Where to now, boss?" asked Tiserae. Fedradin pulled out the silver compass, a moment passed, and he pointed straight ahead, saying, "That way."

They followed Fedradin through the island of Mystike, which seemed to be entirely forest. They saw minimal evidence of animal life, only a few squirrels and minks scampering through the branches. They arrived at a clearing after an hour or so.

It was barren. No grass, bracken, bramble or any other kind of shrubbery grew; there was just dirt and small rocks all around the clearing shaped like a circle. In the center of the clearing, though, there was a strange object. It was made out of rock, but it looked manmade. It was in the shape of a rectangle, five feet long, three feet wide, and seven feet tall. The three foot wide section of the rectangle was pointed towards Fedradin and the group, with what looked like a door on it. To one side of the door, there were four circular shaped holes, the pattern mirrored on the adjacent side.

"It's the tomb," whispered Fedradin. "Tiserae, hand me the bag. The *real* bag." Fedradin referred to how many decoys Tiserae had created. Tiserae handed Fedradin a filled bag, which contained all eight of the rocks that had been protected by the Legendary Eight. "'Right," said Fedradin. "Something might be in that tomb besides the first Demon Caller." Fedradin started placing rocks in the holes. He placed the first four in, then went over to the other side of the door and placed three more rocks in the holes. "Here goes," Fedradin said, as he placed the last rock in the last hole. The door swung outwards as he did so, surrendering a pathetic squeal from the rusty hinges. Fedradin drew out Baxcanador, ready for whatever was inside the tomb. But nothing attacked him. He looked closer into the tomb, to find an object sitting on a pedestal in the middle of the room.

The object was smaller than the rocks from the Legendary Eight, but larger than the crystals he wore around his neck. It was about six or seven inches in diameter, oval in shape. As he picked it up and looked at it more closely, he saw that it had been carved to look like the face of a demon screaming in pain. It felt like it was made out of stone, but it was as light as balsa wood.

Fedradin turned around to face the rest of the group. "Finadek's Treasure," he whispered.

Before any of his friends could respond, Fedradin heard a voice. "So you have first Demon Caller, eh? We'll take that off your hands." From out of the woods walked a man Fedradin had never seen before. "I am Oxlo, one of the Minions. We appreciate the effort you expended getting all those rocks and that Demon Caller. Now, if you would kindly hand us that, we will be on our way."

"We?" said Fedradin. "I only see one of you."

"Is that so?" said Oxlo. Five figures walked out of the woods, standing in front of Oxlo. "Say hello to Coid, Black Heart, Hijimin, Krile, and Axto. If you do not hand over the Demon Caller, we will be forced to kill you."

Fedradin hardly heard Oxlo's last sentence. Axto? He could not believe one of his former Ridders was trying to kill him. Again. "Axto?" cried Fedradin in disbelief, as Kerwan simultaneously exclaimed, "Krile?"

"We killed you, you bastard!" shouted Kerwan at Krile.

"Aparently you didn't do a good enough job," said Krile, with a smirk. As the two brothers started to argue, Fedradin looked over at Black Heart. The woman was nearly identical to Black Arrow: a beautiful blond woman, wearing the same black piece of clothing, tigher, if that was possible. Was this, too, a Uäile? Fedradin decided that it had to be. But where did this Uäile keep its brain? This question did not linger long in Fedradin's mind.

Black Arrow kept her brain in her arrow.

Black Heart must keep her brain in her heart.

"What have you decided to do?" asked Oxlo, smugly. "Am I walking home one Demon Caller richer?"

"You tell me," said Fedradin, thrusting out his palm. A jet of fire emerged, heading directly for Oxlo. Oxlo did not move to avoid the fire, instead he released a jet of water from his hand, extinguishing the fire immediately.

"So you have chosen death for you and all your friends?" asked Oxlo. "Just as I wanted."

TYRATION

There was another boat at the island already. It appeared as though it had been run ashore, then tied hastily to a rock.

"That must be their ship!" said Roger, pointing towards the boat.

"Interesting method of docking," murmured Sgire. Roger, Sgire, and Tyration were all gathered on the deck on a ship that they had commandeered at New Gii. They had asked the crew to sail them to Mystike. Then they had ordered the crew to sail them to Mystike.

"Can you dock at this island?" asked Roger.

"Oh, sure," said the captain, trying to mask his anger. "I'll lay anchor and have one of the crew members row you ashore!"

The anchor dropped into the ocean, as well as a small rowboat, which the three climbed into. A crewmember jumped down to the boat as well, picking up the oars and rowing them to shore. Roger, Tyration and Sgire all got off the boat, and immediately the oarsman rowed back to the boat as fast as possible. Roger saw the captain take up the anchor, make a rude hand gesutre, and sail away.

"Damn it!" yelled Roger after them. "I am your Emperor! You will come back for me!" They didn't.

"I guess we'll have to kill our enemies and take their boat," said Sgire.

"Or we could take it now," said Tyration. "We could make sure that they aren't able to bring the Demon Caller back to the mainland."

"No," said Sgire. "We can't risk them finding another way back. We'll have to fight."

Yay, thought Tyration sarcastically. Suddenly, they heard an explosion.

"What was that?" said Roger.

"It's probably where our enemies are," said Sgire. "C'mon!"

Tyration sighed in exasperation. *Of course. Let's run* towards *the explosion.*

FEDRADIN

"Charge!" shouted Oxlo, who stood still, the figures around him rushing forwards, all going towards Fedradin. Fedradin pulled out Baxcanador, but realized that it would not be very effective against the mob charging at him. As the horde grew closer to him, instead of fighting them off with his sword, Fedradin pointed his palm outward, sending a gust of wind that sent all his enemies flying.

Fedradin saw that the rest of his group ran forwards, each one isolating an enemy. Aserax wound up fighting Axto, Kerwan wound up fighting Krile, Galeb Duhr wound up fighting Hijimin, Fedradin wound up fighting Coid, and Breetex and Tiserae wound up fighting Black Heart. Oxlo backed up and began watching the fight from the treeline of the clearing.

A man was standing about five feet away from Fedradin. He seemed normal, except for the horns which protruded from the sides of his head. Oxlo had referred to the man before as Coid. Coid leapt forwards, swinging outwards with his sword. Fedradin easily parried the blow with Baxcanador. Almost immediately, Coid swung again, and Fedradin blocked that blow as well. Coid kept up this fury of blows, until finally he slowed his pace. In the millisecond that Coid took to regain his breath, Fedradin swept his palm out at Coid's knees, a bar made out of condensed air knocking Coid to the ground. Coid fell, and Fedradin swung his sword down at the falling man. Coid's sword was dangling to the side, his hand out to break his fall, so Fedradin's strike had been aimed at Coid's chest. Fedradin smiled to himself as his sword was about to puncture Coid's heart. *This was too easy.*

Suddenly, Fedradin felt a burning sensation in his right hand, the one that held Baxcanador. Instinctively, he dropped his sword, which fell uselessly to the ground beside Coid. Fedradin saw that what had caused his pain had come directly from Coid's eyes. Each eye emitted a small, thin, red light that hit Fedradin's hand, causing it to sting. Fedradin threw a fireball at Coid, who rolled to the side to avoid it, thus ending his stare of pain, for the red light beams disappeared. Fedradin stole a quick look at his right hand before he went for Baxcanador and saw that there were two circular burns.

Fedradin leapt for Baxcanador, but Coid saw what Fedradin was doing, so he kicked the sword away. Fedradin crashed to the dusty ground, reaching his hand out for his sword, but it was too far away. Fedradin tried to get up again, but Coid beat him to it, the man stamping on Fedradin's stomach and pinning him to the ground.

"Well, well, well," murmured Coid. "Good bye, 'Prince of Destiny.'" Coid raised his sword over his head. But Fedradin wasn't about to give up that easily. Fedradin pushed up with his palm, throwing Coid away with his air powers. After he snatched up Baxcanador, he was about to pursue Coid, when Galeb Duhr and Hijimin, the flayer, came flying out of nowhere, both wrestling for position. As he waited impatiently for them to go away, Fedradin looked over to see that Breetex and Tiserae were advancing on Black Heart.

"Breetex!" Fedradin called out. "I think that's a Uäile! And I think you have to stab her in the heart!"

Fedradin didn't have time to listen for Breetex's response, for finally he was able to get past Galeb Duhr and Hijimin. He found Coid waiting for him, sword in hand.

Fedradin charged at Coid, swinging Baxcanador. Coid easily ducked the swing, stabbing outwards with his own sword. Fedradin sidestepped the weapon, kicking it out of Coid's hands. Coid looked up in shock at Fedradin, sending out a beam of red light. Fedradin pulled out his kappa shell shield, reflecting the beam off the shield and back at Coid. Coid jumped backwards, the beam burning holes in the ground right before his feet.

Fedradin ran forwards, swinging Baxcanador. Coid jumped backwards to avoid the blade. Fedradin advanced, swinging Baxcanador again. Coid, again, avoided the blade by jumping backwards. This process repeated itself many times, until an explosion knocked Fedradin off his feet. It rattled Coid too, so he didn't immediately get up, and when he did, it was at the same time as Fedradin. The two faced each other, Fedradin holding a sword and shield, Coid without either.

"I don't want to kill you, Coid," said Fedradin. "But I will if you don't surrender." Coid did not respond to Fedradin's cocky threat. Instead, Coid fired off a beam of red light. Fedradin used his zappa shell shield to block the beam again, but as he did so, he realized that Coid would be charging (or fleeing). Fedradin lowered his shield, immediately forming a boulder and hurled it. His boulder flew through the air, missing Coid by a good couple of feet.

Coid was actually only a few feet away from Fedradin, leaping through the air towards him. Coid grabbed Fedradin around the shoulders before the Prince could do anything with a suprising amount of force. Coid spun around, using torque to throw Fedradin across the clearing. Fedradin crashed to the ground, Baxcanador and his kappa shell shield flying out of his grasp. He turned to see that Coid was rushing towards him, so Fedradin threw out an invisible wall with his air powers. Coid must have seen Fedradin project the wall with his palm, for the man jumped to the side avoiding collision.

Fedradin tried to get to his feet, but Coid came flying towards him before he could. Literally *flying*. Coid's feet were lifted from the ground, and the man traveled at twice his normal speed towards Fedradin.

Coid knocked him to the ground. Fedradin was about to use his Sage powers on Coid, but his enemy pinned him to the ground too fast. Coid had his hands on Fedradin's wrists, forcing him to face his palms outwards. He also had his feet pinning Fedradin's knees, keeping Fedradin's legs from doing much of anything. Fedradin was not too worried, for Coid was not in a position where it would be easy for him to kill Fedradin. Plus, one of his friends was bound to kill one of their enemies soon, and they would free him from Coid. Suddenly, Coid swung Fedradin's left hand across his body, touching it to Fedradin's right hand so that the palms were facing each other. Coid squeezed the two together with his right hand, while he stuck out his left hand. The sword that Coid had been using came flying through the air, the pommel of it gracefully pushing itself into his grasp.

"That's right. It's one of the Seven Blades," taunted Coid, pressing it to Fedradin's neck. "And I will use it to end your pathetic life."

KERWAN

Kerwan singled out Krile after Fedradin had sent all of them flying. Kerwan leapt forward, grabbing his brother by his shirt and throwing him away from the rest of the crowd. Krile, alarmed, pulled out his wand, for he had been only holding a knife before. When he saw that it was Kerwan who had thrown him, Krile's face visibly relaxed.

"Oh! It's just you, my brother," said Krile, smiling. "I beat you at the swamps and I can beat you again!"

"I beat you at your own temple! *And* I killed you," retorted Kerwan.

"True, true, but then you had the help of a Sage," said Krile. "There is no one to help you now."

"And when you beat me at the swamps, you had the help of an army of dune reapers!"

"Fair point, my brother. Let us settle this now, once and for all, which of us is more powerful!" Kerwan fired off a white spell, which Krile sidestepped. The spell flew until it hit a tree, which it cut down instantly. Krile returned the spell with a blue one of his own, which Kerwan used a green shield to block. The wizards then started to circle each other, like sharks.

It was something Biggs had taught him about wizard duels. One could tell a lot about how their opponent would fight by the way they handled the first couple of spells. It could show weaknesses, vulnerabilities, and other things to exploit. However, as Kerwan gazed at his brother's face, he could sense no fear from Krile, no regret. Krile seemed as confident as ever, and even if he wasn't, his face did not betray him. Kerwan had also learned not to let anything show on *his* face as Krile examined it.

But then, Kerwan saw a slight change in Krile's face. A small movement of his eyes, and a small twitch of the mouth. And Kerwan knew exactly what that meant. At once both wizards started firing spells: white, yellow, blue, brown, purple. Kerwan ducked, dodged, and blocked all the spells that were fired at him, Krile doing the same. Over the course of the battle, Kerwan heard Fedradin call something out to Breetex, but he didn't catch what.

Suddenly, Kerwan saw a black spell fly towards him. He was surprised by Krile. Black spells required the most energy to create, and with the knowledge that the battle ahead would be long and grueling, neither wizard had decided to use them. Until now.

Kerwan threw himself on the ground, the black spell crashing into the tomb, exploding and sending fragments of rock and debris everywhere -but the tomb was not cracked open. Kerwan looked up at Krile, who was running towards him. Kerwan fired three white spells, Krile ducking, side-stepping, and blocking each one.

Kerwan pulled out his warhammer, for Krile was very close to him now. Kerwan swung the warhammer, but he was early in his timing and missed Krile completely. Krile leapt forwards trying to tackle Kerwan to the ground. Kerwan was able to bring his warhammer back around one more time though, and he swung it again, this time the flat end of the weapon catching Krile on the chest.

Krile tumbled to the ground. Kerwan raised his warhammer over his head, preparing to bring it down on Krile, when Krile snaked out an arm and grabbed Kerwan's ankle, pulling him to the ground. Kerwan fell, landing on the ground, hard. Kerwan dropped the warhammer, as Krile jumped on top of him. Krile was holding a knife, which he raised high in the air, above Kerwan's neck. "See you in hell, brother."

GALEB DUHR

Galeb Duhr saw everyone go flying. He saw that Kerwan jumped on Krile, and that Aserax went after Axto, so he realized that he needed to single out an enemy. The least formidable looking one left was a flayer that he heard had been referred to as Hijimin. Galeb Duhr threw himself at the flayer, landing hard on its stomach.

Hijimin gasped as the wind was knocked out of him. Galeb Duhr drew back his fist to punch Hijimin, when the flayer grabbed Galeb Duhr by the shoulders and flung him to the side. Galeb Duhr tumbled across the ground, looking up to see Hijimin running forwards, knife in hand. Galeb Duhr was not concerned about getting stabbed with the knife, for he didn't think it would do any harm to him. Nonetheless, Galeb Duhr rolled to the side as Hijimin brought the knife down, not wanting to find out if it did.

Hijimin pursued Galeb Duhr with the knife, swinging it down, but once again, Galeb Duhr rolled to the side. This pattern repeated itself for a long time, until instead of rolling away from Hijimin to avoid the knife, Galeb Duhr rolled towards the flayer, knocking Hijimin down by taking out his legs. The flayer crashed to the ground, Galeb Duhr jumping upon him and punching his back. Hijimin rolled over, Galeb Duhr falling off his back. Hijimin grabbed Galeb Duhr's legs and threw him towards Fedradin and Coid.

Galeb Duhr hit the ground hard, but was able to bounce right back up again, and was ready for Hijimin as the flayer came running over. Galeb Duhr launched himself at Hijimin, grabbing the flayer around the shoulders, swinging his body around Hijimin, using his torque to bring the flayer to the ground. Hijimin got up once again, and Galeb Duhr charged at him, jumping into the air and kicking the flayer in the stomach. Hijimin flew backwards, Galeb Duhr following him.

The flayer hit the ground right in front of Fedradin. Galeb Duhr landed on top of Hijimin, and he began punching the flayer in the face with his rocky fist. As he did so, Galeb Duhr heard Fedradin yell something to Breetex.

Hijimin grabbed Galeb Duhr's fists, and threw Galeb Duhr far away. Galeb Duhr crashed to the ground, watching as Hijimin came flying across the battlefield at Galeb Duhr. Galeb Duhr tried to get to his feet, but Hijimin pinned him to the ground once more with his foot. Hijimin opened his mouth to say something, when an explosion knocked the flayer to the ground from atop Galeb Duhr.

Galeb Duhr rushed towards the fallen Hijimin, but collided with Hijimin's arm as the flayer stretched it outwards. Galeb Duhr was sent reeling backwards, for only a few seconds, but that was all Hijimin needed to regain his position on top of Galeb Duhr.

"How do I kill you?" wondered Hijimin aloud, enjoying himself. Galeb Duhr struggled fruitlessly against Hijimin's foot, as the flayer pulled out a chisel. "I have an idea..."

As Galeb Duhr watched the oncoming chisel in terror, he thought to himself, *He carries a chisel?*

ASERAX

Once all of her enemies had been sent flying, Aserax jumped on the nearest opponent, a shorter black man by the name of Axto. As she flew through the air towards him, Aserax pulled apart her bow, revealing two deadly blades. She swung the blades downwards at Axto, but the man rolled to the side, narrowly missing getting stabbed in the head. Aserax landed beside him, immediately pulling her blades from the dirt and stabbing them, one after the other at Axto.

Axto caught her wrists, the blades inches from his face. Aserax pushed down with all her weight on the blades, attempting to drive them into Axto's skull. Before she could accomplish this, however, Axto planted both his feet in her chest, pushing outwards and sending her flying.

Aserax hit the ground, fairly hard, getting the wind knocked out of her. As she clumsily got to her feet, Axto came running at her, swinging his halberd at her. Aserax dodged to the side, the axe-like blade passing inches from her side. Axto swung again, this time overhead. Aserax jumped back, spreading her legs to avoid the blade that passed in between them. She landed hard on her bottom, her legs still spread. Axto attacked again, but this time, instead of using the axe-like blade on his halberd, he utilized the spear-like point on the tip of it. He thrust the weapon at Aserax, aiming at her head. Aserax, desperate to avoid the attack, flattened herself on the ground, so that the blade narrowly missed her head, ramming itself in the ground.

Axto started to pull up on the blade, but it was stuck in the soil. As he prepared to pull harder, Aserax seized her chance. She hastily put the two ends of her bow together, missing the first time she tried, so that the blade slipped and cut her finger. She tried again, and this time was successful. She nocked an arrow, but by this time, Axto had pulled his halberd out of the ground and was ready to run Aserax through with the weapon.

As he lunged with the spear-like point of his halberd, Aserax loosed the arrow, the arrow finding its mark in Axto's shoulder. A millisecond later, Axto's halberd found its mark in Aserax, but it merely scraped across the side of Aserax's arm, for the elf had turned to avoid the spear hitting her dead on.

Axto reeled backwards, pulling the arrow from his left shoulder. As he regained his composure, Aserax calmly drew an arrow to finish off Axto once and for all. She pulled the bowstring back as far as her strength allowed, aiming it straight at the head of Axto, who was charging her, halberd pointing out. Aserax was about to release the bowstring, when she heard Fedradin yell out Breetex's name.

Had something happened? Was Breetex hurt? As the thoughts flashed through her head, she turned to see if Breetex was alright. She was relieved to see that he was fine, fighting with Tiserae against Black Heart. And was that a twang of jealously she felt?

This was when Aserax realized she had made a crucial mistake. She turned to the side, arms coming up to protect her side and head. She felt Axto's halberd hit her in the side. Axto had managed to sneak his weapon through her arms, hitting her in the rib with the tip of the weapon. It bounced off, breaking the bone instead of delivering a fatal wound to Aserax.

Even though it wasn't fatal, the wound hurt like hell.

Aserax fell backwards, clutching her side. Axto walked forwards towards the fallen Aserax, swinging his halberd downwards. Aserax rolled to side, the blade embedding itself in the ground. As she rolled, her broken rib pressed against the ground, sending a wave of pain through her body. She yelped out in pain, looking up to see Axto swing his halberd once more. Instead of rolling this time, Aserax pulled apart her bow, using the bowstring to deflect Axto's blade, and because there were nemean lion hair fibers sown into it, the bowstring did not snap. Instead, Axto's halberd went flying back at him.

Surprised, the man hesitated, which gave Aserax a chance to attack. Despite her aching side, smarting finger, and throbbing arm, Aserax managed to lunge forward and plunge one of the blades from her bow into Axto's thigh. The man cried out in pain, falling backwards, while grabbing at his leg.

Aserax crawled atop him, ready to finish him off with one of her blades, when an explosion knocked her from her advantageous position and sent her sprawling on the ground. This time, she could not muster the strength to fight through the pain that now coursed through her body.

Axto had been spared from the explosion, Aserax taking most of its force. He stood up and walked over to her, raising his halberd high in the air. He swung it down with all the force he could muster, Aserax barely blocking the blow with her bowstring. Angry, Axto kicked the bow from her hand, the weapon landing fairly close by.

"You have hurt me, elf! Now you will pay!"

TISERAE

Breetex and Tiserae realized they were the only two who had not singled out an enemy. And there were two enemies left, Oxlo and Black Heart. Breetex charged at Black Heart, pulling her away from Fedradin, who had begun to battle Coid.

Tiserae looked around for Oxlo, but she couldn't find him. Anywhere. She searched. And she searched. And she searched. He was *nowhere* to be found. Tiserae turned around. If she couldn't find Oxlo, then she would go wherever she was needed most. She decided that everyone looked like they were doing fine, except for Breetex who was being beaten back by Black Heart.

I think I know where I'm needed most.

Tiserae's blades protracted from her sleeves as she ran towards Black Heart. Breetex moved aside as he caught out her of the corner of his eye. Tiserae lunged outwards with her right arm, the blade headed straight for Black Heart's chest. The woman saw the blade coming, and turned to the side, Tiserae's weapon passing harmlessly by Black Heart. Before Black Heart had time to use her own sword against Tiserae, Tiserae swung her other blade, this time slicing instead of stabbing. The blade was headed straight for Black Heart's stomach, when suddenly, Black Heart's midsection turned into black mist, Tiserae's blade passing through without leaving a scratch. As soon as Tiserae's blade was through the mist, the mist turned back into flesh, Black Heart giving Tiserae a wink.

"Fool," murmured Black Heart. The woman swung her own black sword at Tiserae, who easily parried it with her own blades. Black Heart swung again and again, the frequency of the swings increasing, instead of decreasing. Tiserae was constantly parrying, blocking blow after blow, until Black Heart's sword finally made contact with Tiserae, the blade scraping against Tiserae's cloak. However, it did not pass through and leave a mark, because of the nemean lion hair fibers that had been sown into it. Black Heart, froze, alarmed at what had just happened, so Tiserae had time to retreat to Breetex.

"Fancy you being here," said Breetex.

"Oh, well, I thought I'd pop in for a drink or two."

"I think that we're up against a Uäile, like Black Arrow."

Tiserae looked at Black Heart more carefully. They and Black Heart began to circle each other, like sharks around a dead, bloody seal. Black Heart was wearing the same outfit as Black Arrow, her looks were quite similar, and for gods' sake, her name was *Black Heart*. "I guess you're right. Where do you think her brain is?"

"Black Arrow's was in her arrow. I'm going out on a limb here and I'm going to say that her brain is in her heart." Black Heart stopped moving. So did Breetex and Tiserae. "You ready?"

"As ready as I'll ever be." The two started cautiously advancing on Black Heart, when they heard Fedradin yell something.

"Breetex! I believe that's a Uäile! And I think you have to stab her in the heart!"

"No kidding," Breetex muttered to himself, sarcastically. Suddenly, Tiserae lunged forward, both blades stabbing towards Black Heart. The Uäile used her sword to block both blades. Tiserae swung again with her blades on her arms, as Breetex threw his tomahawk. Black Heart parried both the attacks with her sword, but the tomahawk found its way into Black Heart's arm. Angrily, she pulled the tomahawk from her arm, black blood rushing from the cut on her arm. Oddly enough, the tomahawk did not cut through her shirt, but the cut was still gushing like an open wound. It was as if the clothing was a part of her...

Tiserae swung again with her blades. Breetex swung with his battleaxe. Black Heart was able to block the blades and get her sword around fast enough to block the axe, but by the time she had blocked the axe, Tiserae swung her blades again, and this time, they made contact with Black Heart's arm, instead of her heart, for the Uäile had turned to the side. Breetex swung with his axe, but as it neared Black Heart's body, she turned her torso to smoke, the axe passing through. However, the Uäile had taken a step backwards, tripped over her own feet and fallen down to the ground.

Tiserae walked over to the fallen Uäile, pressing her sword against Black Heart's chest. Tiserae smiled and pressed down harder with her blade, but before the sword punctured her heart, Black Heart transformed her torso into a black mist, so that the blade passed through without causing harm. Tiserae drew back her blade, and she immediately, the mist turned back into flesh. Tiserae heard Black Heart panting with exhaustion. Good. It required a lot of effort to turn flesh to mist.

Tiserae prepared once more to push her blade through Black Heart's heart. She stabbed downwards, the flesh turning to mist. But instead of drawing her sword back up, she left it in the mist, requiring Black Heart to continuously keep her flesh in mist form. If she let the mist turn back into flesh, Black Heart's heart would form around the tip of Tiserae's blade. Tiserae watched with glee, with Breetex standing next to her, as Black Heart's face twisted in agony.

"She can't hold this much longer," said Tiserae, as she noticed Black Heart's hand go for her sword, which had fallen out of her hand and was lying close by. "Breetex, don't let her get her sword." Breetex was about to kick the sword away, when something changed.

An explosion close to where they were standing and to where Krile and Kerwan were battling it out sent Tiserae and Breetex tumbling across the ground.

Black Heart walked over to them, holding her sharp looking black sword. She smiled sinisterly. Tiserae tried to get up and fight her, but both Tiserae and Breetex watched in horror as a puddle of black goo, identical to the goo that Black Arrow transformed into, slithered across the dusty ground towards Tiserae, the goo building on itself to form Black Heart's exact figure, but without any color or detail. The figure grabbed a shocked Tiserae by the neck and flung her into the ground. Breetex, who was about to get up as well, slowly lowered himself to the ground. How was he supposed to fight *goo*?

The gooey figure melted back down into the black puddle and it slithered back to Black Heart, seeming to recede into her. By this time, Black Heart had arrived at Breetex and Tiserae. Breetex was getting to his feet, battleaxe in hand, but immediately Black Heart disarmed him by slashing her sword across the base of his axe, causing him to instinctively drop the battleaxe. Before he could do anything else, Black Heart delivered a kick to his chest that sent him crashing to the ground. She then delivered a kick to Tiserae's chest, who was trying to stand up, and Tiserae hit her head hard on the ground. Black Heart then stepped on both of their necks, pressing down with her feet, as she examined her sword saying:

"Who's first?"

FEDRADIN

"Hold up!" shouted Oxlo. Coid was about to kill Fedradin with his sword, but as soon as Oxlo uttered those words, he froze, turning to see his master, but he kept Fedradin's hand pressed together with an absurd amount of strength. Fedradin looked around the battlefield and saw a terrible sight. Krile was holding a knife to Kerwan's neck. Hijimin had a...chisel...out and had it on Galeb Duhr's head, in his other hand a rock to drive the chisel. Black Heart was wielding her sword, playing with her two victims, Breetex and TIiserae, who were both pinned to the ground underneath her feet. Worst of all was Aserax. She was bleeding out of her arm and finger, a red flower blossoming on her shirt. He felt a pang of hatred towards his former pupil, Axto, as he stood proudly above Aserax, holding his halberd out towards the elf. However, he was being oblivious to Aserax, who, as Fedradin could see, was inching her arm out towards her bow.

"Hold up, I say, Krile!" shouted Oxlo again. Krile drew his knife back from Kerwan's neck, growling in irritation as he did so. Fedradin looked to see Oxlo, who suddenly materialized from the shadows. Tiserae gasped. "Yes, that's right. They don't call me the Shadow Prince for no good reason.

"Now, why I asked you all to restrain from killing these people right now is because I decided we should give them one more chance to hand over the Demon Caller."

"Never!" spat Fedradin.

"Does that mean we kill 'em, boss?" shouted Axto.

"No, no, no!" shouted Oxlo, as Krile once again pressed his knife against Kerwan's neck. "I will ask Fedradin to rethink that. You see, Fedradin, we have been tracking you, ever since you were just a small baby. We, the Minions, started the fire in the castle. It was an attempt to kill you at a young age. Unfortunately, you escaped with a wizard into the mountains, and when we went after you again, we were deterred by clever defenses by the same wizard. We were about to gather an army to seize you, but then we received a Prophecy. Well, not received, per say, but intercepted. The Prophecy told us that you were the one destined to find the Demon Callers, and we decided that we couldn't kill you. We had to convert you to our side, to help us find the Demon Callers."

"I would never join you!" shouted Fedradin. "You seek to overthrow the LNR!"

"The LNR is overthrowing itself," said Oxlo. "Flyc's attack on the LNR building is tearing it to pieces."

"That was you! That was Erch!"

"All part of the plan," winked Oxlo. "See, we also intercepted another Prophecy, going to that young wizard over there." Oxlo gestured to Kerwan. "Seems he has just as much potential as you to find the Demon Callers. So we sent spies out to observe both of you. To Fedradin, we sent Misk. To Kerwan, I think you remember Utka."

"I knew there was something wrong with that man!" said Fedradin. "I think his it was his eyes."

"Same with Utka!" said Kerwan. "His eyes weren't the same color."

"Yes, yes. I fashioned those two with energy from the Heart, but I wasn't able to equate the eyes."

"The Heart?" said Fedradin.

"Yes. A complicated matter, one that I shall not delve into when you have but minutes to live.

"But I digress. We, the Minions, waited like this for years. Hoping that one of you would find the Demon Callers, so that we could swoop in and seize them from you. Nearly twenty years we spent doing this. Twenty years! We couldn't take it anymore. To observe you closer, we replaced Erch with Flyc at the Gii Games. That still did not satisfy us. Erch came up with a genius plan, which involved making the task of you rallying an army to defeat us even harder by attacking an LNR meeting. As this plan was in action, we sent out more and more spies, until we discovered the identity of a senior member of that nuisance group Thunderflash. We caught him, tortured him until he gave us information regarding the whereabouts of the Demon Callers. All the Demon Callers.

"We made a silver compass of our own with help from the Heart and tracked down the Legendary Eight. Unfortunately, you beat us to every last monster. But instead of chasing you to the seventh and eight monsters, we waited, until the compass finally pointed in the direction of the tomb. We rushed here, and set up and ambush, which you have fallen perfectly into." Oxlo paced around. "You see, Fedradin, we have been manipulating your life from behind the scenes. We have worked you like a puppet, from beginning, middle, and now, the end. Now, along with that information, I would like to tell you something else. We are going to use the Demon Callers to summon an army that will storm the gates of the Celestial Plane. Those bastards sent the demons to the Planes of Hell, locking us up so we could never return. We will take our revenge, putting ourselves in the position of god and ruling over all of the planes, and we will have no mercy, just like the Celestials had no mercy on us."

"The Celestials aren't gods!" said Kerwan. "Gods are gods!"

"You're quite wrong, Wizard of Destiny." Oxlo let the words sink in. "The Celestials were able to store massive amounts of energy away, which they now use to control events on every plane, serving as gods."

"I don't believe you," said Kerwan.

"Doesn't matter," said Oxlo. "Your life will before over momentarily anyway." Oxlo turned towards Kerwan. "Unless! You choose to join our side when the demons take over. You will be spared the demons' wrath and will not be killed today." Kerwan spat at Oxlo. Oxlo turned to Fedraidn, ignoring Kerwan. "How about you Fedradin? You know, we're not so different you and I. We both try to right wrongs when we see them."

"Is that so?" said Fedradin.

"Yes. Shutting the demons away in the Planes of Hell was the worst thing anyone could do."

"Was it?" asked Fedradin, argumentatively.

"Yes! And this is your chance to help fix this problem."

Fedradin looked over at Aserax. She had successfully put her bow back together and had nocked an arrow without Axto noticing. She was now pulling back the bowstring. "As tempting as that offer is...Aserax! Now!" At the same moment as Aserax released the bowstring, Fedradin remembered the trick Coid had showed him. He willed Baxcanador to come back towards him, and it did, the sword flying through the air towards him. However, he had no hand extended to catch the blade. This was intended.

Baxcanador, instead of flying into Fedradin's grip, embedded itself in Coid's shoulder, before the man had a chance to move. Immediately, Coid rolled off of Fedradin, clutching his wounded shoulder. Fedradin, jumped up, pulling Baxcanador from Coid's bloody shoulder.

He ran forwards, towards Oxlo, who was standing shocked in the middle of the battlefield. Hijimin and Galeb Duhr blocked his way to Oxlo again, for they were battling again. However, instead of waiting for them to move by, Fedradin, with a clean swipe, knocked the head from Hijimin's shoulders.

Oxlo, seeing Fedradin charge him, was prepared. Oxlo had a palm out and a sword in the other hand. "You chose death, Fedradin. Now I will give you what desire."

ASERAX

Aserax had fully expected Fedradin to request her to fire the arrow at any given time. He was an observant man, and she was sure he had seen her putting together her bow.

She had had her eyes on Black Heart, who had recently taken down her lover. She had put aside the fears that the woman was a Uäile, and decided that on request, she would shoot Black Heart between the eyes.

Sure enough, the cue came, and Aserax loosed an arrow at Black Heart. The arrow struck the woman between the eyes, right where Aserax had intended the arrow to go. However, her fears were soon realized. Instead of crumpling to the ground, dead, Black Heart transformed into the goo that Black Arrow described Black Arrow had transformed into when he had chopped her head off. Black Heart *was* really a Uäile.

Axto looked down at her, pointed his halberd's spear-like point downwards and thrusted. Aserax put her hands over her head and braced for the impact of the spear, when it didn't come.

She heard the twang of a bowstring.

She heard Axto fall to the ground behind her, presumably dead.

Aserax opened her eyes, to find Roger, Sgire and a man wearing the same outfit as Krile standing at the edge of the clearing. Each one had a surprised look on their face. Roger held the crossbow that was currently empty of any bolts. What were they doing here?

Aserax turned to see Fedradin battling it out with Oxlo. She saw Coid was standing up, blood trickling down his arm. He turned, pulled out his sword and began walking towards Fedradin, who was in an intense battle with Oxlo and didn't notice Coid.

No you don't. Aserax sent an arrow flying at Coid. The man froze in his tracks, his sword seeming to move of its own accord to block her arrow. Aserax rushed at the man, as did Tiserae and Breetex, who had gotten up from the ground. Galeb Duhr and Sgire also moved towards Coid, who was now cornered.

GALEB DUHR

Galeb Duhr was not sure if he could be killed, but he didn't want to find out. The chisel up against his nose was the closest he had ever been to death. But that was when Fedradin yelled out for Aserax to fire her arrow. The arrow struck Black Heart in the head, and she dissolved into a gooey puddle, which receded into the woods.

Hijimin pulled his chisel back, looking over at the chaos that was going on. Galeb Duhr seized the opportunity and head-butted Hijimin, sending the flayer reeling. Galeb Duhr pursued his enemy, but before he could throw another punch, Fedradin ran by and chopped Hijimin's head from his body.

Slightly baffled, Galeb Duhr stood, not sure what he was supposed to be doing. That was when he saw an arrow fly by him, at Coid, who blocked the arrow with his sword. Aserax came flying out of nowhere, attacking Coid, so Galeb Duhr decided to join in. He needed to be of some help.

ROGER

Roger, Sgire and Tyration ran all the way from the shore, coming into the clearing where Fedradin's group was pinned down by the enemy group they had seen earlier. Roger was surprised to see Fedradin's group alive and well, but still, his help was needed. Fedradin looked like he and his group were about to perish.

Suddenly, Aserax shot an arrow, which collided with a woman's head. Without fully registering the fact that she did not fall dead, but instead turned into some black matter, Roger helped the battle by shooting an bolt from his crossbow at a black man who was about to kill Aserax. The man fell dead on the ground, and Aserax stood up, glancing at Roger and his group, and firing an arrow at a man with...horns.

Meanwhile, Roger saw a man dressed like Tyration fighting Kerwan. Roger realized he was needed there. He darted across

502

the clearing to join in the fight. Tyration also realized that the growing wizards' duel was where he was most needed, so he, too, ran over to Kerwan.

SGIRE

Sgire was now left by herself. She saw that the man with horns was now battling Tiserae, Breetex, Aserax and a small rocky monster. She would be hopelessly out matched in the wizard battle and the Sage battle, so she decided to join in the fight with the man with horns.

There were now three fights raging. The battle with Coid. The battle with Krile. The battle with Oxlo. Everyone had avoided the Sage battle, for if one was caught up in that battle, they would be made into mincemeat.

KRILE

Krile was having a difficult time fending off three different wizards. He was shocked to find that Tyration was there. He had killed the man! Then again, Krile, too, had been dead at one point, so maybe he shouldn't be so shocked. Krile shook his head.

He was also shocked to see a young boy fly out of nowhere and begin shooting spells out of his palms. His palms! Since when did wizards not require wands? Krile once again shook his head. Wizards without wands and people coming back from the dead? Crazy!

Three spells flew by his head at once, and Krile was able to dodge all three, but just barely. A blue spell that had flown by singed his cloak. Krile fired weakly back into the crowd of wizards, but was not able to see the effects of his white spell, as he had to drop to the ground to avoid being decapitated by a white spell.

The battle continued to rage for a few more minutes, but soon Krile was forced to abandon his offensive spells and remain only on the defense: projected shields and ducking deadly white spells, until he was tackled by the young boy without the wand. The boy had a crossbow, and now was shoving the bolt in Krile's mouth.

Quickly, Krile swung his elbow outwards as the boy fired the crossbow. Luckily, for Krile, he knocked the crossbow from the boy's grip before the trigger was pulled, so that the bolt flew off, colliding with a tree in the distance. The crossbow clattered to the ground, out of the boy's grip, who was now unarmed. Krile punched the boy across the face with his fist, and he tumbled off of Krile. He was soon replaced with Tyration and Kerwan.

Krile pulled out his knife and slashed at Kerwan, who was currently unarmed, apart from his wand. Krile's knife looked as if it were going to stab Kerwan, until suddenly a bronze knife appeared in Kerwan's hand, the knife blocking the other blade. Krile's knife bounced off, but the wizard was too shocked to do anything else. Apparently, this day was not about to get any more normal.

KERWAN

Kerwan seized his opportunity, while Krile was paralyzed, and he kicked his brother in the chest, sending Krile hard into the dust. Tyration leapt forwards, knife in hand, the look on his eyes telling Krile he was going in for the kill. That was until Kerwan grabbed his arm.

"No! This kill is mine!" roared Kerwan.

"He killed me! I must return the favor!"

Strangely, nay, sadly, for this had become the norm, Kerwan was not fazed by the comment. "He is my brother! And, I've already killed him! I must finish the task!"

Tyration argued, but Krile wasn't listening anymore. He was creeping his hand towards his wand, which had fallen from his grip when Kerwan kicked him.

"No you don't!" shouted the boy. The boy grabbed him from the back and put him into a headlock. "You're going to die. The question is *who* will do the killing."

KRILE

To Krile's delight, he watched as the argument heated up between Tyration and Kerwan so much, that Kerwan swiped outwards with his knife with a roar of anger, slicing the blade across Tyration's neck. The member of Desert Wind let out a cry of pain, trying to stanch the blood with his hand as the life gushed out of him. Kerwan, the rage in his eyes not yet subsided, kicked Tyration in the stomach, sending him crashing into the ground, lifeless as a rock.

Kerwan turned to Krile, who was still being held by the boy. "Now, it's time for you to die, brother!" seethed Kerwan, who was holding the strange bronze knife out in front of him. Krile spat at Kerwan, enjoying the incredible amount of anger that surged forth from Kerwan. With an inhuman cry of anger, Kerwan ran forwards, stabbing his knife through Krile's eye. "And this time stay dead."

ROGER

Roger dropped Krile's body, blood gushing from his eye. The man was clearly dead, Kerwan's knife having done the dirty work. Roger looked to Kerwan to see that the monstrous amounts of rage that had built up inside of him start to subside down, and Kerwan started to realize the horror he had caused.

Krile lay dead in the ground, though Roger sensed Kerwan couldn't care less about his dead brother. Or could he? Krile was the only thing left from Kerwan's past, and he had just killed it in a moment of pure anger.

Roger saw Kerwan's eyes flash to body of Tyration bleeding out in the dust. Finally, he tore his eyes away from the corpses of the men he had murdered and turned to the battle between Fedradin and Oxlo.

Each wizard quickly realized they would not join the fight. The elements swirled around the two as they fought in a dance-like fashion. Earth was flying around, fire shot out of the battle in the form of balls, wind could not be seen but felt as it fly around the field, boiling water splashed about, scalding any who might touch it, and the swords of the two Sages flashed back and forth faster than the human eye could register. In fact, the swords were moving so fast, the sounds of them smashing together could only be heard a few seconds after the initial contact between the blades.

Kerwan turned to the other two. "We can't help him. Even if we shoot a spell into that mess, we risk hitting Fedradin."

"What about them over there?" said Roger, gesturing to the battle with the horned man.

Before Kerwan could respond, the horned man launched himself into the air and started flying away, Aserax lamely shooting a few arrows after him, all of which fell short. The wizards started blasting spells at the man, but it was to no avail. All of their spells missed marginally.

Kerwan sighed and said, "I guess all we can do now is wait."

COID

Coid was shocked to see all of his enemies run towards him at once. There was that girl with the robe, that elf with the knife-bow, the dwarf with all the axes -who picked up his tomahawk on the way over— the weird thing made out of rock, and a girl who belonged in school.

Coid shot his red beams at the elf as she neared him, an arrow nocked on her bowstring. The elf had not expected the beams to hurt, and when they hit her chest, she dove to the side in an attempt to stop the pain.

But he could not rest.

The girl in the robe came charging at him, two razor sharp blades sliding out of her sleeves. Coid shot some beams at the girl in the robe, but instead of burning her, they bounced off the robe, flying back and hitting him in the cheek. Coid stumbled backwards, and when he was finally able to regain his composure, he looked up to see all of the people who had charged him earlier practically on top of him now.

Coid's sword swung out on its own accord, striking something or someone. As it started to swing itself again and again, Coid started shooting out beams of light, while flailing around with his fist.

It was a blur. Robes, rock, blades, axes, arrows, red beams of light. All were thrown together into some twisted mosaic, dancing before his eyes. This lasted a few minutes, until his sword-weilding arm started to ache, and his eyes started to burn from the stress of sending out the painful beams. He was not sure how much longer he could keep up the fight, when he felt his legs come out from under him.

Coid crashed to the ground, landing hard on his bottom. His sword was still swinging itself, but he had stopped lashing out with his fists, and the beams of light had stopped flying. He forced his sword to stop swinging and he scrambled backwards, away from the mob of people wanting his head on a stick.

He saw Tiserae pull out what looked like a glowing marble, and she flung it at him. The marble broke apart on the ground, sending an explosion outwards that caused Coid to tumble across the ground for a while. When he came to a stop and was able to steady himself, he saw the mass of people still rushing towards him. It was now that his fight instinct ceased, and his flight instinct took over.

Coid launched himself into the air, flying away as the group neared him. He saw the elf with the knife-bow shoot some arrows at him, but they all stopped short and plummeted into the trees below. He thought about laughing, until he saw a white beam of light flash by his head. Coid needed to leave.

ASERAX

Aserax watched disappointedly as her arrows missed hitting Coid as he flew away. She saw a few beams of light fly through the air towards the man, and she turned to face the wizards who had shot them.

Krile and Tyration lay dead on the ground, Roger and Kerwan gathered around the bodies. They were shooting spells at Coid as he flew away, but they missed each and every time.

Aserax looked to Fedradin, but the battle was so intense that she didn't want to go anywhere near it to help Fedradin. Neither did anyone else. Their group jogged over to the wizards', in order to determine about what should be done next.

"I think we have to let this battle run its own course," said Kerwan. "I don't see any feasible way to help the battle without putting someone at risk." As if to illustrate his point, a flaming boulder crashing into the ground in between him and Aserax.

"I guess..." said Aserax, her voice trailing off. "I just wish we could help Fedradin somehow..."

"To start we should stop killing each other," muttered Roger.

Kerwan shot him a dirty glance. "I'm not sure I'm quite finished yet." Roger backed away as Kerwan put a hand his dagger. "We can help him by staying out of the way. The last thing he needs is for Oxlo to take a hostage."

FEDRADIN

Oxlo threw a ball of boiling water at Fedradin, who blocked it with his kappa shell shield. The ball splattered against the shell, spraying Fedradin with droplets of hot water. Fedradin put his shield down, to find that another ball of boiling water was headed straight for him. Fedradin threw out his palm, the shield on the forearm of that same arm, creating an invisible barrier upon which the ball of water exploded.

Fedradin had now reached Oxlo, swinging his sword. Oxlo ducked the blade, thrusting his own at Fedradin's stomach. Fedradin battered the sword away from his with the shield, swinging his palm back towards Oxlo to sent flames shooting out of his palm. Oxlo waved his own palm across his body, sending out a sheet of water that smothered the flames instantly.

Fedradin had predicted that Oxlo would do precisely that, so while Oxlo put out the fire, Fedradin created a small rock, which he hurled into Oxlo's stomach. The boulder found its mark, knocking Oxlo backward. Fedradin pursued Oxlo, swinging his sword in a downwards arc. Oxlo was doubled over, but he still managed to get his sword up in time to parry the blow. Quickly, Fedradin swung low, swiping at Oxlo's knees, but the Sage was able to jump back to avoid the swing.

Fedradin pulled back, ready to swing again, when Oxlo swung his palm, firing a ball of boiling water at Fedradin. Luckily, Fedradin had brought his shield down and he was able to deflect most of the water with the shield, but some still splashed onto his shirt, burning his stomach. Fedradin yelped in pain, leaping backwards, and Oxlo followed him, throwing two more balls of boiling water at Fedradin.

Fedradin, using his earth powers, pulled his hands over his head, causing the earth in front of him to leap into the air, blocking the balls of boiling water. Once Fedradin heard both balls of water explode on the wall of earth, he let the land once again smooth out. Oxlo was ready, though, and he charged at Fedradin, hurling ball after ball of boiling water. Fedradin backed up, projecting shield after shield of walls made out of condensed air, until finally he ran straight into the stone tomb, hurting his back.

He clutched his back, gasping in pain, as Oxlo charged forward, stabbing his sword downwards. Fedradin barely managed to roll to the side, Oxlo's sword bouncing off the tomb. Oxlo turned to the fallen Fedradin, stabbing once again at Fedradin. Fedradin threw out a palm, catching the blade in midair with a cushion of air. Oxlo pushed down harder on his sword, put it wasn't able to penetrate the cushion of air. After Oxlo began putting all of his body weight onto his sword, Fedradin released the cushion of air, rolling to the side. Oxlo slammed into the ground, his sword sticking into the dirt, the pommel hitting him in the eye.

Fedradin swung his sword at Oxlo, right as Oxlo pulled his sword out of the ground, the two blades colliding, sending out the metal-on-metal ring. Oxlo and Fedradin both, at the same time, used their Sage powers: Oxlo sending a spray of boiling water at Fedradin, Fedradin sending an invisible punch at Oxlo.

Fedradin turned to the side and was spared the worst of the boiling water, but Oxlo was hit dead-on by Fedradin's punch. Oxo tumbled backwards, sprawling on the ground. Fedradin ran forward, but before he could attack Oxlo, Oxlo threw a ball of boiling water at his feet, forcing him to stop in his tracks to avoid being hit. When it was safe to pass, Oxlo was on his feet, a ball of boiling water hovering above one of his palms. Fedradin, instead of charging at Oxlo, put out his palm, a fireball hovering above it.

They threw them at the same time, the balls colliding in midair, the fireball being extinguished and the ball of boiling water exploding. Thus began a Sage battle. Fedradin started bombarding Oxlo with every element of which he had control. Boulders, air currents, fire, Fedradin threw them all, Oxlo meekly throwing back a few balls of boiling water.

A boulder struck Oxlo, glancing across the Sage's forehead. Oxlo stumbled backwards, clutching his bleeding wound. A powerful gust of wind knocked the wind out of Oxlo, and sent him flying backwards, crashing into a tree. Oxlo bounced off the tree, landing face first in the ground beneath the tree. And he didn't get up.

Fedradin ran over, raising him sword for the finishing blow, when Oxlo snaked his arm out, grabbing Fedradin's ankle and pulling him to the ground. Fedradin hit the ground, hard, surprised by what had happened. Oxlo jumped to his feet, forehead still bleeding, and he kicked Fedradin in the face. Fedradin's head snapped back, and Fedradin fell against the ground, Oxlo pulling out his sword. He raised it over his head, about to swing it down, when a look of hesitation crossed his face. This split-second distraction was all Fedradin needed.

Fedradin shot out a powerful burst of wind, which pinned Oxlo against a tree. Instead of immediately letting Oxlo go, Fedradin decided to run an experiment. He dropped his sword, raised that palm and used it to send a burst of flames at Oxlo, without letting the Sage drop. Oxlo yelped as his clothes ignited, the flames biting into his flesh. Fedradin then used his earth powers to creature a boulder, small, but large enough to do damage. He swung it at Oxlo, hitting Oxlo across the chest. Somehow, the boulder caught fire, so Fedradin threw it behind him. He also felt a substantial energy drain, so he released the invisible force that was holding Oxlo to the tree. Oxlo tumbled to the ground, immediately dousing himself in a sheet of water, which extinguished the flames instantly.

Fedradin watched as Oxlo turned his head towards Fedradin. He was broken, bruised, burned and bleeding, but Fedradin could still see determination on his face. A smile came to Oxlo's face and he charged at Fedradin, sword in hand. He swung his sword, Fedradin easily parrying the blow. Oxlo drew his sword back and swung again; this time Fedradin side-stepped it. Now, Oxlo was angry, he swung again and again, but his swings were getting less frequent and weaker. As Fedradin easily held Oxlo back, he could see pain and exhaustion on his face.

Oxlo slashed outwards at Fedradin, who blocked the sword with ease. Oxlo, weak, stumbled back a few feet, giving Fedradin the opportunity to raise his palm, blasting a strong current of air at Oxlo. Oxlo, too tired to attempt to avoid it, was hit straight in the chest, sending his crashing to the ground once more. As Fedradin ran over to the evil Sage, he saw that Oxlo was not able to get up. Oxlo struggled half-heartedly, but he simply could not muster the strength to get to his feet one more time, just to be knocked down again. Fedradin ran over to Oxlo, putting Baxcanador against Oxlo's neck.

"Good bye, Oxlo," whispered Fedradin. He was about to slice Oxlo's neck, when he saw something flash across Oxlo's eyes. His eyes seemed to turn yellow for a moment, then they reverted back to their original state. Oxlo murmured something faint, and Fedradin just caught it.

"Don't let Erch get the Demon Callers..."

Fedradin was confused for a moment. Then he realized what Oxlo was trying to do. He was trying to trick Fedradin into letting him go, unharmed.

"I will not fall for your trickery!" With that, Fedradin slit Oxlo's neck, the Sage's head slumping lifelessly on the ground. Quickly, Fedradin pulled his dagger from the pouch on his boot, slicing Oxlo's charred shirt. He pulled off what remained of the fabric, and found what he was looking for. A blue crystal hung around Oxlo's neck on a necklace. Fedradin tore the crystal from the necklace, pushing it up against the three merged crystals already on his own necklace. Like the other two crystals, this one fused perfectly.

Fedradin stood up to see Tiserae, Breetex, Kerwan, Glaeb Duhr, Roger, Sgire, some man in a hooded robe, and an injured Aserax watching as he put a palm out, showering the group with water. Fedradin smiled to himself.

He liked his new powers.

Fedradin pulled the first Demon Caller from his pouch. "One down!" he said. "Two to go!"

~Epilogue~

THE SUNLIGHT DID NOT penetrate far into the waters of Lake Strali. It came in rays through the murky water, which were blotted out quite quickly. The guppy liked these rays of sunlight, and spent most of its days swimming around in an undulating forest of seaweed that had grown around the beams of light.

That was until a hungry gar had come along, searching for prey in the teeming forests of weeds. The guppies and sunfish had had to bolt from their familiar homes in the weed as the gar came swimming along, snatching up an unsuspecting bluegill. This particular guppy had been swimming close to the bluegill, the sudden appearance of the gar startling it so much that it started swimming towards the darkness of the lake down below, not stopping until it collided with something hard and metallic.

It was too dark for the guppy to see down in this part of Lake Strali, but after a few moments of swimming against this object, the guppy found that the object had many holes through it. Predators hid in holes. Predators were not good. Holes were not good. The guppy spun around and started swimming the other direction. It was swimming proudly along, until...

SNAP.

The Aboleth had instinctively snatched up the guppy in its powerful jaws. It opened its eyes, one at a time, very groggily. In fact, the Aboleth had not been awake for hundreds of years. The Aboleth pulled to one side, but the chains held firm. The Aboleth pulled to the other side. The chains did not budge. Business as usual.

But yet...

Something was different. Something *felt* different. The Aboleth took a deep breath, the water rushing through its gills. Yes, it was palpable.

War.

War had a distinct feeling, and this was that feeling. War was about to strike Haxter. A war larger than any other.

The Aboleth felt a glimmer of hope. This was its chance. The Aboleth would have its revenge.

The cold had long since stopped taking an effect on him. As the wind whipped across the glaciers, it blew back his thin tunic, but he hardly felt it. He felt something else instead. Slowly, the man opened his eyes, staring across the glaciers.

"He has risen, Immoth."

A voice from behind him responded, "You feel it, too, Master?"

"Yes. He has risen. And he is stronger than ever before."

The coinsword clutched his weapon as the carrack drifted slowly down the Bal-gastar River. So slowly. So *painfully* slowly. He knew this area well, and he also knew it was chock-full of Creopolian river pirates, hence the reason he was needed.

A supercargo had long since taken a liking to his services, and now he served the same shipping company day and night as it sailed up and down the rivers, trading and selling. But the Creopolian plot of land was by far the worst. The city had filled the space in between its three boundaries and now it itched to grow, to expand.

Suddenly, flaming arrows came flying up from the riverside brush, colliding with the deck, the furled up sail -the sail used only to go upriver. A plump man came running up from the below decks.

"Do something!" shouted the first mate. Before the coinsword could respond, an arrow found its way through the mate's neck, and he collapsed dead on the blazing deck. The coinsword turned back to see a force of Creopolian soldiers, not river pirates, rise from the bushes and fling themselves at the side of the ship. He unsheathed his sword. They paid him to fight, he fought. He fumbled for his three-link long bond. Even if it meant death.

His six feet clacked as he climbed Dragonsback Ridge. The sickle-spear he called an *unnak* caught the moonlight, and he admired his weapon. The weapon that would bring Haxter back under his control.

He glanced behind him, seeing his army dutifully following him up the steep slopes, their own *unnaks* waving in the dark. He turned around, letting lose a horrible, insect-like hissing noise. The rest of the Formiant echoed his call, working their way up the ridge with redoubled haste. Vensaaki, son of Xenx, would be the one who brought the Formiant back to their colony of Haxter. But he needed to prioritize. The town of Sequo was not far away.

Glass blowing. A long and laborious process, but he was always rewarded with a great sense of accomplishment when he finished. He was busy adding the finishing touches to a chandelier, when the door to his shop slammed open. A withered, albino man, leaning on a cane, stood in the doorway.

"Can I help-" The glassblower was interrupted by the albino.

"Where is it?" growled the albino.

"Where is what?" asked the confused glassblower.

"Don't play dumb with me!" The albino started walking closer to the glassblower, who stood up, setting down his chandelier with great caution.

"Sir, you must have me confused with someone else..."

"I most certainly have not!" The albino swung his cane at a rack of decorative candleholders, shattering them.

"Hey! You have to pay for those!"said the now angry glassblower.

"Do I? Do I also have to pay for this?" The albino smashed his cane into the chandelier.

"Yes! Yes you do!" A stick, molten glass on the end was heating in a fire. The albino pulled it from the fire, hitting the glassblower across the face with it. "Aaah!" The glassblower collapsed to the ground, a blister forming on his cheek. The albino put the glass back in the fire.

"I believe you have a very rare item reserved for me."

"Think again. I only have one item currently reserved, and I have held onto it only because my grandfather crafted it many years ago for someone who never retrieved it." The albino snarled and struck the glassblower again with the molten glass, leaving it on the man's skin longer this time.

"Where do you keep this item?"

"Why?" The albino struck the glassblower once more with the molten glass.

514

"Alright! It's behind the counter!" The albino walked to the counter and found what he was looking for. It was a vial, which he slipped into his pocket. He turned and walked to the door. Before he left, he turned back to the glassblower.

"I believe I paid your grandfather in advance for this item."

"You ordered it?"

"I did."

"So you're... James of Dire?" wondered the glassblower. The albino walked back to him, pulling the molten glass out of the fire once more. He jabbed the molten glass into the glassblower's eye, pushing down, until the glassblower stopped screaming. The albino dropped the stick with the molten glass, uttering but one word.

"Yes."

END OF BOOK ONE

About the Author

David Vonderheide is a 15-year-old high school student. He got an idea for a fantasy story in third grade, which he wrote and rewrote until finally finishing this book in middle school. He lives near Philadelphia with his parents, brother and chinchilla. Needless to say, this is his debut novel.